DEMON'S GATE

Steve White

DEMON'S GATE

A Baen Books Original

Baen Publishing Enterprises
P.O. Box 1403
Riverdale, NY 10471
www.baen.com

ISBN-13: 978-1-4165-0922-6
ISBN-10: 1-4165-0922-4

Cover art by Clyde Caldwell

First paperback printing, December 2005

Library of Congress Cataloging-in-Publication Number
2003020724

Distributed by Simon & Schuster
1230 Avenue of the Americas
New York, NY 10020

Production by Windhaven Press, Auburn, NH (www.windhaven.com)
Printed in the United States of America

To Sandy, for the love which is the most precious thing I possess.

And to Richard A. Getchell, for allowing Irma Sanchez the use of a great line.

Author's Note

At the risk of belaboring the obvious, *Demon's Gate* is a fantasy. Its setting is not our own world's Bronze Age, although its geography and climatology are markedly similar. It mirrors European prehistory, but with larger and more developed political units and a higher level of sophistication about certain things, most notably theology. (As far as the latter is concerned, a case can be made for the presence of Zoroastrian-style dualism a thousand years early. After all, in the *Demon's Gate* world it's real . . . more or less, as Nyrthim would say.) At the same time, the mundane technology of this world—metallurgy, shipbuilding, construction techniques, chariots and their use, and so forth—is as accurate in terms of our current knowledge of the European Bronze Age as conscientious research can make it.

The pronunciation of the various languages is fairly self-explanatory. Final vowels are always sounded. The *aa* combination in Dovnaan words represents an *ah* sound shading toward *aw*. In words of Nimosei derivation (including numerous names and loan-words in Ayoliysei, such as "Ayoliysei" itself), *iy* approximates a shortened one-syllable form of the sound sometimes rendered as *aiee*.

I make no apologies for using English units of measurement. Metrics would be even more anachronistic. More anachronistic still would be to put fashionable modern sentiments on such subjects as slavery, war, social equality and gender roles into the mouths of the characters.

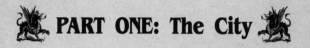

PART ONE: The City

CHAPTER ONE

The mist through which they sailed was unusual for the Inner Sea.

"Nothing to compare to what we're used to, of course," stated Khaavorn.

Valdar smiled. His companion had yet to admit that anything in these regions could compare with home. In this case, though, he had a point. The island of Lokhrein from which they'd departed a moon and a half ago was almost fogbound enough to justify its reputation. Here, the sun kept breaking through rifts to awaken eye-dazzling sparkles on the water. Still, this mist was enough to veil the northern coast of Schaerisa to starboard, and the galley seemed to glide through a pearl-white world of blended air and sea with no land at all.

But then, abruptly, they were out of the pocket of mist and back in the sunlight whose brilliance and clarity almost hurt their northern eyes, under the sky whose blueness Valdar had never gotten used to. Off to starboard was the coast of Schaerisa with its little whitewashed fishing villages. Ahead rose one of the rocky ridges that broke up this island's coast into a series of crescent-shaped coves, forming a headland.

As they drew abreast that headland, a cleft in the ridge gave them a glimpse of what lay beyond . . . and for once, Khaavorn was silent.

They'd heard tales of The City, of course. Khaavorn had scoffed loudly, and in his quieter way Valdar had agreed. But now, as the galley moved on and the cleft fell behind, the two of them turned to each other and exchanged a nervous glance, both wondering if they'd really seen what they thought they'd seen but neither willing to be the first to voice the question. Unconsciously, Khaavorn's hand went to the smooth-worn haft of the heavy war axe that was the weapon, emblem and soul of a Dovnaan warrior. Valdar smiled condescendingly . . . but then realized that his own hand had sought the hilt of his sword.

Then they rounded the headland. Ahead was another rocky prominence, not unlike it. At a bawled command from the captain, the steersmen hauled on the twin rudders and the galley heeled to starboard, turning into the channel between the two capes. Khaavorn and Valdar held onto the rail to keep their footing . . . and stared ahead at the vista for which no traveler's tale had prepared them.

The two curving headlands enclosed a vast harbor, universally conceded to be the finest in the world, rimmed by gentle hills where villas peered forth from groves of olive trees and date palms. Arguably it was two harbors, for it was divided almost precisely in half by a peninsula extending from the harbor's southern shore. The head of that peninsula now lay dead ahead, like a mountain rising from the water . . . not a natural mountain made by the gods, but an artificial mountain fashioned by men like gods, for this was The City.

That was all anyone ever called it. Its actual name was Schaerisa, the same as the island. But it needed no name on any of the coasts and islands of the Inner and Outer Seas that the Old Empire had once ruled. It was simply The City.

It rose in tiers and terraces of stone and masonry and ruddy-tiled roofs, climbing the slopes of two hills. One of those hills was crowned with the temple of Dayu, gleaming with decorative tiles and gold leaf. The other seemed to groan beneath the weight of the imperial palace, whose colonnaded and porticoed façade was like nothing the two of them—the son of one king and the nephew of another—had ever seen, or imagined.

And yet those two hills were only foothills of a conical mountain whose jagged cinder-gray peak loomed above all the clutter of buildings.

A *volcano*, Valdar found himself wondering, *that once blasted its lava out and left the crater that is now a harbor? That's the kind of thing Nyrthim would have wondered about*. He shied away from the thought, as he always did whenever such strange speculations entered his mind, which they they doubtless did at the behest of the old sorcerer's ghost.

The harbor was alive with ships—lean predatory

war galleys and the broad-beamed merchantmen that were their natural prey, tied up at the docks as well as under way. A small but well-kept-up boat approached in a way that somehow exuded arrogance. In its stern stood a middle-aged man who, under his official dress of white kilt and formal over-both-shoulders mantle, suggested gauntness settling into softness. He bore a staff of office.

"What is your business here?" he demanded when his craft had drawn into shouting range. He used the Nimosei that was still the common language of commerce in the lands once ruled by the Old Empire.

"The harbormaster," grunted the captain. He was from the land the imperials still officially called Ivaerisa, where Khaavorn and Valdar had negotiated passage the rest of the way through the Inner Sea, and he had the strongly built hook-nosed look that went with that land's Escquahar blood. Unfortunately, a legacy of suspicion also went with it, here in the New Empire. "This is the *Wave Leaper*, out of Ivaerisa," he called out, leaning over the rail, "bringing distinguished visitors."

"We are uninterested in any louse-infested rebel or barbarian dignitaries you may have brought from Ivaerisa," the harbormaster sneered, using the first person plural in the way of all officials in all times and places. "And the investiture was weeks ago—as I should have thought *everyone* knew by now. Proceed to the commercial docks, along with the rest of the outlanders and the lower orders."

Khaavorn flushed. This was just the thing to bring him out of his paralyzing awe. He pushed the captain aside and glared across the water, axe held so as to be just visible over the gunwale. His Nimosei had been learned in childhood—his family, like many of Lokhrein's ruling clans, blended the bloodlines of the Old Empire's priesthood with those of the conquering Dovnaan. But now he spoke in the Ayoliysei dialect that was the New Empire's ruling language. He and Valdar had acquired it without undue difficulty, for it and the Dovnaan tongue had common roots going back not so very many generations. But Khaavorn's Dovnaan accent was now even thicker than usual—thicker, Valdar suspected, than it needed to be.

"This young gentleman," he declared, waving grandly at Valdar, "is heir to King Arkhuar of Dhulon. An' I meself am Khaavorn nak'Moreg, sister's son to Riodheg, High King of Lokhrein. I've also the honor of bein' half brother to the Lady Andonre, wife of Vaelsaru, chief general of your Emperor . . . who, ye may be sure, will be hearin' of any insolence we encounter from his servants!"

The harbormaster managed to grovel without capsizing his boat. "My humblest and most abject apologies, lord! I naturally never dreamed that this, uh, vessel carried passengers of such eminence. Please permit me to escort you to the imperial moorings." He gestured peremptorily at his steersman, who bawled at the oarsmen, thus confirming the immemorial proverb of the ancient sage Zhaerosa: "Shit flows downhill."

Khaavorn turned to Valdar and smoothed his mustache complacently. "One just has to know how to deal with those sorts of people, that's all," he explained in their more usual Dovnaan tongue.

"No doubt. But was that 'young gentleman' business really necessary? You make me sound like I'm still the callow little twit who arrived in Lokhrein ten years ago begging help from the High King for his old ally Arkhuar."

"And so you are!" boomed Khaavorn. He flung an arm around the younger man's shoulders. "You may have fooled some people into thinking you're a proper warrior of the Dovnaan, foreigner though you are. But I, for my manifold offenses against Dayu, was your mentor. So I know better!"

Valdar grinned, unabashed. "Yes. How well I remember the style of your instruction! It's no exaggeration to say you made me what I am today."

Khaavorn winced. "Now *that* was low!"

He was, Valdar reflected, remarkably little changed from those days, though now in his mid-thirties: tall, powerfully built, with the wide shoulders and heavily developed muscles that came from wielding the heavy war axe from early adolescence. His strong features were likewise of the sort Dovnaan warrior aristocrats were popularly supposed to have—hawklike nose, high cheekbones, heavy jaw—and he wore his hair in their style, long and gathered into a ponytail, with a drooping mustache but otherwise as clean-shaven as bronze razors permitted. But that hair was of a very dark brown, with only a slight coppery undertone, and his eyes were just as dark, a legacy of Lokhrein's older rulers.

Valdar was even darker-haired, and his slender build and straight features were those of the people who had spread the religion of Rhaeie the Mother—and with it the writ of the Old Empire—from the Inner Sea all the way to the cold northern land that was later to be named Dhulon by the Karsha conquerors who'd bequeathed Valdar his tallness and his blue-gray eyes. He wore the same kind of Dovnaan garb as Khaavorn: knee-length woolen tunic, broad belt with studs and buckle of copper, short mantle caught at the left shoulder by a massive gold brooch, the basic color deep blue in his case and forest green in Khaavorn's, edged with elaborate embroidery. But he asserted his heritage by wearing his hair shorter and shaving his mustache as well as his beard.

Neither of them had armor or helmets—this was a peaceful visit—although even without all that bronze they were sweating in the southern spring. But they bore the weapons without which they would have felt naked: Khaavorn's war axe and Valdar's sword.

"They say no one is allowed into the Emperor's presence with weapons," said Valdar, changing the subject.

Khaavorn expressed his opinion with a snort. He automatically lifted his war axe by its haft of fire-hardened wood. The head was a thing of sinister beauty, the product of a tradition that had worked the same shape in polished stone in the days before bronze. The thick blade curved backward in flowing lines to swell into a spiked ball through which the haft was inserted. Behind, the lines continued downward, forming a wicked hook. It was a weapon of terrifying potentialities in the hands of a large, strong wielder—the only kind who could wield it effectively.

"Ridiculous notion! They can't possibly expect a gentleman to go unarmed—even if he's only armed with *that.*"

Valdar smiled easily at the familiar gibe. "You're hopelessly old-fashioned," he said, patting the hilt of his sword. Perfectly balanced, its two-and-a-half-foot blade was a slender leaf-shape designed for cutting and thrusting. It was an import from Khrunetore, whose weapon-smiths had developed a technique of coating bronze with chromium, enabling it to hold an edge keen enough to cut a hair. Some people whispered of demonic assistance. Khaavorn wasn't one of those. He'd merely fulminated loudly about newfangled tomfool foreign innovations . . . and, with no noise at all, learned to use a sword himself.

"Speaking of the imperial presence," said Valdar, shifting subjects again (partly because he knew it annoyed Khaavorn), "the harbormaster's dig about the investiture being over reminded me that there's now just *one* of them."

"Oh, yes." They'd heard the news of old Namapa's death at the newly reconquered imperial island of Sardiysa, where the ship had put in a week earlier. "Naturally I didn't give him the satisfaction of admitting we'd hoped to be in time for it! Hmmm . . . So now Tarhynda is officially the sole Emperor. Well, we can still pay the High King's respects to him." Khaavorn grew subdued. "Some of the stories we've heard . . ."

"I'll keep an open mind for now."

"Of course. And it will be good to see my half sister again. Little Andonre . . ." But Khaavorn's jovial mood was gone. He gazed stonily across the water, and Valdar followed his gaze.

The peninsula ahead was largest at its hilly tip around the volcanic cone where The City rose, so it was more like an island filling much of the center of the great lagoonlike harbor, connected to the south shore by a narrow isthmus. Valdar had heard that a massive wall cinctured that isthmus, though it wasn't visible from here. The Ayoliysei dynasts of the New Empire weren't likely to repeat the mistake of the Old, whose cities had been undefended save by their fleets. But only low sea walls faced the harbor, as became clear as they drew closer.

It also became clear that the harbormaster was exacting a functionary's petty revenge, for his boat was leading them to the naval docks, not to the private ones at the foot of the palace hill—those were, it seemed, too good for semi-barbarian lordlings from former imperial provinces, however well-connected. The quay to which they tied up was closer to the lesser hill on which the temple of Dayu rose in its gilded splendor. Nearby, at the foot of that hill and extending over the water on pillars, was a small shrine to Rhaeie the Mother, in her aspect of Mistress of the Waves.

As they disembarked, they made the appropriate signs of thanks for a safe voyage in the direction of the Mother's shrine. But Khaavorn could not conceal a frown at the temple's ostentatiously subordinate position. It was not his full-blown scowl, however. It was more a look of perplexity. He worshipped Dayu, of course. All Dovnaan warriors did—they even called him by the same name, and the priests were in surprising agreement that the Lord of Light and Good was the same in every land where the Karsha tribes had brought his worship. However, the ancient traditions ran strongly in his family. Valdar understood his companion's ambivalence, for he shared it.

The captain approached after hurried consultation

with a bronze-helmeted officer. "I've arranged for you to be allowed to depart at once." He indicated a gateway in the sea wall, with broad shallow steps leading up to street level. There a crowd had already gathered, shrilly advertising themselves as guides . . . or for other services. "I know a guide who's almost honest. He'll conduct you to the palace, or wherever else you wish to go. Or if you would prefer for me to order litters . . . ?"

"No, just the guide," said Khaavorn with distaste. "We'll walk." He motioned to his servant to collect his belongings. Valdar did the same . . . except that Wothorg wasn't really a servant.

"Come on, Wothorg," he called. "Your pleasure cruise is over."

"Good name for it, in the pond water these southerners call seas," came a bass rumble from beyond the rail, followed by Wothorg, walking without apparent effort under the load he was carrying. He was a descendant of the original folk of Dhulon who'd stared awestruck at the ships that had heralded the Old Empire so long ago. Not as tall as Valdar, he was approximately twice as broad and twice as thick—at least if one counted his paunch, under which lay rock-hardness. His eyes, blue as northern ice, looked out from under shaggy yellow brows. Those eyes seemed squeezed into slits by his rubicund jowls—which, in turn, were barely visible above his dense reddish-blond beard.

When Arkhuar had sent his son—because there was no one else—to seek the help of the High King of Lokhrein, he'd also sent a trusted retainer to guard the boy's back. Afterwards, when Valdar had remained in Lokhrein in Riodheg's service—with the blessings of his father, who thought it the best possible preparation for Dhulon's future king—Wothorg had remained as well. And he was still along now, under the southern sun that caused his blunt red nose to peel continuously.

Not that I need a bodyguard this time, Valdar told himself. *This is just a courtesy call on Tarhynda, now that he's become sole Emperor, to deliver the best wishes of the High King whose existence the Empire has never officially recognized, and to renew the trade agreement for the tin the Empire needs. No pirates or assassins or new tribes of untamed Karsha out of the grasslands this time.*

So no wonder Wothorg is grumbling. He's never happy without a good fight—and without the gales and sleet-storms of the Outer Sea for which he's been pining ever since we entered the straits.

They passed through the sea wall and entered the teeming, bewildering maze of narrow streets. Proceeding in the wake of the guide, they looked around, Khaavorn with studied aristocratic *sangfroid* and Valdar with frank curiosity.

The street was stone-paved, and the buildings—white-plastered, often gaudily painted—crowded close. The people that filled the streets and swarmed about the awning-shaded shop fronts mostly belonged to Schaerisa's native stock: slender, olive-skinned, with curly black hair and regular features. A good many, though, were of the stockier, hook-nosed variety from the island of Alayisa to the east. And the aristocrats who rode in litters on the backs of sweating slaves were apt to be taller and less dark than the common ruck, for many bore the Karsha blood of the

Ayoliysei conquerors from the mainland. And they themselves didn't draw nearly as many stares as might have been expected, for these cosmopolitan streets saw every human variety of the Inner Sea, and many from beyond it.

Valdar wondered—*as Nyrthim would have wondered,* he thought automatically, with the usual accompanying twinge of sadness—how so many people packed so closely together didn't smother in their own waste. But then he recalled tales of The City's underground drains.

Continuing along the street, turning leftward and uphill toward the palace, Valdar began to notice that the poorer classes—most of whom wore nothing more than a loincloth, or a skirt and shawl in the case of the women—didn't look particularly well nourished, and many of them bore the marks of disease. And when a patrol of helmeted soldiers passed, they cringed aside like oft-whipped animals. They also avoided a small square whose very specialized purpose was evident from a row of impaled corpses. Some of these had obviously been there a while; one, indeed, was beginning to decompose badly. Khaavorn gave his nose a fastidious wrinkle.

It was just beyond the place of executions, with the palace looming up above the crowded roofs, that a tough-looking, poorly dressed man lunged from the crowd and attacked with a shout a somewhat more prosperous-looking passerby. The latter defended himself just as vociferously. But neither the attack nor the defense seemed quite right somehow. Neither did the way several bystanders suddenly joined the fight, flailing wildly, knocking over awnings and stalls.

Valdar and Wothorg exchanged a quick eye contact. They knew a staged fight when they saw one.

Valdar started to say something to Khaavorn, who was looking with disdain at this misbehavior by the rabble. But the fight had spread, as such things always do in crowds, and now they were caught up in a tide of screaming rioters.

Valdar drew his sword, forcibly reminding himself to use the flat only. Not that it really mattered—these were the lower classes, after all. Still, he and Khaavorn were Tarhynda's guests, and these were his subjects. He noted with mild surprise that Khaavorn was exercising similar scruples; he saw the Dovnaan grasp his axe handle in both hands and drive the butt of it into the stomach of an attacker, who doubled up with a whoosh of escaping wind. Then, with a heave, he sent the man crashing into a stall. Wothorg was being less cautious; dropping his burdens, he grabbed two rioters, one with each hand, brought their heads together with an alarming sound, dropped them and reached for two more.

Shouts began to rise above the general uproar— shouts in an authoritative tone, for the soldiers who'd lately passed them were now coming back, fighting their way through the crowd. Like most of the New Empire's troops, they were mercenaries: Achaysei from the tributary states on the mainland of Zhraess, ethnic relatives of the Ayoliysei and speaking a related dialect, but descended from a later wave of invaders from the north and altogether rougher articles. They felt no kinship with the denizens of The City's streets, and were clearly taking fewer pains to avoid lethal force than Khaavorn and Valdar had. But they were still a good ways away, their bronze-bladed spears at work beyond a sea of heads . . . the heads of a crowd whose nearer members had suddenly focused their attention on the party from Lokhrein.

As Valdar looked around the circle of faces surrounding them, he felt a touch on his arm. He whirled around, raised his sword . . . and stopped.

"No," smiled the elderly man, through a beard that was a lighter shade of gray than Valdar recalled. "Not a ghost."

"But . . . but you died!" Valdar stammered. "And even if you hadn't, what are you doing here? And—"

Khaavorn heard the exchange, and turned. "Nyrthim!" he exploded. He was about to say more, but the older man gestured peremptorily.

"Plenty of time for questions and explanations later. For now, you must come with me. It's the purpose for which I arranged this little riot."

"*You* arranged it?" Valdar could only gape.

"Come *on!*" snapped he whom Valdar decided must really be Nyrthim—he certainly had the testiness for it. He took a deep breath. "I'll explain one thing right now: I'm here on the Order's business . . . which means the Mother's. And I need your help." He turned toward an alley without looking back. The crowd parted for him.

Valdar and Khaavorn exchanged a look. Valdar, without stopping to analyze his actions, set out after the sorcerer. Wothorg fell in behind him. After a moment's hesitation, Khaavorn scooped up the traveling bag his servant—now down, along with their guide—had been carrying, and followed.

CHAPTER TWO

Away from the paved street with its shops and monuments, they plunged into a different world.

Here, there was no paving. Indeed, there were no streets, really—just footpaths among the squalid, sagging buildings whose upper stories almost met, shutting out the sky and leaving the slum dwellers in a dark underworld.

This is what the hell of Angmanu must be like, thought Valdar, *except that I never imagined it smelling this bad.* These precincts very obviously possessed no connections to the drainage system that was The City's pride. Beyond that, though, Valdar suspected simple lack of self-respect was also a cause of the alleyways' pervasive filth.

But, a stubborn honesty made him ask himself, *how much self-respect can these people possibly have?* The malnourished, disease-ridden look he'd noted before became more pronounced with every step they took into the reeking bowels of The City's slums.

In this setting, Nyrthim's presence became even harder to believe, if that were possible.

Valdar noted, though, that the crowds—*How can they pack so many people into so small a space?* he wondered. *Where do they live?*—parted for the sorcerer like water for the prow of a ship. The little dark furtive people shied fearfully away from his and Khaavorn's size, exotic appearance and, doubtless, sheer aristocratic expectation of being made way for. But there was a different quality to the way they stepped aside for Nyrthim. Many of them made signs with their hands as he passed—signs that did not look like wards against the demons.

They arrived at one of the alarmingly ill-constructed tenements, and Nyrthim gestured them inside. They ascended a stairway so rickety that Valdar wondered if the structure would hold up under his weight and Khaavorn's, much less Wothorg's. But as they passed through the second-story corridor, it became easier to understand where the shoving masses of human flesh in the alleys came from. They passed one old man who was either sound asleep—unlikely, in this pullulating human hive—or else dead. Nobody around him seemed to care very much. They probably had too much else to worry about, for everywhere were the indicia of disease Valdar had noted earlier.

Nyrthim led them into a largish room, sparsely furnished but with a rough brick cooking oven in one corner where an elderly woman—she must have been forty-five if she was a day—prepared gruel that a couple of younger women dispensed around the room. Most of the floor was covered with a scattering of blankets and improvised mattresses fashioned from anything soft that could be found. As Nyrthim led them across the room, they got a look at those—mostly children—who lay on those pallets.

Valdar—product of a time and place and social class so well acquainted with violence that squeamishness was an unknown, unaffordable luxury—felt the unaccustomed sensation of a rising gorge. Khaavorn's jaw, he noticed, was tightly clenched. From behind, he heard a growl from Wothorg, just above the threshold of hearing.

Why is it so quiet? he wondered, listening to the occasional low moans. *Where are the screams?*

But then he looked more closely. He looked into the huge unblinking dark eyes of what had been a lovely little girl of four or so. There was nothing behind those eyes. She had fled to a place where the pain could not follow, and where someone—or *something*—could not find her.

Then, mercifully, they came to a doorway behind a dingy curtain. Nyrthim led them through into a small chamber with a bed, a chest and a few stools. There was also an improvised shelf crammed with scrolls of papyrus from the land of Khemiu, far to the south across the Inner Sea. The papyrus was covered with markings in what Valdar recognized as the imperial syllabary. He stared at Nyrthim wide-eyed. So the sorcerer could *read*? Valdar had never heard of anyone outside the scribe class being able to do that. Indeed, he'd always thought of it as a kind of sorcery in itself.

Nyrthim sat down on the chest. Valdar and Khaavorn lowered themselves gingerly down onto none-too-sturdy-looking stools. Wothorg didn't take the chance; he just hunkered down in a corner and leaned back against a wall that creaked with his weight. One of the women brought in bowls of food and a jar of wine. Valdar had forgotten how hungry he was. Then he tasted the food . . . and forgot again. The wine wasn't half bad by comparison.

"Now we can talk," said Nyrthim. "Speak freely. You can be sure no one here understands the Dovnaan tongue."

"What is this place?" Valdar asked, unable to choose from the array of more important questions.

"My current home. I do what I can for these people; in turn, they keep me concealed—or, at least, try their best to. I've had to move several times in the years I've been here."

Khaavorn cleared his throat. "Yes, well, that brings us to . . . well, that is . . . Angmanu curse it, Nyrthim, what *are* you doing here? Come to that, what are you doing *alive?* Everyone in Lokhrein thinks—"

"Not quite everyone," the sorcerer interrupted with a smile. "Minuren knows. She should. She helped me fake my death and leave Lokhrein, after I explained to her why I needed to come here."

They simply stared at him.

"But . . . but," spluttered Khaavorn, "what do you mean, 'Needed to come here'? You are—or were—the High King's most trusted advisor! And why should the High Priestess of Rhaeie help you do any such thing?"

"Could it," Valdar put in before Nyrthim could even attempt to answer, "have anything to do with what you said to me in the street about 'the Order's business'?"

"Very good, Valdar." Nyrthim vouchsafed him the condescendingly approving smile he reserved for a pupil who'd made an uncharacteristically astute observation. "Yes, I came here to do the Order's work. Minuren knew this, which was why she *had* to help me, however little she wanted to."

"But," protested Khaavorn, "I thought the Order of the Nezhiy was . . ." He stumbled to an agonizingly shamefaced halt.

"Oh, that's all right, Khaavorn. I'm well aware that I'm widely regarded as the last of the Nezhiy. Come to think of it, I suppose that means the Order is now believed to be altogether extinct, doesn't it?"

Valdar avoided the sorcerer's twinkling dark-brown eyes, sharing Khaavorn's embarrassment because that was, in fact, exactly what he'd thought.

"Actually," Nyrthim continued, "there are a few of us left, here and there. But as far as Lokhrein is concerned, there's an element of truth to it." The twinkle departed from his eyes, revealing something that was neither sorrow nor resignation nor bitterness but held elements of all three. "Because, you see, people are right about something else as well: we're not needed in Lokhrein anymore."

Valdar stared miserably at the floor, for the sorcerer—the Nezh, really, although in the popular mind it meant the same thing—had again succeeded in reading his mind.

Nyrthim had seemed ancient to the youth from Dhulon who'd sought him out in the intervals between getting knocked about by Khaavorn in weapon practice. Valdar had sat at his feet listening to lore beyond any horizons he'd known existed . . . and, in the process, being subtly taught to use his mind, for Nyrthim had recognized a mind that could be so taught. But the old man's membership in the Order had seemed merely an odd bit of old-fashioned eccentricity.

Now, into the midst of embarrassment, enlightenment came.

"Nyrthim, you said the Order isn't needed anymore . . . *in Lokhrein*. Does that mean it *is* needed somewhere else? Like here?"

"Sometimes, Valdar, I feel there may be hope for you yet. Mind you, the feeling usually goes away. But yes, I have reason to believe—and Minuren agrees—that there may be something afoot here in The City. The sort of thing the Order exists to combat."

"I'm confused," Khaavorn admitted forthrightly. From Wothorg's direction came a rumble of agreement like a plaintive rockslide.

"Perhaps I'd better explain." Nyrthim seemed to gather his thoughts, stroking his beard. *He hasn't really changed,* Valdar reflected. The wrinkles in his brow, and the creases that ran down from the sides of his long narrow-bridged nose to the corners of his wide mouth, might be a little more deep-graven. Still, he seemed in vigorous condition for his age . . . whatever that age might be.

"How much do you young fellows know about the old religion?" he asked abruptly.

"Well," huffed Khaavorn, "I *am* descended on my mother's side from the Old Empire's priesthood, you know. I carry the bloodlines of those who first brought the worship of Rhaeie to Lokhrein."

"No, no, no! I mean the *really* old religion! Before the Old Empire."

Khaavorn blinked. It wasn't something one ordinarily thought about. "Uh . . . Didn't everyone worship the demons then?"

"'Worship' is the wrong word. They sought to propitiate them, or simply avoid their notice as much as possible. You see, the demons are quite real."

"Why, of *course* they are," declared Khaavorn with sturdy devoutness.

"Yes, yes, Khaavorn. But we're not accustomed to their literal, physical presence nowadays, are we?"

"Naturally not. Dayu cast them out."

"So you've always been taught. And so," Nyrthim added hastily, "it actually happened . . . more or less. But you must clearly understand that before that the demons' existence was not a matter of metaphysical or theological 'truth.' No, it was a thing of red, rending horror. And to understand that, you must understand what the demons really are.

"They are native to a place—a world—which somehow exists alongside ours but is invisible and impalpable to us. They can be summoned to our world, but only with great difficulty . . . at least nowadays. In ancient times, summoning them was far easier. No one knows why. Perhaps our world and theirs are, in some fashion beyond our understanding, drawing farther apart with the passage of time. But for whatever reason, in the old days any tribal shaman or village wise woman could blunder onto the secret. And thus demons began to infest our world.

"At first, they were only minor terrors. You see, there are many kinds of demons, ranked in a strict hierarchy. The lowest-ranking ones are stupid and relatively ineffectual . . . and are also the easiest to summon. In fact, they were the only ones that could be summoned by accident, even then.

"But certain workers in the magical arts began to believe they could *use* these beings to bring them revenge or power or whatever they happened to desire. They began to summon demons *intentionally*, and constantly sought for ways to summon ever higher-ranking ones. They became the first true sorcerers." Nyrthim's face wore a look of weary sorrow. "Fools! They thought the more powerful, intelligent demons would be more useful to them. In the end, they were themselves used. But they never learned. In their deluded pride, they dared to summon the Great Demons themselves. Finally, some madman succeeded in summoning a prince of the Great Demons—the entity we know as Angmanu, the Lord of Darkness and Evil. The world grew ever more horrible.

"Then, almost a thousand years ago, the Old Empire arose. The Nimosei people who brought the working of copper to these islands also brought the religion of Rhaeie the Mother, spirit of the earth that was being violated. Her priestesses gave comfort, with their promise of life after death, and a sense of something worth protecting. But more was needed. They also forbade all summonings. To enforce this—"

"The Order!" blurted Valdar.

"Yes," said Nyrthim after only a brief glare for the

interruption. "The Order of the Nezhiy dates back that far. We traveled west with the explorers and priestesses who spread the Old Empire and its religion through the islands and peninsulas of the Inner Sea to Ivaerisa, and on through the straits and up the coast of the Outer Sea to Arnoriysa and the islands of Vriydansa and Eriysa—"

"Lokhrein and Ehrein," muttered Khaavorn.

"—and on to the northern land that would *later* be called Dhulon," Nyrthim finished, forestalling yet another patriotic interruption. "In every land, our mission was the same: to track down and root out all sorcerers."

"But, Nyrthim," said Valdar, "I don't understand. Everyone calls the Nezhiy 'sorcerers.' Yet you've just told us—"

"Yes. Ironic, isn't it? But that usage is quite correct. And there's a reason. You see, putting an end to further summonings was all very well, but it wasn't enough; it didn't help with the demons that had already been loosed on the world. We learned ways of combating them, found weaknesses to exploit . . . but that still wasn't enough. In the end, because nothing less would serve, we received a special dispensation from the High Priestess of that time to practice sorcery ourselves. We became that which we existed to eradicate.

"Now, to summon the Great Demons requires either a wholesale use of human sacrifice—which the Order has *never* practiced at *any* time!—or else—"

With startling abruptness, Nyrthim clamped his jaws shut as though he feared he might have already said too much. Or so it seemed to Valdar.

Khaavorn, oblivious, spoke up brightly. "Well,

Nyrthim, it doesn't matter now, does it? I mean, whatever may have happened back then, the fact is that Dayu expelled Angmanu and the rest of his foul brood from the world, and now stands guard to drive him off whenever he returns. Well, er, at least that's what we've always been taught."

For once, Nyrthim actually seemed grateful for one of Khaavorn's interruptions. He gave a smile of unwonted gentleness. "Of course, Khaavorn. Of course. Dayu and the lesser gods of light defeated the demons in a great battle in the north. Later, the Karsha tribes carried that good news south and west during their great expansion, two or three hundred years ago. And wherever they went, from here to Lokhrein, they eventually reached accommodations with the old religion—the same sort of accommodations everywhere. So today we worship Rhaeie the Mother and Dayu the Protector. The Order lingered on . . . but with less and less to do. For, as I told you, summonings have become more difficult. No longer do they occur by accident. And to summon one of the Great Demons would be almost impossible today.

"But a couple of years ago I learned—we of the Order have ways of finding these things out, you see—that the demons are returning."

"Uh . . . are you saying that somebody has started summoning them again?" asked Valdar, bewildered. "But didn't you just say that's . . . ?"

"Difficult, but not impossible. Yes. And it's going on here. So now you know why The City, not Lokhrein, was where I was needed."

"But why all the deception? The faked death . . . ?"

"And why," put in Khaavorn with his usual flair for the peripheral issue, "are you staying in *this* squalid place?"

"To both, the answer is the same. Those whom I seek must not be put on their guard. An official visit from the High King's chief advisor—a known member of the Order—was out of the question. So I came in secret, and have remained out of sight while pursuing my investigations. These people have taken me in, for I do what I can to protect them."

"Protect them?" Khaavorn blinked. "I suppose you mean from . . ."

"Yes. Lesser demons now haunt these slums, preying on the poor and keeping them terrorized."

Wothorg spoke up. "You mean . . . ?" He jerked his bearded chin in the direction of the larger room through which they'd passed. Nyrthim nodded. The big Dhulaan's blue eyes grew even icier.

"Have you learned who is behind this, Nyrthim?" asked Valdar.

"I have suspicions . . . but I cannot say until I'm certain. For one thing, it would prejudice your judgment and thus make you less useful."

"Useful?" echoed Valdar suspiciously.

"Yes! From my standpoint, your coming is a gift from Rhaeie. You see, by now the sorcerer—or, more likely, sorcerers—must surely be aware that there is a member of the Order at work somewhere in The City. This limits my freedom of action still further. Also, the suspicions I mentioned before point to social levels *very* much higher than those in which I move."

"I think," said Valdar grimly, "that I begin to see where this is heading."

Nyrthim showed no sign of having heard him. "You, on the other hand, have access to the palace itself. And what's going on is definitely centered there. . . . *No!* Forget I said that. I need proof. And *you* can get it for me."

Valdar took a deep breath. "Nyrthim, we're here as emissaries from the High King to the new Emperor, whom you seem to be implying is somehow involved . . . and, of course, to call on Andonre. All completely aboveboard. We're not here to skulk about the palace."

"Of course not," said Khaavorn, who now grasped what Nyrthim wanted of them. "After all, we're going to be Tarhynda's guests. I mean . . . a gentleman just doesn't *do* that sort of thing!"

"But surely," said Nyrthim, urgency entering his voice, "you must see the importance of this for the High King—especially now that Tarhynda is sole Emperor. He's openly announced his intention of restoring the Old Empire!"

"That's just talk," scoffed Khaavorn.

"So they thought in Siycelisa and Sardiysa . . . before your brother-in-law General Vaelsaru arrived with his fleets and armies! And when you booked passage in Ivaerisa you must have noticed how nervous everybody there is. I can assure you that *they* take Tarhynda's talk seriously."

"He'll never get any further than that," stated Khaavorn, stroking his axehead complacently.

"And at any rate," Valdar put in as Nyrthim rolled his eyes heavenward in exasperation, "Riodheg cautioned us to be on our best behavior. Remember, the situation is awkward. The high kingship's very existence is a standing affront to the New Empire, which has never officially admitted the loss of any of the provinces—including Lokhrein. So if Tarhynda really is serious about reasserting ancient imperial claims, it's all the more reason for us to give him no provocation."

"But," protested Nyrthim, "we're dealing with nothing less than a recrudescence of dark sorcery! A loosing of demons on the world for the first time in centuries! This transcends mere politics. Can't you *see* that?"

"Possibly—if that really *is* what we're dealing with. No, wait, hear me out!" Valdar surprised himself by raising a forestalling hand as Nyrthim started to open his mouth. But he was no longer the youth who'd been this old man's awestruck pupil. "The fact is, you've given us no proof that any summonings have occurred at all. Without such proof, you can't expect us to ignore Riodheg's instructions and violate Tarhynda's hospitality."

"Very well," said Nyrthim quietly. *Too quietly*, thought Valdar, who remembered only too well how the old man usually reacted when anyone doubted his omniscience. "You want proof? All right. I'll show you proof. I'll show it to you this very night . . . unless you lack the courage to follow me!"

Khaavorn surged halfway to his feet . . . but then settled back onto his stool. Valdar slowly released his breath. There were few men—*very* few—who could have said those words to Khaavorn and lived. Valdar wasn't absolutely sure he himself was one of them.

"Do I understand, Nyrthim," said Khaavorn in a voice just as ominously quiet as the sorcerer's had been, "that you're going to take us to see one of these demons?"

"Yes. I believe I know where it can be found."

"Then I'll follow you. Mind you, I don't know whether what you believe is true or not. But *whoever* did what we saw in the next room—whether man or demon—I want to meet him."

"I think I'd like to meet him too," said Valdar.

"You will." Nyrthim's dark-brown eyes held theirs, and would not let go. "Oh, you will!"

CHAPTER THREE

Khaavorn looked down with scant favor at that in which he'd just stepped.

He couldn't really see it, of course. The moon was down, and midnight alleyways of The City had no illumination save the glow from occasional narrow windows and the torches the four of them carried. It was inadequate to reveal the exact nature of what squelched and squished under their sandaled feet . . . which was just as well. The aroma, however, needed no light.

"Is this really necessary?" grumbled Khaavorn. He had no need to hold his complaint to a whisper. No one was abroad. No one ever was, after dark . . . not in this part of The City.

"You two have only yourselves to blame," snapped Nyrthim over his shoulder as he strode along with the confidence of one accustomed to these noisome slums. "Refused to accept my judgment, did you? Demanded proof, did you? Well, you'll get it!"

"But, Nyrthim," inquired Valdar, "how can you be sure we'll find . . . what you're looking for tonight?"

"I'm quite certain one of the lesser demons that have begun infesting The City will be active in this particular district on this particular night." Nyrthim sounded serene, now that his wisdom was being sought. "Their behavior patterns are very predictable, you know, because they're so stupid. This one in particular. Yes, tonight is definitely feeding time."

"Feeding?" echoed Wothorg.

Nyrthim ignored him and settled happily into lecturing mode. "Remember what I said before about the taxonomy of demons? What we're seeking tonight is at or very near the bottom of the hierarchy. Indeed, many people wouldn't refer to its sort as demons at all, reserving that term for the Great Demons—the *Nartiya Chora,* as those beings are called in the old Nimosei tongue. But more properly, the word applies to all *nartiya* varieties, even the—"

A scream split the night—a scream of pain and horror beyond common human conception. Lesser screams of mere panic and terror immediately joined it—and, rising above them all, a hideous sound never made by any creature of this world. It was the very voice of elemental rage and hate.

Nyrthim gestured with his torch and set out at a run—or the closest he could come to a run in this chaos of buildings. The others followed more clumsily, encumbered by their weapons and lacking the older man's familiarity with these alleys . . . and also lacking a sense that seemed to be guiding him even more unerringly than the sound of the screaming. At least they had no panic-stricken mobs to contend with. Everyone was staying indoors. Occasionally a low moaning could be heard from behind shutters.

Abruptly, that changed. They turned a corner and were momentarily thrust backward by a mass of people, fighting and trampling each other to escape from a certain building. Using their elbows, weapons and sheer size, they forced their way through the crush of bodies and into the building, a tenement not unlike Nyrthim's.

"This way!" shouted Nyrthim, who still seemed to know exactly where to go.

Following him, they left the hysterical crowd behind, for the ground-floor corridor he led them down was quite empty. The door he pointed to was as rickety as everything else; Wothorg sent it crashing inward with a single kick. He, Valdar and Khaavorn crowded through . . . and halted, stunned.

The room was open to a back alley, for its window had been ripped open and part of the adjoining wall smashed through. It was like an abattoir. The hard-packed dirt floor was soaked with blood and littered with human body parts.

But none of them noticed any of that, for in the center of the floor squatted . . . something else.

It never occurred to Valdar, even momentarily, to think of it as an animal. Animals, after all, belong in this world. The thing in the room did not. It was *wrong* . . . wrong in every angle and proportion . . . so wrong that at first the mind refused to accept its presence, rejecting the report of the eyes.

After an instant, though, details began to emerge from the initial, confusedly horrible impression. The thing was between the smallest of lions and the largest of dogs in size, though shaped like neither—nor like any other beast Valdar had ever seen. Coarse, bristly hair, ruddy in color, covered everything—albeit in an unpleasantly sparse, patchy way—except the face. At first, Valdar thought that face was human-looking save for grotesquely massive, projecting jaws that held fangs almost long enough to be called tusks. Then he decided that the features were too crude—they were more like those of an ape from the lands south of Khemiu.

The demon had four limbs. The hind legs, on which it now squatted, were grossly overmuscled, and ended in feet with four curved, glistening claws. From behind, a long sinewy-looking tail tipped with a barb lashed back and forth. The forelimbs looked more like an animal's than a man's, but they could clearly be used as arms; for the hands, though clawed as alarmingly as the feet, could grip. At the moment, they were gripping what had once been a child—whether a boy or a girl was unknowable in its present state. The demon was feeding, its face smeared with blood. As they watched, paralyzed, it tore its victim still further apart to reveal more meat.

Then it saw the newcomers. In a motion almost insectlike in its rapidity, it flung the tattered, bloody little corpse at them and, as they flinched aside, bunched the great muscles of its hind legs and sprang at them. Simultaneously, it opened its jaws wide, revealing two tows of upper and lower teeth, and emitted a bellowing, shrieking roar accompanied by a rush of carrion breath whose foulness might, by itself, have rendered Valdar helplessly sick in any other circumstances.

But in his extremity of desperation he let his body act for him. He tried to fend the demon off with the torch in his left hand. With his right, he brought his sword around in a cut that should have cloven the creature to its vitals . . . but which rebounded from the demon's flank, leaving only a shallow cut. This elicited an even more deafening roar from the demon, which smashed the torch from his hand and struck out with claws he barely managed to avoid.

Khaavorn dropped his torch, gripped his axe in both hands and, with a loud war cry, brought it down on the demon's head with all his strength. Simultaneously Wothorg, who'd been getting into a position with swinging room, put all his weight behind his massive bronze-bound club and smashed the demon across the lower back.

It was a combination of blows that would have killed an aurochs of the northern forests. The demon merely staggered, roared even more loudly, and brought its tail sweeping around to catch Wothorg on the flank with its barb and send him sprawling. Then the thing swung on Khaavorn, raking him across the chest with claws that left blood-oozing rents in his tunic, and then dealing him a smashing blow that flattened him.

Before Valdar could take advantage of the momentary distraction, the demon exhibited the same blinding speed as before and turned on him . . . and then hesitated.

Valdar grew aware that Nyrthim was standing perfectly still, holding his torch aloft, eyes squeezed tightly shut, sweat breaking out over his face. And for reasons Valdar knew lay beyond his understanding, the demon's ear-shattering bellow had subsided to a subterranean roar, and its movements were suddenly sluggish and uncertain. It went into an all-fours posture that seemed more natural to it.

"Strike now!" Nyrthim ground out through clenched teeth, as though squeezing out the words without breaking his fury of concentration.

Without sparing time for thought, Valdar sprang. He saw strangely colored blood trickling from his sword cut, and from the gash left on the demon's scalp by Khaavorn's axe. The hide wasn't invulnerable, then. He straddled the demon's back, grasped his sword hilt in both hands and, in an overhand stab, brought the point down on the base of the thing's neck.

It was like trying to punch through well-cured leather. But the sword point penetrated. The demon shrieked and, with a convulsive movement, straightened up and flung Valdar off its back.

The movement left the demon's front exposed. Khaavorn, who had stumbled to his feet, whirled his axe around in a roundhouse sweep that terminated at the demon's midriff.

The shrieking rose in volume as the demon doubled over. Its tail thrashed about wildly, and Valdar, lying half-stunned, forced himself to roll away out of its range. Then Wothorg, moving unsteadily, stood over the demon and gripped the hilt of Valdar's sword, still protruding from the thick neck. He fell forward, and his weight pushed the blade all the way in. The demon convulsed, but weakly.

"Get away from it!" said Nyrthim urgently.

Valdar and Khaavorn helped Wothorg up, and Valdar pulled out his sword. They stepped back from the feebly twitching demon.

"Why—?" began Valdar, still gasping for breath.

All at once, his uncompleted question was answered. The demon stopped moving, and at that instant a brilliant concentrated flame consumed it, leaving only a fine ash on the bloody dirt of the floor. Even the unnatural blood on Valdar's sword blade sizzled and flashed and then vanished.

"That always happens to demons when they die," explained Nyrthim. "The reason why is obscure. It is my belief that—"

"Nyrthim," Khaavorn broke in roughly, clutching the gashes on his chest, "did I understand you to say this was a *minor* demon?"

"Oh, yes: a *Nartiya Zhere*. Just vermin, really— although, as you've discovered, very hard to kill like all demons. And it has abilities you didn't get a chance to observe. For example, it can—like all demons—disappear from sight at will."

"Then why didn't it?" Valdar wanted to know.

"Why should it? It saw no need to escape—it intended to kill the three of you. It would have, too, had I not used one of the Order's ancient techniques to which I alluded before. The trick can't harm a demon, just disorient it . . . and that only momentarily. But we have no time to discuss it. We must get back to my lodgings. Khaavorn's wounds must be attended to, and . . ." He glanced at Wolthrog, who had again slumped to the floor. "I'll do what I can for your retainer."

"What do you mean by that?" demanded Valdar, feeling a chill.

"He was struck by the barb of the demon's tail. It holds a deadly poison. Khaavorn, you're lucky the claws don't. Now *move!*"

Wothorg lay on a pallet, tended by the women. His face had lost its ruddiness, and he was only intermittently conscious, thanks to a liquid Nyrthim had made him drink.

Nyrthim came to join Valdar and Khaavorn beside the oil lamp that was the room's only illumination. His expression was not encouraging. "I've made him as comfortable as possible. In the end . . . I don't know."

Valdar looked up from his wine cup. "Be honest with me, Nyrthim. I'm not a boy anymore."

"I've never known anyone to survive the poison, or even to last this long," sighed Nyrthim. "But the victims I'm accustomed to generally started out malnourished and unhealthy. A large, strong man like that . . . well, we'll see." A little too obviously, he sought to change the subject. "It could have been worse, you know. The Great Demons can shoot poisoned spines from their tails several yards."

"What else can they do?" asked Khaavorn groggily. In addition to smearing an unguent on his wounds, Nyrthim had given him a pain-killing draught that seemed to be intensifying the effect of the wine he'd been quaffing.

"Oh, a great many things. Fly, for one thing, with

great batlike wings. If you saw one, you'd never guess it was even related to what you killed tonight. But the important differences—the ones that make them *really* dangerous—aren't the flashy physical ones. Most important is their intelligence: at least equal to men's. And they can shape-shift, assuming a human form."

Khaavorn simply gaped, struggling to stay awake. Valdar shook his head as though to clear it of horror. "You said there are other kinds of demons as well . . . ?"

"Yes, many kinds. The *Nartiya Serra*, for example, is hairless and scaled, and can breathe water. There never were many of them. More likely to be encountered is the *Nartiya Ozhre*. It is somewhat related to the *Nartiya Zhere* you encountered tonight . . . but altogether more formidable. It is larger, stronger, and even more vicious. It habitually stands upright on its hind legs, and it is better at using its forelimbs—of which it has *two* pairs—as arms. Thus it can grasp weapons, for example. And it is intelligent enough to be trained as a warrior, to fight in units."

"Nyrthim," asked Valdar, almost pleadingly, "who would want to summon these obscenities into the world? Who is doing this?"

"I am as sure of that as I can be without actual proof." Nyrthim glanced sidelong at Khaavorn as he organized his thoughts. "The Order of the Nezhiy is not the only holdover of the old religion. There is another . . . which, unlike the Order, does not enjoy the approval of the priestesses of Rhaeie. You see, after the Karsha invasions not all the priestesses accepted the compromise with Dayu. Some went underground and maintained in the shadows a secret cult of the

Mother that denied the possibility of a male deity. Later, this cult assimilated to itself the last furtive remanents of the even older demon propitiation that had passed for religion before the Old Empire. Over the centuries, this has degenerated into *worship* of demons. Now these cultists hold that the priestesses were wrong to suppress sorcery, for the Great Demons were, so to speak, the chief ministers of Rhaeie. For them, Dayu was the nemesis who broke the power of the demons they worship in secret with bloody rites. Hardly ever do they actually succeed in summoning demons, even of the lowliest kinds . . . until recently. In actuality, they've come to practice human sacrifice for its own sake."

They stared at him, aghast. Khaavorn momentarily shook off his stupor. "You're not implying that this unspeakable heresy exists in *Lokhrein*, are you?"

"Oh, yes. I'm afraid the rot is everywhere. In fact, the cult has two principal centers: Lokhrein, and here in the Empire."

"Are the priestesses aware of this?"

"They are . . . and they're grimly determined to stamp it out. That is why Minuren was willing to help me. When she learned of the summonings here in The City, she realized at once who must be responsible. She knows the cult is especially strong here, and has been growing steadily stronger . . . especially since Tarhynda became co-Emperor three years ago. This is almost certainly no coincidence. I have reason to think the leader of the cult here in The City must be someone very highly placed in his court."

"So," Khaavorn nodded sagely, "now I see why you need somebody in the palace. . . ." But his voice had begun to slur. He slumped forward and began to snore.

Valdar gave Nyrthim a level regard.

"Yes," the sorcerer answered his unspoken question. "What I gave him really was a healing potion. But it was also meant to render him unconscious. It took longer than I expected."

"Why?"

"Because I need to make you aware of certain things . . . things he's not yet ready to hear. You see, matters are actually worse than I just told you. I believe that the leaders of the secret demon cult here and in Lokhrein are now combining forces, and that this accounts for their recent unaccustomed success in sorcery."

"But how could they be acting together? It's such a long way. . . ."

"It would require a human contact—an emissary. Now, the summonings have occurred here, so such a person must have gone from Lokhrein to The City rather than the other way around. And if I am correct that the cult was behind the elevation of Tarhynda to the position of co-Emperor, some preliminary work would have been necessary—beginning with Tarhynda's initial appearance, as though from nowhere, six or seven years ago, just before he married Vaedorie."

"Yes," Valdar recalled. "Old Namapa was childless save for his daughter Vaedorie. Then she married this previously unknown mercenary officer from the province of Carisa, and he began a meteoric rise, even as Namapa sank into his dotage. It was only natural for Namapa to declare his son-in-law his heir, and later his co-ruler. From what we've heard, Tarhynda's assumption of the sole rule is little more than a formality by now." Valdar shook his head angrily. "But nothing happened seven years ago to suggest the forging of some kind of link between the demon cults in the two lands! Admittedly, relations were exceptionally cordial between the High King and Namapa around that time. In fact, that was when Khaavorn's half sister Andonre came here to marry Vaelsaru. . . ."

Valdar's voice trailed off. His eyes widened.

"You've grasped it," Nyrthim nodded. "And now you surely understand why Khaavorn cannot deal with the truth."

Before Valdar could respond, a cry of transcendent agony from Wothorg brought the two of them to their feet. Nyrthim examined the big Dhulaan and shook his head. "It's progressed too far. Nothing can save him. I'm sorry."

"The mercy stroke," Wothorg ground out through clenched teeth, exerting all his massive strength to hold back a scream.

"I have," Nyrthim began, "a quick-acting potion that will—"

"No." Valdar's voice was made of lead.

Nyrthim met his eyes and nodded. He belonged to the priest class, not the warrior nobility, but he understood: Wothorg was Valdar's man. He stood up and began muttering in old languages and making certain signs. The women withdrew to a corner and watched with round dark eyes.

Valdar drew his sword and knelt over the man on whose shoulders he'd ridden before he could walk. He placed the point just below Wothorg's rib cage.

Wothorg actually managed to smile. "When you get

home to Dhulon and tell them how I went, will you make up some good lies?"

"I'll do better than that. I'll tell them the truth. I'll tell them you gave the death stroke to a demon."

Wothorg smiled again. He closed his eyes, and gave a quick nod.

Valdar rammed the sword home, in and upward to the heart. Wothorg jerked and lay still, his face free of suffering.

A low keening arose from the women.

Valdar stood up. His eyes were like cold bluish flame showing through two holes in a mask of bronze.

"Tell me what you want us to do, Nyrthim," was all he said.

CHAPTER FOUR

A terrace at the base of the palace overlooked the open square before the main façade of what was called the New Palace—the area reconstructed and enlarged by the present dynasty. It commanded a splendid view of The City and its teeming harbor.

Andonre nie'Lanoraak, niece to High King Riod-heg of Lokhrein and wife to Vaelsaru, general of the New Empire's armies and conqueror of the western islands of the Inner Sea, leaned on the balustrade and gazed out over the harbor, turned molten by the late-afternoon sun. She ignored the comings and goings of the ships, which seldom failed to delight her. Her eyes were fixed on the harbor's entrance, between the two rocky headlands. Her imagination roamed the seas beyond, from which her husband still had not returned.

She wasn't supposed to know where he was. But she knew.

The entire court had made a great production of secrecy about his departure. Vaelsaru, in his earnest way, had upheld the deception, even with her and their son. On their last night together, he had solemnly assured her he was going on an inspection tour to the big island of Graetess to the south, and she had solemnly pretended to believe him. She truly didn't resent the lie, nor even think of it as a lie. It was simply one of the distasteful things his oath required him to do. And it *was* distasteful to him . . . at least where she herself was the one to whom he had to lie. She knew that. And for that alone she forgave him.

But she knew where he really was. And she wanted him back. Wanted him badly. Wanted him in a way she could never admit to the High Sister.

Nor could she admit it to anyone else around the court, if only because she could no longer face the prospect of listening to the courtiers solemnly farting at the wrong end about the "restoration of the Old Empire." At least she didn't have to endure that with the High Sister, who knew what was really behind all those sonorous platitudes.

It should have been obvious to anyone, though, what a farce the whole business was. *You can't breathe new life into a corpse,* she thought. *Especially an imaginary corpse. The New Empire is exhausting itself with wars of conquest to* restore *something that never truly existed in the first place.*

Of course, not everyone knows that the Old Empire

never was a real empire at all. But they ought to realize it couldn't *have been. No one could have maintained control by force across such distances—and no one ever tried.*

The westward expansion had taken place in two waves, separated by four centuries. First the old Nimosei speakers had carried the religion of the Mother through the islands and peninsulas of the Inner Sea, and on out into the Outer Sea to every accessible island and shore from here to the ultimate northern remoteness of Dhulon. Later, after the discovery of bronze-working, prospectors and traders—increasingly drawn from the newly acquired eastern island of Alayisa—had followed the old sea routes in search of the tin that the useful new alloy required. But neither missionaries nor merchants had ever dreamed of any kind of centralized administration from Schaerisa—not even in the western reaches of the Inner Sea, much less in the wild lands beyond the straits. Those lands had been part of the Old Empire because they'd *wanted* to be, giving their willing but practically meaningless allegiance to the distant, half-mythical emperor who was the secular arm of Rhaeie.

Granted, the emperors had established a firmer control over the home islands once they had bronze-armed warriors to do it for them. And, under pressure from the wealthy Alayisei merchants, an attempt had been made to suppress piracy within the Inner Sea and safeguard the all-important tin supply. But then, about four and a half centuries ago, the old world had begun to go wrong.

First had come the uprising in Ivaerisa. Native Escquahar tribes, unified by chieftains using the metallurgy supplied by Alayisei renegades from the coast, had lashed back and destroyed the imperial settlements that had called them into being. The lands beyond the straits Ivaerisa commanded had been cast adrift in barbarian darkness, all contact with the home islands forgotten.

The Empire had maintained a toehold on Ivaerisa's coast, while the Escquahar had embarked on a saga of wanderings far into the depths of the continent. But shortly even that remnant had gone its own way, no longer able to maintain regular contact with the home islands because of what was happening there.

For those were the years of the great Karsha conquests. The tall pale-eyed warriors from the grasslands north of the Eyxiyne Sea had been spreading west for centuries, imposing their rule and their languages, before acquiring bronze weapons three centuries before. Then their advance—and the Dayu worship they brought—had become irresistible. The Iyomiasei and the Ayoliysei, as they were to become known, had moved south into the mainland of Zhraess, and been partially tamed. At the same time, other tribes had entered the Rhaemu Valley to the west, and encountered the Escquahar from Ivaerisa. From that violent fusion had come the Dovnaan, a people of hybrid vigor who, given another century, flooded down the Rhaemu in the direction of the great island the Old Empire had called Vriydansa, but which they renamed Lokhrein.

By that time, an Ayoliysei dynasty had inaugurated the New Empire on Schaerisa and Graetess. With the passage of time they had expanded to the other islands, and also to Zhraess, bringing the benefits of imperial civilization—as they had redefined it—to their mainland relatives, and to the kindred Achaysei now crowding down from the north.

A shudder of distaste ran through Andonre at the thought of the Achaysei. *Louts! I hear their priests have now decided that Rhaeie is Dayu's wife—which, for them, means utterly subservient to him, locked away while he ruts with mortal women to provide divine pedigrees for drunken cattle thieves who call themselves kings.*

Of course, even the Ayoliysei used to have some odd ideas about Dayu's supremacy, before they became civilized. Even now, even here, there are holdovers of that. And the emperors no longer rule as highest priests, performing the sacrifices and ceremonies that sustain our link with the Mother, but as warlords commanding bronze-armored charioteers. So it is throughout the world in these sad times. And so the Empire must make use of those Achaysei brutes.

We'll change that. We must change it. Even if it means, for now, going along with all the claptrap about restoring the Old Empire—which, in turn, means more wars and therefore more Achaysei.

The High Sister says so. And so I must believe.

She heard footsteps behind her. She had no need to turn and see who was approaching. That shuffling gait was unmistakable.

"Is there any news concerning my half brother and his companions?" she demanded over her shoulder.

"None, my lady," came the odious courtier's simper. "We know only what you yourself heard earlier, from the harbormaster's report and the subsequent inter-rogations of the ship's captain and others. The Lords

Khaavorn and Valdar arrived yesterday, and regrettably became involved as bystanders in a street disturbance. Our efforts to locate them have been unavailing."

Andonre turned imperiously. "I was under the impression, Malsara, that as chamberlain of the court—which technically includes The City as a whole—you were responsible for preventing . . . street disturbances."

"I do what I can, noble lady." As always, Malsara's fawning made her skin crawl.

She wasn't prejudiced against eunuchs, of course. They were necessary—everyone knew that. Originally, they had been required for certain religious purposes. That was no longer the case, but at some point they had attached themselves to the imperial court, where they occupied a position of unique trust due to their inability to found a dynasty, which put them beyond suspicion of the most basic motive for usurpation. At least that was the theory. But . . .

But, dear Mother Rhaeie, they stink *so!* It was true, however copiously diapered they kept themselves. And in Malsara's case, the stench was more than just physical.

He didn't have the stereotypical plumpness. Indeed, he was positively gaunt, and his vulpine features and hard black eyes enhanced the effect. *He must,* Andonre thought, *have been cut at a later-than-normal age.* She wondered if he might feel a certain resentment as a consequence.

The thought crossed her mind, startling in its novelty, that the malice and proneness to intrigue that legend attributed to eunuchs might have something to do with bitterness against the world. She instantly dismissed the notion. *Absurd! What do they have to*

*be bitter about? How else could people of their class
hope to rise to high positions at court? That's why
families compete for the chance to have sons gelded.*

She looked down at him—she was of only average
height for a woman of the Dovnaan aristocracy, but
she would have been taller than Malsara even had he
been standing up straight. "I came here today hoping
for rather more than the nothing you've given me,
Chamberlain. I remind you that the persons in question
are a nephew of the High King of Vriydansa"—she'd
learned better than to say "Lokhrein"—"and the son
and heir of an allied king. If they have come to harm
due to *your* inability to keep order in The City, the
Emperor will view the matter seriously . . . as will the
Empress."

Andonre immediately regretted that last, for Malsara's smell grew even more disgusting. It was a small
price to pay, though, to see his abject terror. "Please
accept my assurances, noble lady, that I am making
every possible effort to—"

"Mama! Mama!"

Andonre turned at the sound of the new voice, the
eunuch mercifully forgotten. A smile transfigured her
face as she watched five-year-old Zhotiyu approaching
at his customary run, his nurse trailing behind and
puffing indignantly.

"Zhotiyu!" she said with unconvincing severity.
"You've been told not to make Corannie chase after
you!"

"Mama," her son gasped, oblivious, "they've come!
They've come!"

"Catch your breath and tell me *who* have come."

"The visitors! The ones you've always told me

about—Uncle Khaavorn and his friend. Is it true they come from a land at the back of the north wind, like Corannie says?"

Andonre forced herself not to smile, or appear to notice the nurse's embarrassment. "No, dear, I don't think so. I come from that land, too. And we got chilled by the north wind often enough, so it must start somewhere else." She tousled her son's hair. That hair was a reminder of Lokhrein, for it was the reddish color of a chestnut horse—almost as red as her own, although the boy's features were already those of Vaelsaru. She knew she would miss that hair when, seven years hence, it was shaved save for the three long locks of adolescence.

She turned to Malsara with a smile. "Well, Chamberlain, it appears that the palace gossip has run ahead of your sources of information."

The eunuch's answering smile was a mask painted on a death's-head of hate. "I can barely contain my elation at the safe arrival of your distinguished countrymen, noble lady. They are undoubtedly in the entry court. If I may escort you . . ."

"We can find our own way, Chamberlain. Corannie, bring Lord Vaelsaru's son."

Andonre swept along the terrace, around a corner to the monumental staircase that led up to the colonnaded entrance court. Guards and functionaries were fussing over two new arrivals.

"Andonre!" boomed Khaavorn. He strode over and embraced her with a spontaneity that scandalized the functionaries. Then he took her by the shoulders and held her at arm's length where he could survey her elaborate ankle-length flounced dress with its embroidered bodice, cut low enough to have raised eyebrows in Lokhrein, even though it didn't expose the breasts altogether as it would have for an unmarried maiden. "Look at you! What a great lady you've become. But you don't look a day older."

"Liar!" Privately, though, she was pleased . . . and knew it was almost true. She might no longer be quite the coltish seventeen-year-old who had voyaged from Lokhrein to an arranged political marriage. But her slenderness had returned as much as could be hoped for after bearing Zhotiyu. (The only child she would ever bear, the physicians had told her, not realizing that she already knew it—and, unlike them, knew why.) Seven years under the southern sun had warmed her complexion without—as yet—drying or wrinkling it. Nor had time faded her coppery-brown hair's ruddiness, or dimmed her hazel-green eyes.

Inwardly . . . well, that was another story.

"An' surely you'll not be tellin' me this great tall lad is your son!" Khaavorn declared, in Ayoliysei for Zhotiyu's benefit.

The boy swelled with pride. "Greetings, Uncle Khaavorn," he said carefully in the Dovnaan he'd learned from his mother but had little chance to practice.

Khaavorn laughed and swept him up into a hug. "Your father sends his best," he told Andonre. "He's as well as can be expected, though he's complained of stiffness lately, and coughs a lot in the winter."

"Thank you. Of course, I heard about mother, last year."

Khaavorn nodded. Andonre nodded in return. There was no need to say more about their mother, nor any occasion for displays of grief. In their world, it was rare indeed for someone in his thirties like Khaavorn to have a living mother. Elaamen, the older of the High King's half sisters, had borne Andonre to her second husband Lanoraak at an unusually late age, a decade after bearing Khaavorn, the oldest of the three sons she'd given her first husband Moreg.

"Aunt Norkhaari is as always, though," said Khaavorn. "She never seems to get any older."

"No, she doesn't," agreed Andonre, recalling the High King's younger half sister, a priestess of Rhaeie. She kept her face carefully expressionless.

Khaavorn drew his companion forward. "You remember Valdar, don't you? A couple of years before you left, I was given the hopeless task of training him."

"At least it forced you to do *something* useful in your misspent youth," Andonre retorted.

"He's misspending his old age as well," Valdar quipped.

"'Old age,' is it? Why, you—"

"Behave yourself, Khaavorn. And of *course* I remember you, Valdar. Welcome to The City." Andonre's eyes met Valdar's, and she thought to see in them a reflection of what she was certain must be showing in hers.

Andonre's fourteenth year had been enlivened by the arrival of the brash young prince from Dhulon, only two years older than she but already living what had seemed a grand adventure—especially after he'd departed with her awesome uncle the High King and his warriors on the war trail to restore the king of Dhulon. He'd walked through her girlish daydreams in those days, his raven hair streaming in the wind of the springtime that all adolescents know will surely never end. His immaterial presence had made it even harder to leave all she'd ever known to marry a much older imperial officer she'd never seen, in a land beyond the sunrise. The daydreams had eventually faded as she'd come to feel, if not love for Vaelsaru, at least a respect so deep as to be—surely—indistinguishable from love. But she'd never entirely forgotten the first time she'd seen Valdar, watched over as always by that great bearlike northern seafarer . . . what had his name been . . . ?

"Where is Wothorg, Valdar? It's hard to imagine you without him on guard at your back."

A barrier clanked down with almost audible force, and what Andonre had seen in those blue-gray eyes guttered out. "Actually, my lady, he was killed in the street brawl which resulted in our getting lost in The City overnight."

A hand went to Andonre's mouth. "Oh, Valdar, I'm so sorry!" Belatedly, she noticed a series of recently mended rents in the front of Khaavorn's tunic—which looked like it had just been cleaned, but still held a telltale rusty discoloration around those stitches. "Khaavorn, were you wounded?"

"How many men did you kill?" asked Zhotiyu eagerly, staring wide-eyed at the war axe hanging from Khaavorn's belt.

"Zhotiyu, that will do! Khaavorn, tell me what happened."

"Oh, just a few scratches," Khaavorn assured her, a little too heartily. "The people we stayed with overnight—we couldn't very well find our way to the palace after dark, you know—were good enough to fix my tunic. Nothing, really. Why, you should see—"

"Yes, yes, I know: I should see the *other* fellows. Khaavorn, I used to wonder if you'd ever grow up. Now I know the answer." Andonre looked around furiously and saw Malsara entering the courtyard. "Lord Chamberlain—"

"I heard, noble lady. I am mortified over this unpleasantness. But what can one expect of the street scum? We will send troops to the district in question at once, to round up known troublemakers. A few public executions should restore the streets to their accustomed serenity."

"I am reassured," said Andonre with a sarcasm to which the eunuch showed no reaction. "I trust you will also search for the body of Lord Valdar's retainer, so that he can be given the proper rites."

"Very well, noble lady." Even Malsara's carefully schooled features failed to conceal his puzzlement: *Why such concern over launching a mere servant into the afterlife?* "On a more cheerful note, I am commanded to invite the Lords Khaavorn and Valdar to a reception tonight, followed by a banquet. But for now, I will have them conducted to their quarters." He clapped his hands, and slaves ran forward.

"Will your husband be there, Andonre?" asked Khaavorn as his belongings were spirited away.

"No. Vaelsaru is . . . at sea. I don't know when he'll return."

"Too bad. I really ought to meet my brother-in-law, you know. Or is it *half* brother-in-law? Well, maybe he'll get back while we're here . . . eh, Valdar?"

"Hopefully." Valdar's eyes met Andonre's momentarily, and they were carefully shuttered. "Until later, Andonre."

They departed, leaving her puzzled. There was something about Valdar's aspect that was strangely at odds with Khaavorn's unaffected joy at greeting her—and also at odds with the Valdar she remembered.

Granted, he's older now—as are we all, except of course dear Khaavorn, who'll always be the same age. And yet . . .

He can't know, surely. How could he?

I must speak to the High Sister about this.

CHAPTER FIVE

"Lokhrein! My word!" The courtier—Valdar couldn't recall his name or title—arched his eyebrows into sickles of insincere incredulity. "I must confess to a certain surprise. We have a tendency, you know, to think of Dovnaan as wild, skin-clad barbarians with flaming red hair."

"No doubt the great distance allows misconceptions to flourish," said another of the courtiers with a condescendingly mollifying smile.

"Aye, that it does," agreed Khaavorn in his carefully accented Ayoliysei. "Why, we've always heard that half of the imperial aristocracy are boy-buggers and the other half are cuckolds. Is it not a wonder, how people's ideas err?"

"I think Andonre wants us to meet someone else," said Valdar into the frozen silence, taking Khaavorn by his left elbow and steering him away. "You're getting better," he murmured when they were out of earshot.

"I rather thought so myself," allowed Khaavorn, either not recognizing irony or choosing to ignore it, Valdar wasn't sure which. But his right hand involuntarily strayed toward his belt, to the axe handle that wasn't there. Andonre had managed to persuade them that weapons could not be worn to a reception where the Emperor would be present. They'd compromised by leaving sword and axe with one of Malsara's ushers at the main entrance. It was small wonder Khaavorn was ill at ease.

The setting didn't help. They were in the same great entrance court where Andonre had greeted them earlier. In the afternoon sunlight of early spring, tiled and painted in a cheerful variety of colors, it had seemed light and airy. But now the sun had set, and in the flickering golden light of torches the court, lined on three sides by tiers of pillared galleries, seemed awesome, hieratic, redolent of ancientness and power.

The chattering throng of courtiers did nothing to dispel the mood—they only added an element of exotic strangeness. The women's gowns were easier to get used to than the men's plumed headdresses, elaborate to the point of fantasy in contrast to the simplicity of their kilt-and-mantle outfits of lightweight white linen.

Valdar had learned by now that this was the New Palace: a wing rebuilt and extended by the Ayoliysei in accordance with their own mainland ideas but on a scale commensurate with the wealth and architectural sophistication of the empire they'd seized. The surviving parts of the Old Palace were falling into disuse. So there was a certain irony—if one knew what to look for—in the consciously archaic court dress, which aped that of the Old Empire. But none of this knowledge banished his sense that the weight of a thousand years' history was pressing in on him.

Malsara, flanked by two of his ushers, appeared and tapped the floor with the butt of his staff of office. This was the signal for everyone to begin filing into the great hall, through a vestibule on the opposite side of the court from the entrance. Once inside, the ushers arranged them according to fixed rules of precedence. Then they waited.

Valdar spent the time examining the hall. It was a chamber of awesome size and mind-numbingly elaborate decoration, the geometric patterns of the tiles contrasting with the startlingly naturalistic frescoes of animals and plants that covered the walls. Along the walls and beneath the frescoes, couches and low tables had been set out, where they would later recline for the banquet. The hall was lit by rows of oil lamps atop tall bronze stands, and a low fire in the circular hearth in the center of the floor. Four massive columns surrounded that hearth, supporting a clerestory that let daylight in and smoke out. Valdar tried to imagine how dazzlingly colorful the hall must look by day. In this light, the colors were muted and the overall impression cavernlike. Against the far wall stood the alabaster throne of the emperors, which had once stood in the throne room of the Old

Palace. The recently deceased Namapa had moved it here. His co-ruler Tarhynda had urged that, just as he'd urged the campaigns of conquest in the islands to the west.

To the right of the throne was a double door covered in bronze and set with semiprecious stones, flanked by guards in the full bronze panoply of chariot warriors. They all waited, attention focused on that door, which led to the imperial apartments.

Presently, a warning cry was heard, coming faintly from the inner reaches of the palace. It was repeated by voices that grew nearer and nearer, until the bronze doors swung open with a crash. In the doorway stood the Emperor and Empress.

Everyone went to their knees as the imperial couple advanced into the hall. Tarhynda sat down on the throne, after which Vaedorie perched on a low stool beside it. This was an innovation for which she herself was responsible. Traditionally, emperors' wives had not held court with them.

The room rose to its collective feet at a signal from Malsara, who moved to the Emperor's side and murmured into his ear. Valdar took the opportunity to study the couple of whom he, like all the world, had heard so much.

Tarhynda was a tall man—almost extraordinarily so—in his early thirties. He was dressed in the rich, deep blue which only the emperor might wear. Instead of the usual courtiers' confections, his head bore only a golden circlet set with a jewel sacred to Rhaeie, confining jet-black hair worn in the fashion of the court: long in the back, with lovelocks hanging down in front of the ears. As a mark of special favor to this select assemblage, he was not wearing the mask of thin-beaten gold which always concealed the imperial visage from the sight of the vulgar. The clean-shaven face thus revealed was long, pale olive in complexion, with straight-nosed, thin-lipped features. Most striking were his eyes: huge eyes of a peculiar deep-gold hue like the amber that came from a northern land to the east of Dhulon. The eyes of a bird of prey. It was, thought Valdar, a face that would have drawn all attention even had its owner not been seated on the alabaster throne.

Vaedorie was renowned as a great beauty. Valdar could see why, even though she was no longer young and did not conform to the conventional aristocratic canons which demanded the tall stature and fair coloring of the Ayoliysei's Karsha forbears. Vaedorie, small and intensely dark, looked like one of the Nimosei wives those northern tribesmen had taken to acquire the property that, in the Old Empire, had passed by matrilineal succession. Thus the foundation for their eventual dominance had been laid. And the tradition was not altogether dead. It had smoothed Tarhynda's road to power as husband of Namapa's daughter, all the more so inasmuch as she still remained childless. There was some concern over the couple's failure to produce an heir. For now, though, most people were inclined to let sleeping succession crises lie.

Valdar became aware that Malsara was motioning him and Khaavorn forward. They approached the throne and bowed as they'd been instructed.

"Welcome," said Tarhynda in a deep, beautifully modulated voice that was as remarkable as his face. "The Lady Andonre has spoken often of her brother.

We are pleased to receive the nephew of Riodheg, *Miynonu* of Vriydansa." The title was a Nimosei word, which the Emperor had doubtless assumed the visitors from the far northwest wouldn't understand. It meant, roughly, a local ruler who held power at the Emperor's sufferance, subject to loose imperial supervision.

Valdar saw Khaavorn flush. He also saw a faint smile touch the corners of Tarhynda's mouth. He decided his initial assumption had been wrong; the Emperor had spoken with full knowledge and intent that he'd be understood.

"The High King of Lokhrein," said Khaavorn, with an emphasis that, to Valdar's relief, stopped short of truculence, "sends his greetings to his brother sovereign." There was a collective scandalized gasp from the courtiers, and a glare from Malsara, but Tarhynda showed no reaction. "He also sends his condolences on the death of the late lamented Emperor Namapa."

This also failed to get a rise out of Tarhynda, although Khaavorn had intended it as something of a barb. It was widely whispered in The City that Tarhynda's expressions of grief at the senior Emperor's death had been no more than propriety demanded.

"Thank you," Vaedorie spoke up from her stool. "My father always regretted the gulf that has, for too long, sundered the Emperors from their loyal subjects in the provinces beyond the straits."

"Yes," nodded Tarhynda. "A state of affairs that we ourselves find intolerable." He smiled charmingly. "But we have learned, to our mortification, that you encountered some unpleasantness on your arrival yesterday."

"A mere disturbance in the streets," Khaavorn assured him. "Our lives were in no real danger."

"Still, we understand your slaves were killed. Such property damage cannot be permitted. Fortunately, thanks to the efficiency of our Chamberlain, the miscreants have been apprehended and dealt with." Tarhynda glanced at Malsara, who gestured to his own underlings. Soldiers—low-ranking ones, armored only in leather—entered bearing a row of X-shaped wooden frames. The flayed skins stretched over those frames were translucent in the lamplight.

"The swiftness of imperial justice inspires awe," said Valdar drily, "considering that the incident occurred only yesterday afternoon."

"The Chamberlain assured us that these were notorious rogues and troublemakers. There could therefore be no doubt of their guilt—if not of this particular disorder, then of something else—so lengthy proceedings were unnecessary." Tarhynda again smiled his winning smile . . . which, Valdar now noticed, rose no higher than his lips. "Be assured that they were kept alive and conscious for the skinning."

"We appreciate your kind consideration." *Of course,* Valdar reflected, *we have only Tarhynda's word for that . . . and, for that matter, that these weren't just some aging, valueless slaves picked at random for the purpose.*

"Please don't mention it. And now," said the Emperor, speaking to the room at large as the frames were removed, "we wish to make an announcement. It will be of interest to our distinguished guest Lord Khaavorn, for it concerns his illustrious brother-in-law's latest triumph."

From off to the left, where Andonre stood with other ladies of the court, Valdar heard a hiss of indrawn breath.

Tarhynda looked in that direction with a smile. "Yes. A swift galley, sent ahead of the main fleet, arrived just hours ago with the news that Lord Vaelsaru's expedition has succeeded in its aim. That aim can now be made generally known." The Emperor let a dramatic pause last just long enough. "Lord Vaelsaru was sent to persuade the recalcitrant rulers of the imperial province of Arvaerness to remember their allegiance. The sight of the imperial fleet—and, no doubt, the reputation of Lord Vaelsaru, mightiest of war leaders—sufficed to compel their submission after only token resistance. Another step has been taken in the restoration of the Empire to the fullness of its ancient glory!"

A chorus of rapturous noises arose from the courtiers, many of whom probably didn't know where Arvaerness was.

"The fleet must have been sailing parallel to our ship, to the north," Khaavorn muttered into Valdar's ear.

"And a couple of days behind," Valdar agreed. He was thinking furiously.

Arvaerness was the Old Empire's name for the mainland region drained by the Rhodamu River, which flowed south to meet the Inner Sea north of Sardiysa and its smaller companion island of Corcyresa (which not even Tarhynda had thought worth seizing). Its connection to the Old Empire had been even more tenuous than most. It had reverted to bucolic obscurity at some point after the upheavals of a couple of centuries ago, and nobody ever thought of it. Everyone—including Nyrthim, Valdar recalled—had been taking for granted that the next move in Tarhynda's game would be westward. . . .

"Maybe Ivaerisa looked like too hard a nut to crack," Khaavorn murmured. "Tarhynda wanted to inaugurate his sole rule with an easy conquest."

"Maybe." But there must, Valdar was convinced, be more to it than that.

"Lord Vaelsaru," Tarhynda resumed, "is remaining with his army in Arvaerness, to which the fleet will return presently with reinforcements. In the meantime he will tour the province's frontiers, to receive the submission of the outlying areas and establish fortresses wherever necessary to assure the Empire's security."

All at once, Valdar understood.

"You realize what this means, don't you?" he whispered to Khaavorn as they let the ushers conduct them, along with everyone else, to their couches for the banquet.

"'Means'? What in Angmanu's name are you talking about?" Hunger always made Khaavorn irritable, and the aroma of the feast was beginning to pervade the great hall. Grilled meats and savory sauces, roast fowl, the broiled fish for which Schaerisa was famous . . .

"*Think*, Khaavorn! Where does Arvaerness have a 'frontier' that would need fortresses?"

Khaavorn blinked twice. "Why, nowhere. Except to the northwest, of course. But no, that's . . ."

"Precisely: the High King's continental possessions in Arnoriysa. All at once, Lokhrein and the Empire have a common border. And for some reason, acquiring that common border was more important to Tarhynda than Ivaerisa and its riches."

The banquet proceeded, and lived up to expectations. But for once, Khaavorn showed little appetite.

Andonre was all alone in the darkness and the silence as she walked through the vast colonnaded halls. No one came to the Old Palace at night. There were too many ghosts.

But Andonre knew her way from long practice, even by the feeble light of her lamp. And she felt no fear in these haunted precincts. She was on the Mother's business.

She emerged from a long corridor into the central courtyard, under the stars and the half-moon. She turned to the right, ascended a broad flight of stairs, and crossed a portico into the room she sought.

It was a place of shadows and dust and lurking rats nowadays. But the three-sided loggia still surrounded the square well in the center of the floor as it had when the priestesses of the Old Empire had descended the staircase in that well to intercede with Rhaeie for the human race.

Andonre descended it now.

Down and down the staircase led, below the public halls and corridors of the Old Palace to its very foundations, where the rough crude masonry dated from a couple of earthquakes back. At the bottom was a small anteroom, one of whose walls was concealed by a heavy curtain.

The palace had been built little by little, expanding until it had overspread the entire hill at the foot of the volcanic mountain . . . including a certain cave, around which it had been organized. Andonre pulled the curtain aside, to reveal a rocky mountainside and a cave mouth. She stepped through, into the holiest place in the world.

She walked along the passageway, seemingly into the very womb of the Mother. Ahead, a light grew. There, she entered the sacred grotto itself, with its icy pool of dark water surrounded by stalactites whose crevices held votive offerings dating back to the earliest days of the Old Empire, or perhaps even earlier. Still older—unimaginably old, in fact—was the stone statue, so crude as to barely be recognizable as a female figure.

Torches were thrust into sconces in the rough walls, and their light revealed two junior Sisters. A third figure—the smallest in the room—was still dressed in a long hooded cloak like Andonre's.

"High Sister," murmured Andonre, inclining her head.

They exchanged the ritual forms of greeting, and made obeisance to the statue—but hurriedly, for the High Sister was clearly impatient. "So, Sister," she demanded as soon as it was proper, "what is behind your half brother's visit?"

"As far as I can tell, High Sister, there is nothing more to Khaavorn's purposes than he says. There seldom is, with him. It is his friend Prince Valdar who concerns me. There is something in his behavior that is . . . closed. He is hiding his feelings in a way that is unlike him."

"You haven't seen him in seven years. He could have changed. At any rate, Dhulon is for the moment unimportant."

"But Valdar is in the service of the High King of Lokhrein." Here, diplomatic fictions and official pretenses could be dropped. "And besides . . . what if he knows something?"

"Bah! How could he? And yet . . ."

"Yes, High Sister?"

"I have learned that a *Nartiya Zhere* vanished in the slums last night—after these men's arrival and before their appearance at the palace."

Andonre had no need to ask how the High Sister had "learned" it. She held her tongue, for fear of letting her true feelings show. She knew what the lesser demons did in the teeming hovels of The City's poor, and she found she could not summon up the proper regret at the death of one of the mindless beings.

"Surely it is mere coincidence," she ventured.

"It *must* be! Only . . . there has been someone, or something, at work in The City recently. We have been encountering certain unanticipated difficulties. It is almost as though . . . No! We are reliably informed that the last member of the vile Order of the Nezhiy is dead. Still, I am concerned about the time your half brother and his companion were out of sight in The City."

"High Sister," Andonre spoke up hesitantly, "remember that Khaavorn, like me, is descended in the female line from the priesthood of the Old Empire. He and Valdar have always rendered all proper worship to Rhaeie. Surely they would never—"

"Ha! 'Proper worship' indeed! They know nothing of the Mother as She truly is. Only we know Her in all Her awesome terror—as all the world knew Her in the great old days before the Old Empire's priestesses rendered Her powerless by denying Her the aid of Angmanu and the lesser *nartiya* who ruled the world for Her. Those priestesses were fools. But the priestesses who came afterwards were worse; they were traitors, turning Rhaeie into a pallid housemaid of the great enemy Dayu! *That* is the Rhaeie your brother imagines when he renders his 'proper worship.'"

"But, High Sister, perhaps Khaavorn and Valdar and others like them can be brought back to the true religion without—"

The High Sister struck her across the face. Her eyes were like burning black coals. "You weak, pathetic little twit!" she hissed. "There is only one way that men—and most women, come to that—can be made to see the truth: abject fear! Thus it was in the old days. Once the people understood that the Mother allowed the *nartiya* to torment them, and that only the Mother could restrain the torment, then they understood what the world is really like! And soon they'll understand it again! That is what we are working toward. That is why we summoned *him*. That is what the Highest Sister sent you here for. Have you forgotten that she ordered you to obey me in all things?"

Andonre's head bowed, for there could be no further argument. "No, High Sister, I've not forgotten."

"Haven't you? I sometimes wonder. You certainly forgot that your marriage to Vaelsaru was merely the excuse for your presence here."

Andonre winced as she had not done when struck. "Zhotiyu's conception was an accident, High Sister. Forgive me for my error."

The High Sister relaxed a little. "Very well—especially considering that it's an 'accident' we've made certain

you can't repeat. Come. There is much to do. We
must make preparations for the ceremony. There is
little time."

"Yes, High Sister."

It never occurred to Andonre to use any other title
for her—not here. In this place, no titles by which
one was called in the world above, exposed to Dayu's
sky, mattered. *No* such titles, however lofty. Not even
the very loftiest.

"Very well," repeated the High Sister. "Let us begin."
She removed her cloak and revealed the regalia she'd
shown the world in the great hall earlier, seated on
a stool at the Emperor's feet.

CHAPTER SIX

Maestor smoothed out a wrinkle in his robe—the robe of the High Priest of Dayu—and spoke with patronizing earnestness.

"So you see, we have reached a stage in our intellectual growth where we no longer need out forefathers' naïve belief in Dayu and Angmanu as *persons*. Now we recognize that they are simply personifications of the impulses—good and evil impulses, respectively—dwelling in the human heart. In this life, we owe it to our better natures to be champions of Dayu and reject the counsel of Angmanu." The High Priest's well-fed face took on a condescending smirk. "The ordinary believer still requires these verbal symbols of ethical concepts which *we*, of course, can comprehend without them."

"I see," said Valdar judiciously. They were leaning against the balustrade of the New Palace's terrace, looking out over The City and its harbor. "You assert, then, that your predecessors were wrong?"

"No, no, no! Not *wrong*, exactly. Just . . . limited. They can hardly be blamed for having been born too early to partake of the theological sophistication to which we have now attained."

"Of course not. And I suppose the lesser demons . . . ?"

"Symbols of the deepest fears of the ignorant—including their fear of their own innermost impulses. We need no longer believe in their *literal* existence."

"No doubt. Still, while in The City I heard some . . . odd stories about things that have been happening there."

"You were among the rabble. One must make allowances for persons of their sort."

"Your ideas are interesting. May I ask if all your colleagues share them?"

Maestor's smug expression sagged a bit. "Not all, unfortunately. Certain members of the priesthood have proven unable to adjust to new concepts. Old Paeliyu, for example."

"Ah, yes: your predecessor as High Priest. Didn't he fall ill and die rather suddenly last year?"

"Yes. Of *course* we were all devastated. And yet . . . I was never able to rid myself of the feeling that his obstruction of my career was rooted not just in stubborn doctrinal conservatism but also in personal animosity—and, starting three years ago, jealousy of the favor the new co-emperor showed to me and others of my persuasion."

"Oh, yes, that's right. Tarhynda's support enabled you to succeed to the High Priest's chair over several of Paeliyu's supporters, didn't it?"

"Indeed." Maestor beamed, dissipating the scowl that had been gathering on his plump face. "He has always been a champion of progressive theological views. Now that he is sole Emperor, I have high hopes for a general housecleaning of the priesthood's higher levels. Indeed, it has already begun."

"So I understand. But now you must excuse me, holy one, for I see that Lord Khaavorn is back. Thank you for your conversation, which has been most enlightening." They parted with further exchanges of courtesies.

"Why were you talking to that pompous fathead?" asked Khaavorn. His initial, automatic respect for the High Priest had not survived closer acquaintance.

"I was seeking enlightenment," Valdar smiled. "Especially on the subject of Tarhynda's intentions—one of which, it seems, is to weaken the priesthood, starting at the top and working down."

"All very interesting," grumbled Khaavorn in a not-very-interested-sounding way, "but where does that leave *us?* We still haven't heard from Nyrthim. You've been putting those messages just outside the eastern stairs up to the terrace, haven't you?"

"Regularly. And they're always gone the next day, so someone must be picking them up for him." There were always plenty of potsherds lying around the imperial storehouses, and Nyrthim had made Valdar memorize a couple of the signs of the imperial syllabary, to represent his and Khaavorn's availability or non-availability the following night. Conveying information by scratching these markings on potsherds was something that still hadn't lost its almost eerie novelty. He wondered if he dared ask Nyrthim to teach him to actually read and write, sometime when they had the opportunity. He'd mentioned the idea to Khaavorn, who found it too unimaginable even for ridicule.

"Well, then, why haven't we heard from him? Didn't he tell you he'd get word to us?"

"Yes, but he didn't say exactly how. Maybe he's encountered difficulties."

"I say we—or one of us, anyway—should go back to his place and find out what's happening."

"*No*, Khaavorn! That's the one thing we mustn't do. We're too visible. Besides, do you really think you could find your way, unguided, through *that*?" Valdar gestured over the balustrade at the incomprehensible warren that was The City. "I'm certain I couldn't."

Khaavorn emitted a growl of frustration as they turned right and climbed the monumental staircase to the entrance court. It was busy at this early-afternoon hour, with much coming and going of the merchants who supplied the court. A wine seller had just arrived with a line of slaves—dark stocky types from Carisa or Lydisa or one of the other provinces on the mainland of Amatoliysa to the northeast—bent under the loads of amphorae they were carrying. The seller, a plump specimen of the same ethnic type, was dickering with one of Malsara's under-chamberlains. He struck a bargain just in time to turn and spot Valdar and Khaavorn.

"Ah, great nobles from afar, do you perhaps require

something exceptional in the way of wines to entertain your guests? Or perhaps to—heh, heh!—weaken the resolves of highborn ladies?"

"Not today," said Valdar shortly. The way these things worked, a merchant would make a gift of his wares, and the recipient would then be obligated to give a gift in return. It went well enough with people like the under-chamberlain, who understood the rules of the game. But aristocrats, lacking all sense of the value of commodities and regarding "niggard" as a deadly insult, would invariably overestimate the amount of gold or jewelry or bronzework their honor required them to bestow. Valdar sometimes wondered what it would be like to have a measuring rod for the prices of things. As it was, however, he hurried on, certain that the wine merchant looked on outland nobles as even easier prey than the local ones.

"But I can supply true novelties! Palm wine of Khemiu; purple grape wine from Graetess normally reserved for the Emperor himself; resined wine from the hills of Zhraess, admittedly an acquired taste . . ."

"Begone," growled Khaavorn as they pushed past. He'd given up bemoaning the unavailability of the good beer of Lokhrein, but he would never be a wine connoisseur.

"Ah, but don't be so hasty, good sirs," the wine seller called out from behind them. "You never know what you'll need to warm you . . . when the wind comes down from Mount Vithfaa."

Valdar and Khaavorn stopped cold, then turned slowly.

It was the recognition signal Nyrthim had told Valdar his messenger would use. It was also one which nobody from Amatoliysa—or anywhere else in the Inner Sea—could possibly know.

"But," said Valdar, "Mount Vithfaa is in the land of the demons."

"All the more reason for it to be cold," said the wine seller, completing the formula.

"So you come from Nyrthim," Khaavorn stated, unnecessarily.

"The Nezh sent me, yes," said the wine seller, in tones low enough to go unheard in the tumult of the entrance court.

"Who are you?" asked Valdar. "How do you know Nyrthim?"

"My name is Zhassu. And the Nezh placed me in his debt by what he did for certain of my kindred. I am now able to work off some measure of this debt through my ability to enter the palace without suspicion. It is fortunate that I saw the two of you here, thus saving me from having to invent excuses to roam about without getting an Achaysei sword in my belly. My sense of gratitude to the Nezh is great but, like everything else, not infinite."

"So you bring a message from him?" Khaavorn demanded brusquely.

"Yes, indeed. His instructions to the two of you are as follows: tonight, when the moon is at its highest, conceal yourselves outside the villa occupied by the Lady Andonre. If she emerges, as the Nezh is certain she will, follow her to—"

"*Andonre?*" Khaavorn remembered to keep his voice down, but his eyes blazed and his hand went to his axe handle. "What are you saying, you ball of rancid grease?"

"Mercy, mighty lords! I only repeat the words of the Nezh."

"Then you got his words wrong, fool! The Lady Andonre has nothing to do with any of this."

"Khaavorn," said Valdar quietly, "Zhassu wouldn't have the password if he wasn't trustworthy. Besides, merchants have to have good memories."

"But why should Nyrthim want us to follow Andonre? It doesn't make any sense."

"I'm sure Nyrthim's reasons will become clear to us in time. Remember, he knows things we don't." *Or, at least, that* you *don't*, thought Valdar guiltily. With the passage of time, and with the silence on the subject he must maintain in Khaavorn's presence, what Nyrthim had told him had faded into unreality. At times, he'd begun to wonder if it could really be true . . . or if he'd ever really heard it. Now it had come back, unwelcome. He turned to Zhassu, avoiding Khaavorn's eyes. "Go on; what are the rest of Nyrthim's instructions?"

"Only that you are to follow the lady wherever she goes, and observe . . ." Zhassu's eyes flickered warily to Khaavorn and Khaavorn's axe. "And observe whatever transpires. Then go to the place where you have been leaving the potsherds. I will be waiting there, to take your message to the Nezh."

Khaavorn was still seething. "I don't see why we can't just tell Andonre, and—"

"Remember, Khaavorn, Nyrthim swore us to secrecy."

"Yes, yes, I know. But this is Andonre we're talking about! Surely he didn't mean to include her. . . . Oh, all right, Valdar. We'll do it Nyrthim's way."

The palace complex didn't cover the entire hill at the foot of the volcanic cone, not even after the expansion that had created the New Palace. Some old villas from the days before that expansion had survived and been renovated, though now they found a tight fit in the remaining open spaces.

One such villa was to the southwest of the Old Palace, in an angle between that looming hulk and the New Palace. It overlooked an ancient semisubterranean gallery that ran alongside the Old Palace and gave access to it, but was now seldom used.

Valdar and Khaavorn slipped out of the New Palace by moonlight, and sidled along the base of its terrace wall, through a narrow passageway—an architectural oversight, really—between the old and new constructions. Ahead was the villa, which had been bestowed on General Vaelsaru after his conquest of Sardiysa, and where his wife was currently residing. Just inside the passageway, they settled in as comfortably as possible and waited.

"So what did you think of the chariot practice this afternoon?" asked Valdar to make conversation.

"Impressive." Khaavorn genuinely sounded impressed. The chariot was relatively new to the Dovnaan, and they still tended to think of it largely as a form of prestige transportation, carrying the wealthiest of warriors to battlefields where they alighted and butchered each other in traditional ways. Only in recent years had Riodheg, acting on Nyrthim's counsel, begun to change that. This afternoon, while Valdar had been sounding out Maestor, Khaavorn had accepted an invitation to go over the isthmus to a field on the main island where the Achaysei mercenaries honed their skills. "They've got the heavy chariots from Amatoliysa, you know: the kind that can carry two spearmen as well as the charioteer."

"Hmm. But they don't do what we were hearing about from that emissary from Khemiu, do they?"

"Of course not! These Achaysei in Tarhynda's service are *gentlemen.*"

In Khemiu, and in the flat plains to the east, the chariot was used—devastatingly—as a platform for archery. But not among the peoples descended from the Karsha. Not even the Dovnaan, who also numbered the Escquahar—noted archers—among their forebears. They'd upheld that tradition of expertise with the bow . . . as a hunting weapon. But to use it against men, killing at a safe distance enemies into whose eyes you had never looked over a shield rim, was somehow dishonorable. Nor did one particularly relish being killed in such a manner oneself, however much dishonor might accrue to the killer.

"Still," Valdar mused, "I understand Tarhynda is hiring bands of foot archers."

"I heard that, too. Bad business."

"I heard something else, from one of the merchants."

"Merchants!" Khaavorn put an infinity of contempt into the word.

"Yes, I know. But this one was telling me that in eastern Amatoliysa they're learning to work . . . I forget what he called it, but it's the black mineral that you always see seams of in the mountains."

"You mean . . . for weapons? Like bronze?"

"Yes, though apparently they haven't been able to make it as good as the best bronze."

"What's all the fuss about, then?"

"It's *common*. There can never be many bronze weapons, even though copper is fairly easy to find, because the tin is so scarce it usually has to be brought in from far-off lands. But if weapons—even average-quality ones—can be made in great numbers, there could be larger armies than we've ever seen, or even imagined. Maybe even *tens* of thousands of men!"

Khaavorn looked blank. "But no matter how many weapons you have, there simply aren't that many men in the warrior class."

"Well, of course you'd have to go beyond the nobility and their retainers. Train able-bodied peasant lads, maybe . . ."

"Ha! And what if chopping up their betters became a habit? Ever think of that? And besides . . . what's the *point* of war, if you have to let the riffraff in?"

"You're probably right. This new metal will never catch on. Why, armies of that size would require organization. You'd have to bring in a lot of scribes."

"Dayu forbid! Nothing against Nyrthim, of course," Khaavorn added hastily. "I know: he can read and write. He's entitled to his eccentricities. But there *are* limits." He gave his head a decisive shake and spoke with great earnestness. "No. It's important to keep war restricted to the Right Kind of People. Otherwise, it just wouldn't be *fun* anymore."

Valdar was about to reply when he saw a flicker of light in the entrance to the villa. He motioned Khaavorn to silence.

A slender, cloaked woman emerged, carrying the oil

lamp Valdar had seen. She looked around cautiously, then walked quickly toward a crumbling staircase leading down into the gallery.

Khaavorn sucked in a breath. The figure's face could not be seen in the moonlight, but there could be no doubt of who she was.

"To Angmanu with all this sneaking around!" he whispered harshly. "Let's just tell her we're here and—"

"No, Khaavorn!" Valdar understood his companion's feelings. Not even the knowledge he possessed immunized him from a sense of absurd unreality. "We must do as Nyrthim told us."

Khaavorn subsided, muttering. They waited until Andonre had vanished down the steps, then followed her. They cautiously descended the steps and entered the passageway. The moonlight streamed in through shallow windows just under the ceiling. Ahead flickered the light of the oil lamp. They followed it with the silence of experienced hunters.

Presently, Andonre turned to the left and ascended a stairway. The two men followed her into a series of halls and corridors where ancientness lay even thicker than the dust. By the time they emerged into the Old Palace's central courtyard, the moonlight seemed dazzlingly bright to their dark-adapted eyes.

Andonre had almost reached a wide staircase leading up to a portico. They waited until she had entered the portico, then darted across the courtyard.

Beyond the portico was a square chamber, its center occupied by a stairwell with loggias on three sides. There was no sign of Andonre.

They walked to the head of the staircase. It led

downward into a darkness unrelieved even by Andonre's lamp.

"She must have gone down," said Khaavorn.

"No doubt," said a voice from the entrance, "inasmuch as there is no other way in or out of this chamber."

They whirled. By the time they were facing the loggia, Valdar's sword was out and Khaavorn was in fighting stance with his axe. A familiar figure stood in the moonlight.

"What are *you* doing here, you oily toad?" rasped Khaavorn.

"The Nezh wished to have a second string to his bow, as it were," explained Zhassu. "He asked me to follow the two of you as you followed the lady." His lightness departed abruptly. "He was afraid this would be her destination—and that you would try to continue to follow her, not realizing that matters have now gone beyond you."

Valdar gave the wine seller a narrow regard. "Your knowledge of this affair—and your loyalty to Nyrthim— are greater than you've led us to believe."

"Never mind that. You must come with me. We need the Nezh."

Khaavorn had looked ready to explode with indignation at the merchant's sheer effrontery in following them. Now, bewildered astonishment deflated him. "Nyrthim? But where is he?"

"Nearby. I will lead you there. But come quickly!"

"I obey no merchant!" snapped Khaavorn.

"Khaavorn, we must follow him," pleaded Valdar. A sudden inspiration: "Andonre may be in danger."

"What?" Khaavorn glared at Zhassu. "Well, what are you just standing there for, worm? Take us to Nyrthim at once."

They crossed the courtyard and plunged into the Old Palace's corridors and halls. Zhassu had brought an oil lamp, and he seemed to know his way through this maze. *Khaavorn and I would starve to death before we could find our way out,* reflected Valdar—a thought he found more unsettling than the thousand years of ghosts these precincts were widely believed to harbor.

· They descended a series of narrow, time-worn stairs and came to a doorway, open to the night. The moonlight revealed the rocky hillside at the base of the palace, with the roofs of The City below. *It must,* thought Valdar, *have been a sally port in ancient times.*

"We must be cautious," whispered Zhassu, "for troops patrol the hillside." He slunk forward and peered out the doorway. "I do not see the Nezh."

"If this is some kind of trick," growled Khaavorn, "I'll feed you your balls, if any."

"No! I swear by Rhaeie!"

Valdar pushed forward and looked. A crude stairway curved down from the door to a ledge of the craggy slope, about half again the height of a man below. Shadows moved near its base. "Soldiers!" he hissed. "Two of them."

"The Nezh must be hiding from them." Zhassu sounded relieved.

Khaavorn shoved him aside and joined Valdar at the opening. The approaching pair were common soldiers, wearing helmets and corselets of hardened leather, armed only with spears and daggers.

"They must be within shouting distance of other patrols," whispered Valdar. "This will have to be quick."

Khaavorn nodded, and loosened his axe from the thong that held it to his belt. Valdar likewise readied his sword. They exchanged a look, then crept out onto the landing just outside the doorway.

The soldiers paused at the foot of the steps and gazed down the slope. Valdar and Khaavorn looked at each other again, nodded, and leaped down together.

They landed behind the soldiers, who spun around, stunned by the sudden rupturing of their nightly routine. There was no time for an outcry. The one facing Khaavorn brought up his spear in desperation, but it was no use. The descending axe broke the spear shaft without even slowing down and crashed into the soldier's skull with a force that ignored the leather helmet.

Valdar's man tried a spear thrust. Valdar twisted aside and grabbed the spear with his left hand, pulling it forward. The spearman, pulled off balance, stumbled forward and went to his knees. Valdar brought his sword around and up, then chopped down at the base of the man's neck, not quite decapitating him.

There had been very little sound. Zhassu, at the top of the stairs, stared goggle-eyed.

"It's as I told you, Zhassu," said Nyrthim, stepping out from behind a boulder. "Say what you will of these men, they are awesomely efficient killers. Unsubtle to the point of crudity, but efficient."

"Well, Nyrthim," said Khaavorn as he wrenched his axe out of the skull in which it was wedged and used the kilt of the skull's owner to wipe off the blood and brains clinging to it, "I trust you have an explanation for all this."

"Later. At the moment, we have no time to waste. From the fact that you're here, I gather that—"

"Yes," Zhassu confirmed. "She's gone down to the grotto."

"Then it's as I feared. Come on!"

They retraced Zhassu's route through the Old Palace, crossed the courtyard and entered the chamber of the stairwell. Nyrthim paused at the top of the steps, turned, and gave them a stern regard.

"Down there," he stated, "it is essential that you follow my instructions instantly and without question. Your lives, and more than your lives, will be at stake. Is that clear?" They all nodded meekly, even Khaavorn. "Very well. Let us proceed."

They descended the stairway by the light of Zhassu's lamp, through strata of ancient masonry. When they reached the anteroom at the bottom, Nyrthim motioned to the wine seller to extinguish the lamp. He opened the curtain and led the way into the cavern, toward a faint light and barely audible sounds that sent a chill sliding along Valdar's flesh.

They approached a grotto, the source of the light and the sounds. Nyrthim gestured to them to flatten themselves against the cave walls. Then they crept forward until they could peer from behind crags flanking the opening.

The grotto was of great extent, and its floor was below the level of the entrance. So they looked down over the scene playing itself out by torchlight beside a pool of black water. A circle of figures surrounded a stone slab, evidently a natural outcropping of the floor. The figures, as far as could be told through their cloaks and hoods, seemed to be female—with one very tall exception. That one was leading a droning chant in a language Valdar had never heard.

On the slab a naked black-haired young woman lay spread-eagled on her back, her wrists and ankles tied to bronze spikes driven into the stone. She was conscious but seemed lethargic, as though drugged with opium poppy from east of the Eyxiyne Sea, for she was as oblivious to the dank chill as to the bronze dagger that the tall figure held over her.

"Where is Andonre?" whispered Khaavorn. "What have they done with her?"

"Quiet!" hissed Nyrthim with a withering glare.

The chanting quickened and rose in volume, building to some kind of obscene crescendo.

Khaavorn ignored the sorcerer's warning. He pushed forward for a better look. Nyrthim reached out to restrain him. Between them, they dislodged a pebble. It rolled and bounced its way down to the floor of the grotto, hitting the back of one of the female figures.

Distracted, she turned and looked. As she did so, her hood fell partially away, revealing a lock of reddish hair, distinctive in this part of the world.

"Andonre!" Khaavorn croaked, through muffling layers of shock.

Her face was a sickly pallid color, and she looked as mesmerized as the sacrificial victim, though not in the same drugged way. No, her expression was one of horror and revulsion held grimly in check by some imperative that would not allow her to flee from the grotto but kept her feet immovably in place. Valdar had never seen such a look on her features. But there was no possible doubt that it was she.

Andonre's turning attracted the attention of the tall leader. He jerked his head up furiously and barked at her, causing his own hood to fall away.

Valdar stared full into the long, regular-featured face with the great golden eyes, and he plunged into a pit of horrified unreality as deep as the one into which Khaavorn had fallen seconds before.

Nyrthim, clearly, was as stunned as he was. Zhassu, however, was not.

Well, of course not, thought Valdar. *Zhassu is a commoner. He's never seen that face, just the gold mask that covers it in public.*

And yet . . . neither has Nyrthim! So he can't know who that is.

So why does he look so stricken?

All at once, the chanting finally climaxed and, with a scream of unholy exultation, the tall man brought the knife slashing across the victim's throat.

At the last split second she came out of her trance and began a scream. It ended immediately in a ghastly gurgle, as a second mouth—a blood-red one—appeared, grinning horribly from one jaw angle to the other.

As she died, a wavering, misshapen shadow appeared on the wall of the grotto . . . even though there was nothing there to cast it.

At that moment, the man below thrust out his right hand with its bloody dagger and pointed at the cave mouth, his amber eyes blazing . . . the eyes that had managed to discern the intruders in the shadows beyond. He screamed, and all the women turned to follow the pointing knife.

That scream galvanized Nyrthim. "Run!" he snapped. "We must get away!"

"Andonre!" sobbed Khaavorn, rooted where he stood.

"Come *on*, Khaavorn!" Valdar grabbed his arm and dragged him away. He was too shattered to resist.

They raced down the passageway as fast as the feeble light of Zhassu's lamp permitted. Valdar caught up to Nyrthim and spoke as he ran.

"Nyrthim, why were *you* shocked? How could you *know*?"

"Why . . . what . . . ?" The sorcerer looked bewildered in a way Valdar had never seen, or imagined. "What do you mean?"

"You've never been to an exclusive reception in the palace. Otherwise, the Emperor only shows himself in that gold mask. So . . . *how did you know that was Tarhynda down there?*"

Nyrthim stopped dead and grabbed Valdar's arm with surprising strength. His eyes bulged. "Tarhynda? Are you saying that was *Tarhynda*?"

"Why, of course it was. That's why I'm asking how you . . . But you *didn't* know it was he, did you? You couldn't! So what *did* you see that caused you to look so stunned when his face was revealed?"

Nyrthim's expression was no longer one of bewilderment. It was one of dawning horror. "So," he finally breathed, "it all comes together. Now I understand everything . . . including the reason Tarhynda was so eager to conquer Arvaerness." He blinked several times, as though seeking to dispel a nightmare from which there could be no awakening. "Valdar, we have to get out of here with this knowledge!

Although . . . I fear we're merely fleeing to meet the world's end."

Before Valdar could think of a reply, they heard a sound that sent them running headlong without pausing for further conversation. It was a sound they'd heard before, in the slums of The City.

It was the roaring of demons.

CHAPTER SEVEN

They emerged, gasping for breath, from the passageway that gave access to the Old Palace, and tumbled into the hiding place where Valdar and Khaavorn had waited earlier. They had long since left the hideous roaring behind, and there was no other evidence of pursuit.

"Perhaps," speculated Nyrthim as he got his breathing under control, "you weren't recognized. He just saw a movement in the tunnel."

"So," asked Valdar, "should we just go back to our guest room and pretend nothing has happened? Or do you want us to go back with you to your place?"

Nyrthim stared at him in disbelief. "You must be joking! But no, I suppose you can't possibly understand, can you?" The sorcerer seemed to pull himself together, and spoke with his wonted imperiousness. "Forget all that. We must leave The City at once—tonight!—and take ship for Lokhrein!"

"*Lokhrein?*" Valdar looked, rather desperately, at their two companions. But there was no support there. Zhassu was even more winded than the rest of them, and too exhausted to take much interest. Khaavorn was still moving in a kind of shocked apathy that made him almost unrecognizable to anyone who knew him.

"Lokhrein?" Valdar repeated. "But, Nyrthim, how will we find a ship in the middle of the night?"

"We'll take the Ivaerisei ship you two came on. I arranged for it to be ready for departure—the captain owes favors to certain people in The City who owe *me* favors, you see. I was afraid that it might be needed tonight . . . although I never dreamed that we'd have *this* news to take to Lokhrein."

Valdar was about to ask for an explanation of just what *this* was, when Khaavorn's glazed eyes suddenly cleared. "Lokhrein," he said, as though only just realizing what was being discussed. "We're going to Lokhrein? Good. But first we have to go back and get Andonre."

"Andonre?" chorused Nyrthim and Valdar.

"Yes! She's being held here against her will. We have to rescue her, take her with us. . . ."

Nyrthim grasped Khaavorn by both shoulders and held his eyes. "Khaavorn, listen to me. Andonre is beyond your help. She is a member of the demon cult I told you two about."

"*No!* That's a lie. They've got some kind of hold over her. Yes, that's it! They've corrupted her since she came to this damned place!"

"No, Khaavorn. It's as I told Valdar—"

"You knew?" Khaavorn stared incredulously at Valdar. His hurt was visible in the moonlight. "Why didn't you tell me?"

"I should have," said Valdar miserably, with a glare at Nyrthim.

"You wouldn't have believed it, Khaavorn," said the sorcerer. "You *couldn't* have believed it. But now you've seen. Now you know—however much you may try to deny it to yourself—that Andonre is lost to you. All we can do is get away and take the word to the High King."

"But, Nyrthim, why is it so urgent? Granted, it's terrible that the Emperor is a demon worshiper. But why is that an immediate threat to Lokhrein?"

"No, you really don't understand, do you?" Nyrthim looked weary, older and, somehow, taller. "I had hoped to spare you lads this knowledge, but I see that I cannot. Savor these, your final seconds of innocence." He paused for a moment that was not as long as it seemed. "The Emperor is *not* a demon worshiper. *The Emperor is a demon!*"

"You're mad," Valdar heard Khaavorn say. Or perhaps he said it himself—afterwards, he was never sure.

"Would that I were! I wish with all my heart that this nightmare was only a madman's imaginings. But I fear it's all too real.

"Remember I told you the Great Demons—the *Nartiya Chora*—can assume human form? Fortunately, the form they take is always the same. Either they lack creativity or they are limited by nature to a single pattern: very tall . . . and the face is a remarkable one. Extremely long and attenuated, with unnaturally regular features, narrow bladelike nose . . . and, most distinctive of all, enormous amber eyes."

"But," Valdar began, "how could he . . . ? But of course! Most people never see his face, only the golden mask."

"Even if they did, how could they recognize him for what he is? It's been centuries since a Great Demon walked the earth. The description of their human aspect is part of the lore of the Order.

"I had truly believed it impossible, nowadays, to summon a Great Demon. It took the combined resources of the demon cults of Lokhrein and the Empire. Yes, it all becomes clear now. Tarhynda appeared from obscurity shortly after Andonre arrived." Khaavorn winced as though struck. Nyrthim ignored him and continued. "Vaedorie went through the motions of marrying the creature they had summoned—we need no longer wonder why they're childless!—and thus put him in position to succeed to the throne. According to their beliefs, they've brought in one of Rhaeie's great ministers to rule the world for Her as it was in ancient days. But I assure you that it is *he* who is using *them*. It explains everything he's done since taking power . . . most of all, the seizure of Arvaerness, creating a frontier between the Empire and the High King's lands." As he often did, Nyrthim halted abruptly as though stopping himself from saying too much. "So," he finished shortly, "you can see why tonight is none too soon for us to depart for Lokhrein."

Khaavorn raised his head from its slump of misery. "Nyrthim, I've never denied that your wisdom is beyond my comprehension, and I'll accept what you've told me about Andonre being . . . being . . ." He couldn't finish.

He shook his head violently, as if to shake foulness from it. "But I won't leave without Zhotiyu."

"Zhotiyu?" Nyrthim stared, taken aback.

"Yes. If what you've said—and what we've seen—is true, then he must be gotten away from Andonre. Away from this vile place!"

"Khaavorn," began Nyrthim gently, "I know the boy is your nephew, but—"

"There's more to it than that! He's also the High King's great-nephew. Have you forgotten about the succession?"

Nyrthim fell silent. So did Valdar, for in fact he *had* forgotten about it. The great chieftains of Lokhrein chose the High King from among the royal kindred. But at present . . .

"The royal kindred are a bit thin on the ground just now," Khaavorn continued, paralleling Valdar's thought. "Riodheg himself is childless. My stepfather Lanoraak is related to the royal house only by marriage, and at any rate he can't live much longer. Neither I nor my brothers have produced heirs yet." By-blows didn't count, of course. "What if something happens to us before we do? That would leave—"

"All right," Nyrthim cut in heavily. "I can see there's no dissuading you. It is even conceivable that you may have a point, for once. But we won't all embark on this expedition to rescue your nephew, for it is essential that *someone* survive. Valdar, you and I will go directly to the ship. Zhassu, you will go with Khaavorn as he essays this exercise in bravado."

"Me?" The wine seller's voice broke in a squeak.

He and Khaavorn eyed each other, and it was difficult
to know which was more distressed over the sorcerer's
pairing.

"Yes, you. Khaavorn could not find his way to the
docks unguided. Meet us there. If we're not there,
leave without us. If the ship is already gone when
you arrive, find another ship. Do whatever you have
to do, but remember that you *have* to get to Lokhrein and tell the High King . . ." Once again, Nyrthim
seemed to catch himself. "Tell the High King what
we've learned . . . and tell him to prepare for war.
Also, tell the High Priestess Minuren about Tarhynda.
She will . . . understand certain things. I charge you
on your honor to do this!"

"But . . . All right, Nyrthim. I'll remember." Khaavorn
gave Valdar's shoulder a squeeze before turning to
Zhassu. "Come on, merchant."

"Very well, barbarian," muttered the wine seller,
too low for Khaavorn to hear.

The oddly matched pair slipped away toward the
darkened villa. Valdar watched until Khaavorn vanished from sight.

"What was it you decided at the last moment not
to tell him?" he asked Nyrthim pointedly.

"We've already wasted quite enough time on explanations. Come along. At some point when we have more
leisure, I *may* decide you're able to deal with it."

Nyrthim led the way back down the passageway.
As he followed, Valdar looked back over his shoulder,
troubled.

The propylon of Vaelsaru's villa was deserted;
there was no need for guards here within the palace

precincts. Khaavorn slipped quietly in, axe in hand. Zhassu followed, holding the lamp unsteadily.

Khaavorn had been a frequent visitor here during their stay, and he knew the way to the nursery. They ascended the stairs and crept down a hallway to a small room where the moonlight streamed through the open shutters to reveal a small bedstead and a scatter of toys, including a wooden sword with which Zhotiyu had doubtless slain armies of imaginary demons. . . .

Khaavorn knelt beside the bed. He ruffled the chestnut hair with a strong man's clumsily careful gentleness. "Zhotiyu, wake up," he whispered.

"Mmm . . . ?" The boy turned over and opened bleary eyes. "Uncle Khaavorn?" he mumbled.

"Quietly, Zhotiyu. Listen, we're going on a trip."

Zhotiyu blinked, still more than half asleep. "Where's Mama?"

"Your mother couldn't be here." For an instant, Khaavorn's face wore a look Zhotiyu wouldn't have understood even if he had been awake enough to see it clearly. "She said she wants you to come with me. Up, now!" He picked up the small, unresisting form, motioned to Zhassu with a jerk of his chin, and slipped out the door.

They were just entering the propylon when Corannie, Zhotiyu's nurse, appeared on the porch, her face contorted with fury and fear for her charge. She screamed and pointed, and guards rushed past her. Zhotiyu, now at least half awake, panicked and began wailing and struggling in Khaavorn's arms.

"Hold him!" ordered Khaavorn, passing the boy to the nonplussed Zhassu. He then raised his axe and swung it around his head with a loud Dovnaan war cry, then launched himself at the guards.

These carried shields of hardened hide stretched over wooden frames, as well as spears. But they didn't have time to form up into a concerted rush. The one in the lead raised his shield, but Khaavorn brought his axe down with a force that shattered it, and the arm holding it. He kicked the injured man out of the way, made a quick recovery with his axe, and caught the edge of another shield with the weapon's hook. A quick yank left the guard without protection, and the axe whirled down and shattered his skull. At appreciably the same instant, Khaavorn grabbed a thrusting spear with his left hand, wrenched it out of its owner's grasp, and flung it back at him. The guard went down, moaning and clutching the spear shaft that protruded from his shoulder.

The remaining guards drew back, apprehensive. For a moment the standoff held, and Khaavorn coolly took stock of the situation. Something wasn't right . . . *Oh, yes! Where's Corannie?*

From behind him he heard a child's scream, a woman's shriek of triumph, and a bleat of protest from Zhassu. He risked a look over his shoulder, just in time to see Corannie, who'd circled around, snatch Zhotiyu away from the wine merchant.

Before he could do anything—even hurl a reproach at Zhassu—the guards saw their opportunity and charged. He turned back to face them in fighting stance, axe raised. . . .

The inner doors crashed open, shattered. A familiar stench filled the propylon, and an ear-shattering roar overrode Corannie's scream.

The guards halted, paralyzed, but Khaavorn felt no inclination to take advantage. He turned and stared nightmare in the face for the second time.

Not that the creature was really anything like what he'd seen, his first night in The City. Oh, there were enough points of resemblance to awake the same skin-crawling, stomach-churning sense of horrible wrongness. But this thing added something else: a dimension of terrifying awesomeness. For it stood erect, half again the height of a tall man and disproportionately massive. It had four arms, ending in what were inarguably hands. Each of the lower pair held a club that made the one Wothorg had wielded look like one of Zhotiyu's toys. And its crude, tusked face, although just as hideous as the one Khaavorn had seen buried in an eviscerated child on that other night of horror, held something more ... a gleam of brutish intelligence in the eyes under the shadowing shelf of bone.

Yes, that's right, he thought in a corner of his brain that had walled itself in against what was happening and could think clearly. *Nyrthim did say something about a bigger, stronger kind of demon—the* Nartiya Ozhre, *or some such Nimosei name—that stands up like man and has four arms and can be taught. . . .*

With the same impossible quickness Khaavorn had seen before—even more impossible in something this size—the demon sprang to where Corannie stood frozen in a state beyond panic. It reached out one of its upper arms and snatched Zhotiyu from her. Then it raised its other upper hand. Long, curved claws appeared, growing out of the fingers—they must, Khaavorn thought, be retracted on the hands that held the clubs and the writhing five-year-old. With a roar, the demon slashed downwards.

Khaavorn had once seen a man killed by a bear. This was infinitely worse. Corannie simply fell apart into slices, spurting blood and other fluids, and collapsed into a shapeless heap.

Zhotiyu, though conscious, had ceased to scream. He hung limp in the grip of the huge, misshapen hand. His eyes stared, unblinking; his mouth worked, but no sound came.

Two more demons like the first one appeared behind it in the ruined doorway.

Zhassu was the first to become capable of motion. "Run!" he screamed, and bolted past the guards. They immediately dropped their weapons and followed him.

Khaavorn did something he had never done before, the possibility of which he would have indignantly denied. He turned and ran.

Afterwards, he had no clear recollection of that flight. He let Zhassu lead him back through the Old Palace and out the ancient sally port. They scrambled down the rocky hill slope until they were among the buildings of The City.

On and on they ran. At some point, Khaavorn became aware that he had at least kept his axe.

Finally, the harbor appeared between the close-packed buildings ahead. Off to the side, lit by torches, Khaavon recognized the shrine of Rhaeie they had passed on their arrival—could it have been only a few days ago?

"There, lord, there: the ship!" yammered Zhassu. It was, indeed, the ship in which he and Valdar

had come. And Nyrthim had spoken the truth about
it being ready for departure. The captain and his
dozen crewmen stood about muttering uneasily in
the torchlight. Zhassu ran forward and spoke to the
captain in rapid-fire trade Nimosei. Then he turned,
beaming, to Khaavorn.

"The captain says we can depart at once, lord."

"But where are Nyrthim and Valdar?"

"They're not here, lord," said the captain. "Please,
we must hurry."

"We'll wait for them!"

A note of desperation entered the captain's voice.
"Lord, there is much confusion in The City . . . wild
rumors. People are claiming to have glimpsed strange
things. No order has come down yet forbidding depar-
tures, but I expect it any time now."

"I'll not abandon my friends!"

"Lord," said Zhassu, speaking deferentially but meeting Khaavorn's eyes, "staying here and dying will not
make up for the fact that we lost the boy."

The shame Khaavorn had been holding tightly in
check broke loose and tore at his guts. He grabbed
the merchant by the throat and forced him to his
knees. With his other hand, he raised his axe. "How
could you understand a matter of honor, you peddler
of donkey piss misnamed wine? And besides . . . what's
this *we*? I'm going back to Lokhrein. What makes you
think you're coming?"

"I must leave this place," rasped Zhassu through
his constricted throat. "I was seen with you at the
villa. Things will be done to me that—"

"That's not what I meant. Why should I take
you?"

"I have contacts with certain merchants in Ivaerisa, who owe me debts. How do you expect to pay for your passage?"

Khaavorn relaxed his grip and lowered his axe a bit. He had nothing in his possession but that axe and the clothes he wore. It was the sort of thing a gentleman could of course not be expected to think of.

"And remember," said Zhassu, pressing his advantage, "the Nezh said you were not to wait for him and the Lord Valdar. The message you bear to your High King is too important."

Yes, Nyrthim did say that, didn't he? thought Khaavorn. *And he placed me on my honor.*

So my honor requires me to run away for the second time in a single night.

"Come on," he growled, releasing Zhassu and starting for the gangplank. The wine merchant followed, moaning softly about what was probably going to happen to the business under his brother-in-law.

The soldiers had departed and the slaves were still cleaning up the mess in the villa.

"But surely it can't be true," said Andonre dully. She had cried all the tears her soul held, and they had not washed away the agonizing realization: *Zhotiyu was gone.* Now that realization was all the universe held for her.

"It is," Vaedorie insisted. She poured more wine into the cup Andonre had already emptied twice. "Your half brother and his friend kidnapped your son. By now, they've gotten away and are doubtless taking him back to Lokhrein. We sent the *Nartiya Ozhre* to try and prevent it, but they were too late."

"But . . . but . . ." Andonre tried to think straight. But it was hard . . . so hard. "But Corannie . . ." She almost gagged at the recollection of her first sight of that which had been Zhotiyu's nurse. "The *Nartiya Ozhre* killed her—I could tell. Why?"

"Apparently she was killed by accident in the confusion. Never mind—that's not important. What matters is getting your son back—or, failing that, taking vengeance."

"I don't want vengeance!" Andonre's voice was an unsteady wail. "All I want is Zhotiyu!"

"Of course, dear, of course." Vaedorie's voice became soothing. "That's what we all want. But we can only get him back if our great plan succeeds. And its success depends on *you*. So you see, now you have even more reason than ever to obey the Highest Sister and give me your full cooperation. It's the only way you'll ever see your son again.

"And besides, surely you can now see these men for what they are. You owe them nothing! Forget blood ties and childhood infatuations. Now you know whom you can and can't trust."

"Yes . . . I suppose you're right."

"Of course I'm right, dear. Now you must get some rest." The Empress gestured to some slaves, who led the unresisting Andonre toward the stairs.

Vaedorie did not linger. She returned to the Old Palace and descended to the lower level, seeking a certain room. Malsara awaited her in the corridor outside.

"Have those idiot guards been dealt with?" she demanded.

"Yes, lady. All the surviving guards who were present at the villa have been located and killed."

"Good. And who knows about—?" She gestured at the barred door.

"Only those who stand guard."

"Make arrangements to have them killed when they're no longer required."

"Lady . . . these are some of my most useful men."

"Don't argue with me, you nauseating piece of filth! All that matters is keeping the secret. But no; one other thing is important as well." Vaedorie stepped to the door and gazed through a narrow slot at the bare cell and the five-year-old boy it held. He lay curled tightly into fetal position on the floor of the cell, sucking on his fingers, staring fixedly into nothing.

"It is important," Vaedorie resumed, "that the brat remain unharmed. He must not be molested in *any* way. Are you and your 'useful men' quite clear on that?"

"Yes, lady," the eunuch assured her hastily. "But I don't understand—"

"Of course you don't. But there are reasons, involving the sacrifice. And besides . . . I see no reason why he should be allowed to become inured to pain before that." For a moment, Vaedorie's face wore a look that chilled even Malsara's soul.

The moment passed, and she was businesslike again. "Now I must go. *He* will be back soon."

"Back, lady?"

"Yes. *He* decided to take a personal hand in the search for the fugitives." Without further explanation, Vaedorie swept out of the passageway.

The two of them crouched behind a disorderly pile of bales on the dock, watching the Ivaerisei ship vanish into the darkness. It didn't take long—the moon had set. But Valdar fancied he could see the vessel long after the night had swallowed it.

"I could have taken that patrol, Nyrthim," he groused, not for the first time. "Then we wouldn't have had to waste time circling around, and we wouldn't have missed the ship."

"It was out of the question."

"But we came so close!" They had even been able to see, from a distance, Khaavorn and Zhassu boarding the ship . . . without Zhotiyu.

"The risk was too great. I have reason to know there are demons involved in the search for us—and not just the kind you already know."

"You mean—?"

"Yes. Higher demons—the *Nartiya Ozhre* of which I told you. We could not run the risk of *them* appearing while you were occupied with a patrol."

"All very well. But now we're stranded here in The City."

"No, we're not," corrected the sorcerer, maddeningly serene. "Indeed, this may have worked out for the best."

"I beg your pardon?"

"I know a captain who is involved in the amber trade. He is due for departure—and he owes me a favor. We'll go to earth for a short time, then take ship with him. He'll take us to where we can set out on the amber trail."

"The *amber trail?* Nyrthim, that's half the world away from Lokhrein!"

"I see your weakness for imprecise terminology remains unabated," said Nyrthim peevishly. "Granted, this route won't take us to Lokhrein. But we're not going there."

"We're not?"

"No. The amber trail *will* take us up to Khrunetore territory. From there, we can make our way to Arvaerness. There's something to be said for our going there, as long as we have Khaavorn going to Lokhrein to warn Riodheg and Minuren—which he will do if it's humanly possible. In a sense, I'm glad he and Zhassu failed to secure his nephew. They'll have a better chance of winning through without a child to burden them. And as for us ... Yes, the more I think about it, our presence in Arvaerness may become crucial indeed.

"But now let's be on our way—cautiously. There are worse than the *Nartiya Ozhre* abroad this night."

"Worse?"

"Yes. I have reason to believe Tarhynda may be indulging himself a bit. I don't think his personal intervention will pose a serious danger to us. One thing the Great Demons *can't* do is see in the dark. But he undoubtedly misses his natural form, and seeks for excuses to reassume it."

Just then, Valdar heard something overhead. It was like the beating of vast, leathery wings. He looked up, and for just an instant he could have sworn an unnatural shape occluded the stars.

"Quickly, now!" hissed Nyrthim.

They slipped away into the alleys.

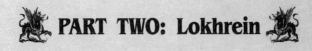

PART TWO: Lokhrein

CHAPTER EIGHT

Beating against the prevailing northwest winds, it took twenty days to reach Ivaerisa. Not all of Khaavorn's growling and Zhassu's whining could change that.

Once ashore, Khaavorn watched with no good grace while Zhassu did whatever incomprehensible things he did, huddling conspiratorially with various business associates or—more often—relatives of business associates. In the end, they boarded a ship bound for Lokhrein to pick up a load of tin.

She was not unlike the vessel on which they'd voyaged from The City: a single-masted sixty-footer, designed to carry the maximum cargo and therefore differing from the sleek war galleys, and not just in being tubbier. Rather than carrying a large number of oarsmen and their provisions, she depended on her sail, using her eight oars mainly for maneuvering in and out of harbor. Also, the captain didn't carry much in the way of stores, but put ashore every few days to take on water and obtain grain and vegetables by whatever means seemed appropriate in the locality. (Khaavorn loved to taunt Zhassu with the old witticism about how to tell a pirate from a merchant: if you're armed, he's a merchant.) Still, they made good time, especially since the captain was one of those daring souls who would sometimes sail on through the night instead of seeking a sheltered bay, as long as the weather portents were good.

Zhassu grew less plump on the austere shipboard fare—especially after they passed westward through the straits. Then he lost all appetite, and also lost most of what little he did eat. He was a seasoned mariner . . . on the Inner Sea. The tricky currents of the straits were bad enough. Then they encountered what were considered mildly turbulent waters in the Outer Sea, and the merchant was leaning over the rail emptying his guts to the crew's vocal amusement and Khaavorn's grim smile.

At least Zhassu could keep his mind occupied trying to learn enough of the Dovnaan tongue to get by. His aptitude for languages—always a useful quality for a merchant—helped make up for Khaavorn's deficiencies as a pedagogue.

They followed the coast northward until it turned east and then curved northward again. Soon they were passing the shores of Arnoriysa, where the High King's protection ran, and the captain's dealings with the shore folk grew noticeably more respectful. Then they reached the cape where the coast turned east again.

There, they waited in the shelter of the headland for a south wind. Finally, none too soon for Khaavorn, the wind shifted and they struck out at dawn heading due north, leaving the coast behind.

It took a day and a night. The captain and crew had done it before, as had Khaavorn going in the opposite direction, and Zhassu had occasionally been out of sight of land in the Inner Sea. But there was still something about that empty desert of water that gnawed at the pit of the stomach. It was casting oneself a little too unreservedly on the mercy of the gods—especially in these treacherous seas. Zhassu fidgeted nervously every time the wind picked up and the sea grew choppier. But the night finally ended, and in the morning light the western tip of Lokhrein appeared ahead and to starboard.

"We must have drifted a little to the west," commented Khaavorn. "There's the Island of the Stones, almost dead ahead." He pointed at the round island ahead, which fell astern as the captain shifted sail and headed for the mainland.

"This must have been where the explorers of the Old Empire first landed," said Zhassu, squinting at the island. On the coasts of Arnoriysa they had seen many of the standing stones that those ancient missionary/prospectors had raised to the honor of Rhaeie. Similar stonework could be seen on the island they were leaving behind.

"Maybe they landed on this island, but they weren't the ones who put up those stones. Those are tombs, built later by the Escquahar. Nyrthim told us about it, once. He said it was just after the Escquahar threw off the Old Empire. At the same time some of them were going north by land to the Rhaemu Valley, others went north by sea. That island was the first place they stopped, and it's a sacred burial ground for those of them who still live in western Lokhrein. But most of them moved on further north, to Ehrein." Khaavorn chuckled. "I still remember a few things from Nyrthim's history lectures, even though Valdar always paid more attention to them than I did." At the recollection of those two, whom he felt he'd never see again, his mood changed abruptly. He fell into a silence which Zhassu wisely refrained from breaking.

They resumed sailing along the coast, working their way eastward along Lokhrein's southern shore through a chronic chill drizzle. Eventually they reached the mouth of a wide stream, near the greatest concentration of tin mines. This was where the trade ships put in, and a small settlement had grown up. Behind the marshy shore rose a dark-green forest of oak, beech and some birch. It couldn't, in short, have possibly been mistaken for anywhere in the Inner Sea, least of all The City.

"It may not be grand," Khaavorn said, more to himself than to Zhassu, "but it's *clean.*"

"If you say so." Zhassu didn't sound altogether convinced.

As they stepped ashore, Khaavorn drew a deep breath of the misty air, and was home. He looked around with the widest smile the wine merchant had ever seen him wear. Not that Zhassu really noticed, in his misery.

"Is it always like this?" he asked desperately.

"Oh, no," Khaavorn assured him. "This is almost summer. Wait till winter—it's *much* worse!"

Zhassu moaned and pulled his cloak more tightly around him.

Khaavorn led the way to a hut that catered to various needs of sailors. He procured a beaker of amber-colored liquid and drank deep. Then he expelled a long sigh of pure, beatific contentment.

"Here," he offered, handing the beaker to Zhassu.

"Ah, yes: this 'beer' you're always waxing lyrical about." Zhassu took a tentative swallow, and gagged. "Are you sure we're supposed to *drink* it, and not soak our feet in it?" he gasped.

Khaavorn grinned wolfishly. "Welcome to Lokhrein, merchant!"

Zhassu took on a look of calculation. "I think I see a potential market for my wares in this country."

"Wine? In *Lokhrein*? Never!" Khaavorn quaffed the remainder of the beer. "Come on. We need to get started."

"Are we going to the seat of your High King?" inquired Zhassu.

"No . . . not directly. First we're going to the steading of my stepfather Lanoraak. There, I'll send for my brothers, and maybe Aunt Norkhaari." Khaavorn's face grew as clouded as the sky, and his homecoming joy vanished. "The family must be told what has happened—that is my duty. And I need to ask their advice on what to do next."

They set out westward, following forest trails, eventually entering a countryside of cleared meadows. Here were villages of thatched-roofed cottages of wattle and daub over timber, inhabited by peasants who grew grain and fed pigs. These people—mostly descendants of the old inhabitants of the land, although by now they could speak the Dovnaan tongue—worked the lands of Lanoraak, and Khaavorn had a claim on their hospitality.

Finally they emerged onto the high downs, where the steadings of the great Dovnaan houses stood, surrounded by the cattle herds that were their principal wealth, and the mounds of the warrior tombs. Presently, Lanoraak's steading appeared in the distance.

It was typical, surrounded by a ditch and an earthen embankment topped by a wooden palisade. The half-timbered hall was, to Zhassu's eyes at least, larger but very little better than the hutments of the peasant farmers. Less typical was the household it contained, for normally a noble's sons—and their wives—lived with him until he died and the eldest inherited. But the widowed Lanoraak had no son, and there was only the usual collection of armed retainers, captured slave women, semiitinerant craftsmen and others that made up the extended noble household that was the essential unit of Dovnaan society.

On the plain outside the earthwork, a chariot was racing along, watched by shouting spectators and trailing a crowd of squealing children. Khaavorn recognized the warrior riding it, and the clouds lifted from his soul for a moment.

"Khaaradh!" he roared. "Showing off, as usual!"

The chariot warrior looked incredulously toward him, and grasped his charioteer by the shoulder in a signal to rein in the horses. Before the chariot had come to a full stop, he flung himself out of it and ran toward the newcomers.

"Careful, little brother!" greeted Khaavorn. "You'll hurt yourself."

"At least my bones aren't brittle with age!" laughed

Khaaradh. He was, in fact, slightly bigger than Khaavorn in all dimensions, and somewhat fairer, with hair and eyes of a tawny brown. He grasped his oldest brother by the arms and surveyed him as though confirming the reality of his presence, before blurting out what was uppermost in his mind. "Theidre is pregnant again!"

"Well, well! Congratulations!" Khaaradh's wife had already borne one child, but it had died in infancy, as happened as often as not. Anyway, it had only been a girl. "You're determined to be the first of us to sire an heir, aren't you? Even if he *is* a half-breed!"

They exchanged playful cuffs at the jibe. Theidre was the daughter of one of the Escquahar-descended nobles of Ehrein. Her marriage to Khaaradh had been part of the web of political matches Riodheg and his counselor Nyrthim had woven. Like Andonre's. . . . Khaavorn's mind flinched away from the thought.

"But what are you doing here, Khaavorn? We didn't expect you back so soon. And where's your friend Valdar?"

Khaavorn's expression went shuttered in a way that puzzled Khaaradh. "Time for questions and answers later, little brother. I might ask what *you're* doing here."

"Oh, Akhraworn is here too. We're on our way to the High King's steading at Kintara, and this is on the way. So we stopped to visit Lanoraak—he hasn't been in the best of health lately, you know." Khaaradh's puzzlement deepened. "You don't exactly look overjoyed."

"Take no offense, Khaaradh. The look on my face is that of a man who'd been hoping to be able to put something off and now finds he can't." Khaavorn sighed in a way that was, in Khaaradh's experience, not like him at all. "Well, let me go in and greet

Lanoraak. And . . . congratulations again. For Theidre to bear you a son has become even more important than you know."

The hastily organized feast in honor of Khaavorn's unexpected arrival was over, and the guests had made their unsteady departure—not half as unsteady as Zhassu thought it should be. He'd been amazed at the quantity of beer the Dovnaan could drink without losing consciousness. Truth to tell, he'd been amazed at the amount of it they could manage to consume, period. Maybe it had something to do with the quantity of roast pork that accompanied it. He had forced himself to put away enough of both to avoid seeming unsociable. Lanoraak and various others had looked somewhat askance at the swart foreigner, but as a companion of Khaavorn he could hardly be excluded.

Now he sat in the darkened hall beside the low fire in the hearth from which the slaves had removed what was left of the pig, alone save Khaavorn, his brothers and his stepfather, for the time had come to answer the questions Khaavorn had managed to deflect throughout the feast.

Lanoraak gazed out from beneath shaggy gray brows. He had been a strong man once, though only medium-sized. Now his muscles had shrunk into stringiness, his movements were stiff, and he coughed enough to make Zhassu wonder what this land's winters must be like for him. But the shrewdness for which he'd always had a name was unimpaired. He had grasped, without being told in words, that his oldest stepson had things to say that could not be said easily, even in this circle. So he still didn't press Khaavorn, but made conversation instead.

"So, Khaavorn, I'm honored indeed that you came here first, rather than to your own steading."

"It was too far out of the way." Khaavorn's situation was untraditional. He had, as eldest son, inherited the lands of Moreg his father. But . . . "Anyway, I've got nothing to worry about. I'm certain cousin Dhaaroveg is managing it for me better than I could."

"Yes, he's a smart boy. And I know your duties as one of the High King's Companions prevent you from being there yourself. Mind you, I say no word against Riodheg, nor allow any to be said under this roof. Still, back in my day . . ."

It was one of Riodheg's many innovations: a body of warriors permanently attached to the person of the High King, drawn from the most noble families of Lokhrein but also including foreigners like Valdar. Those warriors did his bidding at once without having to be summoned from their steadings, and spent the rest of their time perfecting themselves in the new techniques of warfare he was introducing. It was a tremendous honor to be chosen, of course. But quite a few steadings had absentee landlords nowadays.

"Back in your day," grinned Khaaradh, "we didn't even *have* a High King!"

"I'm not *that* old! As a young whippersnapper I fought under Udheg when we smashed the . . . But you've heard about that once or twice, haven't you? Ah, well. So many new things, these days . . ." Lanoraak gave Zhassu a slantwise glance, and cleared his throat. It turned into a coughing fit. "Anyway, Khaavorn," he finally wheezed, "tell us about your journey."

Khaavorn wore the expression of a man going into battle. "I scarcely know where to begin. First of all, Nyrthim is alive. Or rather he *was* alive when Valdar and I were in The City. Now he's surely dead . . . as is Valdar."

"What?" demanded Akhraworn, the middle brother. He was as dark as Khaavorn, but smaller. He gave the scowl that was as habitual with him as a boyish grin was with Khaaradh. "But everyone knows that Nyrthim—"

"No! Let me finish! This is going to be difficult to tell."

Khaavorn had to bellow them back into silence a few times as he struggled to put into words what had happened in The City. He had dreaded Lanoraak's reaction when he told of the glimpse he'd had when Andonre's hood had slipped in the grotto. But the old man only half-stood, then sank back onto his bench, eyes glazed and mouth half-open with shock. Khaavorn wasn't sure how much of the rest of the story he heard, although a flicker of awareness was visible as Khaavorn unflinchingly described the loss of Zhotiyu. By the time he was done, there were little more than feebly glowing embers in the hearth.

"And so," he concluded, "I'm back, to carry out Nyrthim's instructions and warn the High King to prepare for war. But I've had time on the voyage to do some thinking." He pretended not to notice Zhassu's look of pointed skepticism. "I can see now that I can't go directly to Kintara and blurt out the tale to Riodheg."

"Why not?" Khaaradh's puzzlement was palpable. "Why the secrecy?"

"I have no way to know how deep the rot has

gone here in Lokhrein. There could be members of this demon cult in the High King's innermost circle. Remember, someone must have arranged for Andonre to be sent to—"

Something snapped in Lanoraak at the mention of his daughter's name—his only child, whom he'd loved with an intensity rarely lavished on girl children. He surged to his feet. "No! It can't be. Not Andonre. It's a lie!" He stopped, and looked confused. "But no, Khaavorn, I know you would not lie. You must be mistaken. Or maybe Nyrthim is. No, I won't call it a lie—"

"*I* will!" Akhraworn rose, glaring. "I call it a lie, and I'll not listen to such filth about Andonre." He'd never been unduly fond of his half sister—indeed, it was hard to recall *anyone* he'd ever been unduly fond of. But any reason for a quarrel was as good as any other.

Khaavorn also rose, and leaned forward until their outthrust jaws weren't far apart. His hand rested on his axe handle. "Do you call *me* liar, you little prick?"

Akhraworn paused. Whatever his shortcomings, suicidal tendencies were not among them. "No, of course not. But maybe these foreign demon worshipers deceived you somehow, with their foul arts. Did you ever consider that? Or maybe even Nyrthim, for some mysterious reason of his own."

"Rubbish!"

"But by his own admission he deceived everybody with his faked death."

"Weren't you listening? His reason was—"

"So he says! But how do you know you can trust him? No, it *must* be something like that. I simply can't believe that Andonre is—"

"I can," Khaaradh broke in.

The shouting match came to a stunned halt, for Khaaradh was the last one any of them would have expected to say those words. Open, boyish Khaaradh, so likeable that even Akhraworn liked him. Khaaradh, who had never spoken ill of anyone in his life. Khaaradh of the sunny smile . . .

Now his face was a mask of tightly controlled hurt.

"It comes back to me now," he said dully. "Andonre and I were always close as children—partly because I was nearest to her in age, I suppose. Remember all the time Aunt Norkhaari used to spend with her?"

"Why, of course," said Lanoraak. "Norkhaari was in charge of her religious instruction." The young Andonre had been considered fortunate to have such a teacher: a high-ranking priestess who was also a half sister of the High King.

"When Andonre was about twelve and I was fifteen or sixteen, I happened to overhear the two of them together. The things I heard Aunt Norkhaari telling her . . ." Khaaradh shuddered with the memory of foulness. "Afterwards, I asked Andonre about it. She was very upset that I had heard. She told me it was a secret, and made me swear never to tell anyone. I swore. Afterwards, as the years went by, I forgot about it—it was so unbelievable to begin with, it came to seem like just a bad dream, and finally faded. But now . . . this brings it back."

Lanoraak spoke into the silence. "Norkhaari had a lot to do with arranging Andonre's marriage to Vael-saru. If memory serves, she was the first to suggest it. Afterwards, Nyrthim came to believe it had been his own clever idea all along. You know how he can be, that way."

Khaavorn sat down again and put his head in his hands. "Dayu help us! If this is true, it makes it even more impossible for me to go to the High King. I'd be accusing his own half sister. Besides, how can I trust *anyone* around him?"

At first no one had anything to say. Then Zhassu spoke up diffidently. "Lords, if I may be permitted to speak . . ."

"Shut up, bladder," snarled Akhraworn.

"You are talking to a guest of my house," said Lanoraak sternly. He immediately looked surprised at himself, but of course there was no going back now. "Let him speak."

Zhassu turned to Khaavorn. "As I recall, the Nezh told you to take the news not just to your High King, but also to the High Priestess of Rhaeie in this land. He said she would 'understand certain things.' Perhaps you should seek her counsel on how best to proceed."

Khaavorn raised his head. "That's right! Nyrthim *did* say to tell Minuren what we'd learned about Tarhynda. And he didn't say I couldn't go to her first."

"But," said Akhraworn, forgetting for once to be truculent, "how will she react when you accuse one of her priestesses?"

"I don't know. All I know is that I need advice, and that Nyrthim trusts her. Is she at Khlaastom, Lanoraak?"

"As far as I know."

"Then that's where we'll go. You three go directly to Kintara—we'll meet you there. Zhassu, we leave in the morning!"

CHAPTER NINE

They set out from Lanoraak's steading on a northwesterly route across the downs, riding a borrowed chariot. It was a new experience for Zhassu. Khaavorn, for all his impatience, finally slowed down in response to the merchant's moans. Zhassu expressed scant appreciation, continuing to declare that his skeleton was jolted apart and that henceforth his knees would bend the wrong way. Silently, he wondered how Khaavorn—now acting a charioteer, normally a role for a retainer—could actually wield weapons from the platform. He himself could barely hold on, clutching the thong attached to the rim, even when the horses were being held to a walk.

Toward the end of the journey, Khaavorn swung

west, giving a wide berth to Riodheg's seat of Kintara, for he had no desire to meet anyone he knew just yet. Then he turned northward again, and the land grew more wooded, cut up with small streams that flowed north and west into the Saabrinol Channel beyond which lay the mountainous land of Khymbron, where the Dovnaan had never settled and the high kings were alien invaders. They followed one of the streams until a cluster of hills could be glimpsed over mist-shrouded marshland and swamp.

To the southeast, a low ridge extended out into the marsh. Here, a grizzled old man sat patiently beside a raft. Khaavorn spoke to him briefly. He nodded, got on his raft and poled it off from the shore, soon vanishing into the mist. Khaavorn sat down to wait. Zhassu gave him an interrogatory eyebrow lift.

"He's gone to ask permission for us to come to the island," explained Khaavorn. "He's been here forever—the only one who knows the way."

A slight breeze picked up, and the mist parted enough to glimpse the top of the main hill. A circle of standing stones crowned it. Zhassu eyed it dubiously. "Even in the Inner Sea, one hears stories of a great stone circle on this island. That's not it, is it?"

"Oh, no. This one dates back to the Old Empire. The one you're thinking of is well to the east of here, on the high downs. It's much newer; it was built by the stoneworkers of the Old Empire to the specifications of a great chieftain of the early Dovnaan conquerors, for the worship of Dayu in his aspect as guider of the sun."

"Sun?" Zhassu's eyebrows rose even higher. "In *this* country?"

Khaavorn gave him a hurt look.

Presently the boatman returned. His raft also held a slightly-built, dark-haired young woman in the light-green robe of a priestess of Rhaeie.

"You may come," she told Khaavorn with a gravity beyond her years. "The High Priestess will receive you." They boarded the raft, loading it to its maximum capacity, and the boatman pushed off.

Neither Khaavorn nor Zhassu was burdened with an overly active imagination. Indeed, that lack was one of a number of characteristics they had in common—however indignantly each of them would have denied the possibility of any such commonality. But now, gliding through the marshes surrounding the island of Khlaastom, they both found they were not immune to the feeling, so common among visitors to this place, of entering a region where time itself stood still—or, at least, ran more slowly—so that the mists of ancient-ness had not yet lifted.

Ahead, dry land took shape out of the vapors. They disembarked and walked a short distance to a grove of huge oak trees at the base of the hill. The young priestess walked ahead and took her place beside the two women—one middle-aged, one very old—already standing beside a crude stone altar of unguessable age.

Khaavorn stepped up to the woman standing between the maiden and the crone, and bowed very low.

"Greetings, Khaavorn nak'Moreg, warrior of the Dovnaan," she said in a throaty voice that would have commanded all attention anywhere. "Usually, men are admitted to these precincts only for good reason—and may not pass beyond this grove at all. But you have a name for being respectful to the Mother as well as to Dayu of the warriors."

"I try to be, lady," Khaavorn mumbled. "And, as I told the boatman, I come on the High King's business." *Even if the High King doesn't know it just yet,* he mentally amended. "Could we speak in private?"

"You presume too much," said Minuren sternly, "even though you are descended, through your mother Elaamen and her mother Ykhraame, from the priestesses of the Old Empire who brought Rhaeie's worship to this land."

The same could obviously not be said of Minuren herself. Unlike the two priestesses who accompanied her, both of whom had the dark fine-boned look that marked the Old Empire's bloodlines in these islands, she was to all appearances pure Dovnaan aristocrat: tall and large-framed, with brown hair beginning to show a few silver threads, fair skin, gray eyes and strongly marked features. She also had a natural stateliness that was all her own.

"And who is this?" She indicated Zhassu, who clearly was prevented from groveling only by uncertainty as to its propriety.

"This is Zhassu, from Amatoliysa—"

"A humble wine merchant, most holy lady," stammered Zhassu.

"—whom I met in The City. I've just returned from there."

"The City?" For an almost imperceptibly short moment, Minuren's serenity wavered. It was only a tiny ripple on the still surface of a very deep lake. But it emboldened Khaavorn, in this place of ageless sacredness where he did not belong, and he stood up straighter.

"Yes, lady. I went there with Valdar nak'Arkhuar." Khaavorn recalled, with a twinge of sadness, how he could always annoy Valdar with the bastardized Dovnaan form of his name. It had been one of their games . . . never to be played again. "We encountered Nyrthim there."

Minuren stiffened. "Nyrthim died year before last!"

Khaavorn sighed. "Lady, I intend no disrespect, but time is fleeting. Nyrthim told us how you helped him fake his death and depart for The City. He also told us the reason why, and recruited our aid. Zhassu is another confidant of his. So we are all parties to the secret now, and need engage in no pretenses. I'm here because Nyrthim charged me to bring you an account of what we learned . . . and because I need you to tell me what to do."

The other two priestesses looked paralyzed by outrage, but a smile ghosted briefly at the corners of Minuren's wide mouth. "You may continue."

"Thank you, lady. But prepare yourself for ill news."

Khaavorn launched into the tale. Minuren did not interrupt. Her face set into grim lines when he provided confirmation of her fears and Nyrthim's by describing their first encounter with a demon. She grew even grimmer when he came to his glimpse of Andonre, but showed no other reaction; it was nothing of which she and Nyrthim hadn't already been fairly certain. But then he told of Nyrthim's revelation of the Emperor Tarhynda's true nature . . . and her face became a colorless and expressionless mask of shock. He pressed on with the rest of the tale, hoping she was hearing him.

"Anyway, lady," he concluded, "Nyrthim made me promise to tell all this to you as well as to the High King—he said you'd 'understand certain things.' Oh, and I almost forgot; he mentioned something about how this explains why Tarhynda was so eager to take over Arvaerness, with its common border with the High King's lands in Arnoriysa. Do you have any idea what he meant by that, lady? Uh . . . lady? *Lady?*"

Khaavorn sprang forward and caught Minuren as her legs gave way and, with a sound halfway between a cry and a moan, she collapsed. The two priestesses helped lower her to the ground, glaring furiously at Khaavorn.

"What *is* it, lady? Nyrthim also reacted this way. Tell me why."

A little color began to seep back into Minuren's face. She shook her head. "No, Khaavorn. This involves things you may not be told."

"You can trust me, lady." Had he but known it, Khaavorn's mustache failed to hide a rather comical pout.

"I know I can. It is not a question of trustworthiness. It is only that you are not ready to hear certain things. Take no offense—and feel no disappointment! Believe me, the stewardship of this knowledge is no privilege for such as Nyrthim and myself. It is a burden and a curse, and I wish with all my heart that Rhaeie in her mercy would wipe it from my mind as though it had never been there! Then I could spend whatever time is left to us in happy ignorance, not knowing of the world's end until it is actually upon us and the Mother herself dies."

Khaavorn's hand went to his axe handle, and his voice was like a clang of bronze. "Not if I have anything to say about it, lady!"

Minuren smiled gently, and reached out and gave his arm a squeeze. "You are a good man, Khaavorn nak'Moreg, and you almost give me hope. Almost . . . but not quite. For I fear we have entered the end times, when your kind of goodness—all the strength and loyalty and courage and honesty in the world—can avail us nothing. But . . . just in case they can . . ." Minuren got to her feet, shaking off the priestesses' assistance, and her invisible robe of regalness descended on her anew. "You must carry out the rest of your charge from Nyrthim. Go at once to Kintara and tell the High King that an invasion of Arnoriysa is imminent. He must gather his fighting men and prepare to resist. Tarhynda *must* be kept out of Arnoriysa. Whatever poor shred of hope remains to us depends squarely on that."

"I'll tell him, lady. I don't understand, but I'll tell him."

"Do so—and tell *only* him. Who else knows all this?"

"Only my father-in-law and my brothers. They had a right to hear this news about Andonre from my lips."

"Yes, yes—but did you also tell them about Tarhynda?"

"Why, uh . . . yes, lady. It was part of the story, and—"

"Well, I suppose it can't be helped now," sighed

Minuren. "But they must tell no one else. And you must tell no one but the High King."

"I won't, lady. And I'll swear them to secrecy."

Zhassu cleared his throat. "Ah, lord, about the tale your brother, the Lord Khaaradh, told us . . ."

"Yes! My youngest brother recalled something that happened in his youth." As Khaavorn related the story, Minuren kept her features under tight control. "Mind you," he concluded, "I don't necessarily accuse a priestess of Rhaeie. But as long as the possibility exists that Aunt Norkhaari is somehow involved . . . well, she's at Kintara, and so it makes things awkward."

"Yes, it does, doesn't it?" Minuren's control slipped for an instant, revealing the face of a person feeling a pain at which she knows she shouldn't really be surprised. "Norkhaari," she said slowly, to herself rather than to Khaavorn. Then she shook herself and spoke briskly. "Clearly, it is necessary for me to go to Kintara myself."

"Uh . . . how soon can you be ready to depart, lady?"

"No, no, not with you. There are certain things I must do here first. Besides, you can travel faster without me. Go at once; I will arrive later."

"Very well, lady." Khaavorn turned to go. Then he paused and faced Minuren again, and his eyes did what the rest of him could not: they pleaded. "Lady, if this is true about Norkhaari, does it mean . . . well, is it possible that Andonre isn't truly lost to this abominable demon cult? Maybe she just had bad advice."

"Perhaps, Khaavorn." Minuren allowed her compassion to show for just an instant. Then sternness closed down over it again. "You naturally wish to believe this.

It may even be true. But you must not allow that wish to make you forget what is at stake here."

"I know my duty to the High King," Khaavorn protested.

"Khaavorn, we are speaking of matters beside which the high kingship of Lokhrein is a small thing indeed! Your sister's fate cannot be allowed to weigh in the balance. I, too, hope she can be saved. But if she cannot, you must be prepared to let her go without a moment's hesitation. Can you do this?"

"I think I can, lady. I think I must." Khaavorn turned away and headed toward the raft.

As he turned away, he had no way of knowing that Khlaastom was being watched.

Not closely. The High King's seat at Kintara was twelve miles to the southeast. But from the highest point of that isolated peak, beside the great hall, the cluster of hills that was Khlaastom could be glimpsed in the hazy distance.

It wasn't the only element of the impressive view. The hill of Kintara sloped away on all sides, ringed with massive earthworks and ditches, although the bluebells and primroses of spring were now past their prime. To the east was a rise that marked the edge of the high downs. But Norkhaari nie'Khorleg gazed fixedly to the northwest and that hill that seemed almost an island in a sea of mist.

When Udheg, the previous High King, had defeated and killed her father Khorleg, he had taken Khorleg's wife Ykhraame in accordance with immemorial practice. He hadn't killed Ykhraame's two daughters, though, as he would have killed a male child. Indeed, he'd been indulgent by his own lights, keeping Elaamen—ten at the time—in his household until she was old enough to be married off to his henchman Moreg. The six-year-old Norkhaari—already whispered to be precociously apt at the uncanny ways that blossomed like dark flowers on her mother's bloodline—had been largely forgotten in the excitement of Ykhraame's pregnancy by her new lord. She'd been even more thoroughly forgotten when Ykhraame had given Udheg the son she'd never been able to give her first husband—and died doing it. Norkhaari had watched her die, to the sounds of drunken revelry from the hall as Udheg and his cronies had celebrated the birth of Riodheg. Afterwards, she'd remained in the darkness a long while with the cold stiff thing that had been Ykhraame, and whatever the killing of her father and the rape of her mother had left of her childhood had ended.

After a time, Udheg had taken notice of her, if only as something that had needed to be tidied away. Not knowing quite what to do with the dark, quiet little girl with the unnaturally expressionless face, and not wanting to be bothered with the problem, he'd packed her off to Khlaastom to be trained as a priestess of Rhaeie.

She had spent her adolescence and early adulthood there. She had learned much—more, in fact, than her teachers knew. For she had soon been approached by certain priestesses who had told her they knew older, truer, harsher secrets—secrets that must never be revealed, least of all to the High Priestess. That last had been no problem for Norkhaari; she'd had much practice at concealing her thoughts. So they had taken her to see certain forbidden rites. The first time she'd seen a victim sacrificed, it had been a young boy. She'd pretended to herself that the boy was Riodheg, who had killed her mother, and smiled one of her very rare smiles.

Having found her true vocation, she had applied herself to it with an intensity that had caused her to rise in the ranks of the secret cult far more rapidly than she had in the official hierarchy. She sometimes regretted that. The possibilities, if she'd become High Priestess . . . ! But Minuren had overtaken her. She permitted herself a certain bitterness about that. After all, she thought, it didn't exactly hurt Minuren to be a protégé of Nyrthim. . . .

Norkhaari had been in her early twenties when Udheg had died. The five great chieftains had been unable to agree on a successor, for various ambitious claimants had sought to set aside the seventeen-year-old Riodheg . . . permanently, if necessary. Nyrthim had spirited the young heir out of danger, and war had raged beyond Khlaastom's encircling marshes. When Riodheg had finally prevailed, partly due to Nyrthim's counsel, the sorcerer had been in a position to influence the choice of a high priestess to succeed old Nakeiren, who had died shortly thereafter.

Other changes had also come, for a messenger had arrived at Khlaastom with an invitation from the new High King to his half sister. Minuren had welcomed the opportunity to place a priestess in the entourage of the High King—especially one to whom he was tied by blood. Norkhaari had departed for the new seat Riodheg was constructing at Kintara, at a neutral remove from the steadings on the high downs and their rivalries and jealousies. There, her double life had continued, with new opportunities to advance the cult . . . especially when she'd been put in charge of the young Andonre's religious instruction. . . .

A footfall broke her train of thought. She turned, with the smile that was, by now, so well schooled that she could even bestow it on Riodheg without great effort. This time it took no effort at all, for Khuonar was approaching.

A nephew of the chieftain of the steading of Naklore on the high downs, Khuonar looked the way most Dovnaan warriors only wished they looked: very tall, massive of shoulders and chest, with hair and mustache like an alloy of copper and gold. He enhanced the effect with a great deal of gold jewelry and a splendidly embroidered tunic and mantle of dark red. His gray eyes held an expression Norkhaari still had the power to ignite in them, and which always filled her with self-satisfaction. She had come late to sex—at least with men. But the priestesses knew certain secrets of prolonging the appearance of youth (though not life itself), and at forty-eight years she could still arouse the lust of a man like Khuonar, young enough to be the son she'd never had. Her hair was still as black as ever, a vivid contrast with the violet blueness of her eyes. Her figure was still good, though more petite than her culture generally favored—just as well, in her view, for at least she didn't sag.

"You sent for me?" said Khuonar, keeping his voice as correct as his hands—there were other people about—and letting his eyes speak for him. Norkhaari did not reciprocate his look. Their affair was pretty much at her discretion, its main purpose to make him her responsive tool. Sometimes, though, it served purely recreational functions for her. This was not one of those times.

"You must alert your supporters to hold themselves in readiness," she said without preamble. "An emissary is coming from the Empire."

"From the Empire? But how can you—?"

"I have my sources of information. There is no need for you to know the details. Suffice it that the emissary will be here soon, and will present certain demands to Riodheg."

"What demands?"

"Oh, nothing—just some minor territorial concessions in Arnoriysa. That's unimportant. The point is, you must speak out in council in favor of acceding to those demands. Thus you will demonstrate your usefulness to Tarhynda. And if your arguments carry the day in council, it will hasten the day when—"

"Yes!" Khuonar's eyes lit up, then clouded over with second thoughts. "But what if Riodheg refuses the demands anyway, and it comes to war?"

"Then you will, of course, accompany Riodheg to Arnoriysa with the war host. And . . . everyone knows how accidents can happen in war. You can arrange for one to happen to Riodheg. And I will make sure Tarhynda knows of your service to him."

Khuonar frowned, and Norkhaari wondered if she'd been a bit too nakedly cynical. "Uh . . . I don't know. I don't like it. . . ."

"Khuonar, dear, we've been over all this before. I have the Empress Vaedorie's assurance that Tarhynda really has no intention of trying to rule Lokhrein directly. That would be impossible. No, he'll just appoint a *miynonu*, a ruler who gets the benefit of the legitimacy the Emperor alone can confer, in exchange for mere formal gestures of homage. And if you continue to do as I advise, *you* will be that ruler!"

This time the light in Khuonar's eyes flamed up into a blaze—and not just one of ambition. He stepped closer to Norkhaari, inhibitions forgotten. "Let's go and—"

"No, idiot! There are people watching. You'd better go. We must remain discreet . . . for the time being. Soon, there'll be no further need of it."

Khuonar grinned at the implied promise. He turned to leave, then paused. "Oh, I have some information, too. A friend who was at Lanoraak's steading just arrived here today. He mentioned that Khaavorn is back from The City."

"What?" This was unexpected.

"Yes. Remember, he and Valdar nak'Arkhuar were going there? He wasn't expected back so soon. No sign of Valdar. But Khaavorn should be returning here soon, I would think. Uh . . . what's the matter?"

Norkhaari wasn't listening. She was doing the kind of mental calculations that the priestesses were taught, and which seemed a kind of magic to everyone else. Tarhynda's emissary had left the city with Vaelsaru's fleet, so as to depart for Lokhrein as soon as the Arvaerness campaign reached its inevitable conclusion. So he wouldn't even know of Khaavorn's arrival at The City, much less his return. Khaavorn, then, would have information from The City more recent than his. And . . . what would have motivated such a hasty return? And where was Valdar?

Norkhaari shook her head as though to clear it of profitless speculation. "Never mind. It's not important.

Just remember what you must do. Your . . . no, *our* future depends on it."

Khuonar's eyes burned, but he remembered himself and departed with nothing more intimate than a small bow.

Norkhaari turned back to the northwest and her contemplation of the distant hill of Khlaastom. She genuinely liked Khuonar. And, she told herself, it might even be true. He might actually be appointed puppet ruler of Lokhrein . . . just at the moment when such an honor ceased to matter. That would be typical of Tarhynda. (Or whatever his *real* name was, among his own kind . . . assuming that they had names, as Norkhaari was fairly certain they did.) He had a sense of humor, of sorts; it was the most unexpected thing about him, and possibly the most alarming. It would amuse him to make Khuonar *Miynonu* of Lokhrein at the precise moment when Lokhrein—like every other component of the present, corrupt world—ceased to exist, swirling down into the cauldron of chaos from which the true worship of Rhaeie must reemerge.

The thought reminded her of Vaedorie. She, like Khuonar, was in for a surprise.

Norkhaari had never actually met Vaedorie, of course. But from the messages they had exchanged, and conversations with the carriers of those messages, she had formed a fairly definite impression of the Empress's character and motivations. Vaedorie pictured what was to come in the only way she could: in her own image. Vaedorie visualized a universal Empire where she sat at the side of Tarhynda and exercised limitless power to dispense fear and inflict pain.

Vaedorie had *no* idea.

CHAPTER TEN

To Zhassu, the stronghold of Kintara looked much like Lanoraak's steading writ large. Very large.

It was an isolated hill, terraced with earthwork ramparts. The innermost ring of those had been topped with timber battlements—rather sophisticated fortifications for this country, Zhassu thought condescendingly as they entered through a northeastern gate whose guards clearly knew Khaavorn. It enclosed over fifteen acres of uneven elevation, rising to a summit ridge crowned by the great hall. Below was a scattering of lesser buildings—dwellings, stables, workshops, kitchens, storerooms, armory, and others of less obvious function—all surrounded by a vital workaday clutter and filled with a bustling crowd that made Zhassu feel a little less out of place. Granted, none of his Amatoliysei countrymen were in evidence, nor anyone else from quite that far afield. But there were dark hawk-faced Escquahar descendants, some from Ehrein—they were dressed in much the same style as the locals—but others from Ivaerisa. There were a couple of blond hatchet-faced visitors from the Khrunetore realms, and various sorts that Zhassu could not identify.

Most of the crowd, however, were Dovnaan as was to be expected, and many of them wore the sumptuous tunics and gold-brooched mantles of the warrior nobles—including the three who now advanced through the crowd to meet them.

"Khaavorn!" greeted Khaaradh. He and Khaavorn clasped each other's forearms in the standard greeting. "What happened? Did you see Minuren?"

"Yes, little brother—but keep your voice down about it. One of the things I learned from her is that I've already blabbed too much. The three of you mustn't repeat any of what I've told you."

"Are you saying we're a lot of garrulous old women?" bristled Akhraworn.

"Besides," added Lanoraak glumly, "do you think we *want* everybody to know about Andonre?"

"*Any* of it," repeated Khaavorn. "For the present, no one can be told except Riodheg himself . . . and he *must* be told."

"Well, you're in luck," said Lanoraak. He jerked his chin in the direction of the great hall. "He's holding court now, and he's eager to see you. We told him you're back—no, calm down, Khaavorn. That's *all* we told him."

"Is Aunt Norkhaari in there with him?" demanded Khaavorn.

"Why . . . no, I don't think so. She's here at Kintara, but now that you mention it I haven't seen her lately. No telling what she's up to."

"Good." Khaavorn's sigh of relief puzzled the others. "Let's go."

"Wait, Khaavorn," protested Khaaradh. "You just got here, and you look like Angmanu himself. Wait a while—freshen up, grab a bite to eat and some beer."

Zhassu gave a silent but heartfelt cry of agreement as he alighted stiffly from the chariot, convinced that his shins would never be the same again. This time, Khaavorn had spared neither the horses nor him. Their clothing was caked with mud and spattered with horse spittle, and to Zhassu's amazement the mention of beer actually sounded inviting.

"No time," muttered Khaavorn. He did, however, compromise to the extent of walking stiffly to a horse trough and splashing water over his head. "No time," he repeated with a little more vigor. "I've got to see the High King while Norkhaari isn't there. Come on, Zhassu!"

They climbed the path to the summit. As they went, they encountered men who knew Khaavorn, and accumulated a small crowd. Zhassu, ignored, studied their destination. The great hall was wooden, of course; the Dovnaan only raised stones in honor of the gods. Zhassu prepared to feel condescending.

The feeling died as they entered and his eyes adjusted.

Massive, elaborately carved timber columns around

a central hearth upheld a raftered ceiling. The light from clerestory windows brought out the gleam of bronze weapons hanging from the walls among furs and tapestries, and of gold vessels on the heavy tables. But then they approached the man sitting in the high oaken throne, and Khaavorn bowed . . . and Zhassu ceased to notice the barbaric magnificence of the hall.

Riodheg nak'Udheg, High King of Lokhrein, was forty-two. But he was in such obviously superb condition that Zhassu had no trouble believing the stories that he still sometimes engaged in weapon practice with the young sparks among his warriors to keep them humble—or as humble as the Dovnaan ever got. This, despite the sprinkle of salt in the darkness of his thick wavy hair and short well-trimmed beard. That beard, combined with the sweeping mustache which the warrior class usually wore in conjunction with a clean-shaven face, was something of an individual touch. But it wasn't eccentricity—that was a word that would never have occurred to anyone in connection with Riodheg. Rather, it was a stately declaration that here was a man to whom no rules applied but those of his own devising. As though in compensation, he was dressed conventionally, though richly, in deep burgundy and gold.

None of which, Zhassu realized, could fully account for the way one stopped looking at anyone else in the vast hall.

"Welcome back, nephew," Riodheg called out to Khaavorn in a vibrant baritone, raising a gold-chased tankard of beer. A chorus of boisterous greetings from Khaavorn's friends at the tables accompanied him. "Sit here beside me and drink. You look like you've come in great haste. And who is your companion?"

"Zhassu of Amatoliysa." Khaavorn saw no compelling reason to go into details, such as the fact that Zhassu was in trade.

"Let him be welcome in this hall." A shadow crossed the High King's face. "But Lanoraak tells me that Valdar did not return with you."

"No. I fear he died in The City, though I did not actually see him fall."

Riodheg winced as though from the bite of edged bronze. "May Dayu guide him to where the Mother will take him to the Land Beyond." Sounds of agreement filled the hall. Almost all these men had liked Valdar, even though they hadn't always known quite what to make of him. "And now I'll have to send word to Dhulon, letting my old ally Arkhuar know his son has died in my service."

"It was the service he chose."

The High King gave a headshake of self-reproach. "Forgive me for dwelling on my own loss. I know he was a particular friend of yours. But it seems I've suffered all too many losses in the last year or two . . . starting when Nyrthim died. But enough! You must tell me the tale of your journey, and of how Valdar met his end."

"Ah, well, nak'Udheg, as to that . . . odd you should mention Nyrthim." Khaavorn's eyes went swiftly around the hall. Lanoraak had been right: there was no sign of Norkhaari. Still, the hall was fairly crowded. "It's to tell you the tale that I've come here. But grant me a favor: let me relate it to you in private."

Riodheg's eyes widened. This was odd behavior

indeed among the Dovnaan, who loved nothing better than telling an audience of their fellows a good story, and improving on it with each retelling—and Khaavorn was a Dovnaan of the Dovnaan. "But, nephew, everyone wants to hear—"

"I've been told that it's for you alone to hear, nak'Udheg."

"Told?" Riodheg's voice went sharp. "By whom?"

"By the High Priestess Minuren." Khaavorn watched the High King's dark eyebrows rise. "And, before that, by Nyrthim."

"*Nyrthim?*" Riodheg's face wore a look of bewilderment that made it almost unrecognizable. A perplexed buzz of conversation began among those nearby, and spread outward.

Khaavorn leaned closer to the High King and lowered his voice. "Uncle, you know me. I'm not a clever man like Valdar, and I understand nothing of these deep matters. But I've looked upon horror. And I've been charged to convey that horror to you, and *only* to you. I beseech you, speak with me alone."

Riodheg gave him a gravely thoughtful regard. "Since you put it that way, I can hardly refuse. Very well: let's go and—"

"Nak'Udheg!"

The breathless outcry came from Kaayeg, a warrior Khaavorn knew well. He came running in wearing a helmet and carrying a shield, for he was currently in command of the guard.

"What is it, Kaayeg?" asked Riodheg irritably. Rulers do not relish being interrupted.

"Nak'Udheg, it's an emissary from the Emperor!"

"From the *Emperor?*" Riodheg was nonplussed. So

was everyone else in the hall. This wasn't something that happened every day. Indeed, it had *never* happened in the memory of anyone present, nor in the memory of anyone's father or grandfather.

"Yes! He landed a few days ago—a messenger from the coast just arrived, barely ahead of him."

Riodheg turned back to Khaavorn. "It seems, nephew, that your news will have to wait."

"But, uncle, couldn't we just—?"

"No." Riodheg's tone remained affable, but he clearly meant to be obeyed. "We must prepare to receive Tarhynda's representative. Who knows? Maybe he'll have some word as to Valdar's fate."

The imperial embassy was marvelous to behold. People came from miles around to gawk at its arrival.

Even the elements cooperated, and the sun glinted off the bronze helmets and spearheads of the honor guard that led the procession. Then came a line of slaves carrying the requisite gifts; people's eyes grew round at the glimpses of gold and jewelry, and the number of amphorae. Finally, flanked by more bodyguards and an obvious scribe, slaves bore the litter containing the emissary himself, straining to keep it level as they ascended the hill.

Riodheg and his household warriors waited at the summit, in front of the great hall. Khaavorn, standing beside the High King, wondered how the ambassador would react to that. He'd seen The City, and he knew the Emperor would have made an emissary come to him, through corridors and halls and courtyards to stand and bow before the alabaster throne. He dismissed the thought. *This is Lokhrein, and this imperial popinjay can think what he likes of the way we do things!* He concentrated on studying the popinjay as the slaves set the litter down.

With spring shading into summer, it was a very warm day by local standards, and the ambassador was wearing imperial court dress with no evidence of discomfort. *If this was winter, he'd have to wear a cloak over it or freeze his balls off,* thought Khaavorn grimly, observing the lightweight linen kilt and mantle. The wraparound headdress was fantastical even for an imperial noble, with peacock plumes no one here had ever seen before. The man himself was medium-tall, with the medium coloring typical of the New Empire's half-Ayoliysei ruling class.

He bowed to Riodheg—a less profound bow than he would have given the Emperor, but an inarguable bow nonetheless. It was the first indication as to how he'd been instructed to behave toward the High King of Lokhrein. Another followed, when he spoke in heavily accented but fluent Dovnaan, rather than the trade Nimosei Khaavorn had expected.

"Lord, I bring greetings from Tarhynda, Emperor of Schaerisa and Graetess and all the isles; King of Arzholsa and the other imperial provinces of Zhraess; lord of Carisa and Lydisa and all the other imperial possessions in Amatoliysa; suzerain of Sardiysa and Siycelisa and the other islands of the west; master of Arvaerness; and protector of all lands which owe allegiance to the Empire."

Khaavorn released his breath. He'd half-expected to hear the High King addressed as "*Miynonu* of Vriydansa." Instead, the ambassador had neatly avoided the entire issue by giving Riodheg the general purpose

honorific "lord." It wasn't the mode of address favored
by Dovnaan nobles, who used the patronymic standing alone as a mark of respect without the servility
they weren't about to show to anyone. But at least
it wasn't provocative. Likewise, he hadn't included
Lokhrein/Vriydansa in his catalog of lands Tarhynda
claimed to rule. Still, that final phrase was something
of a catchall. And it seemed to Khaavorn that he'd
placed a subtle emphasis on the words "master of
Arvaerness."

"Convey our greetings to the Emperor Tarhynda in
return," said Riodheg. "And by whom do I have the
honor of sending them?"

"I am Tavazhalava of Baersa—the least of His Imperial Majesty's servants. He has, nonetheless, entrusted
to me certain small gifts, which I now have the honor
to present." He motioned to his guards, who led slaves
forward to display their burdens. The *oohs* and *ahs*
from the crowd grew louder. Last came the amphorae.
"Finally, His Imperial Majesty sends the finest grape
wine of Graetess."

Riodheg's eyes gleamed. "Ah, yes! I once had some,
while campaigning in Arnoriysa. I thank the Emperor.
Come into the hall, and we'll drink some of it together."
He gave Kaayeg orders to see to accommodations for
the ambassador's guards and slaves, and led the way
into the hall. Khaavorn followed, pointedly avoiding
looking at the crowd of lesser lights where Zhassu
doubtless wore an expression of smug vindication.

The great hall was crowded. Riodheg's court did not
usually adhere to rigid rules of seating precedence,
but this was a special occasion. The ambassador sat
at the High King's left at the head of the main table.

To Riodheg's right was his wife Khvemunare, wearing the same tight-lipped look of sour discontent she had worn for most of her childless political marriage. Seated down the length of the table were the High King's kindred and Companions. Khaavorn, though also a member of the latter group, sat among the former . . . and so did Norkhaari.

The High King's half sister sat not quite directly across the table from Khaavorn, not far down from the head. A few places further on down was Khuonar nak'Thaaleg, heir presumptive to his uncle the childless chieftain of Naklore. His eyes kept straying to Norkhaari, who occasionally met them. Their affair was more or less an open secret.

"So, Lord Tavazhalava," said Riodheg after the initial pleasantries had been spoken and the wine duly sampled. (There was also beer for the conservatives like Khaavorn.) "You must tell us of your journey. It was a long one—an epic one, even—from The City to this island in one stretch."

The ambassador seemed to weigh his words. "Actually, lord, my journey was in two stages. First I accompanied General Vaelsaru to Arvaerness. But doubtless you already know of his campaign there."

"So I do. I received news of it from my lands in Arnoriysa. But having been abroad with General Vaelsaru, you probably missed the visit of my nephew Khaavorn to The City, from which he has just returned. Khaavorn, did you meet Lord Tavazhalava there?"

"No, nak'Udheg, I didn't have the pleasure. Indeed, the Emperor announced the conquest of Arvaerness at the reception where I was presented to him."

"Hardly 'conquest,' Lord Khaavorn," Tavazhalava

demurred. "One cannot 'conquer' one's own domains. General Vaelsaru was sent merely to reestablish order in what is, after all, an imperial province of ancient standing."

"*Very* ancient," Khaavorn muttered. There were a few splutters of laughter around the table. They died a quick death under Riodheg's glare.

"But I should have mentioned in the course of the introductions," said the High King into the silence he'd created, "Khaavorn is the brother-in-law of General Vaelsaru."

"Ah!" The sharp regard Tavazhalava had been giving Khaavorn since he'd learned of the latter's visit to The City grew even sharper. "But of course! You must be the brother of whom the Lady Andonre has spoken so often."

"Yes." Khaavorn had no intention of letting the subject of Andonre be opened, though his undiplomatic shortness drew a warning glance from Riodheg. "But it occurs to me, Lord Tavazhalava, that if you were already in Vaelsaru's entourage when he departed The City, the Emperor must have been planning to send an embassy here to Lokhrein even before the 'restoring of order' in Arvaerness."

"The Emperor is noted for his farsighted plans," acknowledged Tavazhalava obliquely.

"No doubt. He is noted for a great many things." Khaavorn took a fortifying gulp of beer and leaned forward, no longer troubling to dissemble despite the warning look gathering like thunderclouds on Riodheg's face. "But surely those 'farsighted plans' involve more than just a courtesy call on the High King. So why don't you share with us your real reason for being here?"

Tavazhalava gave a sigh of languid resignation. "I had hoped to be able to put off such matters at least until after dinner. But I reckoned without the—how shall I say it?—refreshing forthrightness for which the Dovnaan are so justly renowned. I see now that I must come directly to the point." He turned back to Riodheg. "You have already demonstrated the excellence of your sources of information, so you are doubtless aware that the Emperor is committed to restoring imperial civilization to all those lands that once basked in its light."

"Including Lokhrein?" inquired the High King quietly. Without taking his eyes off Tavazhalava's, he motioned with his hand and stilled the low rumbling that had begun to arise in the hall.

Tavazhalava spread his hands. "Surely, lord, you cannot deny that your country—which we still habitually call Vriydansa, in imitation of our ancestors—first received civilization as a gift of the Old Empire, from which it—"

"—was cut off four hundred years ago," Riodheg finished for him.

"The mere passage of time cannot alter the fundamental forms of allegiance which all peoples, however backward, recognize—such as that which a child owes to its parent. The Emperor feels that it has been all too long since any expression of this allegiance has been forthcoming from Vriydansa to its parent the Empire."

This time there was a roar, not a rumble, and there was no suppressing it. Grudgingly, Khaavorn found himself respecting Tavazhalava's nerve. Of course, tradition held an ambassador's person sacred. Still, judging from everything Khaavorn had ever heard about Riodheg's father—and dimly remembered, for he'd been nine when the old bastard had died—that tradition wouldn't have stopped Udheg from splitting Tavazhalava's skull with an axe.

Riodheg, though, continued to speak in a level voice. "Actually, Lord Tavazhalava, time alters *all* things. Children grow up . . . and parents die, as the Old Empire died. Its orphaned children here in Lokhrein continued to keep the worship of the Mother alive—and when the Dovnaan arrived, they joined with those imperial descendants. Both sorts of blood flow in my own veins."

"But now the Empire—without which, by definition, civilization is impossible—has been reborn."

"Bah! The New Empire is no more a resurrection of the Old Empire than we here in Lokhrein are. Even as the Dovnaan arrived here, the Ayoliysei and the Iyomiasei and the rest of the Karsha tribes from Zhraess overran the old imperial islands and came to see the civilization they'd conquered as something to be cherished and defended. Well, so do we! We hold at bay the untamed Dovnaan tribes that still live in the Rhaemu Valley. In our own way, we are as much the heirs of the Old Empire as you are. *In our own way!*" Riodheg rose to his feet. His voice was still controlled, but now he let it out to fill the hall. "The Old Empire was held together by the willingness of many lands to acknowledge the supremacy of the Mother's first home. That's gone now. We've traveled too far along our own road. The Old Empire never tried to enforce this island's submission—and Tarhynda can't enforce it now!"

The High King's final words were almost drowned out by the thunder of affirmation that shook the hall. Khaavorn was on his feet and shouting with the rest, but a calm portion of his mind thought: *This is it! This is the war that Nyrthim and Minuren told me to warn Riodheg of. There's no stopping it now.*

He waited for Tarhynda's ambassador to hurl the imperial anathema, making war an accomplished fact.

Tavazhalava waited for the noise to die down, then spoke in tones of judicious thoughtfulness. "Actually, the Emperor has reached somewhat similar conclusions."

Riodheg, for the first time in Khaavorn's experience, looked as completely taken aback as though he'd been struck in the belly. He looked, in other words, like Khaavorn felt—and everyone else as well, judging from the silence of stunned bewilderment in the hall.

"Indeed," continued Tavazhalava with a smile, "it is self-evident to all intelligent men that any sort of direct imperial rule across such distances would be impractical to the point of absurdity. Under these circumstances, no purpose would be served by insisting on some meaningless gesture of fealty. Rather, the Emperor feels that surely some accommodation can be reached. It is for this very purpose that I am here."

"Continue," said Riodheg, sinking, deflated, back onto his throne.

"The only real areas of possible disagreement are in the province of Arnoriysa, which now shares a common border with territories under the direct control of the Empire. I am empowered to agree to a boundary adjustment which will assure the legitimate security needs of the imperial province of Arvaerness . . . and of Lokhrein." Tavazhalava gave a graceful smile of concession as he pronounced the Dovnaan word. "The scribe who accompanies me has, in written form, a detailed description of the revised boundary line the Emperor proposes. Informally, let me say that the contemplated modifications are rather trivial."

So, thought Khaavorn, *all that horseshit about allegiance was just a bargaining point*. It confirmed the impression that had been growing on him ever since the ambassador had spoken to the High King in Dovnaan: Tavazhalava might look like the courtiers Khaavorn had seen in The City, but the resemblance was deceptive. Unlike those decorative parasites, he served the interests of his Emperor—about whose true nature, Khaavorn was prepared to believe, he had no idea—in the field. And he was good at it . . . altogether *too* good for Khaavorn's taste.

Riodheg stroked his beard thoughtfully. "This must be thought on. I shall take counsel with my advisers. Not," he added with a wistfulness that came to him all too often these days, "that I have Nyrthim to advise me any more."

It was those final words that pulled Khaavorn out of the slough of forgetfulness into which he'd been sinking.

Nyrthim had told him to seek Minuren out. And Minuren had told him: "Tarhynda *must* be kept out of Arnoriysa! Whatever poor shred of hope remains to us depends squarely on that."

And everything this ambassador has said has been a ploy for territorial concessions in Arnoriysa . . .

As though from a great distance, he heard Norkhaari's

voice. It was not customary among the Dovnaan for women to speak in council. But this was a social function of the sort to which women were invited. And her priestess's robe conferred a prestige that made her difficult to suppress. "I believe you should consider this seriously, brother. After all, there is much in what Lord Tavazhalava says. We *did* receive the truth of Mother Rhaeie from the Empire. We owe them much for that." Her eyes strayed toward Khuonar, who jerked as though at a signal, and rose to address the High King.

"The words of the Priestess Norkhaari cannot be ignored, nak'Udheg. Neither can the fact that our possessions in Arnoriysa now share a common border with the Empire—a border across which is an army led by General Vaelsaru."

Tavazhalava gestured delicately. "I wasn't going to put it that way, but . . ."

"These considerations will be given full weight in council," said Riodheg gravely. "But for now, let us—"

"*No!*"

Every eye in the hall was on Khaavorn as he sprang to his feet and interrupted the High King. The general rumble—the sound of the uncertainty into which Tavazhalava had maneuvered the crowd—was momentarily stilled.

"No, nak'Udheg!" Khaavorn repeated. "This thing must not be. Not an inch of Arnoriysa must be yielded to Tarhynda!"

"This matter must be considered carefully, Khaavorn," Riodheg frowned. "Of course you will have the opportunity to air your views. But why are you so vehement?"

"Because," began Khaavorn—and stopped cold. He'd forgotten where he was: a hall filled to the rafters with people, including Tarhynda's representative.

"Yes, why?" goaded Khuonar with a sneer.

"Uncle, before Lord Tavazhalava arrived you agreed to see me privately, because I had things to say that were for your ears only. Those things touch directly on why we must refuse Tarhynda's demands. The High Priestess Minuren says so." Norkhaari started, and a buzz of talk arose. "I ask you—I *beg* you—to let me relate my tale to you."

"I agree," said Norkhaari, catching Khaavorn flat-footed. "Brother, you should certainly give our nephew a private audience as he requests. And," she continued smoothly, "I will accompany the two of you. After all, Khaavorn says that Minuren has taken an interest in this. So, as the only priestess of Rhaeie present, I will represent her."

"That seems only reasonable," Riodheg nodded. "Your insights should be of value. Well, Khaavorn?"

Khaavorn swallowed hard, and wished desperately that Minuren would walk into the hall. But the doorway remained disobligingly empty.

"No, nak'Udheg. I must ask that it be you and me alone."

Norkhaari stiffened and glared at him, and a low growl arose from Khuonar.

"What is the reason for this request, Khaavorn?" asked Riodheg with a frown.

"Yes!" snapped Khuonar. "What possible reason could you have for seeking to exclude a priestess of Rhaeie?"

Khaavorn ignored him and addressed the High King.

"The tale I have to tell, uncle, is of truly evil things. I have reason to believe—and Minuren agrees—that Norkhaari may be somehow involved."

The hall erupted in a buzz of scandalized incredulity, overridden by Khuonar's roar. "How dare you make such an imputation, dog?"

Lanoraak, Khaaradh and Akhraworn were immediately on their feet beside Khaavorn, bellowing their support for him. "Who are you calling dog, you son of a long line of cattle thieves?" demanded Lanoraak, shaking his fist, before a coughing fit overtook him.

Khuonar's relatives rose, raging. "Lanoraak, you'll answer to me for that, you conniving old snake!" raved a man even older than Lanoraak, through sparse teeth.

"Enough!" commanded Riodheg. "That will do!" With the families lining up, he smelled a feud brewing. It was a subject always on the mind—and in the nightmares—of any high king of Lokhrein.

Khuonar got his breathing under control. "Nak'Udheg, I demand satisfaction from Khaavorn nak'Moreg for the insult he has laid on my . . . friend, the Lady Norkhaari, your own half sister."

Khaavorn also brought himself to heel. He could not allow himself to be sidetracked from his mission, on whose importance Nyrthim and Minuren had been in agreement. "You can have satisfaction, Khuonar—later. But for now . . . Uncle, I must speak to you first. This cannot wait."

Khuonar barked laughter. "So you seek an excuse to put off answering for your lies. In addition to being a slanderer, you're also a coward!"

All at once, everything was forgotten except the scarlet mist that filled Khaavorn's eyes. Without remembering having climbed onto it, he was advancing down the tabletop toward Khuonar, who followed suit, scattering drinking jacks to the vocal indignation of the drinkers. They both retained enough presence of mind not to wield their axes in the presence of the High King. But they were upon each other, grappling and roaring with inarticulate fury, before their respective relatives pulled them apart.

"I SAID ENOUGH!" Riodheg's voice was like the thunder of Dayu, and it brought instant silence to the hall. "Lord Tavazhalava, you must think we are savages here."

The ambassador made a gracious gesture, wordlessly disavowing any such notion—which, in fact, was precisely what he'd been thinking all along.

Khuonar's pale-gray eyes and Khaavorn's dark-brown ones bored into each other as the restraining hands gradually released them. "Nak'Udheg," grated Khuonar, "as a matter of honor I challenge Khaavorn nak'Moreg to meet me at once . . . the old way."

Riodheg's face lost a shade of color. "As I have told Lord Tavazhalava, we strive to uphold civilization here. This is exactly the kind of thing we've been trying to get away from. I am resolved to see it consigned to the past."

"I have been insulted," said Khaavorn without breaking eye contact, "and I issue the same challenge. When both parties wish it, Uncle, you must permit it."

"That is the law," stated Norkhaari, with a vindictive smile in Khaavorn's direction. She clearly was in no doubt as to the outcome of what was about to happen.

The High King sighed deeply. "Very well. So be it: the old way."

CHAPTER ELEVEN

"You realize, of course, that this is mad folly," muttered Zhassu. He had managed to catch up with Khaavorn and his brothers and stepfather as they strode down from the summit. Now he kept abreast, puffing with exertion and anxiety. "You shouldn't have accepted this challenge."

Khaavorn gave him a sharp glance, then opened his mouth . . . and closed it. Some things are too obvious to put into words. "I had to," he settled for saying.

"But what if you—Rhaeie forbid!—are killed without having told your High King the truth about Tarhynda, as the Nezh charged you to do? All will be lost."

"I suppose you'll just have to tell him yourself," grinned Khaavorn.

"*Me?*" Zhassu's voice broke in a squeak. "He'd never listen to me. The only status I have here is that of your guest. If you die . . ." Zhassu fell silent as he contemplated the unpleasant possibilities.

"Your confidence in me is deeply reassuring."

They reached an oval area enclosed with a wooden fence, normally used for weapon practice. A crowd was gathering at the fence as everyone in Kintara flocked to watch. There were two gateways, on opposite sides. They stopped at one, and looked across at Khuonar and his relatives and friends. The High King and various notables, including Tavazhalava, were taking seats on a raised bench. Norkhaari was there, sitting stiffly as somehow befitted her peculiar status in this affair.

Zhassu looked around, adrift on a sea of alienness. "Uh . . . isn't someone going to bring your armor, and that of your opponent?"

"Armor? Weren't you listening? We're doing this the old way."

"Yes, I remember hearing that. I was going to ask you what it means, exactly. . . ."

But Khaavorn was listening no longer.

First he twisted his ponytail into a rope and looped it around through the bronze ring that held it, forming what looked to Zhassu oddly like a handle at the back of his head. Then he removed his mantle. Then his tunic. Then everything else save his gold and amber jewelry, and his loin strap. Through the latter he thrust a bronze dagger.

Zhassu watched, open-mouthed. Then he looked across the enclosure and saw that Khuonar was in the same state of virtual nudity.

Khaaradh wordlessly handed Khaavorn a very basic

shield of hide stretched over a wooden frame. Khaavorn took it in his left hand, and hefted his war axe with his right. Then he and Khuonar walked through their respective gates, entering the enclosure . . . and it was as though they'd entered the past as well.

Since times beyond the memories of anyone's grandfather's grandfather, the Dovnaan had measured a warrior's courage in inverse ratio to the amount of personal protection he wore. Oh, they weren't incapable of changing with the times. Nowadays they rode chariots into battle, wearing all the up-to-date bronze and hardened leather armor they could afford. But deep in their heart of hearts, they saw this as a regrettable decline from the ideal. When honor, rather than the soulless practicalities of warfare, was involved, a warrior could still insist on the old way. It wasn't done very often anymore, for Riodheg was known not to favor it. But the custom still had a force which not even he could defy in extreme cases.

So it was that Khaavorn and Khuonar advanced on each other, for all the world like two tribesmen of the first Karsha tribe to come west from the grasslands, save that their axeheads were bronze rather than polished stone.

And, thought Khaavorn, telling himself what he would never have admitted aloud in Zhassu's hearing, *Angmanu curse me for a fool, to have agreed to it. If Valdar were here, he'd be splitting his sides laughing!*

Khaavorn was a seasoned veteran of war as Riodheg had trained his men to wage it. With the newfangled panoply of bronze helmet and armor, that experience would have given him the advantage. But in this kind of fighting, little counted but strength and endurance. And Khuonar was the bigger, stronger and younger man.

For a moment they circled each other warily, to an accompaniment of shouts from the fence. Then, with a roar, Khuonar sprang, swinging his axe in an overhand sweep. Khaavorn got his shield up in time. Tearing pain shot through his left arm as the heavy axehead rebounded from it.

Besides which, his mind gibed on, *I'm out of practice at this sort of thing.*

At least the pain served the purpose of reigniting his anger. He gave a roar of his own as he swept his axe around, forcing Khuonar to jump back. Khuonar recovered quickly, though; he brought his shield down, almost catching Khaavorn's axe haft with its lower edge, and swung his own axe back up for another powerful stroke.

Khaavorn was back on the defensive, and stayed there. Khuonar advanced inexorably, landing one smashing blow after another on Khaavorn's weakening shield, pushing at Khaavorn's body with his own shield. Khaavorn retreated, unable to free his own axe for a return stroke. Soon they were both soaked in sweat, breathing in ragged gasps—Khaavorn more than Khuonar.

But still Khaavorn watched his opponent through narrowed eyes, waiting.

Then, almost imperceptibly, Khuonar paused between axe strokes to shift his grip on the weapon's haft.

Ha! flashed through Khaavorn's mind. *Experience counts for something after all!*

It was a standard maneuver. Having established

a repetitive pattern of hammerlike blows, Khuonar was reversing the axe in his hand to bring the hook into play, grabbing the edge of Khaavorn's shield and jerking it away. But Khaavorn, expecting it, launched himself forward in the split second Khuonar's adjustment of his grip took, and brought his axe down to thud against Khuonar's shield, rocking him back.

Seizing his advantage, Khaavorn pressed forward, raising his axe again. But Khuonar, caught off-balance, reacted without pausing to readjust his grip, swinging his axe hook first in a sideways sweep that went under Khaavorn's shield. Like the beak of some bird of prey, the bronze hook gouged into Khaavorn's left thigh and ripped out, tearing flesh and muscle.

Breathtaking pain shot through Khaavorn, and his left leg gave way under him.

With a scream of rage and triumph, Khuonar flung away his shield, gripped his axe in both hands, raised it high, and brought it down with all his strength.

Khaavorn, struggling to rise, managed to interpose his shield.

The bronze axehead crashed through the shield, gashing the arm holding it. The force of that blow smashed Khaavorn flat onto his back. With another roar, Khuonar braced his feet and pulled on his axe to free it for a final, killing stroke.

It remained where it was, caught in the torn oxhide and splintered wood of the shield.

Khuonar stared at it stupidly for some fraction of a second, then tugged on it with frantic desperation.

Khaavorn had kept his grip on his axe. Without even trying to swing it, he thrust it upward, ramming the head with its spiked ball into Khuonar's exposed stomach just below the solar plexus.

With a *whoosh* of expelled air, Khuonar doubled over, and his grip on his axe loosened.

Khaavorn flung away his shield, and his opponent's axe with it. Ignoring the white-hot pain in his thigh, he staggered to his feet and gripped his axe two-handed. Khuonar, still trying to breathe, looked up just in time to see that axe's onrushing edge, before it split his face and crashed into the brain behind.

Khaavorn heard nothing of the shouting from the spectators, for the pain he'd been holding at bay would no longer be denied, and his exertion had caused his wounds to bleed more freely. He sank back down to the bloody dirt beside that which had been Khuonar. But there were things that must be done.

First he removed Khuonar's gold chains and bracelets and put them on, as was expected of him. Then he drew his dagger, knelt over the body, and began sawing at the neck. Khuonar hadn't been dead long enough for the pressure behind his jugular to have altogether abated, and blood gushed forth. By the time Khaavorn stood up, holding Khuonar's ruined head by the loop of hair which *was*, in fact, a handle, his arms were scarlet to the elbows. Amid the cheering, he heard the sound of someone being violently sick, to the vast amusement of those standing nearby. A glance confirmed that it was Zhassu.

He limped over to stand before the High King and Tavazhalava—whose color, he noted with satisfaction, was not particularly good—and held the head aloft as tradition dictated. "Nak'Udheg, I claim the favor you granted me earlier, of speaking with you in private."

"That is your right, Khaavorn," said Riodheg gravely.

"Furthermore," said Khaavorn, riding the momentum of the moment and trying to think clearly, "I ask that Norkhaari nie'Khorleg be excluded from our deliberations." Norkhaari had been sitting like a statue of pale ivory, her huge dark blue eyes staring fixedly at Khuonar's head. Now she blinked her shock away and rose slowly to her feet, fury mounting visibly in her.

"No! I protest, brother. Anything that concerns Mother Rhaeie is my business."

"The reason is as I said earlier, nak'Udheg: the possibility exists that she may be implicated in the vile and depraved things of which I must tell you."

"I cannot be excluded on the grounds of these wild, unsupported allegations from one whom I thought to be a true kinsman!"

"I take no great pleasure in this, Aunt. But the High Priestess herself told me my news was for the High King's ears alone. She'd say as much if she were here."

"But she's *not* here!"

"Yes, I am."

The new voice brought instant silence. Khaavorn turned, as the crowd parted to reveal Minuren, advancing from the gate through which she'd passed unnoticed. Two junior priestesses accompanied her, as did the old ferryman, who doubled as a porter.

"See to Khaavorn's wounds," she ordered the priestesses briskly. Then she turned to Riodheg, whose jaw hung as slack as everyone else's. "Greetings, nak'Udheg. I regret that I didn't arrive sooner. Perhaps I could

have prevented . . . this." Her gesture took in the
enclosure and the headless corpse lying in a pool
of blood. "But if it had to be, then you should give
thanks to Rhaeie and Dayu that your nephew won.
Otherwise, all would truly be lost."

Norkhaari recovered quickly. "High Priestess, I'm so
relieved to see you! I have been the victim of monstrous
imputations—from my own nephew, no less!"

Minuren turned an unreadable expression on her.
"So you deny these 'imputations'?"

"Of course . . . But no, they are too vague to even
deserve a denial!"

"The High King must hear the specifics, then—as
I already have. And I say they are serious enough
to warrant his hearing them in private. Nak'Udheg,
I suggest that you assign men to keep the Priestess
Norkhaari confined to her own quarters while you
and I confer with Khaavorn."

"Of course," the High King nodded. "Kaayeg, see
to it."

Norkhaari looked from Riodheg to Minuren to
Khaavorn, letting her gaze linger on each just long
enough to let its inexpressible hatred register. Then she
marched stiffly off, accompanied by two warriors.

"Could I bring Zhassu with me, Uncle?" asked
Khaavorn, from the ground, where his thigh wound was
being dressed. "He was there, too, in The City."

"Very well, if the High Priestess has no objection.
Khaavorn, come to my quarters as soon as you've
dressed. Lord Tavazhalava, will you excuse us?"

The High King's private quarters were in a wing of
the great hall. By the time they were all there, seated

around a heavy table amid the carved wood and tapestries, Riodheg had recovered his kingliness.

"So, Minuren," he began, "I gather that you have already heard Khaavorn's tale . . . and that you believe it. Why?"

"Because, nak'Udheg, everything in it squares with what I know, starting with his meeting with Nyrthim."

"*Nyrthim?*"

"Yes. He did not die when you and everyone else believed he did. His death was faked . . . with my help."

Riodheg had half-risen from his chair. Now he sank back into it, stunned anew.

"Why?" he managed.

"That will become apparent from the tale. Proceed, Khaavorn, and leave nothing out."

Khaavorn did as he was bidden. He occasionally called on Zhassu for confirmation, and Minuren interrupted him a few times to emphasize some point or other.

But the High King broke in hardly at all. He sat, holding Khaavorn with his brooding eyes and taking it all in with far less shock than might have been expected. *But then,* Khaavorn thought, *he was in Nyrthim's care when he was young, as well as receiving the lore of the Old Empire from the priestesses. No one knows how much he learned—things beyond the ken of the rest of us. He's not like his father, who was—let's face it—just an extremely capable butcher.*

When the tale was done, Khaavorn's final word vanished tracelessly into silence. Finally the High King sighed deeply.

"So . . . Nyrthim is dead after all. And the demons are back. And one of them sits on the throne of the New Empire." Another sigh. "Minuren, why did you not tell me about this demon cult?"

"In that, nak'Udheg, I was mistaken. I thought I could deal with it myself, without the help of anyone except, perhaps, Nyrthim. Besides, I shrank from letting anyone outside the priesthood to know that we—any of us—could be capable of such things. So I blame myself for both pride and cowardice. And yet . . . would you have been able to accept the idea that your niece Andonre might be a part of it, as I've suspected for some time?"

Riodheg winced, and the lines on his face deepened. It was, Khaavorn reflected, easy to forget that his uncle was only eight years his senior. He seemed so much older.

"Well," the High King finally gusted, "I suppose I'll have to accept it now, won't I? But as for my half sister . . . Khaavorn, you have no direct proof of Norkhaari's involvement, do you? Just your brother's childhood recollection of some overheard conversation?"

"Well, no. Of course, she was Andonre's teacher, and Andonre—"

"But that's still not direct evidence. It's just an inference from circumstances—*circumstantial evidence*, I think the ancient sage Zhaerosa called it." A gleam of desperate hope began to grow in the High King's deep-set eyes. "She must be given the opportunity to defend herself, to answer these questions."

"Yes, yes," said Minuren impatiently. "But in the meantime, surely you can see why Tarhynda must be kept out of Arnoriysa. That's the important thing." Her eyes met Riodheg's in a moment of silent communication from which Khaavorn was excluded.

"Lords," Zhassu spoke up hesitantly, "perhaps the message brought by Lord Tavazhalava has some bearing on this."

Khaavorn struck the table with his right fist. (His left arm still hurt.) "That's right! Lady, I forgot that you've only just arrived. You weren't here when the imperial emissary told us, in effect, that concessions of land in Arnoriysa are Tarhynda's price for not pressing the Empire's claim to this island."

Minuren went pale. "Of course. It fits with everything else. Tarhynda would be only too delighted to get what he wants without fighting. The overlordship of Lokhrein means nothing to him. All the claptrap about restoring the Old Empire, and all the wars in the Inner Sea supposedly fought in its name, have just been foundation stones for this demand—it's what Tarhynda has been building up to all along. And we *know* one particular bit of territory those 'concessions' are going to include, don't we?"

With her last words, Minuren's eyes locked with the High King's. Once again, the two of them were alone in silence with whatever secret knowledge they possessed. Watching them, Khaavorn began to believe that the High Priestess had been right: he himself, and the world at large, were better off without that knowledge.

"Yes, we do know," Riodheg finally said. He straightened up, and his voice deepened. "As soon as I reject Tarhynda's proposal, I will immediately summon all the chieftains. I will also send word to my allies in Ehrein."

"Yes," nodded Minuren. "The isles of the west must stand together in this. We are now the shield of the whole world—the only shield it has, whether it knows it or not. And we no longer have Nyrthim."

"No, we don't." The hurt and loss returned to Riodheg's face for a moment. "But . . . to get back to Norkhaari: as I said before, there is not enough evidence to condemn her as yet. She must be given the right to present a defense. I've always sought to do justice; I must do so now. In fact," he continued with the smooth eagerness of an intelligent man rationalizing freely, "I'll send the word to the chieftains and allies *now*, and tell Tavazhalava that I can't give him a reply before consulting with them. And then I'll give Norkhaari a hearing before doing that. That'll gain us more time."

"Very well." Minuren looked dubious. "Your desire to be fair to her does you credit. I only hope you—and the world—won't regret it."

CHAPTER TWELVE

The messengers had been sent out, to summon the five great chieftains of the high downs who were entitled to style themselves "kings" and whose counsel Riodheg must seek before deciding how to respond to Tarhynda's proposal. Or so Tavazhalava had been told—it was the official reason he was being kept cooling his heels at Kintara.

Other messengers had also departed, without the ambassador's knowledge. They had further to go, for they were to assert Riodheg's claim to the support of his allies across the water: the ones in Ehrein, and also Arkhuar of Dhulon, who probably wouldn't be able to contribute any aid in time to affect the issue.

The high downs, on the other hand, were close, and

one by one the kings arrived. Kedhorn nak'Thaaleg of Naklore was the first. He had some hard looks for Khaavorn, but couldn't really make an issue of the killing of his cousin Khuonar—who had, after all, issued the initial challenge. Maair nak'Ronar of Noveg, Araapar nak'Konorn of Therthak, Meneth nak'Paardholorn of Uaala, and Faalnar nak'Komaal of Fimnokh followed. The last of those five traditional kingships had been the power base from which Udheg, through his unrivaled ability at murder and slaughter, had elevated his own blood into a primacy new to this island. Faalnar, a cousin, had held the kingship since Riodheg had established his own seat at Kintara—an innovation which had caused those five touchy grandees, proud of their relatively pure Dovnaan lineage (whatever that might mean), to wonder if he might be trying to aggrandize himself into something more than *primus inter pares*. Partly as a consequence, Faalnar was Riodheg's staunchest supporter among the five. Riodheg could place more reliance on the backing of the lesser chieftains like Lanoraak, most of whose families had mingled their blood with the heirs of the Old Empire and the Escquahar of the west. Those, too, were arriving in response to the High King's messengers.

But the arrival of the last of the big five was the signal for pointed suggestions from Tavazhalava, who seemed disturbingly well informed on the workings of the high kingship.

"Surely, lord," he urged, managing to convey impatience without letting his suavity slip, "it is now appropriate for you to formulate a reply to the Emperor."

Riodheg gazed at him from under lowered brows. "You constitute yourself, then, as the arbiter of what is and is not 'appropriate' in my hall?"

"Indeed not, lord! I apologize for my infelicitous choice of words. Still and all, the fact remains that the kings *have* arrived, so there is no further obstacle in law or custom to finalizing this matter. And surely a prompt resolution can only be to the advantage of both parties."

"Perhaps, Lord Tavazhalava, perhaps. I will give the matter my earnest consideration. But first I must deal with the case of my half sister, the Priestess Norkhaari. After that, Tarhynda will have his answer."

Later, Riodheg repeated the conversation to Khaavorn, Minuren and Lanoraak. "I can put Tavazhalava off no longer," he concluded. "We'll bring Norkhaari in, and I'll turn jurisdiction of her over to you, Minuren. Then I'll put Tarhynda's proposal before the kings."

Khaavorn put forth a question that had been on his mind. "When you do, Uncle, will you openly announce what Tarhynda really is?"

Minuren frowned. "Would that be wise? We'd be letting Tarhynda know that *we* know—which he doesn't, as yet. What would be the advantage?"

"To rouse the kings into refusing Tarhynda's demands and setting out on the war trail," said Lanoraak.

"Oh, they'll do that in any case—if the proposition is presented to them in the right way," said Riodheg confidently.

"I wouldn't put it past Tavazhalava to talk them into accepting it," said Lanoraak with the pessimistic relish of the elderly. "He's smooth as an eel, that one."

"I have no intention of giving him the chance. They'll hear it from *me*, and by the time I'm done they'll be so enraged they'll fling it back in Tarhynda's face. Don't worry; I know how to handle them."

"But, Uncle," Khaavorn persisted, "what if they seem to be having second thoughts?"

"*Then* it will be time to reveal what we know. We'll hold it in reserve for that possibility."

Minuren looked troubled. "I hope it doesn't come to that. It would be better if we can stop Tarhynda without people ever knowing just what it really was that we stopped. The knowledge that such things are possible should not become widespread; no good can come of it."

"Well, we'll see how matters develop," said Riodheg. He seemed to understand Minuren's qualms while at the same time being impatient of them. "For now, let Norkhaari be brought before us tomorrow."

It was done as Riodheg commanded, the following afternoon. He sat at the head table with the five kings, splendid in the rich colors favored by the Dovnaan, and Tavazhalava. The other chieftains and their personal retainers, as well as the High King's Companions, packed the hall. Minuren sat beside Riodheg, waiting.

Kaayeg approached the High King and muttered something into his ear. Riodheg frowned and made an equally inaudible reply, and Kaayeg hurried off.

"What was that about, nak'Udheg?" asked the High Priestess.

"Oh, just something he thought I'd want to know without delay. A couple of days ago, a child was reported missing. Now the body has been found . . . or a least what *could* be the body, in a condition that makes it hard to be certain. Horrible. After all this"— Riodheg indicated the crowded hall—"is done with, we'll have to look more closely into . . ." Riodheg's voice trailed off. Like Khaavorn, who was seated a few places down the table, he saw the color draining from the High Priestess' face as though from a broken pot. "Minuren, what is it?"

"Riodheg," she said with breathless urgency, "you *have* been keeping Norkhaari *closely* confined—haven't you?"

"Why . . . yes. Well, closely enough. She hasn't been allowed to leave Kintara, if that's what you mean. But after all, she *is* of the royal kin. Naturally, I gave orders that her privacy be respected."

Minuren went even paler. "Merciful Rhaeie! Do you realize—?"

"Shush!" Riodheg cut her off, for Norkhaari was entering the hall, escorted by two warriors who, together, must have outweighed her by a factor of almost four. Minuren did her best to compose herself.

Norkhaari, on the other hand, looked quite composed—altogether too much so under the circumstances, Khaavorn thought uneasily. She wore her priestess' robe, of which there existed as yet no grounds for divesting her.

"Norkhaari nie'Khorleg," began the High King formally, "you are under suspicion of involvement in forbidden and abominable practices. I have determined that these suspicions are supported by sufficient reasons to turn you over to the High Priestess Minuren for further examination. You will be given into her charge and conveyed to the sanctuary of Khlaastom for this purpose, under armed escort."

Something was bothering Khaavorn. At first he couldn't put his finger on it. Then he realized what it was: a faint but undeniable odor. His sensitivities in such matters were not exactly overdeveloped, for in his world the various aromas of life, including the ripest, were not disguised. But this was not part of the accustomed olfactory background. And yet it was somehow familiar . . .

Norkhaari gave Riodheg a singularly inappropriate smile. "What, Brother? Does the blood we have in common suddenly count for nothing?"

"You stand accused of the summoning and worship of demons." A stunned silence filled the hall. "I cannot allow anyone's lineage—anyone's!—to shield such foulness. I can only hope that the charges will prove untrue, and that you are not involved in such a betrayal of the faith of Rhaeie."

The odor seemed stronger now. Khaavorn saw from their expressions that others were noticing it. Minuren, however, wore a subtly different look, as though she were sensing, with senses other than smell, a wrongness that went beyond any mere stench.

Norkhaari's smile curled into a sneer. "'Untrue'? Oh, it is true enough, dear Brother, to the extent of your ability to understand it. But when you say I am 'involved' you say too little. I am the Highest Sister!" Riodheg's jaw fell, and as Norkhaari spoke on, her expression continued to transform, until the sneer became a less-than-human snarl. "But 'betrayal'? What a joke! The betrayal happened hundreds of years ago,.

and the betrayers were the priestesses of the Old Empire. Pretending to worship Rhaeie, they sold out to the archenemy Dayu like whores spreading their legs for copper trinkets. And now their corruption has eaten away at the world like a growth until all that now remains is the corruption itself, frozen into a great, pompous, lifeless monument to the futile stupidity of men! The old world is dead now—the world as it was intended to be, and as it actually was before the life-destroying lie of a *male* god entered into it and poisoned it. It cannot be restored. But another world like it can be born out of chaos. And I have assured the coming of that chaos. Nothing can stop it now—least of all you, Riodheg, you bastard who clawed your way into the world through my mother's torn, bleeding body!"

Everyone in the hall sat in horrified fascination. But Khaavorn had ceased to listen, for he had finally remembered when and where he'd smelled the odor that had entered into the hall behind Norkhaari. He was also remembering what Nyrthim had said that same night, about the *Nartiya Zhere* he and Valdar and Wothorg had just killed at such cost: "... *it can—like all demons—disappear from sight.*"

"Enough, Norkhaari," he heard Riodheg say, in a voice of mingled sternness and sorrow. "You have condemned yourself out of your own mouth. You will now accompany Minuren to—"

"Oh, no, Brother. I think not." Norkhaari's smile was suddenly back.

Khaavorn surged to his feet. "Uncle! Beware! There is—"

But it was too late.

Afterwards, Khaavorn was never sure just what it was he had expected. Regardless, there was in fact no blinding flash of light, no puff of varicolored smoke, no thunderclap of sound—indeed, no sound at all. There was only a wavering of the sort one observed through the heated air rising above a fire. But this was a wavering of reality itself, in the area between Norkhaari and the head table. . . .

The memory that Khaavorn had been living with ever since his first night in The City suddenly crouched there in all its hideous solidity, and it was like awakening from a nightmare to find that the nightmare is real.

The moment lasted too small a fraction of a second for paralysis to sink home. The *Nartiya Zhere*—it must, Khaavorn thought, be the only sort of demon Norkhaari could contrive to summon, in such limited time and with only one sacrificial victim—emitted the remembered ear-shattering roar, and sprang forward with the remembered insectlike swiftness.

Khaavorn, alone among those in the hall, had seen its like before. So while the others remained frozen into stunned immobility, he bounded across the table, ignoring the stiffness of his wounds, and, with a shout, committed the *lese majesty* of yanking his axe from its belt thong.

Not the head, he reminded himself as he raised the axe aloft two-handed and rushed to intercept the demon. *That's a waste of time.* He swung downward, aiming for the base of the almost nonexistent neck.

The seemingly impossible quickness of the demon's movements made accuracy difficult. At the last instant, the demon twisted toward him, glaring at him and opening its grotesquely prognathous jaws wide to display its double rows of carnivore teeth and emit a shrill blast of hate. The descending axe hit the shoulder, leaving a shallow gash and causing the demon to stagger. Khaavorn jumped backwards to avoid a vicious sweep of the barbed tail, for he remembered Wothorg.

Less than a second had passed. But the abrupt explosion of violence had been sufficient to bring everyone else out of shock. The hall erupted with shouts and screams and turmoil. From each side, members of Riodheg's Companions rushed in to interpose themselves between the demon and the High King.

With a shrieking roar, the demon turned on them in a blur of slashing, rending motion. Blood sprayed, severed limbs flew, and bodies collapsed in a welter of butchery. The few weapon strokes that connected merely glanced or rebounded from the unnaturally tough hide, or bounced off bones that were harder than the finest Khrunetore bronze. Those blows did not even slow the demon down as it advanced into the crush of human bodies in the hall, rending and tearing them.

Beyond the demon's reach, people were being trampled in the stampede for the door.

But Khaavorn had had time to regain his balance, despite his wounded left leg. He got in behind the demon, carefully avoiding the thrashing tail, and raised his axe. Then, with all the strength he could summon up, he brought it down on that tail.

It was like cutting a thick skein of tough leather. But the hard-driven axe went through. The barb and a couple of feet of tail lay on the floor, still twitching feebly with an independent residue of life.

The demon filled the hall with a sound that threatened to rupture every eardrum. It whirled around to find its tormentor.

Khaavorn, still struggling to pull his axe out of the wood floor into which it had sunk, knew himself for a dead man.

Then, with a loud war cry, Khaaradh sprang forward and swung his axe around hookfirst. It gaffed the demon's throat from the side. With a convulsive effort, Khaaradh jerked back. The hook ripped out, pulling the demon's windpipe—or the equivalent thereof—like a rope dripping with unnaturally colored blood. The demon's roar died in a ghastly gurgle as a final heave parted that rope.

Khaavorn finally freed his axe. He heaved it aloft slowly—his arm wound was beginning to catch up with him—and struck the demon in its already-ruined throat, leaving its head attached to its body by little more than its spine. The creature toppled slowly over onto its back.

Now warriors closed in from all sides, clearly wanting nothing so much as to chop the expiring demon into an unrecognizable mess.

"Get back," Khaavron shouted to them. He grabbed one of them by the arm, and then another, pulling them away. He was barely in time, before the all-consuming flame he remembered incinerated the demon at the moment of its death.

The hall was suddenly silent save for the moaning and cries of the wounded.

"So, Khaavorn," breathed Riodheg, who stood among the warriors and the mutilated bodies, "this is what you described to me?"

"Yes, Uncle. A *Nartiya Zhere*, Nyrthim called it—the least of demons." Khaavorn finally let his left leg give way under him and sank, groaning, to the floor. He gestured at the wounded men. "Those who were struck by the tail barb . . . give them a clean, quick death. It's the only mercy the world still holds for them."

"Norkhaari must have summoned it," said Minuren, who had remained behind the head table. "They will—for a while, anyway—obey whoever summons them. She must have brought it with her when she entered the hall."

"Norkhaari!" Riodheg blinked with recollection, and looked around the hall. "Where is she?"

A hasty search revealed no trace of the priestess—the Highest Sister, as they now knew her to be.

"And that," said Minuren grimly, "is precisely why she summoned the demon. In the chaos it created, she slipped away—doubtless with the assistance of her 'Sisters.'"

"We'll find her."

"You won't."

"And," resumed Riodheg, "where is Lord Tavazhalava? We still have business to attend to."

"Here, lord." Tavazhalava's peacock-plumed headdress appeared over the rim of the head table, under which he'd been hiding. He surveyed the slaughterhouse that the great hall had become. "Ah . . . perhaps this is not the best possible time to—"

"On the contrary! I can imagine no better time." Riodheg stalked back around the table, his feet squishing in blood, and stood between the High Priestess and the cringing imperial emissary. He ran his eyes over the kings of the high downs. Meneth was wounded but conscious. Maair lay dead in a tangle of his own guts, but his son was there, cradling his head. The others were all hale. Riodheg mounted to the top of the table and looked out over all of them, his eyes flashing with the fury he was holding in check—a rage that had burned his mind clean of all reasoned, calculated intentions as to what he was and was not going to say.

"What was just unleashed in this hall was merely a small part of something truly abominable—something of which my nephew Khaavorn has returned from The City to warn us. Now we all know his warning is true. The demons of Angmanu are returning, admitted into our world by a dark alliance of demon worshipers from this island and the Empire. Even the Great Demons, the worst nightmare of all, are back. One of them squats in The City, wearing the semblance of a man as the old tales tell us they can do. And that false man is the Emperor Tarhynda! A demon sits on the alabaster throne of the Empire!"

A gasp went through the hall like a shuddering wind. Tavazhalava, speechless for once, stared at Riodheg as though the High King had grown a second head. It confirmed Khaavorn in his belief that the ambassador had no knowledge of what his Emperor truly was.

"And now," Riodheg went on, "Lord Tavazhalava has come bringing the gracious words of this demon Emperor to us, his subjects. He demands our submission—"

A collective growl arose from the survivors in the hall. It wasn't the truculent bellowing Riodheg's words might have aroused in other circumstances—not after what had just happened in this hall. It was quieter, and more dangerous.

"—but will condescend to forego that submission if we surrender land in Arnoriysa."

"No! No!" The shouting easily drowned out Tavazhalava's feeble, stammering efforts at a demurral. Riodheg let them go on a few seconds before motioning for silence. Then he turned to the emissary.

"You have your answer, Lord Tavazhalava. We reject your proposal, and anything else from the foulness you serve. I allow you to depart unharmed because I have no proof that you serve it knowingly. In fact, I believe that you do not."

Tavazhalava finally found his voice, and when he spoke all diplomatic equipoise was forgotten. "Madness!"

"Get out! Take our reply to your Emperor . . . and to his depraved Empress, who summoned him into the world! If they want even a fistful of Arnoriysa's dirt, they'll have to fight for it. And . . ." Riodheg's voice dropped, and he spoke to Tavazhalava alone and not to the hall at large. "Ask yourself about things you've seen, things you've wondered at, things that didn't seem quite right."

For a short but nonetheless real moment, Tavazhalava hesitated. Then he seemed to draw around himself the ancient dignity of the Empire. "Madness," he repeated. "You can't possibly win. You and your handful of barbarian buffoons will be facing the armies of the Empire, led by Lord Vaelsaru himself."

"At least we'll be fighting for Dayu, and for Rhaeie— and for the Earth that *is* Rhaeie. Perhaps Vaelsaru will begin to wonder just what it is *he* is fighting for. Now go, while I can still guarantee your safety."

~ ~ ~

"Well, little brother, you occasionally have your moments," said Khaavorn as they strode toward the High King's quarters. Actually, he limped rather than strode, favoring his reinjured left thigh. "That stroke to the demon's throat . . ."

"Actually," admitted Khaaradh, "I didn't think of it myself. I'd been talking to Zhassu, and he mentioned something of the sort."

Khaavorn looked over his shoulder in surprise. The wine merchant—who had been invited to this conference for his familiarity with the Empire—spread his hands in a self-deprecating gesture. "The Nezh once told me the throat is an area where they are relatively vulnerable."

Before Khaavorn had a chance to inquire as to the circumstances, they arrived at the inner chamber. Various advisors were already there, including Lanoraak.

"Welcome," said Riodheg. "You stepfather was just giving his views on imperial strategy."

"Well, nak'Udheg," said Lanoraak, "one thing I'm certain of is that they'll invade Arnoriysa in the autumn. Remember, Vaelsaru's army is made up of mercenaries. They don't have farms they have to return to for the harvest."

"You're doubtless right," the High King acknowledged. "We'll have to depend on the Companions and any local retainers in Arnoriysa who can be in the field at that time." The warrior nobility's retainers were basically farmers, with small holdings worked by themselves as well as by peasants descended from times before the Old Empire.

"Another problem," said Khaavorn, "is the matter

of chariots. We'll have to ship ours across the water to Arnoriysa. Of course, Vaelsaru has had to do the same thing. But he's been at it longer."

"Also true," nodded Riodheg. "Of course, I'm hoping that won't be decisive."

Khaavorn nodded, and ran over the subject in his mind.

The light, mobile chariot invented by the Karsha tribes of the grasslands, with its six-spoked wheels and specially bred and trained horses, had long since been refined into a highly maneuverable instrument with its axle positioned well to the rear. Against the disciplined infantry of the eastern kingdoms, a rigid tactical doctrine had come to regulate its use. The chariots would advance at a canter or at most a fast trot, while the noble archers who rode them rained volley after volley of high-trajectory arrows down on the opposing formation until it broke up. Further west, in the lands from which the New Empire drew its Achaysei charioteers, infantry was little more than an armed mob and the chariot had come into its own as a shock weapon, charging at high speed. For this a heavier chariot had evolved, with the axle near the center for stability at the expense of maneuverability.

Riodheg had introduced that to Lokhrein. And now he was hoping to change it.

"One piece of good news," he announced. "I've heard from Taalorg of Ehrein and Kaailtraam of Fortrein. They're going to honor their pledges, and will be here in time to accompany us to Arnoriysa."

Sounds of relief arose from everyone present. The Escquahar to the west and north were good fighters . . . and better archers. Khaavorn was in no mood to quibble about the use of the bow in war at this particular time. And Riodheg, he knew, had some original ideas about its use.

"What about Arkhuar of Dhulon?" he asked.

"There hasn't been time for a reply from him. We can only hope he'll be in time. I feel safe in saying we all have a healthy respect for those northerners."

"Yes," said Khaavorn, joining the chorus of agreement. "I remember Wothorg . . ."

Riodheg's deep eyes rested on him. "Yes, you told me what happened to him. He'll be missed . . . now more than ever. And so will Valdar."

Khaavorn inclined his head in response, and his thoughts went back to his last sight of his friend, now surely dead, his irreverent but goodhearted laugh stilled forever.

And yet . . . I never actually saw him and Nyrthim die. . . .

Khaavorn shook off the thought. *Don't cling to false hopes,* he chided himself. *They can't have survived. The most you dare hope is that they met a decent death, in battle against men.*

But the tiny doubt refused to leave him.

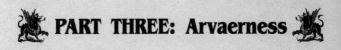

PART THREE: Arvaerness

CHAPTER THIRTEEN

Northwest of Zhraess, the tributary of the Inner Sea known as the Iylaetica stretched north toward the mountainous heart of the continent, the destination of Nyrthim's acquaintance, the amber merchant.

The ship's route led past old-established imperial islands like Cercyrsa and Ibvacsa . . . and also past the maze of islets known as the Aechiynads, among whose reefs and rocks lurked a dark wiry race from Dayu knew where, incorrigible pirates all. Valdar's sword drank deep one night, while their ship sheltered beneath a pine-crowned cliff and those scavengers emerged from a hidden inlet and tried to board them. That sword-work helped pay for their passage.

At length they struck out westward across the

Iylaetica and followed the coast north to the mouth of a wide river. Proceeding upriver, they presently came to a settlement—little more than a camp, really—which had the air, common to all times and places, of being inhabited by people who were there to gain the wherewithal to go somewhere else. For this was the southern terminus of the amber trail, and the captain sought out a trader from Khrunetore.

It was the way the amber trade worked. The Dhulaan, and kindred folk from the shores of the cold sea to the east of Dhulon, brought the precious stuff down along the river valleys to the lands of Khrunetore, where they traded it for gold that the Khrunetoraan had obtained from further east by trading the tin that only a few lands, including theirs, bore. Thus they acted as the middlemen of the trade, bringing the amber south to resell for the finished products of imperial civilization. Valdar would find none of his countrymen here.

The captain grumbled to everyone who would listen that the whole trade was drying up because the Khrunetoraan had less and less tin to devote to it. They had better uses for it, having become bronze workers of some renown themselves. Eventually, though, he did his business, communicating haltingly in trade Nimosei with a tall ash-blond Khrunetoraan named Khudrogar. The latter agreed to let Nyrthim and Valdar accompany his party on his return trek to the north in exchange for a few extra trinkets—the captain's final payment on whatever obscure debt he owed the sorcerer—and for the pair's services as a healer and a guard respectively.

They followed the river and its tributaries through a

countryside of the sort Valdar had become accustomed
to in the lands around the Inner Sea. Then the land
grew steadily more rolling, with numerous lakes. They
stopped at villages built on pilings over the adjacent
wetlands, to buy food from villagers who had learned
to covet trinkets from civilized workshops.

And as they progressed northward, the titanic
Aelphon Mountains grew nearer, looming in range
piled upon range, their peaks clothed in white even
in summer.

They ascended a pass Khudrogar knew from long
experience, leading through high meadows, green with
summer, between the majestic peaks. Gradually, they
began to descend, and followed rivers that flowed
north into the great Iystaer.

There, Nyrthim and Valdar parted company with
the traders, whose route led across the Iystaer and
continued northward into the Khrunetore realms.
Instead, they turned west and followed the Iystaer
toward its source. Valdar had fashioned a bow, and
between his hunting and the hospitality of the riverside
villages—clusters of rectangular houses whose wood-
pole structure was covered with mud and roofed with
thatch, set in clearings in the ageless forests—they
survived.

Passing the tiny lake that was the source of the
mighty Iystaer, they passed through a hilly country
into the upper reaches of the valley of the Rhaemu,
which flowed north to eventually empty into the narrow sea beyond which was Lokhrein.

The Rhaemu Valley, though outside Riodheg's
sphere, was the original home of the Dovnaan who
had migrated into Lokhrein a couple of centuries

before, and the people still spoke dialects of the same tongue. Nyrthim and Valdar had little trouble making themselves understood in the villages and in the hill forts that lorded it over them. It would have been easy to arrange for transportation by boat down the Rhaemu and eventually to Lokhrein. But that was not Nyrthim's intention. Instead, they struck out westward, skirting the ill-defined northern frontier of Arvaerness, toward the headwaters of the Liyzher River, which ran west to the Outer Sea. Around the Liyzher's middle course was the debatable border region between Arvaerness and Arnoriysa. Here they avoided villages and forts alike—especially the latter, which were either in fief to the Empire or occupied outright by its troops.

It was in one of their overnight camps that Valdar tried yet another strategy to worm information out of Nyrthim.

They were in the midst of a rolling mixture of forests and meadowland like most places north of the Aelphons. Nyrthim claimed that in his boyhood, grandsires had insisted there had been more forest in their own youth—and that *their* grandsires had remembered a time when there had been still more, and also more rain. By this point in their trek, Valdar felt the present era had quite enough rain.

They'd camped by the shores of a small tributary of the upper Liyzher under a thickly forested bluff. Valdar had done some spearfishing, and as the sun sank behind the hills they sat across the fire from each other finishing off the last of their supper and removing tiny bones from between their teeth. Valdar thoughtfully stroked the black beard he'd grown in the course of their travels. It wasn't yet full and fluffy by any means, but at least it was past the itchy stage. Nyrthim's gray beard had only gotten longer. At first Valdar had worried about the old sorcerer. But Nyrthim's well-cured stringy toughness had been up to the rigors of their journey. Even crossing the mountains, he hadn't slowed Valdar up too much.

"You know, Nyrthim," said Valdar with calculated casualness, "I think I've figured it out."

"Congratulations. *What*, exactly, have you figured out?"

"Why Tarhynda is going to go to war with Riodheg and invade Arnoriysa. You haven't been particularly informative about that, even though you made some vague promise, that last night in The City, to let me in on it eventually. As a matter of fact, some would say you've been downright evasive. But I think I've worked out for myself what Tarhynda's game is."

"Have you indeed?" Nyrthim's eyes narrowed in the firelight.

"It started to become clear to me while listening to the captain going on about the amber trade." Valdar leaned back and launched into what he hoped was a proper impression of an insufferably cocksure young know-it-all. "What it's really all about is *tin*. Tarhynda may be a demon, but the empire he rules still can't get along without bronze. Now, the Khrunetore realms have become producers of finished bronzework; they're no longer interested in shipping their tin off to be alloyed into bronze by others. So Lokhrein has become the Empire's chief tin supplier—on terms with which the Empire has never been particularly happy. But now the Escquahar in Ehrein have learned to work in bronze. Sooner or later, they'll take all the tin Lokhrein can supply, and provide the high kings with the bronze weapons they need. Where will that leave the Empire? No," he finished, for all the world as though he believed it, "Tarhynda's purpose is to nip that little problem in the bud by conquering Lokhrein outright so he'll have the tin under his direct control."

"Most ingenious. You are, of course, entitled to your opinion." Nyrthim's expression did not match his words, and Valdar forced himself not to grin. The sorcerer was a natural teacher. He was simply incapable of letting a smug airing of ignorance go uncorrected.

But Nyrthim's self-control appeared to be putting up a good fight. Valdar decided a further nudge was indicated.

"Of course," he said pensively, "that still doesn't account for all the dark hints you were dropping that night, outside the Old Palace. Let's see, how did you put it? Oh, yes: it was what you *didn't* tell Khaavorn. As I recall—"

"Oh, all right! You'll have to know eventually, I suppose." Nyrthim took a deep breath. "It has to do with what I was telling you and Khaavorn that first night you were in The City, about the old religion and how we of the Order became known as sorcerers."

"I *knew* it!"

"I know you did," said Nyrthim quietly. Valdar sank back, deflated. The sorcerer's next words were unexpected. "Have you ever heard of the Shrine of the Lake?"

"Why . . . of course." Everyone knew of the ancient

shrine somewhere in Arnoriysa . . . although no one seemed quite sure just exactly where. It was very holy . . . although no one seemed clear as to just exactly why.

"Of course," Nyrthim echoed. "What you don't know is that it was established by the Order." His voice dropped, and his eyes glowed catlike in the gathering dimness. "I am about to reveal to you a secret that has been the exclusive property of the Order for more than half a thousand years. You must swear by the Mother, according to the formulas in which I will now instruct you, that no rewards, no entreaties, no threats, no torture—of yourself or of your loved ones—will ever wring this secret from your lips!"

White-faced, Valdar nodded. He then followed Nyrthim through a series of questions and responses calculated to freeze the blood of anyone contemplating dissimulation.

"Now, then," Nyrthim said briskly after it was over, "what I told you and Khaavorn was true . . . as far as it went. And it went as far as Khaavorn—and, I thought at the time, you—were ready to hear. To summon a *Nartiya Chora*, one of the Great Demons, is almost impossible today. Summoning Tarhynda took the combined resources of the demon cults of Lokhrein and the Empire. Each of them must have known something the other didn't, and possessed certain lore that the other lacked, which was why they needed Andonre as a courier. And it must have required human sacrifice on a scale and of a nature about which I do not care to speculate. In ancient times, as I explained, these things weren't quite so difficult. But even in those days, summoning a *prince* of the Great Demons—which would, I truly believe, be quite out of the question today—was a supreme feat of sorcery. Nevertheless, someone whose name no tradition has preserved managed to do it . . . and brought Angmanu into the world.

"Now, as I explained to you and Khaavorn, the Order was forced to fight sorcery with sorcery. And, like the black sorcerers we strove against, we found ourselves trapped in the inexorable need to summon ever more powerful demons. But we never—*never!*—yielded to the temptation to do it the easy way, ripping open the veil between the worlds with the death agony of human sacrificial victims. Instead, we found other ways. Slower, more difficult ways, but clean ones."

"Clean?" Valdar shook his head. "Can any summoning of demons ever be clean?"

"Not really," Nyrthim admitted. "Perhaps we deceived ourselves. But it was a necessary self-deception, as the grim struggle went on and we were forced to more and more unthinkable measures. Finally, we were driven to the ultimate extremity, which we'd hoped to be able to avoid. There was no other way to save the world from drowning in a cesspit of horror and agony. The Order summoned *another* prince of the Great Demons."

"But, Nyrthim, why should that have been necessary? In the end, Dayu drove out Angmanu and the lesser demons."

"Yes, so he did." Nyrthim held Valdar with eyes that held a sorrow too great for mere pity. "You still don't understand, do you?"

All at once, Valdar did understand. And the foundations of his life seemed to crumble away, revealing nothing beneath him, leaving him falling endlessly through a chill void of unthinkable, meaningless chaos.

"No," he heard himself whisper. And he felt his head shaking as though activated by a will of its own. "No. You can't mean . . . you can't be saying that *Dayu himself was a demon?*"

"A prince among the Great Demons, to be exact. Nothing less than one of his own kind would serve to counteract Angmanu. The Order had hoped that he could be isolated, rendered powerless by depriving him of the services of his lesser demons. We underestimated him."

Desperately, Valdar sought for some handhold by which he could cling to what he'd always been taught. "So, Nyrthim, are you telling me that there are such things as *good* demons, and that the Order summoned one?"

"No," said Nyrthim with merciless finality. "I doubt if our concepts of 'good' and 'evil' are really applicable. Perhaps it is only in their interaction with humans that these beings appear to be essences of pure, uncomplicated malevolence. Among themselves, they may have more complex motivations. They may even have some equivalent of an ethical system."

Valdar's bewilderment deepened. "Then why did the Order summon a *second* monster like Angmanu into the world? Wasn't one bad enough?"

"The head of the Order then was a certain Haerne. Most people have never heard of him, given the veil of secrecy that surrounds the events of that time. A pity, for if any man has ever deserved to be worshiped as a god, it was he. He somehow learned that unlike ordinary demons, who work together about as well or as poorly as men, the princes of the Great Demons hate even each other. Bring two of them into contact, and they will forget everything except that hate, destroying each other without a thought for the consequences. So Haerne took the greatest calculated risk in history.

"But even in those desperate times, we would not resort to the abomination of human sacrifice. Remember I told you we used other ways? Those ways involve certain places where . . . oh, how shall I explain it to you? There are places where the barrier between our world and that of the demons is weaker than elsewhere. The Order had learned how to use those places. It involved certain rituals, and a clear demarcation of the space involved—a space which is somehow congruent in both universes." Nyrthim smiled. "Have you ever wondered why those circles of standing stones were put up in the days of the Old Empire? What they were for before the Escquahar adopted the technique and used it for marking tombs?"

"You mean the Order—?"

"Yes. Those were the places where we created what we called 'gates' and brought in demons to fight other demons. But none would serve to summon a prince of the Great Demons. Finally, though, Haerne—who, as I said, must have been the greatest genius who has ever lived, or ever will live—found a place where the wall between the universes was so weak as to be almost nonexistent. And he invested it with special holiness, making it the only place in the world where one of the demon princes could be summoned without a holocaust of victims."

"So," said Valdar, "the Order brought Dayu through that 'gate.'"

"Dayu and a full retinue of lesser demons. Such a wholesale tearing down of the 'wall' is, in the nature of things, an all-or-nothing proposition. At any rate, Haerne's terrifying gamble worked. Dayu and Angmanu tore into each other with insensate ferocity, in a battle that swirled away toward the northeast. In the end, they destroyed each other and most of their subordinate demons. The Order could deal with what was left.

"Meanwhile, the primitive Karsha tribes had witnessed the visible manifestations of that titanic struggle. They worked what they'd seen into their myths, which they later brought south and west."

"So," said Valdar slowly, "we've been worshipping a demon all this time." He gave a short, rather horrible laugh. "You know, while we were in The City, I had a conversation with Maestor, the High Priest of Dayu. He assured me that in our enlightened times, nobody except peasants believes any longer in the literal existence of gods and demons."

"Yes." Nyrthim's expression could no longer be seen in the twilight, but Valdar could almost hear his weary smile. "Religion has frayed out into philosophical aridity among 'advanced thinkers' of the sort Tarhynda naturally wants in the upper echelons of the priesthood so that, like a tree, it will die from the top. It's an old story, you know. By denying the existence of evil, people think they've abolished it. In fact, all they've done is render themselves defenseless against it. However," the sorcerer continued sternly, "Maestor and his ilk are right in one sense. Dayu and

Angmanu, whatever their real nature, *have* become symbols for all that we instinctively recognize as good and evil respectively. It's not really true to say, as you just did, that 'we've been worshiping a demon.' Rather, we've taken Dayu as we believe him to have been and made him the embodiment of everything of value in the masculine virtues. His name has become a vessel into which we pour everything that we know we *ought* to worship. That's a very different thing from the *knowing* worship of demons that we saw in the grotto under the Old Palace."

"And," Valdar nodded, "it would be gone if people knew the truth."

"You understand, then, why I felt Khaavorn wasn't ready for this."

"Yes—and why you swore me to secrecy. But, Nyrthim, this is all in the past. What does it have to do with what Tarhynda is up to now?"

"Everything. You see, Valdar, the gates of which I've told you still exist. It is inherent in their nature that, once created, they are permanent."

"What? But in that case, why can't demons just come swarming through them?"

"Only the knowledge possessed by the Order—or the older way of human sacrifice, which can be used in conjunction with gates—can actually *open* them. And at any rate, the ever-increasing difficulty of summoning demons has rendered most of them effectively useless even if some madman *wanted* to use them. But they still exist, including the ultimate gate of which I've told you, through which Dayu came . . . the one which you know as the Shrine of the Lake."

It took a moment for Valdar's mind—still reeling

from too many revelations in too short a time—to assimilate the connection Nyrthim had made. But when it did, an avalanche of consequences came roaring down on him. He leaped to his feet. "Nyrthim, are you telling me that this 'gate' is in *Arnoriysa*?"

"Which Tarhynda has been laying the groundwork for taking over," said Nyrthim, finishing the other's thought. "And now we know why, don't we? He wants to pervert the power of the Shrine of the Lake for his own ends. Even at this late date, a sufficiently horrific ritual of human sacrifice performed within the precincts of the shrine could open a floodgate to the demonic universe."

Valdar sat back down. He had reached a stage beyond shock and stupefaction, and found he could think clearly. "How much of all this does the High King know?"

"He knows a great many things, through his mother's family. And Minuren knows the rest. If Khaavorn has managed to win through with the news of what Tarhynda truly is, Riodheg will know what must be done."

"Yes. He'll lead his warriors to the defense of Arnoriysa. And I should be there with him! For Dayu's sake—well, you know what I mean—why didn't you take passage down the Rhaemu when you had the chance? That way, we could at least join Riodheg for this final twilight battle."

"You're letting your glands and your muscles do your thinking for you," snapped Nyrthim. "That's only to be expected of Khaavorn, of course, but I'd hoped for better from you. Consider: Tarhynda will have to be present for the consummation of his grand plan. And it was from Vaedorie and Andonre that he learned of the Shrine of the Lake and its potentialities. So he'll bring them to Arvaerness with him, preparatory to the invasion of Arnoriysa. And . . . if memory serves, you and Andonre shared a certain attraction in your adolescent years."

Valdar's jaw dropped. "You mean—?"

"Of course that's only one possibility," said Nyrthim, a little too hastily. "We'll have to be alert to *any* opportunities that present themselves. But the point is that we'll be present at the epicenter of the colossal events that are about to unfold, and therefore in the best possible position to influence those events."

Valdar showed no sign of having heard the sorcerer's last three sentences. "You scheming, cynical, heartless old—"

"This conversation grows tiresome." Nyrthim drew his cloak around him and rolled over onto his side. "I suggest you get some sleep. We have a long day ahead of us tomorrow, for we're entering the borderlands of Arvaerness and there's no telling what we may encounter."

CHAPTER FOURTEEN

They continued their descent, working their way down the tributary to its confluence with the Liyzher.

Here in the Liyzher valley, on the south side of the river, they were in what was, at least arguably, Arvaerness proper . . . and Valdar began to notice differences in the hill forts.

It went beyond differences in construction—box ramparts with timber frameworks filled with earth or stone rubble, not mere heaped earthworks. There were also *more* of them here than one saw elsewhere, and distributed in a network spaced more or less regularly along the river valley. And in some cases, roads had been or were being smoothed between them, covered with wooden trackways over which wheeled carts rumbled. Valdar didn't like it. It wasn't the usual haphazard arrangement of the strongholds of dominant warrior clans. No, it was the systematic control of a large area without regard to the kinship of the people inhabiting it. Unnatural.

They continued to skirt the forts, but it became more and more difficult to avoid the comings and goings of imperial messengers, supply trains and troops. They took to trails higher in the hills, from which the river could be glimpsed below, through foliage turned the dull green of late summer.

It was on such a trail that the attack came.

They were shaggy, wild-looking creatures, wearing the tattered remains of this region's usual sort of tunics eked out with wolfskin mantles that gave a certain amount of protection. Their arms were just as motley: clubs, flint axes, some assorted ill-maintained bronze weapons, and a few bows which they used none too well. A dozen of them appeared from behind the underbrush and the trees, uttering cries that presumably served to intimidate most travelers.

Not a tribe, thought Valdar. *Rabble. A gang some local bully assembled from among the people displaced when Vaelsaru's army moved into this valley.*

Even as he thought this, Valdar's well-conditioned reflexes were acting for him. He grasped the pole he'd been using as a walking stick and thrust it into the belly of an attacker who'd bounded over a fallen log and was leaping for him with a scream. The man's breath whooshed out of him in midair and he fell with a thud. Valdar heard an arrow whir past his ear. He turned in the direction from which it had come and flung the pole in the archer's face. It gained him a second in which to draw his sword and raise it into the path of a descending flint axe, severing the haft. The man was staring at the stump of wood in his hand as Valdar brought the sword swooping around, thrust it into his midriff, and withdrew it with a gut-spilling twist.

Valdar spared an instant for a glance around. Nyrthim had his back to a tree, and was flailing away with his own walking stick, holding two attackers at bay. Valdar ran toward him.

A wild figure appeared in front of him—probably the chief, for he bore a sword of his own, not yet nicked and bent entirely out of shape, which he swung two-handed at Valdar's head.

Uses it like a club, thought Valdar contemptuously as he ducked and simultaneously brought his own sword down in a cut that almost severed the chief's left arm.

Then stars exploded in his head as a wooden club descended on the back of his head. It was only a glancing blow, for he'd been in motion, but it staggered him and he went to one knee. He looked up at the men crowding around him. He slashed out with his sword and cut a man's legs out from under him, sending the others into a hasty retreat. The one who'd hit him from behind raised his club again . . . and suddenly had an arrow through his throat. A scream ended in a blood-spraying gurgle, and the man sank to his knees.

A crashing sound and a chorus of shouts came from up the trail, and a monster appeared.

The bandits, or whatever they were, fled screaming.

Valdar stood rooted to the ground, and his sense of reality reeled as he stared. The thing had the lower body of a horse, and its four hooves thundered as it rounded a bend in the trail. But it had the head, torso and arms of a man. Those arms were about to loose another arrow from a short compound bow.

But then, before Valdar could join his erstwhile foes in their panicked flight, he remembered something.

It had been on the pastures outside Kintara, where the chariot horses for the High King's Companions were grazed. Valdar had happened to be watching when the old retainer who served as chief groom had sent one of the boys who assisted him on some errand. The boy, deciding he'd rather ride than walk, had startled Valdar by grasping a horse's mane and swinging himself awkwardly up onto the animal's back. He'd made a *tchk* sound with his mouth and used his knees to nudge the flanks of the horse, which had broken laboriously into a walk. He hadn't gone far when the chief groom had bellowed at him to dismount, and cuffed him soundly after he'd done so. *And quite right, too,* Valdar had thought. *Doesn't that young idiot know a horse can't carry a man—or even an adolescent boy—any distance?*

But the tableau had lasted long enough for Valdar to store it in his memory, so that now the image his eyes were seeing resolved itself in his mind. It was no monster, but a man sitting astride a horse—or, rather, what looked like a horse, only larger. Others followed, riding after the running bandits. The first one loosed his arrow at the fugitives, then put his bow away in a deerskin case behind his back that also held arrows. Then he picked up a bridle that had hung loose while he'd been controlling his mount with his knees and plying his bow simultaneously, and walked the horse over to face Valdar.

Valdar stood up, shaking his head to clear it, and gripped his sword cautiously. But the man gave a friendly wave and a smile split his bearded face. That beard was brown, and his features had a generally Karsha cast, but his gray eyes were slightly tilted and his cheekbones were high. He was wearing some kind of soft leather helmet, laced under the chin, and a short gray-and-green tunic that had seen much wear. His feet were leather-shod, and his legs . . . it took a moment for Valdar to grasp that they were enclosed in some kind of garment that separated into a pair of cloth tubes, one for each leg, fairly close-fitting and gathered into the shoes. Valdar had never seen the like, but it looked practical for riding a horse as this man did, sitting astride on a kind of blanketlike cloth pad strapped to the huge animal's barrel.

"Ho! Good fighting!" he greeted in the Ayoliysei that was the common language of the polyglot imperial army, barbarously accented but with the fluency of long practice. "We've been looking for those scum. You were doing pretty well yourselves."

"Thank you," said Valdar. "Still, your assistance was most welcome. To whom are we indebted for it?"

"I am Rupaeranz of the Yaszykh tribe. These are my men," he added with a gesture that took in his fellow riders, now returning from their pursuit and occupying themselves with dispatching the wounded with the long bronze daggers that were the only weapons they carried besides their bows.

"Ah, yes," nodded Nyrthim, approaching and looking

Rupaeranz and his mount over with frank curiosity. "I have heard that the Kynaeraan tribes have been breeding horses for size and strength, and have produced a strain capable of carrying a man fast and far."

"Still a good idea to rest them whenever you can." Rupaeranz dismounted in a smooth motion, revealing himself to be of average height. His legs, unsurprisingly, were somewhat bowed. They must, Valdar thought, be very muscular, inside those . . . whatever they were called; Rupaeranz evidently spent a lot of time clinging to a horse's barrel.

"You're a long way from your home on the grasslands north of the Eyxiyne Sea," Valdar observed.

"True." Rupaeranz gave the forest around them a sour glance. "Can't even get off a decent shot here, at any range, without tree branches getting in the way. But men came from the trading posts at the river mouths, offering rich gifts for the families of men who would take service under Lord Vaelsaru. And, of course, we'd all heard tales of him." There was a chorus of agreement from the other riders, who'd begun to gather around. "We knew there'd be good plunder, following him."

"I can see why he wanted such men as yourselves," said Nyrthim ingratiatingly. "Everyone knows that the Kynaeraan have learned to ride horses—and, indeed, use the bow while doing it—in a way beyond the comprehension of other peoples. Although I imagine you've picked up a thing or two from those imperial trading posts. This, for example." He gestured at the bronze bit in the horse's mouth, to which the bridle was attached. "It resembles what you see on Achaysei chariot horses."

"Chariots!" snorted Rupaeranz. His men chimed in with a chorus of derisive noises. "Their day is done. We can ride circles around them and fill them with arrows. But," he interrupted himself with stately barbaric courtesy, "may I know with whom I have the honor of conversing?"

Valdar and Nyrthim exchanged a quick glance and, seeing nothing to be lost by it, gave the mercenary captain their actual names. "From Dhulon," Valdar added, not wanting to mention Lokhrein to one of Vaelsaru's men. "It's a land to the north of here, about—"

"I've heard of it," said Rupaeranz. "You, too, would seem to be a long way from home."

"We were traveling with a party of traders on the amber trail, heading home from the Inner Sea." Valdar didn't elaborate on what they'd been doing by the shores of the Inner Sea in the first place, and Rupaeranz was too well bred to ask. "We had to separate from the traders because of a blood quarrel." Valdar launched into a story he and Nyrthim had previously agreed on. "So," he concluded, "we decided to strike out westward. We'd heard that Lord Vaelsaru was in charge here in Arvaerness, so we thought things would be better here."

"And you were right," declared Rupaeranz, to an accompaniment of affirmative growls from his men. As Valdar was to learn, opinions of Vaelsaru among his troops ran the gamut from deep respect all the way to idolatry. "But say," Rupaeranz resumed, changing the subject, "that's a rare fine sword you've got there. Khrunetore work?"

Valdar gave him a sharp look, but saw no larcenous intent, only friendly curiosity. "Yes."

"And you certainly know how to use it. Listen: why don't you come with us to Castranaenom? It's Lord Vaelsaru's headquarters, although he's off on an inspection tour just now. Once he gets back . . . Well, he likes to hire warriors in groups, like my men and me. But he's got a special unit of good swordsmen from all over the world. You can get in—especially with a good word from me. And, Nyrthim, you said you're a healer, right? Lord Vaelsaru hires them, too. Keeps a whole unit of them around, to patch up his wounded. That Vaelsaru!" Rupaeranz shook his head and clucked his tongue at the thought of such an unheard-of innovation. "What do you say?"

Valdar and Nyrthim made another quick eye contact of wordless agreement. They had, after all, wanted to establish themselves as close as possible to Vaelsaru.

"Thank you," said Valdar. "We may just take you up on that."

"Good! You won't regret it. And," Rupaeranz added with a broad wink, "neither will I. We get a reward for any new recruits we bring in. So let's be off."

The fortress of Castranaenom was at a bend in the Liyzher, crowning the cliffs that overlooked the river. The hill sloped away to a shoreline covered with untidy acres of huts, sheds and tents, where large numbers of laborers worked at constructing the barges that lined the riverbanks. Those workers, Valdar reflected, probably included relatives of the bandits he'd fought. The bandits were simply the ones who'd gotten away when the imperial slave hunters had swept through their villages.

"Lord Vaelsaru must plan on operations downriver,"

Nyrthim commented to Rupaeranz as he walked with Valdar to the left of the leader's horse. This was how they had traveled. For a horse—even one of these horses—to carry *two* men was even more out of the question than it would have been for Rupaeranz and his men to wear armor.

"No doubt," said Rupaeranz, clearly wrestling with his conscience. His conscience lost. He leaned over and spoke with hushed self-importance, in the immemorial way of soldiers passing on information from Rumor Central. "I'm not supposed to tell you this, but the word is we're going to be invading Arnoriysa, beyond the river to the northwest."

"Won't that mean fighting the High King of Lokhrein—that's the big island to the north where the tin comes from?" asked Valdar cautiously. "I think he owns Arnoriysa."

"Probably." Rupaeranz' interest in the larger strategic picture had definite limits. "So the plunder ought to be good—they say this king is rich as hell. I've also heard that the women from Lokhrein are something else! Tall, redheaded, with tits like you wouldn't believe! Terrible tempers, though; I was talking to this man who knew somebody who once lost two teeth getting one of 'em in the right mood. He said it was worth it, though; she was like a weasel in heat afterwards."

Valdar wasn't listening, for they had come through the last of the terraced outerworks on the hill slope and were approaching the main gate.

Castranaenom was the linchpin of Vaelsaru's network of fortresses, and it looked it. Valdar observed the construction of the rampart with a professional eye. It was basically similar to the forts they'd seen before: timber beams laid in alternate directions to form a boxlike structure. But here the filler was stone, so it was basically a stone wall anchored by wooden members passing through. The overall layout was likewise unique in this part of the world, with its arrangement of mutually supporting bastions and curtain walls. The place was clearly impregnable if defended by men resolved to hold it.

The enclosure held a variety of buildings, many of them substantial. Rupaeranz saw to the stabling of the horses, then led his two new recruits to a hut within the innermost enclosure.

"Have to check you in with Siytta first," he explained. "He's the commander of Lord Vaelsaru's personal guard—the outfit I said you could get into, Valdar—which makes him pretty much the second in command, and also the . . ." Rupaeranz struggled unsuccessfully against the limitations of a cultural background that included no such concept as "chief of staff."

Siytta proved to be a stocky, grizzled veteran whose features—thin-lipped and hazel-eyed, but dark-complexioned and with thick black brows almost meeting over a substantial nose—reflected ancestors from both the Ayoliysei aristocracy and the peasantry of the Amatoliysei provinces. He listened without comment to a fulsome account of Valdar's fighting skills by Rupaeranz, for whose judgment he evidently had a certain grudging respect. Then he eyed the newcomers narrowly. "From Dhulon, eh? I understand that King Arkhuar of that land is an ally of Riodheg of Lokhrein. I've heard he even has a son serving in Riodheg's Companions."

Valdar swallowed hard, and told himself he shouldn't

be surprised. One of the things Vaelsaru was famous for was the care he took to inform himself about his potential enemies, using any sources of information that came to hand—or that he could cultivate. Some imperial nobles grumbled that it wasn't quite gentlemanly. They didn't grumble very loudly, though.

"That's true, lord," he said. "But we left because of a blood feud with certain of the king's relatives."

Siytta's rock-hard face creased in a slight smile. "I gather you already know we're going to war with Riodheg." He glanced sourly at Rupaeranz. "What a surprise!"

Rupaeranz was all innocence. "But I never told them anything about—"

"Oh, never mind. It doesn't matter now. Remember the emissary we brought with us, who went on ahead to Lokhrein?"

"Yes." Rupaeranz's brow furrowed with effort. "Lord Tazha . . . er, Tala . . ."

"Tavazhalava. Anyway, he came back empty-handed. And now war is imminent." Siytta seemed to relish the opportunity—a rare one, Valdar suspected—to tell Rupaeranz something he didn't already know. "While you were gone, the Grand Chamberlain of the palace arrived—Lord Malsara." Siytta put the "lord" before the eunuch's name with obvious effort. "He's brought word that the Emperor is going to be arriving soon, with major reinforcements."

"The *Emperor?*" blurted Rupaeranz. "Himself?"

"Yes, and *herself*. The Empress is accompanying him."

Valdar, watching Siytta and Rupaeranz, thought he saw a shared look between them: a look of distaste which they weren't quite ready to share with fresh-caught recruits.

"Anyway," Siytta continued, "Lord Vaelsaru has been informed by courier. He's on his way back now, and will summon all forces except bare-bones garrisons to rendezvous here with the army the Emperor is bringing." Siytta relaxed a bit, and even smiled. "He has even better reason than that for hurrying back. Who do you suppose came here with Lord Malsara?" Nobody spoke, of course, and he answered his own question with a look of knowing lasciviousness. "The Lady Andonre! Lord Vaelsaru's wife."

Valdar forced his face to remain expressionless. He hoped Nyrthim was doing the same, but didn't dare look.

"Anyway," Siytta resumed, addressing Valdar and turning abruptly businesslike, "I don't care that you're from Dhulon. We've got men from every land you could name and quite a few you couldn't. We'll see if you're good enough for the guards tomorrow. For tonight, you can bed down with Rupaeranz and his throatcutters. Just don't drink any of the fermented mare's milk they get drunk on."

"Good stuff," the mercenary maintained stoutly.

As they left Siytta's office, however, Rupaeranz was uncharacteristically silent, even subdued. "You seem preoccupied," Nyrthim probed.

"What? Oh, nothing. I was just thinking about some of the rumors we've been hearing, about . . . but no. I'm not one for loose talk."

"Actually," Nyrthim prompted, "we've heard a few rumors ourselves, about things that have been going on in The City. Stories about . . . well, about demons."

Rupaeranz stopped in his tracks and whirled to face Nyrthim. "Don't *ever* say that aloud!" he hissed. "Do you hear me? Lord Vaelsaru has had men flogged within an inch of their lives for repeating the stories about the Emperor summoning demons. And anyway, there's no truth to that. It's not the Emperor; *he* wouldn't be mixed up in that kind of thing." Rupaeranz glanced over both his shoulders, and his voice dropped still lower. "No. It's *her*."

"Her?" Nyrthim echoed.

"The Empress! Everybody knows she's a witch. She must have the Emperor under a spell or something. Ensorcelled, or whatever they call it."

"And now she's coming here with him," Valdar observed.

"Yes," said Rupaeranz glumly. He shook himself, and spoke more normally. "Anyway, that sort of thing is no concern to the likes of you and me. Just forget I said anything, will you? As you know, I'm not one to repeat rumors."

"Of course not," Nyrthim deadpanned. "Oh, by the way . . . do you happen to know where Lord Vaelsaru's wife is staying?"

"Angmanu take it, I only just learned she's here! But she must be in Lord Vaelsaru's quarters." Rupaeranz indicated a long low building of sturdier-than-average construction at the very back of the fortress, at the top of the cliff. His eyes narrowed. "Why do you ask?"

"Oh, just curious. I've heard she's from Lokhrein—a niece of the High King, no less."

"I've heard that too. I imagine it'll be kind of awkward for her, considering. . . . But that's also no concern of ours. Come on, let's get you settled in."

CHAPTER FIFTEEN

The next morning, on the practice field, Valdar disarmed a series of swordsmen without hurting them any more than necessary. He finally capped the performance by doing as much for two of them together.

Siytta was sufficiently impressed to take him into the guards at once, and even furnished him with armor from a common stock maintained precisely for the purpose of outfitting promising but impecunious recruits. It represented, he explained, an advance against future loot.

Nobody in the world had yet conceived of any such thing as a uniform. But the panoply was the standard one of elite warriors, which for centuries had made them invincible against anyone who couldn't afford the

armor: crested bronze helmet with adjustable cheek
guards, bronze greaves to guard the knees and shins,
and a corselet and round shield to protect everything
between. The last two were of hardened leather, which
was actually better for such purposes than sheet bronze.
Valdar kept his own sword, of course; it could hardly
have been improved upon.

At the same time, Nyrthim joined Vaelsaru's cadre
of healers. They were, he condescendingly informed
Valdar, mostly little better than village leeches. But
he managed to appear no better himself, although it
took an effort he considered—and made quite clear
that he expected Valdar to consider—nothing less
than heroic. He had no wish to call special attention
to himself.

All the while, they took every opportunity to sur-
reptitiously observe the long building, hoping for a
glimpse of its occupant.

They never got such a glimpse. If Andonre was in
fact there, she stayed in seclusion. If she got any fresh
air, it was in a small enclosed area behind the building, called by courtesy a garden, out of sight of such as
themselves. Or perhaps she took walks on the cliff-top
parapet behind that area, overlooking the river.

So matters stood when Vaelsaru returned to Castranaenom.

The entire garrison was drawn up to greet the
cavalcade of chariots. Valdar stood among the guards,
flanking the long house, on whose tiny porch stood
Siytta, Malsara, the nobleman named Tavazhalava
whom Siytta had mentioned . . . and Andonre, looking
strangely pale and tense.

The possibility of recognition didn't worry Valdar. After hearing of Andonre's presence here, he'd abandoned his intention of shaving the beard he'd grown, and his helmet hid a good part of what the facial hair didn't. He also relied on the human tendency to see what one expects to see, for Andonre would hardly be expecting to see him among the ranks of her husband's guards. As for Malsara, he and Valdar had barely met.

That they'd revealed their actual names before learning of Andonre's presence was unfortunate. But it was too late to do anything about that now.

The chariots began to rumble through the gate, the dust of travel somewhat dimming their brazen splendor and that of their occupants. Those were imperial, but mostly mainland Achaysei rather than the nobility of the islands. Their armor was much like that of Valdar and his fellow guards, but more splendid, with horsehair plumes waving over the helmet crests, and lacquer and semiprecious stones adorning the leather and bronze. Richly colored cloaks streamed behind them with the wind of their passage as they entered the courtyard and displayed their mastery of their horses by drawing themselves up in two lines.

Then the long bronze horns on the parapet gave their deep-throated call, and the drums thundered. A solitary chariot entered the courtyard, and the shouts of "Vaelsaru!" drowned out the drums.

The great general—the brother-in-law Khaavorn had never seen, Valdar thought—was in his forties. He held his magnificent helmet in the crook of his left arm, revealing short dark-gray hair beginning to recede from the temples. Equally graying was his close-trimmed chin beard—somewhat old-fashioned in upper-crust imperial circles. But he rode his chariot like a man half his age, standing erect to his full height, which was several inches above average. Despite the dust kicked up by the chariot horses, the sun glinted from his ornate sheet-bronze cuirass that was more an emblem of rank than protection. He raised his right hand in response to the army's acclamation, and his strong features wore an expression that managed to be stern without being remote. The shouting redoubled in response. Valdar joined in because it was expected of him, and because it helped conceal the sickness he felt at the realization that this army, led by this man, was about to descend on Lokhrein.

Vaelsaru's chariot drew to a halt, and he alighted and proceeded, alone, along the ranks of warriors that lined the way to the porch, dispensing greetings along the way. Rupaeranz and his Kynaeraan horsemen were drawn up close to the guards, and Valdar heard Vaelsaru's deep baritone as he came abreast of them.

"Ah, Rupaeranz! I should have known you'd be ready for the bloodletting. Just leave some of the loot and women for the rest of the army, will you?"

Amid the laughter of the eastern riders, Rupaeranz swelled visibly with pride at having been recognized. Like many successful leaders, Vaelsaru had a phenomenal memory for faces, and knew that the sweetest sound any man can hear is that of his own name. Valdar's depression deepened.

Vaelsaru resumed his progress toward the porch . . . and, for the first time, his eyes met Andonre's.

His expression wavered for a moment, before self-discipline closed over it again. He advanced the last few steps and gave Andonre the brief embrace that was all propriety permitted in this setting. Then he turned a carefully controlled face to Malsara, and spoke in an even more controlled voice—but one which Valdar was close enough to hear.

"Welcome to Arvaerness, Lord Chamberlain. I thank you for conveying my wife safely. But . . . why did you bring her at all? Was it necessary to subject her to the hardships of such a journey, and the dangers of a newly subdued province?"

"It was on the Emperor's express command that the Lady Andonre accompanied me, Lord Vaelsaru," said the eunuch smoothly. "He had been led to believe that Arvaerness is now quite safe, due to your glorious victories."

"Whoever led him to believe that knows nothing about backwoods provinces," snapped Vaelsaru. "And, furthermore, what about my son? The message I received said nothing about him. Is he here too? If not, whose care is he in back at The City? I want to know . . ." Vaelsaru's voice trailed off. Risking a sideways look, Valdar could see why. Malsara wore a look of embarrassed apprehension, and Andonre had gone even more pale and expressionless.

"What is this all about?" demanded Vaelsaru, almost too quietly for Valdar to hear.

"Perhaps it would be best if the rest of us withdraw," said Malsara carefully. "I'm sure you and your wife would appreciate some time alone together, after the long separation. And . . . she has news for you that is not for the ears of common soldiers."

"Yes, I believe you're right. I'll confer with you later, Lord Chamberlain. Siytta, dismiss the men."

As he walked away, Valdar wondered what the mystery was about. And he wondered why Andonre looked on the verge of a breakdown.

In his austere quarters, Vaelsaru sat on the edge of his bed amid the wreckage of his life, staring at the floor and seeing nothing.

Across the bed, facing away from him, Andonre slumped, sobbing woefully. She had thought she'd already wept all the tears she would ever have in her. But she had discovered whole new reservoirs of them as she'd faced her husband and spoken aloud the tale of Zhotiyu's kidnapping. And Vaelsaru had no comfort to give her.

"And so," Andonre gulped, when she could finally speak, "I *wanted* to come here. It was too painful for me in The City, among all the familiar places that reminded me of Zhotiyu. And besides . . . I needed you." This was all true, as far as it went. But soon, Andonre knew miserably, the lies would have to begin.

"But I don't understand." Vaelsaru spoke in a dead, hollow voice, still not looking at her. "Why would your half brother and his friend have wanted to take Zhotiyu?"

"I don't know!" wailed Andonre. Above all other considerations, her husband could not be allowed to know of what Khaavorn and Valdar had glimpsed in the grotto. Instead, he had to be told the story in which Vaedorie had instructed her. She turned and looked at Vaelsaru's back "Uh . . . the Empress thought of one possible reason. After they learned you were here in Arvaerness, maybe they were afraid Lokhrein would be next."

"But that's never been the plan! All that Lord Tavazhalava was instructed to ask for were certain concessions in Arnoriysa. I've never wanted war with Lokhrein."

"But *they* didn't know that. So maybe they saw you as a threat, and believed that they could neutralize you by holding your son as a hostage."

With a convulsive motion, Vaelsaru sat up straight, and he turned to face her. "What? You mean they think that by threatening Zhotiyu's life, they can force me to . . . to betray my oath to the Emperor?" The dull shock in his eyes began to be replaced by anger. "But how could Khaavorn be capable of such a thing? Using a child—his own nephew, at that—as a coward's weapon! It doesn't sound like him, from everything you've ever told me."

"Maybe I didn't know him as well as I thought I did," said Andonre quietly.

It was, she reflected, going much as Vaedorie had foreseen. The High Sister had told her the kidnapping of Zhotiyu might prove useful by igniting in Vaelsaru a rage that would burn away masculine fatuities about honor among enemies and the like, and make him fight harder. Andonre had found distasteful the whole notion that there could be a bright side to what had happened to her son. But of course she'd held her tongue, and now she carried out her instructions.

"Well, if that's what they think, they're wrong." Vaelsaru's voice began to rise from its slough of dull despair, and his eyes held a look that very few men had ever seen and lived to describe. "No blackmail can make me forswear my oath. And if they harm a hair on that boy's head, I swear by Dayu I'll make Arnoriysa—and Lokhrein, too—a desert!" He halted abruptly, and reached out to take his wife's hand. "I'm sorry," he murmured. "I know it's your native land we're talking about. And I'm sorry for . . . this whole situation. I know how difficult it must be for you. The choices you're being forced to make—"

"I made my choice when I married you, my darling." With an inward sigh of relief, Andonre let herself sink back into the truth.

Vaelsaru took her in his arms, and her tears welled up anew.

Malsara rose and gave a smile of unctuous insincerity as Vaelsaru entered the room. Tavazhalava and Siytta rose with him.

"Ah, Lord Vaelsaru, I trust the Lady Andonre is well."

"As well as can be expected, under the circumstances." Vaelsaru sat down at the small table, and the others followed suit. The room was a small one, as the rooms at Castranaenom tended to be. The days were getting shorter, for autumn was approaching, and the servants had lit the stone lamps against the encroaching dusk.

"We've just heard the news," growled Siytta. "I want you to know that I . . . I and all the men . . ." He stumbled to a halt, unable to voice what he felt.

"Yes," Tavazhalava filled the silence. "Simply appalling. You and the Lady Andonre have my most heartfelt sympathy."

"My thanks to you both." A sudden thought penetrated the grayness that blanketed Vaelsaru's soul. "Lord Tavazhalava, didn't you tell me that you met my wife's brother Khaavorn while you were in Lokhrein?"

"Indeed I did. It was largely due to his intervention that my embassy failed. He had some sort of wild story from his recent visit to The City." Tavazhalava chuckled. "He also fought a duel which for sheer barbarity surpassed even—"

"Yes, yes. But did he say anything about having my son in captivity? Anything about what might happen to the boy if it came to war?"

Tavazhalava blinked, and looked thoughtful as he began to see what Vaelsaru was driving at. "Er . . . no. Actually, there was no mention of your son whatsoever. Not even after the consequences of a refusal of our demands became offensively clear. Curious, when you think about it."

"So it is." Vaelsaru's brow furrowed. "And did you happen to encounter a friend of Khaavorn's named—?"

"It's quite obvious, " Malsara cut in hastily, "that they're holding the boy in reserve, as it were. Not that it will do them any good. We all know, my dear Vaelsaru, that your loyalty is beyond suspicion. In fact, His Imperial Majesty is relying on that."

"I am gratified to hear you say so."

"Then let us turn our attention to other matters. Am I correct in supposing that the message you received by courier mentioned the Emperor's imminent arrival?"

"You are. It also mentioned—to my disbelief, I must admit—that the Empress is accompanying him."

"So she is." Malsara's tone grew fawning. "Now you can see the genuineness of the Emperor's confidence in your pacification of Arvaerness. It isn't just *your* wife he is prepared to put at risk here."

"Point taken, Lord Chamberlain. But I gather he is also bringing reinforcements—even though he must have departed long before he could have learned of Riodheg's rejection of Lord Tavazhalava's offer."

Malsara looked momentarily nonplussed—but only momentarily. "Actually, the Emperor anticipated all along that it would come to war. This is not a reflection on your diplomatic skills, Lord Tavazhalava, only a realization that those skills would probably be unavailing with crude, mindless barbarians like the Dovnaan."

"My wife is of Dovnaan blood," said Vaelsaru with ominous mildness.

"Er . . . that is . . . of *course* I meant to except the Lady Andonre, who has abundantly demonstrated her capacity for civilization. She is, one might say, a credit to her race. But," Malsara hurried on, "it is as you have surmised. In addition to a large contingent of the household troops, the Emperor has engaged more Achaysei charioteers, some of them with the new, heavier chariots from eastern Amatoliysa."

"I've wondered how well they'd work in this terrain," Siytta remarked, his professional curiosity aroused.

"Nor is that all," Malsara continued. His voice was not the high-pitched screech that was popularly supposed to characterize eunuchs. Now it dropped still lower, and his gaunt face sloughed off its mask of false affability. "In addition, the Emperor is bringing reinforcements of, shall we say, a very special kind."

For an instant there was a dead silence of incomprehension. Then Vaelsaru stood up so abruptly his chair went crashing over backwards.

"You don't mean—?"

"But I do." Malsara's black eyes held a feverish glint.

Siytta and Tavazhalava now understood. They stared openmouthed.

"Demons!" Siytta finally breathed. He made a sign that the priestesses of Rhaeie taught.

"More specifically, *Nartiya Ozhre*: physical giants, very difficult to kill, and trainable as weapon-bearing troops. The Emperor is bringing a heavily armed unit of *twenty* of these beings. Neither the Dovnaan nor any other enemy will be able to stand against them."

Vaelsaru carefully righted his chair and lowered himself back into it. "We've heard rumors of things that have been going on in The City," he said slowly. "Dark sorcery, summoning demons to prey on the people. I've punished men for spreading such talk."

"And quite rightly! Rest assured that these beings have not been induced to enter the Emperor's service by any of the . . . alarming and distressing means we hear of from olden times. It would not do to have such rumors circulating among the ignorant common soldiers."

"Then how *were* they summoned?" Siytta asked bluntly.

Malsara's hooded eyes slowly swung toward him. "The details are unimportant. Suffice it to say that the *Nartiya Ozhre* have responded to the Emperor's innate personal force, for which all his loyal subjects hold him in such reverence."

Siytta rolled his eyes toward the ceiling, drawing a warning glare from Vaelsaru. Tavazhalava maintained the expressionlessness of a seasoned diplomat. Malsara showed no sign of having noticed any of this as he rhapsodized on.

"I may also tell you that the Empress, whose qualities of goodness and wisdom are as far above the merely human as is her beauty, has been instrumental not only in securing the loyalty of these beings but also in keeping their . . . ardent natures under control. So, Lord Vaelsaru, now you can see why it is necessary for the Empress to accompany her lord, whatever the hardships and dangers."

"Indeed." Vaelsaru wore a carefully neutral expression as he framed his thoughts into acceptable words. "Has anyone taken into account the effect these rumors—these *false* rumors—of dark sorcery may have on our enemies' will to resist?"

Before Malsara could respond, Tavazhalava cleared his throat nervously. "In that connection, Lord Vaelsaru . . . Well, I never mentioned this to you on my return from Lokhrein because it seemed so absurd. But when Riodheg rejected my proposal for a border adjustment—which he did, as you may recall, after a rather violent demonic manifestation—"

"Yes, so you told me."

"—he not only repeated the unfounded rumors of sorcerous summonings in The City, but also added an element which, to repeat, was so utterly farfetched that I—"

"*What*, exactly, was it that he said, Lord Tavazhalava?"

Malsara's eyes seemed even more ophidian than ever, and his voice could not be described other than as a hiss.

"Well, please bear in mind that I'm only repeating his ravings. He claimed that the Emperor has not merely summoned demons but is, in fact, a . . . well, er, a demon himself, in human guise!" Tavazhalava gave a nervous laugh, and his gaze flitted around the room in search of reassurance.

Malsara shattered the dead silence with a sound which counterfeited—badly—a normal human laugh. "How utterly predictable! This barbarian warlord, in understandable despair at the thought of having to face the might of the Empire, was desperately casting about for something to tell his followers that would rouse them from their habitual drunken stupor and induce them to fight. So he appealed to superstitious fears." The eunuch gave another humorless chuckle. "I must admit, he has a certain low animal cunning. He has instinctively grasped the principle that if an assertion from an authoritative source is sufficiently preposterous, the common herd will assume it *must* be true because no one would have dared to make it up. The ancient sage Zhaerosa termed this technique 'the big lie.'"

"All very well, Lord Chamberlain," said Vaelsaru heavily. "But the fact remains that Riodheg's men—who, by the way, we should not underestimate, if my sources of information are to be believed—will, indeed, fight with fanatical desperation if they think that they are defending their hearths and homes from demonic forces. All the more so when the . . . reinforcements the Emperor is bringing provide a kind of confirmation to all the talk of demons."

"I disagree. Riodheg's pathetic ploy can only work to our advantage. When these ignorant bumpkins see the *Nartiya Ozhre* advancing on them, they will be paralyzed by terror. I doubt if we'll even have to fight a battle. They'll flee in panic, wetting themselves with fear!"

"You are entitled to your opinion, Lord Chamberlain. However, my responsibility to the Emperor requires that I proceed from less optimistic assumptions. Furthermore, I must consider the effect of this news on my own men's morale. The prospect of fighting alongside these, uh, *Nartiya Ozhre* could prove . . . unsettling."

"That's one way to put it," muttered Siytta.

A note of impatience, tinged with habitual malice, entered Malsara's voice. "The maintenance of discipline in your own ranks is your responsibility, Lord Vaelsaru. Is it only my imagination, or do you yourself find the Emperor's commands 'unsettling'?"

Vaelsaru surged to his feet. "I have never once failed to carry out the Emperor's commands! I will not permit my loyalty to be questioned!"

Malsara shrank back, afraid that he might have gone too far. "Oh, no, Lord Vaelsaru, I never dreamed of impugning your loyalty. I only question your . . . enthusiasm for the Emperor's decisions as to how to prosecute this war."

"Angmanu take it, I never asked for these 'reinforcements'! My army could have dealt with Riodheg unaided. He's more formidable than those of you back in The City seem to appreciate, but we could have handled him. What's the *need* for this . . . this . . . ?"

"It is the Emperor's decision. It is not for us to

question or for him to explain." Malsara made himself seem ingratiating. "I can, however, tell you that he is motivated by a desire to leave nothing to chance. He wishes to make our victory even more certain than it would be if left to you and your fearless men." The eunuch grew even more oily. "And can you truly disagree, my lord? After all, think of your son! The more overwhelming our victory, the greater our chance of rescuing him." Emboldened by Vaelsaru's silence, he pressed on. "I also assure you—so that you can assure your men—that his and the Empress' powers are such that there is nothing to fear. There is no danger of these demons failing to obey his will."

The other three looked dubious, but no one cared to be the first to speak their doubts.

CHAPTER SIXTEEN

There was, Valdar decided, one good thing about the fermented mare's milk to which the Kynaeraan horsemen were addicted. It tasted so putrid that he was in little danger of drinking enough of it to get befuddled.

Rupaeranz suffered from no such limitations. Since they'd come outside to sit under the stars by the horse corral, seeking refuge from the worse-than-usual smokiness of huts overcrowded by the mass influx of troops into Castranaenom, he had put down at least three to Valdar's and Nyrthim's one. And it was starting to show.

"I don't like to spread rumors," he said with the careful enunciation of incipient intoxication, "but everybody knows that there are demons coming with the Emperor—that he's got a whole bodyguard of 'em."

"I've heard that, too," Nyrthim assured him, feigning tipsiness. Rumor had, of course, outrun the official announcements. Rupaeranz had been uncharacteristically moody. This, however, was the first time he'd taken enough alcohol on board to share the general whispers with Valdar and Nyrthim. They'd been maneuvering for such an opportunity.

They'd also decided against revealing what they knew about Tarhynda. Rupaeranz wasn't ready yet.

"Of course," Nyrthim continued, "I suppose it's not too surprising. After all, the Empress *is* coming with him, and considering what you told us about her. . . ."

Rupaeranz looked around nervously, and dropped his voice. "Yes! That must be it. She's behind it." He took another swallow.

"I suppose this means we'll be fighting on the same side as demons," said Valdar, pretending to take a sip. "I'm not sure how I feel about that. Are you?"

"I don't know!" snapped Rupaeranz with the sudden anger of his condition. "I don't know what I think about anything anymore. I don't know why Dayu permits it." His face cleared as he remembered the one basic truism to which he could cling. "But it must be all right. If it wasn't, Lord Vaelsaru would tell us—and he wouldn't be following the Emperor. *He'll* explain everything to us."

"Of course," said Nyrthim. "Lord Vaelsaru wouldn't be a part of anything untoward. Unless . . ."

"Unless what?"

"Well . . . what if Lord Vaelsaru was under the same kind of influence as the Emperor?"

"Huh?" Rupaeranz blinked and tried to concentrate. "Lord Vaelsaru? Influence? What're you talking about?"

Nyrthim leaned forward and looked the mercenary in the eye. "Rupaeranz, you are right about the Empress and her demonic practices. What you do not know is that the Lady Andonre is also involved. The two of them are in league."

Rupaeranz reeled unsteadily to his feet. "Lord Vaelsaru's wife? You're crazy! What makes you think—?"

"Have you ever heard," Nyrthim asked steadily, continuing to hold Rupaeranz' eyes, "of the Order of the Nezhiy?"

"Of course," said the mercenary, settling back down to the ground under that steady regard. "I've heard all the old stories."

He would have, too, thought Valdar. The grasslands north of the Eyxiyne Sea were the original homeland of the Karsha. The Kynaeraan had absorbed the blood of tribes drifting in from still further east but their traditions were elementally Karsha. Whatever his features might look like, Rupaeranz had lapped up the tales of the ancient struggle against Angmanu and his demons along with his mother's milk.

"It's more than just old stories, Rupaeranz. The Order is not altogether dead. There are a few Nezhiy left. And I am one of them."

The mercenary simply stared, his normally narrow eyes like saucers.

"I can vouch for him," said Valdar. "I can also tell you that what he says about the Lady Andonre is true. And believe me, I find it harder to accept than you do. You see, I know her. I knew her when she was a girl."

Rupaeranz swung his stare back and forth between the two of them. "So you lied to me."

"Not exactly," Nyrthim denied. "Admittedly, there were things we didn't tell you. But it was necessary. We had to get into this fortress—"

"To spy on Lord Vaelsaru!" Rupaeranz was on his feet again, and one hand was on his dagger hilt.

"No, Rupaeranz. We bear Vaelsaru no ill will."

"But . . . you say his wife is a witch. . . ."

"Yes, I fear that is true. But he, of course, doesn't know it. And we have reason to believe that she, unlike the Empress, may not be utterly evil. This is why you are in a position to aid us."

"Aid you?" Rupaeranz echoed faintly. He made a visible effort to wrench his mind free of alcohol. "No! I'll never betray Lord Vaelsaru."

"We're not asking you to. All we ask is that you get us in to see the Lady Andonre. By helping us in this, you'd also be helping Lord Vaelsaru. All we want is to free him of the evil influence which the Empress is exercising over him through his wife."

Rupaeranz squatted on his haunches, his face a study in inner conflict. "All right. The Lady Andonre goes for evening walks on the parapet back there behind her quarters, overlooking the river. I know one of the guards to the inner compound, and he owes me a favor. Tomorrow night, I'll arrange for *you* to be there." He pointed at Nyrthim.

"Not both of us?"

"No." Rupaeranz shook his head emphatically. "It

wouldn't be fitting. You, Nyrthim, are old. So it ought to be all right." Valdar smiled at the mercenary's solicitude for the virtue of his commander's wife. But then Rupaeranz' eyes hardened. "Besides, I still can't be sure I can believe any of this. You, Valdar, will wait with me—unarmed. If anything happens to the Lady Andonre, a lot worse will happen to you."

"Fair enough," said Valdar steadily.

A three-quarter moon spread a rippling trail of silver on the waters of the Liyzher as Andonre walked out onto the parapet atop the cliff. She paused a moment to drink in the beauty of the scene. But then the moon slipped behind clouds, leaving her in a darkness that mirrored the inside of her soul.

Vaelsaru was out among the makeshift camps that were spreading like fungus on the slopes on the fortress' landward side. He was nearly always busy, these days. It was, she admitted to herself, probably just as well. Whenever they were together, Zhotiyu's absence gaped like a void between them. Their self-conscious attempts to talk about other subjects only made it worse.

It was, she knew, worse for her than for Vaelsaru. For her, it was a *second* burden, piled atop the lie she was already living.

At the same time, in a perverse way, she was almost grateful for the tragedy that they now had in common. In this, at least, she could be honest with him. And in addition, it gave her something else her life had lacked for a long time: unambiguous clarity of purpose, free from all doubts and misgivings. She was now nothing more than a vessel containing grim determination to get Zhotiyu back.

She had, of course, questioned Tavazhalava about his visit to Riodheg's court. Her desperate eagerness had collapsed into dull depression on learning he had seen or heard no sign of Zhotiyu. She hadn't been able to bring herself to inquire as to Khaavorn and Valdar, such was her unabated hurt and anger at their monstrous betrayal.

She was thinking about it when the clouds rolled away, and a flood of moonlight revealed that she was not alone on the parapet.

Her heart thudded as she stared at the tall, cloaked figure, obviously not one of the guards. "Who are you?" she asked quietly, drawing her own cloak more tightly around her—odd, she hadn't noticed the early autumn chill before—and drawing a breath for a scream.

"Perhaps you remember me, Andonre," said the stranger, stepping closer and lowering the cloak from his gray head. "I remember you very well. I remember the day you were born."

Her breath caught in her throat as girlhood memories appeared, ghostlike, in tangible form. "Nyrthim? Is it you? But . . . I thought you'd died."

"Amazing, the number of times I hear that. But I can hardly complain, having started the rumor myself." Nyrthim's chuckle was humorless and short-lived. "Since you remember me from your girlhood, you must recall that I am a member of the Order of the Nezhiy. And therefore you know why I am here."

Andonre concealed her alarm, and drew herself up with the hauteur she had learned at the imperial court. "I haven't the least idea what you are talking about."

"I have little time, Andonre," Nyrthim said sternly. "So don't waste any of it with denials. I know everything. I know about the demon cults in Lokhrein and the Empire, and I know that you are the human link between them. And . . . I know what Tarhynda really is."

This time Andonre could not keep herself from gasping. Hopefully, Nyrthim would attribute it to outrage at injustice. "How dare you utter these wild accusations? I only have to raise the alarm, and the guards will make sausage meat out of you!"

The sorcerer took another step toward her, and he seemed to grow and transform in a way for which the moonlight was surely to blame. "Enough of this! I was in The City, trying to protect the people from the demons you and Vaedorie had summoned. I was in the grotto beneath the Old Palace with Khaavorn and Valdar. So I know these things. I merely believe that you, unlike Vaedorie, are not hopelessly mad and irredeemably depraved. It is on the strength of that belief that I have gone to some small trouble to be here tonight. Until I hear it from you personally, I cannot believe that you would knowingly betray your High King, your people, the human race in general—and the Mother."

Andonre barely heard the last four sentences, in her shock. *So he was with them. . . .* But then Nyrthim's last words ignited her shock into rage.

"Yes, Nyrthim, I admit it: I am one of those who seek to bring back the great old days when Rhaeie ruled alone, in all her terrible beauty, before the Old Empire was brought down in ruins by Escquahar rebels and Karsha barbarians."

"The blood of both flows in your veins, Andonre."

"I can't help that. But so does the blood of the old priestesses—the *true* priestesses, before Rhaeie was sold to the worshipers of the great nemesis Dayu like some slave girl on the block. You dare to speak of betrayal, Nyrthim? The Nezhiy, and those deluded priestesses who gave them their head, were the real betrayers."

"So now you seek to use the same means we did, the Shrine of the Lake—oh, yes, I know about that too—to admit new hordes of demons into the world?"

"It is the only way. This world must fall into cleansing chaos before the old world can be reborn. It wouldn't be necessary, save for your original betrayal. And nothing has changed!" All the anger Andonre had kept bottled up for lack of a flesh-and-blood target came boiling to the surface, and her face took on a snarl from which the sorcerer actually recoiled. "You're betrayers still. You've just admitted you were with Khaavorn and Valdar when they robbed me of my son!"

Nyrthim's jaw fell. "What are you saying?"

"You heard me! And don't pretend you don't know what I'm talking about! They kidnapped Zhotiyu as they were fleeing from The City. The High Sister—the Empress—told me about it later. She didn't know you were involved, but . . . Nyrthim? Nyrthim!"

Incredibly, infuriatingly, the sorcerer was no longer listening to her.

"So," he finally breathed. "It all becomes clear now." He pulled himself together and turned back to the furious woman before him.

"Andonre," he said in a voice of urgent intensity, holding her eyes against her will, "you must believe me.

Khaavorn did, indeed, intend to abduct Zhotiyu—or, as he saw it, rescue him—"

"Then you *do* admit it!"

"—but he *failed!* He and a companion went to get the boy. They became separated from Valdar and me. We saw them board their ship. And Zhotiyu was not with them."

"So you say! I'd wondered how Khaavorn could be capable of such a thing. *You* probably persuaded him to do it!"

"No. I permitted it—as I probably shouldn't have—but it was his idea. And can you really blame him? We had just seen what you and Vaedorie and Tarhynda and the others had done in that cavern." Nyrthim saw Andonre wince, and remembered the sick look they'd glimpsed on her face when she had turned toward them in that grotto. He pressed his advantage. "But I repeat: he did not succeed! He departed for Lokhrein without Zhotiyu."

"Why should I believe you?"

"You remember me well enough to know I do not lie. Besides, you can verify it for yourself. This Lord Tavazhalava has been to Lokhrein. Ask him if he saw Zhotiyu there, or heard him mentioned." Shrewdly: "But I see you have already done so."

Andonre turned away abruptly. She gripped the parapet and stared out over the moonlit river for a few heartbeats, in a silence which Nyrthim left unbroken. Then, just as suddenly, she whirled back to face him.

"But Zhotiyu is *gone!* I should know that, shouldn't I? If you and Khaavorn and Valdar didn't take him, who did?"

All at once, Nyrthim's years seemed to catch up with him, bearing with them a heavy burden of sorrow. "I believe I know who, and why. It makes a hideous kind of sense, for I now see what Tarhynda's plan is. I repeat: Tarhynda's plan. You see, my dear, you—all of you, including Vaedorie, who at least deserves it—have been duped. You're like the ancient sorcerers who first brought the Great Demons into the world in the days before the Old Empire. They thought they could use these beings, but ended by being themselves used. Tarhynda, you may be assured, has his own agenda, which has nothing to do with yours or Vaedorie's. He has no interest in restoring humankind to some fantasy of the good old days before the coming of the Karsha and the worship of Dayu. No—his aim is to destroy humankind. For that, he needs to bring in his fellow *Nartiya Chora* in vast numbers. There is only one way to do that in the present age: use the Shrine of the Lake in conjunction with human sacrifice."

"But what does all this have to do with Zhotiyu?" demanded Andonre.

Nyrthim didn't answer. He only looked at her, his dark eyes full of pity.

All at once, her hands flew to her mouth and her eyes bulged.

"No," she finally whispered. "You're not saying the Empress—?"

"She and Tarhynda had other motives as well. Think about it. By making you believe we were responsible, she bound you even more tightly to her. What you've been saying here tonight makes that clear enough. I daresay it also helps to stiffen your husband's determination. But, yes, their primary use for him is as the victim for the sacrifice they plan."

"But . . . but why Zhotiyu? Any slave would do as well!"

"I'm afraid not." Nyrthim fell into the well-remembered lecturing mode which, under the present circumstances, set Andonre's teeth on edge. "You see, there are certain qualities of sacrificial victims which enhance their efficacy. No one understands just why this is, but the effect is well attested from ancient times. One of these qualities is blood relationship to one of the persons performing the sacrifice, or even to someone associated with those persons. The closer this blood relationship is, the better. That of parent and child is best of all.

"Another such quality," the sorcerer went on inexorably, "is susceptibility to pain and terror due to lack of experience in such things. An innocent young child from a loving, privileged home—"

"Stop!" Andonre turned away and steadied herself on the parapet as she drew deep shuddering breaths. "You're lying. You must be lying."

"I could swear an oath that you would have to take seriously. But I don't really think I need to. Look within yourself, Andonre. Take an honest look at what you know from personal observation about Vaedorie's character—things you've felt obliged to deny to yourself because she is the leader of your cult."

"She's only the leader in the Empire," said Andonre dully. "The Highest Sister is my Aunt Norkhaari. She arranged for me to be sent to The City."

"Norkhaari!" Nyrthim closed his eyes and heaved a sigh that held sadness but little real surprise.

"Yes. Tavazhalava says her role was revealed while he was in Lokhrein, but she escaped."

"Norkhaari," Nyrthim repeated. "Your old teacher. Of course. How well it all fits!" He sighed again, and stepped closer to her. "Andonre, my dear, it is perhaps not too late to undo all that has been done. But there is no time to waste, and you must follow my instructions unquestioningly. First of all, you must tell your husband everything: the truth about Tarhynda, the truth about who has his son—"

Andonre's reaction caught him flat-footed. From her lethargic slump against the parapet, she shot erect and glared at him, eyes flashing green flame. Belatedly, he recalled that this was, however much she might deny her heritage, a daughter of the Dovnaan warrior nobility.

"You don't understand, Nyrthim. Vaelsaru has sworn his oath to the Emperor. He renewed it when Tarhynda assumed the sole rule. His honor is his life—and that is *not* just a slogan where he is concerned! If he knew these things, with his oath still in force . . . well, it would put him in an insoluble dilemma. It would destroy him inside." Womanlike, she turned abruptly practical. "And if he *did* decide that he must turn against Tarhynda, it would destroy him *period.* It would mean slow death by torture—something he's incapable of even considering when his honor is involved."

"Hmm . . . You know, that might not be the worst of all possible outcomes. If a wedge could be driven between Tarhynda and his best general—the one with the best chance of conquering the portion of Arnoriysa that includes the Shrine of the Lake—"

"NO!" Andonre's vehemence rocked Nyrthim back on

his heels. "Put that out of your mind. I'll have nothing to do with any plan that will so endanger him."

"But, Andonre . . . perhaps you don't understand what is at stake here—"

"No, Nyrthim. *You* don't understand." Andonre laughed unsteadily. "You see, the Highest Sister made one mistake. When she arranged for me to be married off to Vaelsaru, she never considered one possibility." Andonre gave another laugh, which turned into a sob. "The possibility that I'd actually come to love him!"

She fled along the rampart, leaving Nyrthim standing alone in the darkness.

CHAPTER SEVENTEEN

The Emperor's arrival was reminiscent of Vaelsaru's, but dwarfed it.

Once again, Valdar stood with his fellow guards as they inhaled the dust of the chariots and cursed the sunny dryness of the day. This time, Vaelsaru headed the welcoming committee—which, on this occasion, didn't include Andonre. Rumor had it that she was indisposed. Valdar could easily believe it, knowing what had passed between her and Nyrthim.

Vaelsaru and the other dignitaries stood on the porch of the long house. That house had been hastily enlarged by the addition of apartments suitable for the Emperor's household—although Malsara, who had been growing steadily more imperial in his manner as

his master and mistress approached, made no secret
of his doubts as to just how suitable they were. The
slaves who had worked on that enlargement had
been a mere handful compared to the army that had
toiled to repair and extend the trackways leading to
Castranaenom. This was partly to ease the way of
the chariots—especially the new, heavier ones from
Amatoliysa—but mostly because Malsara had informed
Vaelsaru that the Emperor was bringing a train of
wagons, including an unprecedentedly heavy one
designed as private living quarters in the field.

The imperial couple rode in one of the new
chariots, behind the masses of troops, chariot-borne
and afoot, which made up the vanguard. The drums
and trumpets sounded for them as loudly as they
had for Vaelsaru. But this time those sounds did
not awake a spontaneous counterpoint of cheering
from the massed army. Mostly, there was only an
uneasy sullenness, and what cheering there was
seemed forced.

Tarhynda wore a tunic of imperial deep blue and
a version of ceremonial armor that blazed with precious stones. His face was hidden behind the imperial
mask of beaten gold—for which Valdar was deeply
grateful, as he was having trouble enough keeping his
fear and loathing under control even without actually
looking on the visage which he now knew for what
it was. Vaedorie stood to her full height—well short
of Tarhynda's shoulder—and visibly gloried in the
unconventionality of her appearance in public, riding a
war chariot. She wore a costume designed to enhance
the effect: a version of Tarhynda's, with the richly
encrusted sheet-bronze armor molded to fit her—and,

indeed, emphasize her—in a way that gave a whole new significance to the term "breastplate."

No question about it, the two of them would have held every eye—at any other time, and with any other set of guards . . .

Those guards marched in two files, flanking the imperial chariot on either side—at a goodly distance from the horses, which seemed oddly skittish. The guards marched in a silence that seemed incongruous, given their eight feet and more of height, squatty massiveness and unguessable weight. They marched in a way that suggested rigid control of a capacity for impossibly rapid movement.

The thick hide with its sparse, rusty hair—on full display, for they needed no armor to supplement their natural protection—was as Valdar remembered from that night of madness in the slums of The City. But as for the rest, he could only think back to Nyrthim's description of the *Nartiya Ozhre*, the warrior demons which could be trained to use weapons. Weapons they had, clutched in the hands of their lower pairs of arms, which looked even stronger than the upper ones: bronze-bound clubs and crude axes, which Valdar wasn't sure he would have been able to lift off the ground with both hands.

But worse than any of this was the sense of wrongness, of something that shouldn't exist in any sane and wholesome world.

The rest of the army was feeling it too, Valdar could tell. Even the earlier dutiful cheers had died, and everyone stood rooted to the earth in a silent paralysis of horror.

Is this army going to shatter like thin ice? wondered

Valdar. *All it would take would be for one man to scream....*

But then Vaelsaru, holding himself tightly in check by sheer force of will, stepped forward and bowed. "Welcome to Arvaerness, Your Imperial Majesty," he said in a loud, firm voice. And the moment passed; for Vaelsaru, as Valdar realized anew, was the heart and soul of this army as well as its brain.

Tarhynda acknowledged his general's greeting and alighted from the chariot. But Valdar had ceased to pay attention. He was watching the wagons that were now passing through the gate.

They were, of course, drawn by teams of oxen. Horses, straining against their choking chest-strap harness, could pull nothing heavier than a chariot. They would have been particularly out of the question for the big, enclosed wagon of which Malsara had spoken. It was, indeed, the largest Valdar had ever seen, and for all its flourishes of woodworking and brightly colored paint it looked more sturdily constructed than it needed to be. It had windows, as befitted what they'd been told of its function—but they were tiny, and heavily barred with bronze, which seemed an inexplicable extravagance ...

Unless, of course, one knew what he and Nyrthim knew about Zhotiyu's kidnapping, and the probable reason for it.

Valdar stared long and hard at those little windows, but glimpsed nothing.

Vaelsaru, Siytta and Tavazhalava rose to their feet and bowed as the Emperor—no longer wearing the mask—entered the room.

Malsara accompanied his master, making clear by his demeanor that he regarded the bows as directed at himself as well. Also present was the Empress, still in her absurd dress armor. Vaelsaru carefully kept all disapproval out of his face.

"No ceremony," said Tarhynda with a smile. He appropriated the chair that was normally Vaelsaru's. "Be seated, everybody. Let informality be the watchword." His smile decreased by a barely visible iota. "Within the limits of decorum."

They all lowered themselves into chairs and stools that crowded the small meeting room. Vaelsaru, in a chair no lower than Tarhynda's, was relieved that the two of them were no longer standing—he wasn't used to dealing with men taller than he was. But now he had to meet that disturbingly strange golden gaze directly.

"Now, then, Lord Vaelsaru," began Tarhynda, "we are pleased to see that you have been working with your usual industry, and that all is in readiness for the autumn campaign. We are eager to commence the pacification of the province of Arnoriysa—and the chastisement of the barbarian scoundrels who abducted your son."

"Thank you, Lord of the World," said Vaelsaru, using the full form of address.

"'Lord' is quite sufficient. We are, after all, under field conditions. Remember: informality!"

"Thank you, lord."

"We assume you have also made preparation, in accordance with the instructions we sent by the Lord Chamberlain, for the accommodation of our . . . personal guards."

A chill that had nothing to do with the advancing season invaded the room.

"Yes, lord," said Vaelsaru in a neutral tone.

"You'll find they are very little trouble. They require only the most rudimentary shelter, being almost impervious to heat and cold. Admittedly, they *do* consume a fair amount of meat, which they prefer raw."

"So the Lord Chamberlain informed me, lord. We may have to send foraging parties further afield, and increase our levies on the nearby villagers. This may occasion resentment—even resistance."

"Why, in that case," said Tarhynda with a pleasant smile, "the problem solves itself. If the peasants rebel, the levies can be laid on them and their families *directly*, not just on their livestock. And after all, what are peasants but two-legged livestock? The *Nartiya Ozhre* will certainly not object. In fact, it will be very much to their liking."

Vaelsaru kept his voice and his features under tight control. "It may not be to the liking of my men, lord. They already feel a certain degree of disquiet—"

"Yes," Vaedorie interjected acidly, "we noted that our reception lacked the unrestrained enthusiasm we had expected."

"—and while they feel no kinship with the local population here in Arvaerness, the fact remains that these people are *people*, if you take my meaning. Disciplinary problems could result from . . . what you are suggesting."

Tarhynda's smile did not waver, but it ceased to mean anything more than the expression fashioned in gold on his public mask. Vaelsaru wondered if it had ever meant anything more than that.

"You need not concern yourself with 'disciplinary problems,' Lord Vaelsaru. Such problems are a thing of the past, now that our personal guards are here to enforce discipline. Fear of them should suffice to maintain order. And if it does not . . . well, in the course of suppressing any outbreaks of mutiny, they can at the same time supplement their supply of their favorite food."

Vaelsaru started to rise from his chair. Siytta stared with apprehension, and Malsara with venomous anticipation. The sight of both helped Vaelsaru to clamp self-control down on himself. He drew a deep breath and pushed words, one at a time, out past clenched jaws.

"This is not how I am accustomed to dealing with my men, lord."

Vaedorie leaned forward, eyes glinting. "*Your* men, Lord Vaelsaru? You mean the *Emperor's* men, don't you? You merely command them for him. You would do well to remember that."

"I do, lady. And for that very reason, I feel constrained to point out that whatever successes I have achieved in the Emperor's name have been due in no small part to the fact that the soldiers trust me. They know I expect obedience and will not tolerate insubordination; but they also know my discipline is fair and my punishments not excessive. An army controlled by terror will be a . . . less effective instrument of the imperial will."

Malsara spoke, shedding the last vestige of his pretence of deference to Vaelsaru like a snake sloughing off its dead skin. "Your successes have been due entirely to the Emperor's sagacious plans, of which you have been merely the executor! They have had nothing to do with your coddling of the troops—including hired ruffians from every land under the sun. Indeed, one can only speculate as to your motives in seeking to cultivate their personal loyalty to you—to you, rather than to their Emperor!"

When Vaelsaru finally broke the shocked silence, he dared not permit himself to speak much above a whisper. "Lord, must I listen to this?"

Tarhynda leaned back in his chair and spoke in a languid drawl. "Well, Lord Vaelsaru, we can hardly ignore the views of our Lord Chamberlain, can we? He has our complete confidence. And, being—ha, ha!—incapable of founding a dynasty, *he* at least cannot be suspected of laying the groundwork for a usurpation."

The word had been released into the air of the little room. Vaedorie looked on with undisguised vindictiveness—as did Malsara, after a momentary wince at Tarhynda's offhandedly malicious reference to his condition. Tavazhalava clearly wished he were somewhere else. Siytta sat immobilized by anxiety over what his commander might say or do.

But Vaelsaru only lowered his head. "I am sick at heart that I so displease you, lord, and that I . . . can no longer be of service to you."

"We will inform you when your services are no longer required!" There was no longer any possible doubt as to the nature of Tarhynda's smile. "In the meantime, you need to be more mindful of your oath to us, and less concerned with currying favor with your men—for whatever purpose. Fear will keep them obedient: fear of the *Nartiya Ozhre*, who obey only us and our Empress. Never forget that.

"And now, let us discuss plans for the reconquest of Arnoriysa. We are impatient to begin." A strange expression came over the long, straight-featured face—an expression of eagerness beyond common conception. "*Very* impatient."

Vaelsaru looked at that odd expression, and into those even odder golden eyes. Unbidden, there came a recollection of what Tavazhalava had said he'd heard in Lokhrein.

He thrust it from his mind angrily.

Valdar and Nyrthim stood atop the cliff beside the walls of Castranaenom, watching the parade of barges crossing the Liyzher to its north shore.

"Here he comes, Nyrthim," said Valdar, indicating the figure walking up the slope from the fortress' landward side, with the characteristic bowlegged roll of men who'd been set on horses' backs before they could walk. "You know, it would simplify things if we could just tell him everything."

"No! When I returned from my talk with Andonre to prevent him from—with deep regret, no doubt—slitting your throat, I told him everything he needs to know and is ready to hear."

"But if we could just tell him the truth about Tarhynda—"

"As I've repeatedly explained, the fewer people who know that, the better. It's bad enough that you and Khaavorn know it."

Before Valdar could formulate an adequate reply, Rupaeranz joined them. "The advance guard is almost all across the river by now," he muttered. The barges had been carrying heavy infantry whose duty was to secure the landing area on the north shore. "After the last of them, my men and I are to cross, and scout ahead into Arnoriysa. So I won't be able to delay much longer. Have you heard anything further from the Lady Andonre?"

"No," admitted Nyrthim. "Matters still stand as I told you before. She recognizes—or at least is beginning to suspect—Vaedorie's evil. She even knows who really kidnapped her son, even though she still shrinks from the knowledge. But she can't bring herself to take any action that might harm Vaelsaru."

"Well of *course* not!" Rupaeranz' huffiness brought a smile to Valdar's lips. But it immediately subsided back into the moodiness that had characterized the mercenary since his first sight of Tarhynda's demonic bodyguards. He no longer doubted Nyrthim's word as to what the sorceror was or what he was doing here. Nor did he doubt that Vaedorie was behind the abduction of Vaelsaru's son, whatever the official version that had been fed to the troops. Nyrthim had sternly warned Rupaeranz that the truth was not to go any further, thereby assuring that it would.

"But what are we going to *do*?" he demanded as the three of them walked down the slope, skirting the walls.

"At the moment, we can do nothing. You must depart with your men. We will cross over later, with Vaelsaru and the imperial party. If nothing else, I'm certain Andonre won't betray us. And she may change her mind. I imagine it must be torture for her to look at that wagon."

They reached the level area in front of the main gate, and entered what resembled a bazaar. Ever since the Emperor had arrived, purveyors of various supplies had been pouring in: local farmers, peddlers from further afield, and, most recently, traders from afar with caravans of pack animals loaded with more exotic items.

As they approached the caravan of a wine seller, Valdar couldn't help smacking his lips—it had been so long since he'd tasted the quality wines for which he had acquired a taste in the Inner Sea while with Khaavorn on the diplomatic mission that now seemed to belong to another lifetime. Now, of course, anything except the rough local wines—and, Dayu forbid, fermented mare's milk—was beyond his means in his current persona.

Still, this all reminded him of an earlier time . . . those amphorae . . . the voice of the trader, seeking to peddle his wares to individual soldiers as well as Vaelsaru's supply officers. Yes, that voice, issuing from the plump figure up ahead . . .

"—I can supply novelties! Purple grape wine from Graetess, fit for the Emperor's table—"

"No," said Valdar faintly. And then: "*Zhassu?*"

The wine seller heard his voice, and turned. They goggled at each other, and started to open their mouths.

Nyrthim stepped forward and spoke firmly. "We might be interested in your wares. But let us go someplace where we can discuss terms in private."

Valdar and Zhassu both blinked, and remembered they weren't supposed to know each other. They let Nyrthim lead them—and the thoroughly bewildered Rupaeranz—behind a line of wagons.

Zhassu was the first to regain the power of speech. "But . . . but I thought you were dead!"

"I *do* wish people would stop saying that!" said Nyrthim testily.

"The question is," snapped Valdar, "what are *you* doing here? And where is Khaavorn?"

"Lord Khaavorn is well. He and I delivered the message as we had been charged."

"Yes, so we've heard. Oh, by the way, Rupaeranz," Valdar added, "this is Zhassu, who accompanied the Lady Andonre's half brother to Lohkrein."

"And now," Zhassu continued, "he is in Arnoriysa—or about to land there—with the High King and his warriors. I was sent ahead, with sufficient supplies of wine—some of which, amusingly enough, was supplied by the Emperor himself as a gift to the High King—to make my role plausible."

"A spy," said Rupaeranz sourly.

"An obtainer of information," Zhassu corrected primly. "It was felt that my lifelong familiarity with the Empire fitted me for the role. However, my primary mission is to watch for the arrival of the Priestess Norkhaari. You see, she—"

"Yes, we know about her," said Nyrthim heavily. "Andonre told me."

Zhassu started. "*She* is here? I've already learned that Vaedorie came here with her . . . husband. But this makes my mission even more urgent. Norkhaari was found out in Lokhrein, but she escaped." He described the escape, to his listeners' horror. "It must be assumed that she will come here. And with both Vaedorie and Andonre present, then the entire leadership of the demon cult will be present!"

"Indeed," Nyrthim nodded. "Something must be done."

"Before *anything* can be done," said Valdar suddenly, "we must be able to trust each other."

"Whatever do you mean?" inquired Nyrthim blandly.

"I mean sharing the entire truth—including, Zhassu, the truth about *you*."

The wine merchant blinked, and glanced nervously at Nyrthim, who had gone expressionless.

"It's pretty obvious," Valdar continued, "that you're not just some wine merchant with a vague sense of obligation to Nyrthim. I think it's time we knew the truth."

"Ummm . . ." Nyrthim cast a glance in Rupaeranz' direction.

"We've asked Rupaeranz to trust us, Nyrthim. It's time to start trusting him."

"Very well," sighed the sorcerer. "As you know, the Order of the Nezhiy was originally drawn from the Old Empire's priesthood. But there were never enough of that sort. The Order recruited helpers—a kind of lay brotherhood, known as the Nezharatiy. Men who had other occupations—"

"I really *am* a wine merchant," put in Zhassu.

"—but who had the aptitude for the work, within certain limits. And they served as a link between us and the world, for unlike the full Nezhiy—whose identities were always known—they led a double life. "

"And," said Valdar slowly, "they survived to the present day just like the Order iteslf. But in secret."

"Yes. It was useful to have them in reserve, so to speak. I imagine, Zhassu, that you were particularly useful in Lokhrein recently, from what you've just told us."

"I was able to be of some small use in dealing with the demon Norkhaari summoned," Zhassu allowed. "I conveyed certain information to Lord Khaavorn's brother Khaaradh."

"For which you'll never get any credit," said Valdar, staring at the wine seller—or the Nezharat, as he decided he must now think of him. Rupaeranz simply stared.

"Too true." Zhassu emitted a sigh of theatrical self-pity. "We *never* get the credit we deserve. But this has been in my family for many generations, so we ought to be used to it by now."

"And now, Valdar," said Nyrthim with an air of getting down to business, "if you're *quite* satisfied that you've been taken into our innermost confidence, perhaps we can turn to Norkhaari's imminent arrival—which, as Zhassu has surmised, brings matters to a head. We can no longer simply wait for Andonre to change her mind. We must force the issue."

"Whatever it is you plan to do," said Rupaeranz suddenly, "I'm with you. I know Lord Vaelsaru would never have anything to do with all this witchcraft if he only knew about it."

"You're probably quite correct," said Nyrthim. "So we must make sure he learns the truth."

"But Andonre told you she wouldn't allow that," protested Valdar.

"Once we have crossed over and are on the march into Arnoriysa, I believe an opportunity may present itself to do what must be done without alienating Andonre—or, at least, to put her in a position where she *must* go along with us."

"What are you plotting now?" demanded Valdar. "If it involves any harm to Andonre—"

"Oh, no. Not really. For now, we must continue to wait—but not for much longer. In the meantime, the three of you know all you need to know."

Try as they might, they could get nothing more out of him.

PART FOUR: Arnoriysa

CHAPTER EIGHTEEN

The imperial army followed the Liyzher downstream, proceeding westward along the river's northern bank. They moved slowly through the gently rolling meadowlands, keeping pace with the flotilla of barges.

Eventually, of course, the army would have to part company with the barges, striking north into Arnoriysa, whose southern boundary the Liyzher's lower reaches traditionally formed. For now, however, it was far easier to let the river's flow effortlessly carry most of the stores and the heavy wagons—including the great enclosed one that the Emperor had brought—through country where the trackways were primitive at best.

They marched in a carefully preplanned order,

behind a scouting screen of Kynaeraan riders. The chariot-riding nobles naturally occupied the van. Behind came the infantry contingents, in the regional dress of various imperial provinces, or of foreign lands from which they'd been hired: stocky Lydisei in their oddly shaped leather caps, Sardiysei whose curiously flat bronze helmets sported short horns (not very practical, Valdar had been heard to remark), dark wiry archers from Graetess, and so on. The center was occupied by Vaelsaru's own, very cosmopolitan elite guard unit of heavy infantry. In the rear trailed the inescapable crowd of camp followers, including Zhassu.

The Emperor's "personal guards" were not part of the formation. They floated with stolid patience on a pair of barges. Ashore, they would have caused too much trouble with the horses, which could not endure their smell in close proximity. Besides, Vaelsaru and Siytta had managed to convince Tarhynda that they should be kept as isolated as possible, for as long as possible, from the human troops. This was the obvious way to do it. Only occasionally did the men on the left flank, closest to the shore, glance out over the water and shudder as they glimpsed those hulking inhuman shapes sitting hunched over.

Finally, the time came when the army must turn north. The barges were poled over to grind ashore on the Liyzher's north bank. The wagons which must accompany the invasion were manhandled ashore. The outriders were called back as the army reorganized itself for the march north, where it expected to encounter Riodheg's forces, believed to have already landed in Arnoriysa.

Thus it was that Zhassu and Rupaeranz found themselves sitting and drinking under the stars near the riverbank, with the Emperor's great wagon in sight, indulging in the kind of drunken resolves that can sometimes have unforeseeable consequences.

Theirs was one of those improbable friendships that always seem strangely inevitable after the fact. Of course, Rupaeranz first had to get over his conviction that the wine merchant-*cum*-Nezherat was a spy. It also helped that Rupaeranz loved to talk and Zhassu was a good listener.

But in the end, the decisive factor may simply have been that Rupaeranz acquired a taste for wine.

"You know, Zhassu," he said, speaking around a suppressed hiccup, "I've never liked wine all that much. But *this* stuff . . ."

"Jush . . . that is, *just* don't get used to it. Rare stuff—very expensive." Zhassu seldom overindulged in his own wares. When he did, he was one of those whom alcohol caused to speak with careful profundity.

"Right! When a man's right, he's right. And you're right." Rupaeranz nodded emphatically to emphasize the point still further. "Never a good idea to acquire expensive tastes, I always say."

"Is that what you always say?"

Rupaeranz was still nodding, having forgotten to stop. "Damn right! You might end up not bein' able to afford 'em sometime. Then where would you be?" He tried to take another drink, but found it difficult to hit a moving target. So he finally stopped the motion of his head.

"Good point," acknowledged Zhassu. "But don't let

it become generally known. People might stop drinking overpriced wine. Then where would *I* be?"

Rupaeranz blinked with puzzlement a few times. Then enlightenment dawned and he spluttered with laughter, spraying an oblivious Zhassu with wine. By the time he caught his breath, his hiccups were gone.

They drank for a few moments in companionable silence. Then their attention—such as it was—was distracted by a sound of voices from the direction of the Emperor's great wagon. Tarhynda and Vaedorie were both at some kind of conference with Vaelsaru at the latter's tent, elsewhere in the camp, and the wagon stood dark, with half a dozen guards in the light of a torch thrust into the ground. It was those guards' voices they had heard, calling out to some passing acquaintance in their boredom.

The sight of that wagon was enough to bring a scowl to Rupaeranz' face. "When is Nyrthim going to let us do something?" he muttered. "He still hasn't told us his brilliant plan . . . if any."

"Perhaps," said Zhassu, even more owlishly than before, "he's waiting for an opportunity that can only arise when we're on the march northward."

"Bah! By then it may be too late. They say—not that I'm one to repeat rumors—that Riodheg is already on his way south to meet us. I tell you, Zhassu, Nyrthim is just dithering. He's waiting for a perfect opportunity that will never come. Don't get me wrong: he and Valdar are good sorts. But they think too much. That's the problem with most civilized people. No offense meant."

"None taken."

All at once, the stillness of the night was broken

again, this time by a chorus of distant shouts, and a flickering light. A small fire had broken out somewhere.

As Zhassu and Rupaeranz watched, the guards at the imperial wagon held a huddled colloquy in the torchlight. Their words could not be made out, but their decision soon became evident. They ran off to help fight the fire, with one grumbling exception who remained to watch the wagon.

"Zhassu," said Rupaeranz in tones of tipsy portentiousness, "I have reached a decision."

"Mmm?"

"Yes, a decision!" The mercenary got carefully to his feet—not quite carefully enough, for he lost his balance and fell backwards onto Zhassu's plump lap. Cursing, he got back up, and this time he managed to stay upright. "Nyrthim is never going to get off his scrawny old butt and act. It's up to us!"

The wine merchant's jaw dropped and his eyes grew round. "Us?" he repeated faintly.

"Yes! This calls for men of action!" Rupaeranz thumped himself on the chest and almost toppled over again. "Nyrthim has told us what—or *who*—is probably in that wagon, right?"

"Yes, but—"

"Well, I ask you: when will we ever have a chance like this again?" Rupaeranz pointed unsteadily but dramatically in the direction of the great wagon and its one guard. "It's now or never, Zhassu!"

Zhassu stood up, and began to sway alarmingly. He and Rupaeranz managed to steady each other.

"But . . . but . . . I'm no fighting man, Rupaeranz!"

"Ah, don't worry. I'll take care of that sort of thing.

All you have to do is distract that guard. Just walk past him and act drunk. It'll be easy—you *are* drunk!"

In fact, realization of what the mercenary was proposing had gone far toward sobering Zhassu up. So had outrage at the injustice and sheer gall of Rupaeranz' last remark. But before the wine merchant could muster a crushing retort, his companion started off along the line of smaller wagons, keeping out of sight as his barbaric hunter's instincts reasserted themselves even through a haze of wine fumes. Nearing his destination, he gestured to Zhassu to proceed.

A lump of fear congealed in Zhassu's stomach, and he didn't move.

Rupaeranz gestured again, more peremptorily.

Zhassu discovered he was more afraid of being left alone here than he was of going along with the mercenary's crazy plan. He swallowed, took a deep breath, and stepped out into the torchlight, walking a weaving line that brought him close to the guard, who was leaning on one of the wagon's state-of-the-art, multiply-spoked wheels.

"Greetings, brave warrior!" he slurred.

"You're as drunk as you are fat." Being left behind while his fellows sought excitement had done the guard's mood no good at all. "Get back with the rest of the camp followers where you belong."

"Ah . . . I seem to have lost my way. . . ." While Zhassu temporized, Rupaeranz slipped out of the shadows behind the guard. His right hand held the long Kynaeraan dagger.

"Go, before I help you along with a sword-point up your ass!" The guard stood up from his leaning position and stepped away from the wagon to shoo Zhassu away.

It gave Rupaeranz his opening.

The mercenary sprang the last few feet, and his left arm went around the guard's neck, forcing the chin up and exposing the throat. Zhassu averted his eyes as Rupaeranz made a quick sideways motion with his dagger.

"Hurry!" snapped Rupaeranz. He wiped off the dagger and put it away, and drew the late guard's sword. He also yanked the torch out of the ground. "The other guards won't be gone forever."

A folding stepladder gave access to the wagon's door. That door was secured by something Zhassu recognized: a large wooden bolt with holes in the top through which wooden pins dropped. A hole to the side, he knew, admitted a key which pushed the pins up. He explained all this to Rupaeranz. "But we don't have the key," he finished.

Rupaeranz evinced little interest. He grasped the guard's sword overhand and plunged it into the wood behind the bolt. Then, unconcerned with bending the bronze, be pulled back, wrenching the bolt out of the doorframe with a splintering sound. Then he kicked the door open.

"That's one way," admitted Zhassu.

The interior was dark. Rupaeranz thrust the torch forward, revealing an interior swathed with hangings and cluttered with gleaming bronze. There were two narrow beds, one along each side. On one of them, a small figure lay motionless.

Rupaeranz gave Zhassu a look of silent inquiry.

"Yes." Zhassu remembered Zhotiyu from that night

of horror in The City. He stepped over to the bed
and shook the boy vigorously. The only response was
a low moan. Zhassu frowned. Even the sleep of childhood shouldn't be this deep. Then he pulled back an
eyelid and gazed at the eye beneath.

"He's not dead, is he?" rasped Rupaeranz.

"No. He's been drugged. I know the stuff—it comes
from eastern Amatoliysa. It must be how they've kept
him quiet whenever there was any danger of anyone
noticing him. I imagine he's been in this state almost
continuously since their arrival at Castranaenom.
Look!" He indicated Zhotiyu's face, which had a pallid, pinched and generally unhealthy look. The bones
stood out sharply, as though he hadn't eaten properly
in a long time.

"And they call *us* barbarians!" Rupaeranz growled
something in his own language that sounded unmistakably like a curse. He scooped the child's limp form
up in his arms. "Let's get out of here!"

Privacy is always at a premium for an army in the
field. Nyrthim and Valdar had managed to find it in
the healers' tent where Nyrthim worked—at least late
at night, after everyone else had gone to bed. So far,
the sorcerer and his colleagues had had little to do
but set bones broken in accidents and dispense ineffectual remedies for the runs.

"So, Nyrthim," said Valdar with an air of elaborate
patience, "when are you going to reveal the fine
points of your plan—or the coarse ones, for that
matter—to us?"

"When the time is ripe," replied the sorcerer with
his accustomed air of irritating omniscience. "In these

matters, timing is everything. It is absolutely essential that we not move too soon and upset the delicate balance of—"

A corpulent figure half-ran and half-fell through the tent flap and collapsed, gasping for breath.

"Zhassu!" exclaimed Valdar. "What—?"

"It isn't my fault," stammered the wine merchant. "He made me do it!"

"Who made you do what? Talk sense!"

"Rupaeranz! He—"

The mercenary came staggering through the tent flap, went to his knees, and deposited the small form he was carrying on the ground.

Valdar stared at the tousled chestnut hair. "No," he breathed.

Nyrthim, who had never seen Zhotiyu, nevertheless began to grasp the truth. "This isn't . . . ?"

"I'm afraid he is," nodded Valdar.

"It wasn't my idea," Zhassu repeated miserably.

Rupaeranz looked up with the obvious anticipation of approval displayed by a cat who deposits a slain rabbit's guts on the kitchen doorstep. "The wagon was left almost unguarded. It was an unforeseeable opportunity. With the tactical flexibility I have developed over the course of many hard-fought battles, I decided . . ." He trailed to a wretched halt under Nyrthim's glare of gathering fury.

"Clowns!" spat the sorcerer. "You have ruined everything!"

"They *did* rescue Zhotiyu," Valdar felt compelled to point out.

"We are here to save not a single child but the world, including all the children in it. And," Nyrthim added a little more gently, "I don't think we'll be able to keep even Zhotiyu safe for long. Listen! The alarm has been raised." A tumult of shouts could be heard in the distance.

Nyrthim began to pace, talking more to himself than to the others. "What's done is done. Rhaeie—with the help of a pair of sots—has presented us with this moment. We must use it in whatever way we can." He stopped abruptly in his pacing, and whirled to face Valdar. "We can't stay here. This tent will be searched, along with everything else. We must take Zhotiyu to the last place anyone would expect: to his mother."

Valdar could only stare.

"Vaelsaru has surely left to organize the search," Nyrthim continued. "Andonre will be alone in their tent. If she sees Zhotiyu with her own eyes . . . well, how she will react is unpredictable. We've been cast into chaos—all we can do is ride its winds."

Rupaeranz stood up, eyes alight. "Yes! We must seize the moment! Let us take the boy—"

"Valdar and I will take him," said Nyrthim crushingly. "You and Zhassu have done quite enough for one night. You will return to your accustomed haunts and pretend innocence when the searchers arrive. Come, Valdar."

Valdar hung a heavy cloak loosely from his shoulders. Then he picked up Zhotiyu, who was beginning to stir and murmur in his drugged sleep. Letting the cloak fall around the child's form, he followed Nyrthim from the tent.

As they flitted through the night, they were like invisible disembodied spirits in the uproar of the camp. Even the area around Vaelsaru's tent was only sketchily guarded—and they had spent time earlier in the day scouting out the approaches to it. They slipped through, taking advantage of the dark and the confusion, and hid behind some bales of provisions.

All was quiet in the tent's immediate vicinity. Nyrthim was evidently right about Vaelsaru's absence. Valdar turned the semiconscious boy over to the sorcerer and approached the tent.

There was lamplight inside it, and the sound of two voices—but both of them were female. Valdar couldn't make out words through the heavy material, but he heard something in a tone of command and a voice he recognized as Andonre's. The tent flap opened, and a servant girl emerged on some errand.

Quelling his distaste for what he must do, Valdar slipped up and grasped her from behind. His left hand closed over her mouth before she could scream. With the knuckles of his right, he rapped her as lightly as possible behind the ear. She went limp. Lowering her gently to the ground, he tore strips from her light linen clothing with which to bind and gag her. Then he motioned to Nyrthim, and crept up to the tent flap. He lifted a corner of it and peered inside.

In the light of the stone lamp, amid the heavy hangings, Andonre stood with her slender back to him. That back was held at an angle of tenseness, and she was rubbing her hand together in her stress.

"Andonre," he called quietly, stepping into the tent.

She whirled, and stared wild-eyed. Belatedly, Valdar remembered the beard he had grown.

"Andonre, it's me, Valdar," he said hastily.

Her scream died in her throat and something ignited in her eyes. "Valdar? Nyrthim told me you'd come with him, but . . ." The light in her eyes died. "What are you doing here?"

Instead of answering, Valdar lifted the tent flap. Nyrthim entered, bearing Zhotiyu.

With a cry that encompassed a whole spectrum of emotions, Andonre sprang forward and took the child in her arms, weeping.

Something broke through the wall of drugs that separated Zhotiyu from the world. "Mama?" he mumbled.

Andonre stared at the wasted five-year-old face. "What have you done to him?" she demanded furiously.

"Oh, *think* about it, Andonre," snapped Nyrthim with his trademark irritability. "Would we have brought him to you in this condition if we were responsible for it? On the other hand, if what I told you before about Tarhynda's and Vaedorie's intentions is true, then this makes perfect sense. Zhotiyu obviously can't live long this way. But he doesn't *have* to live long, does he? He only has to survive until they can get him to the Shrine of the Lake—and this army is already on the march in that direction. You *know* I'm right, Andonre!"

Andonre's head dropped. She looked sick. She clasped Zhotiyu to her, rocking him, making small noises.

"When will Vaelsaru be back?" asked Nyrthim with sudden, unaccustomed gentleness.

"Probably not until morning," she said numbly. "He's inspecting the entire perimeter of the camp."

"Well, then," sighed the sorcerer, "we'll have to find a place to hide you and Zhotiyu tonight. Gather up what you need and—"

A chill breeze slid along the back of Valdar's neck as the tent flap opened behind him. And the flickering lamplight cast a shadow against the hangings—a misshapen shadow that Valdar had glimpsed once before, as he'd fled from the grotto beneath the Old Palace.

Andonre screamed, and held Zhotiyu even more tightly.

Valdar turned . . . but it was Tarhynda who stood inside the opening, in human form but somehow casting that monstrous shadow. Vaedorie stood behind him, eyes glittering with a fever of hate.

"Someone you know has just arrived tonight," said the Emperor pleasantly.

He gestured. Norkhaari stepped into the tent. Her garments were travel-soiled.

Behind her, the tent was ripped away, revealing two of the *Nartiya Ozhre*. They tore it apart, flung it to either side, and advanced past their master.

"Take them alive," commanded the Emperor, "but not necessarily undamaged, except for the boy."

Fear and despair somehow cancelled each other out in Valdar. He whipped out his sword and shouted a defiant Dhulaan war cry.

Out of the corner of his eye, he saw Nyrthim's features contort with concentration. All at once, the advancing warrior demons took on the look of sluggish disorientation he'd seen on the *Nartiya Zhere* in the slums of The City.

Tarhynda frowned.

Norkhaari stepped forward, her eyes tightly shut and her face locked into the same silent fury of concentration as Nyrthim's . . . and the demons' paralysis broke. Shaking themselves, they roared deafeningly and resumed their advance.

Afterwards, Valdar had only disjointed recollections of what happened. He remembered delivering a perfect drawing cut to one of the demons' upper arms, and being almost blown off his feet by the bellow of rage and pain as the unnatural blood flowed. He remembered glimpsing Nyrthim being struck to the ground. He remembered Zhotiyu, now aroused from his torpor, screaming hysterically for his mother as he was wrenched out of Andonre's arms.

Then came a shattering blow to his head, and it all dissolved in an instant of sickening pain before the merciful darkness took him.

CHAPTER NINETEEN

Valdar regained consciousness, and immediately wished he hadn't.

It wasn't just the nauseating spike of pain that drove through his head. No, the true agony was the stiffness—but he didn't become aware of that until he tried to move.

He was sitting on a hard wooden floor, with his back to a wall. His arms were stretched above his head, secured to the wall, keeping him sitting upright.

He opened his gummy eyes and looked around at the interior of what had to be the Emperor's wagon. Even the dim light—it looked like late afternoon—through the tiny, heavily barred windows hurt his eyes and intensified the pain in his head. Among the sumptuous wall hangings and rich bronze implements, his own sword hung from a peg, tantalizingly out of reach. He looked up and behind, and saw the bronze ring, bolted to the wooden wall, to which his wrists were tied. He tried to shift position, and a cry of agony escaped his lips like a living thing with a mind of its own.

"You're awake."

He turned his head—carefully—in the direction of the familiar female voice. Andonre was to his left, about an arm's length away. She must have been conscious longer, for she had gotten up onto her knees, relieving the excruciating position of the arms. Beyond her, Nyrthim was still slumped, breathing raggedly. Dried blood was caked in his gray hair.

"He's never awakened," Andonre answered Valdar's unspoken question. "Sometimes he's stirred and talked in his sleep."

"Are you—?"

"They didn't hurt me much." Her clothes, Valdar saw, were torn, and a bruise spread on her exposed right thigh. The left side of her face also looked battered. But no blood showed. "I was conscious when they brought us here. I haven't been able to sleep much."

"Of course not. And Zhotiyu . . . ?"

"They took him. I don't know where." Andonre's voice and face were controlled. Too controlled.

With startling abruptness, the door opened. Norkhaari and Vaedorie entered. The former's expression was unreadable; the latter's face fairly rippled with vindictiveness. At first they said nothing.

Andonre broke the silence, in a voice still under

unnaturally tight control. "Where are my son and my husband?"

"Don't speak until you're spoken to, you traitorous bitch!" hissed Vaedorie. "Remember your place."

"My place is no longer under you. By your lies, and by what you have done to Zhotiyu, you have forfeited my loyalty."

Vaedorie bared her teeth in a rictus of hate, and her hands unconsciously formed themselves into claws.

"No," said Norkhaari quietly.

Vaedorie turned to face her, and for an instant their eyes locked in a contest of wills which Valdar could dimly understand. Vaedorie was the Empress, accustomed to instant, cringing obedience. Norkhaari was a priestess from a half-barbarous former province . . . but she was the Highest Sister. And it was Vaedorie's eyes that slid aside.

Andonre spoke directly to Norkhaari, ignoring Vaedorie, and her self-control began to fray. "I've known you and trusted you since I was a child. If that means anything to you at all, tell me where my son is . . . and don't let him die!"

"So you know." Norkhaari glanced at the still unconscious Nyrthim. "Of course; he would naturally have told you. So you understand that Zhotiyu is no longer yours—he belongs to a greater purpose. Where he has been taken is none of your concern. As for Vaelsaru, he has been told that Riodheg's spies have kidnapped you. Later, your body—intact enough to be recognizable, though just barely—will be 'found' and shown to him. It will turn him into a force of nature that exists only to wreak vengeance against Riodheg. This, too, is a necessity you must understand."

"What I understand," said Andonre in a cold, empty voice, "is that everything you ever told me was a monstrous lie."

"Monstrous, perhaps, but not altogether a lie," said a new voice. "As my presence attests."

Tarhynda bent low as he passed through the door.

Valdar prepared himself for death, or worse than death, in forms beyond his mind's capacity to imagine. He also prepared himself to watch Andonre suffer the same, helpless to protect her.

Norkhaari and Vaedorie said nothing. But their aspect underwent a change. They looked like servants awaiting instructions.

Vaedorie came out of it first. She approached her "husband" with a look of avid hunger, and gestured toward Andonre. "Let me—"

"No." Tarhynda gave an imperious gesture that encompassed both her and Norkhaari. "Leave us."

Without a word, the two women departed.

"I see," came a familiar voice, "that any questions about who is the master have been resolved. But then, they think of you as a minister of Rhaeie."

Valdar glanced sharply to the left, beyond Andonre. Nyrthim was regarding Tarhynda with steady eyes. *All the talk must have awakened him,* Valdar thought. *Or . . . could it be that he's aware of Tarhynda's very presence, in ways that have nothing to do with hearing or sight or smell?*

Tarhynda gave the sorcerer a look of what Valdar could have sworn was approval. "I see you're not wasting effort by trying your Order's mind-confusing tricks."

"What would be the point? The old stories tell us that the technique has no effect on the Great Demons."

"Quite right." Tarhynda nodded. He picked up a light folding camp stool, set it up in front of the three prisoners, and seated himself with crossed legs. His face wore an expression of carefree, guileless charm. "It works well enough with the simpleminded *Nartiya Ozhre* and the practically mindless *Nartiya Zhere,* to use the names the old Nimosei gave them. But we of the *Nartiya Chora*—the Great Demons, as you call us—are merely aware of an irritating mental intrusion, mildly distracting but not really disorienting."

Valdar struggled to fight off a sense of unreality. In all his gut-churning imaginings, the very last thing he had anticipated from the demon-emperor was chattiness.

"So." Nyrthim's voice took on what Valdar recognized as a note of shrewdness. "I suppose it would be even more pointless to try it with a prince of the Great Demons, such as you plan to summon."

Tarhynda looked genuinely shocked. "What are you thinking of? Surely you must know—or at least have guessed—that by this point in time it is quite impossible, by any technique or combination of techniques, to summon what you term a 'prince of the Great Demons.' That's the whole point!"

If Nyrthim wasn't puzzled, he counterfeited it well. "Perhaps you'd better explain."

"Yes, I see that I must." Tarhynda's eyes took on a faraway glow. "And it's so *good* to be able to discuss these matters with someone who at least has an inkling of them, unlike. . . ." He gestured at the door through which Norkhaari and Vaedorie had exited.

"Aren't you afraid we'll tell them?" asked Nyrthim mischievously.

"Not at all. You underestimate the human *will to believe*—always a potent weapon in our arsenal. But no, you don't really underestimate it at all, do you? You know perfectly well that they'd rationalize away anything they learned."

"Too true," Nyrthim acknowledged sadly. "But you were saying . . . ?"

"You of the Order have correctly surmised that we—*Nartiya* in the old Nimosei tongue, 'demons' as you prefer nowadays—are native to another world. Or, to be more accurate, another *universe*. Actually, there are many universes—possibly an infinite number. They all had their beginning at the instant of the . . . Your language lacks the terminology. It even lacks words for the numbers involved. But long ago, the entire universe of worlds and stars and the void between them was . . . compressed into a very small volume, less than that of an acorn, and at the instant after it exploded outward there were far more dimensions than the four you know, before most of them collapsed into—"

"Talk sense!" blurted Valdar, irritated beyond fear.

Tarhynda gave him a quelling glare, then turned back to Nyrthim, whom he obviously considered the only human present worth talking to. "As I was about to say, it follows that these universes aren't really 'parallel.' Think of them as . . ." He sought for an analogy his listeners would understand. "Visualize the spokes of a wheel, that are spaced more widely the further they are from the hub. With the passage of time, they are growing 'apart,' in multidimensional terms."

"And therefore harder to pass between," Nyrthim nodded.

"You understand more than I thought. The 'neighboring' ones—the 'adjacent spokes' if you will—are so similar as to be almost identical. Sometimes a human will spontaneously transpose between them, changing places with his or her opposite number *without even noticing.* It accounts for any number of puzzling occurrences—lost items, lapses of memory, slight personality changes in close acquaintances. On very rare occasions, transpositions occur between universes that are more dissimilar in various ways—for example, time unfolds at an infinitesimally faster or slower rate, resulting in a different local time, and there are always at least minor differences in geography. In the case of more 'distant' universes—these terms are *so* imprecise!—the differences become more profound." Tarhynda gave them a condescendingly knowing smile. "There was a notable instance of this in your own history. The individual involved managed to adapt to your world, and even made quite a name for himself as a maker of proverbs.

"Now, we 'demons' arose in a universe that is very 'remote' from yours—say, a quarter of the way around the 'wheel.' Conditions there are quite different, although there was a near-human race . . . which," Tarhynda added offhandedly, "we naturally exterminated."

"I don't understand," said Nyrthim. "Why didn't the early sorcerers' first feeble summonings bring humans from 'nearby' universes?"

"It doesn't work for humans. My race has a unique quality of interdimensional portability. What you call 'summonings' draw us, starting with our weakest-minded varieties, like metal to a . . . but you wouldn't know about that, would you?"

"But you can't travel between universes by yourselves?" Valdar queried.

"Surprisingly shrewd," Tarhynda acknowledged, deigning to notice the younger man. "And quite correct; we must be summoned by humans. Not that this was ever a problem in the past. Your own old tales recount the typical sequence of events. Once established, we've very seldom even had to force the local humans to summon still more of us. They're all too willing—avid, in fact." The demon's façade of urbanity exhibited its first crack as he gave a sneer of cold contempt. "So it's always the same, in universe after universe. Once humans summon us into one of their worlds, that world is doomed."

"*We* will stop you!" rasped Valdar.

"Don't be even more ridiculous than your nature requires you to be." Tarhynda took on a look of pleasurable reminiscence. "I personally recall a certain world, very similar to yours in geography. As a matter of fact, it was the source of the spontaneous transposition to your world I mentioned earlier. But remember what I said about slightly varying time rates in different universes? This one was three or four thousand years ahead of yours at the time we entered it. Your world now is like an image of the ancient history of theirs, distorted like what you see when you're looking at your face in a disturbed pool of water.

"In all that time, they'd been able to do things

you've never dreamed of. What a world of machines! They had chariots that moved themselves. They had ships that flew, and others that sailed under the sea. They had devices that could project their voices and even their images across thousands of miles. They even had machines to *think* for them—which may have been why they had largely stopped doing it for themselves. Their arts had plumbed the invisible essences of life and of matter itself. Indeed, unique among all worlds, their first accidental summonings were the result of experimentation into what they thought to be the farther reaches of the natural world. But after that, it went the way it always goes—even though they had weapons that spat fire, weapons that made yours look like toys. They even had weapons that released the energies of the sun itself, and could lay waste to an entire city in a single inconceivable ball of fire. When all other hope was gone, they finally used those weapons against us, despite the damage they wreaked on their world. And they killed a lot of us. But it did them no good in the end. Their world succumbed like all the others." The demon leaned forward, amber eyes glowing, and Valdar wondered how he could ever, for even an instant, have mistaken this creature for human. "If *those* people, with powers beyond any gods you have ever imagined, couldn't stop us, what makes you think *you* will with your pathetic bronze swords?"

Valdar met those horrible eyes and did not look away. "We stopped you once before," he said quietly.

Tarhynda's human semblance flushed with fury. "That was a temporary setback, due entirely to Dayu—one of those you refer to as the princes of the Great

Demons. He was something unique in our history. In terms you can understand, he was a wolf who chose to be a sheepdog."

Even at this moment and in this place, Valdar couldn't help turning to Nyrthim with an I-told-you-so look. "Then you were wrong! Dayu *was* a good demon."

"In a certain sense, perhaps," Nyrthim allowed drily. He turned back to Tarhynda. "But since you're telling us so much else, tell us about these princes of the Great Demons."

"It can do no harm. They arose in the course of our conquests of many worlds, as the result of a . . . your languages lack the word. But you know about the breeding of livestock, and surely you've noticed that occasionally an animal will be born with characteristics inherited from neither of its parents, and pass those characteristics on to its own offspring. The princes represented such a spontaneous change in our race. To all appearances, they are ordinary *Nartiya Chora*. But they have extraordinary powers. And they exude a powerful . . . Once again, vocabulary fails. Suffice it to say that the rest of us *must* obey them. In the actual presence of one, we cannot even *wish* to disobey him!" For a fleeting instant, Tarhynda's face clenched with an emotion for which, Valdar suspected, no human language held a name. Then the demon composed himself and his expression smoothed itself out. "They also have another quality, of which your predecessors somehow learned: an absolute inability to tolerate rivals of their own kind. A few moments ago, I compared them to wolves. A better comparison would be lions, among whom there can be but one dominant male in each pride. Ever since they arose among us, our worlds have been riven by their unending wars of extermination. On some worlds, we have died out altogether."

"Justice of a sort," Nyrthim murmured.

Tarhynda leaned forward again, and this time those huge golden eyes gleamed. "Ah, but now I have an unprecedented opportunity! Using the gateway your Order fashioned at the Shrine of the Lake, in conjunction with the sacrifice of this female's son, I can bring in limitless numbers of my fellows from my own world and others—but the princes cannot follow! They have always been the hardest of all to summon, and by now they simply *cannot* be summoned to this world from any of ours, even at the Shrine of the Lake. We will be free of them! This world will be our refuge from them."

For the first time, Andonre spoke up. Her voice held something that sent a shiver up the spine of Valdar, who was not altogether unacquainted with violence on all its levels. "You're forgetting one thing. Nyrthim explained to me that you want Zhotiyu for your victim because of his relationship to one of the people performing the ceremony. But I *won't* be performing it! No torture could make me. So he'll be useless to you."

Nyrthim cleared his throat with embarrassment. "Ahem! If you recall, I said that a blood relationship with someone *associated* with those persons would also serve."

"But I'm not associated with them anymore! I renounce them and curse them! And I ask Rhaeie to forgive me for having been such a fool as to be taken in by even greater fools such as they."

"I'm afraid it's not quite that simple." Tarhynda's expression was unreadable, even though their eyes had adapted to the darkness as the light filtering through the bars of the windows had turned to dusk. "Your prior association with them still counts for something. Don't ask me the reason; we understand the *whys* of these things no more than you. It will count for still more if you are alive at the time of the sacrifice, and present to watch it but helpless to prevent it. This will disappoint Norkhaari, who had thought she was being terribly clever by using your faked murder to enrage Vaelsaru . . . and Vaedorie, who had hoped to wield the knife herself. But that is the least of the things in which they will be disappointed." Now, even in the dimness, there was no mistaking Tarhynda's smile.

Abruptly, the demon stood up. "I have lingered too long. There are things to be done. I must instruct the guards—humans, for I am still keeping the *Nartiya Ozhre* as isolated from the camp as possible—to be especially watchful." He gave Valdar an accusatory glance. "After all, you ruined the lock to this wagon when you spirited the boy away."

Valdar's mouth had barely begun to open when he clamped it shut. If Tarhynda didn't know he and Nyrthim had confederates still at large in the camp, Valdar saw no purpose to be served by enlightening him. Nyrthim, of course, also kept silent—and Andonre didn't know.

Tarhynda departed. The gray twilight between the bars deepened to blackness. They waited in darkness and thirst and hunger and general misery.

Valdar finally managed to stand up and examined the bronze ring to which he was tied. He braced his feet against the wall and pulled with all the strength his agonized, bleeding wrists would let him exert. The wood creaked a little, but there was no perceptible give. He stopped, cursing with frustration.

Time passed. There seemed nothing to say.

After so much silence, the creak when the door opened was startlingly loud.

Three guards entered, holding torches. They were Asshyrhim, from a land far to the east of Amatoliysa: squat dark men with the full, curly, blue-black beards their people cultivated. They wore cuirasses of hardened leather scales, and helmets of the same material.

Valdar was surprised that this particular guard duty had been entrusted to mercenaries from the far end of the earth. On reflection, though, it wasn't surprising at all. Tarhynda could hardly use Vaelsaru's elite guards—Valdar's own erstwhile unit—or anyone else who would have recognized their general's allegedly kidnapped wife. The Asshyrhim—barely able to speak the Ayoliysei of the army—probably knew only that one of the prisoners they were guarding was a woman.

Judging from their expressions, and the tone in which they muttered to each other in their own language, that was all they needed to know.

They inserted their torches into sconces and advanced on Andonre.

Knowing how futile it was even as he did it, Valdar shouted and kicked out at them.

One of them grabbed his ankle and yanked his legs out from under him. With breathtaking pain, his bound wrists caught his entire falling weight.

The Asshyr knelt over him and planted a knee in his abdomen. "Quiet, pig-shit!" he rumbled in barely intelligible Ayoliysei. "Maybe we use *you* next." Valdar recalled what he'd heard about the sexual habits of the Asshyrhim. He watched as the other two grabbed Andonre's desperately writhing body. One of them held a hand over her mouth while the other began to tear at her clothes.

The door crashed open, and Rupaeranz was through it, lunging with his long Kynaeraan dagger. The man who was undressing Andonre turned just in time to have his throat ripped out. His assistant, startled, let his grip loosen enough for Andonre to bite his hand. As he yelped in pain, the Asshyr holding Valdar down surged to his feet and turned on Rupaeranz.

Grimly holding onto the rope that secured his wrists, Valdar swung his legs out and clenched them around his erstwhile captor's thick midriff, immobilizing him.

Rupaeranz recovered from his lunge, brought the dagger back, and hurled it at the man Andonre had bitten. It wasn't designed to be a throwing knife, but it sufficed. The Asshyr wore a startled look with the hilt protruding from his left eye socket.

The third Asshyr, with a mighty heave, managed to free himself from Valdar's legs. The effort propelled him forward—face to face with another Kynaeraan who had just entered. The new arrival drove his dagger forward with a force which, combined with the Asshyr's momentum, sent the point punching through leather scales, cloth, flesh and muscle, and into guts. A vicious twist, and the dagger was out, pulling some of those guts with it. Simultaneously, the Kynaeraan's left hand shot out and grasped the throat of the Asshyr, whose scream died aborning. That grip did not loosen until the Asshyr was beyond screaming.

The wagon's interior was thick with the stench of death.

"This is my cousin Straekau," said Rupaeranz, introducing the other Kynaeraan, who grunted. "Yes, I know," he added hastily, with an apprehensive glance at Nyrthim, "I wasn't supposed to tell anybody. And he doesn't know everything. But he knows he hasn't got any use for demons, or for those who summon them." Straekau grunted with more emphasis. "And of course you already know . . ." Rupaeranz gestured toward the door, where Zhassu was entering, wrinkling his nose.

"*I* don't know any of you," said Andonre. "But I've never been so glad to see anyone."

"Neither have I," admitted Nyrthim.

"Time for introductions later," said Valdar. "Cut us down!"

The keen-edged daggers made short work of the ropes. Valdar and Andonre collapsed to the floor, rubbing circulation back into their arms and legs. Nyrthim was also down—but not moving as readily. As soon as he could walk, Valdar went to the far wall, grasped his sword, and felt much better.

"Come on, Nyrthim," he urged. "We've got to get out of the camp."

The sorcerer shook his head. "I'm too badly hurt. I could never make it. And you and Andonre would never make it with me slowing you down. No, you two must go and—"

"I'm not leaving without Zhotiyu!" flared Andonre.

"Use your mind, Andonre! You have no idea where Tarhynda has him. If you stay here to search for him, you'll only be recaptured, and all this will have gone for nothing."

"I'll go to Vaelsaru and—"

"And what? Even if you could reach him, what would it accomplish but the deaths of you *and* your husband? No, you and Valdar must go north and find Riodheg's army."

"But Zhotiyu . . . and Vaelsaru . . ."

"I'll still be here, as will Zhassu. We'll be working from within to find a solution that will allow both of them to live. I make no promises—you'd know such a promise would be a lie. But I swear by Rhaeie to do my best."

Rupaeranz' teeth gleamed in a grin. "Come, Valdar! I'll gather my tribesmen and we'll cut our way out of the camp!"

Nyrthim gave him a withering look. "Your approach to life has proven appropriate *once* tonight. Don't press your luck. How could Valdar and Andonre keep up with you, even if you gave them horses?"

This, Valdar knew, was true. Rupaeranz had let him practice riding astride the Kynaeraan mounts a few times, but it was no substitute for a training that had begun in early childhood. The experience had also taught him that those outlandish garments that encased both legs separately might just have a practical function. Andonre had never even tried.

"We'll steal a chariot for them," Rupaeranz insisted stubbornly. "My men and I will escort them."

"Stealing a chariot makes perfect sense," the sorcerer nodded. "But you must *not* be seen to be involved, Rupaeranz. Have you forgotten your oath to Vaelsaru?"

"Good point," said Straekau, with the grunt that seemed to be his standard conversational embellishment. Rupaeranz looked sheepish. His night's work could be rationalized as having been directed against the witch-empress rather than against Vaelsaru. But any action that would irrevocably cut his ties to the general could only make an oathbreaker of him.

"Besides, Rupaeranz, I have other plans for you—plans that will not violate your oath. This, too, I swear. But for now . . ." Nyrthim painfully rose to his feet. "Help me, Zhassu. Get me to your tent—I'll be able to hide among the camp followers." Before Zhassu could reach him, he stumbled. Valdar and Andonre caught him.

"We can't leave you here, Nyrthim!" cried Andonre.

"You can't take me with you!" He clasped their shoulders. "Go! The fate of the world goes with you."

Valdar, Andonre, and the two Kynaeraan hurried silently through the fortunately moonlit night. The wagon's position near the river was not far from the chariots and the corral that held their horses. A couple of judiciously stealthy killings got them through the guards. They carefully untied a team of horses and led them to a chariot of the sort Valdar wanted.

It was little changed in its essentials from those the Karsha had developed for war on the grasslands centuries earlier: light, with the axle positioned well to the rear, allowing great speed and maneuverability at the cost of being able to carry only two. Now in his element, Valdar hitched the two horses to the traces,

and hefted the whip attached to the side. Then he
helped Andonre up onto the platform. She held onto
the balance thong attached to the upper rim, and
took up the stance of one not entirely unaccustomed
to this kind of travel.

Valdar reached down and grasped Rupaeranz' shoulder. "Thank you. Whatever happens, I owe you my
life."

The mercenary looked worried. "Do you think
Nyrthim will be able to do . . . whatever it was he
was talking about? I mean, if you're going to join
Riodheg, my oath to Vaelsaru will force me to fight
you." He shook his head with perplexity.

"I know that Nyrthim generally keeps his promises,
even if he isn't always perfectly clear as to just exactly
what he *is* promising. But remember what he said: for
it to happen, you mustn't be suspected of involvement
in our escape. So go!"

Rupaeranz and his cousin went. Valdar waited to
give them time to get far away, conscious all the
while of Andonre's warm proximity. Then he grasped
the reins, and cracked the whip over the horses. The
chariot sprang forward.

Guards came running, but they leaped out of the
way of the onrushing chariot. Valdar glanced upward,
and remembered what Nyrthim had taught him about
the patterns in the sky. It was far enough into autumn
now for him to see the closely spaced line of three
white stars, with the bright bluish one some distance
"below" them to the south, and the equally bright
ruddy one a roughly equal distance "above." Some
people claimed to be able to see the outline of a
warrior, or a hunter, in those stars.

Even at that moment, he couldn't help remembering what Tarhynda had told them, and he wondered if the stars were arranged in the same patterns in the skies of all the earths.

But there was no time for such thought now. He concentrated on driving through the moonlight toward the ruddy star. Behind them, the shouts from the camp grew fainter.

CHAPTER TWENTY

The meadowlands north of the Liyzher were flat near the river, gently rolling further north. Valdar was able to maintain a steady pace—though not too fast, out of caution as well as to prevent exhausting the horses—until the moon began to set behind some dark low-lying clouds. Then he began looking for shelter.

He found it in a village beside a small stream, much like every other village in this part of the world. It was deserted, for the peasants had fled at the approach of the imperial foragers, taking their livestock, and were doubtless huddled in the woods. Valdar knew there would be nothing to eat, nor was there. He tied the horses inside a rickety pen, then searched the huts for any items he and Andonre could wrap themselves in against the chill of night, for they had fled with nothing but the clothes they wore—somewhat torn, in Andonre's case—and Valdar's sword.

There was little to be found; peasants had little to begin with. Taking the few animal hides he had turned up, Valdar led the way into what seemed the most substantial of the huts.

"Aren't you afraid they'll find us here?" wondered Andonre.

"No. It must have taken time to organize a pursuit, and they can't travel safely in darkness any more than we can. But they'll arrive in the morning. We'll have to leave at daybreak."

"Of course." Andonre sank down onto the hard-packed dirt floor, finally letting exhaustion and grief overtake her. But her eyes remained open, staring.

Valdar sought for something to say—something more intelligent than that he was sure Nyrthim would find a way to save Zhotiyu.

"Uh . . . I'm sure Nyrthim will find a way to save Zhotiyu," he finally said.

A very tiny smile flickered at the corners of Andonre's mouth. "You needn't try to reassure me, Valdar." The smile abruptly died. "Even if it could be done, I wouldn't be worthy of it. All this is my fault. Everything that has happened and will happen to me, I deserve. But . . ." She squeezed her eyes shut, too late to stop a tear from trickling from one corner. "But Zhotiyu doesn't!"

"Oh, come!" said Valdar with desperate heartiness. "Don't take all the blame on yourself. You were only used. Vaedorie and Norkhaari are the ones who are truly vicious and ruthless and depraved and . . ." *And now have Zhotiyu in their grasp,* an inner imp jibed at him. He halted, recalling an axiom of the ancient sage Zhaerosa: *"When you find yourself in a hole, stop digging."*

But Andonre showed no sign of having made the connection—or, for that matter, of having heard anything he'd said. "And now," she continued in the same bleak voice, "I've betrayed the one person I hadn't already betrayed: Vaelsaru."

Sheer amazement broke Valdar free of his verbal paralysis. "*Vaelsaru?* Because you fled from the camp tonight? But what else could you have done? You heard Nyrthim—"

"You don't understand! In all the years of living a lie, he was the only thing in my life that was *real.* So I've clung to him like a castaway at sea clinging to a floating log, lest I drown in self-hatred, for I think some part of me knew all along that I was being used for something that was wrong. He was all I had. And now I've lost him."

"Surely he wasn't all that was worthwhile in your life," Valdar improvised frantically, kneeling down beside her. "You must have had good memories . . . clean memories. Think back. Why, I can remember you when you were fourteen—the day I arrived at Riodheg's hall."

For the first time, something other than dull dead despair flickered to life in Andonre's eyes. "Can you truly remember me on that day?"

"Of course! You were slender as a living sword blade, so vividly alive, so—"

"—Painfully skinny," she finished for him. But now her eyes held an inarguable twinkle.

"Rubbish! I had eyes for no one else that day."

"Liar! But keep on doing it." She smiled at the remembered scene. "I think I fell in love with you then."

A moment passed before Valdar trusted himself to speak. "Er . . . you were only fourteen."

"I know. But the feeling didn't stop. I felt it every time I saw you for the next three years."

Without remembering having done it, Valdar found he had lowered himself down to lie beside her. He also found himself speaking words he had never intended to utter, knowing as he spoke them that no good could come of them. "I think I can remember every time we were together those three years. When you left, I felt less alive."

She reached out an unsteady hand and touched his shoulder. "Hold me."

"No, Andonre. I mustn't." But with that touch, all the longing he had felt in those bygone years of his first manhood reawakened and returned in a rush. He took her in his arms.

In the midst of the hostile night, their bodies sought each other hungrily.

Even after the bare two or three hours of sleep he finally got, long-accustomed reflexes brought Valdar awake at dawn. He shook Andonre until she stirred and opened her eyes. For a moment they stared at each other, unsure of what to say.

"Uh, we have to be going," he finally managed.

"Yes, I suppose we do," she sighed. And all at once their aching bones and chilled skin and empty bellies and desperate circumstances came crowding oppressively back, to join the new complication that had just entered their lives.

They got up stiffly and went to the stream to drink and splash icy water in their faces. Valdar untied the unenthusiastic horses—they had found only scanty grass to nibble—and hitched them to the chariot. The horses got under way sluggishly but finally fell into their drilled-in rhythm, and the biting wind blew the grogginess from the two humans' heads.

The sun rose over the eastern horizon, and Valdar kept it to his right as he drove on, for they had no plan save to fare northward, toward Riodheg.

As they went, the meadowlands with their stands of autumn-colored trees became somewhat more rolling, so the horizons grew wider. They both scanned those horizons constantly, for any sign of the oncoming army of Lokhrein.

They had splashed across a stream and ascended the hillslope on its far side when Andonre suddenly gave a cry and pointed behind them. Chariots were topping a distant ridgeline. More appeared even as he watched, spread out over a goodly extent in a manner unpleasantly reminiscent of a fisherman's net.

They've found us, thought Valdar, hunger and bone-weariness forgotten. *Still a good ways behind . . . but with well-fed horses.* Across the distance, the wind brought shouts faintly to his ears. Their pursuers had seen them.

"Hold on!" he snapped at Andonre, who gripped the balance thong with white-knuckled force. He gave the horses a vicious whip crack, and they sprang forward, scrambling over the crest, and careening down the reverse slope with reckless momentum.

But by the time they next topped one of the low ridgelines and attained a vantage point, the pursuing chariots had gained perceptibly. And behind them, Valdar could glimpse dark masses of infantry in the distance—presumably light-armed troops, to have kept so close to the chariots. And, peering far to the southwest, he could make out what had to be the Kynaeraan riders, flanking the chariots.

So this isn't just a hunt for us, he thought. *Vaelsaru has flung his whole advance guard northward. Which means the main body of the army must have gotten under way and is now following somewhere behind.*

He lashed the flagging horses into renewed efforts. But each upward slope was a greater struggle than the last. And, inexorably, the imperial chariots closed in.

It was on one of those slopes that the horse on the left finally collapsed. Its mate slewed wildly, bewildered, and the chariot began to tip. Valdar grasped Andonre by the arm and leaped free. They hit the ground together, rolling to a halt. Valdar scrambled to his feet and stared at the oncoming chariots. He could make out details like faces now.

He grasped the hide Andonre had been using as a shawl, wrapped it around his left forearm in lieu of a shield and raised his sword. Then his eyes met Andonre's for what they both knew would be the last time.

"Run, Andonre!"

"No. They won't risk throwing javelins while I'm with you. Vaelsaru must have ordered them to take me alive."

The sheer dishonor of using—however unintentionally—a woman as a shield, coming on top of everything else, was almost more than Valdar could bear. But the part of him that never quite stopped thinking told him that he wouldn't be able to delay them while she fled—the chariots on the flanks would merely press on after her.

"Get behind me, then." He assumed fighting stance and awaited the first of the chariots. Now he could see individual features . . . the charioteer's big nose, the way the warrior's beard bristled out from between the cheekpieces of his helmet . . .

Like a thunderclap, a line of chariots burst over the ridgeline behind him, practically going aloft and crashing back down to earth. Louder than that crashing were the Dovnaan war cries of their riders. Valdar's expert eye recognized the heavier shock chariots, less maneuverable than his and those of his pursuers. But here and now they had neither opportunity nor need for maneuvering. They plunged downhill to crash into the line of imperial chariots, in a melee where tactics had even less place than they usually did in this milieu's warfare.

Before Valdar could recover from his stunned surprise, one of the Dovnaan chariots thundered past him and sideswiped the imperial chariot he'd been staring at mere moments before. The warrior brought his great war axe around to chop unerringly into the vulnerable spot over his opponent's cuirass where neck met shoulder. Blood fountained. Then the chariots were past each other and the imperial charioteer lost control. His capsizing chariot crushed the life out of him.

The Dovnaan chariot came back around. Its warrior tossed his axe aloft, caught it, and laughed, for the

battle joy was on him. Like all of Riodheg's elite, he
was armored like his imperial counterparts, with bronze
helmet and hardened leather cuirass. From under that
helmet hung mustaches and a ponytail darker than the
Dovnaan average, and that cuirass was worn over a
tunic of a distinctive forest green.

"Khaavorn!" yelled Valdar.

The big Dovnaan clapped a hand on his charioteer's
shoulder, signaling him to halt. His eyes bulged as
though he'd seen a ghost, which was precisely what
he thought he was seeing. "Valdar? But you . . ." He
looked again, and his expression of bewilderment grew
positively comical. *"Andonre?"*

"It's a long story, Khaavorn, and there's no time
to—*Khaavorn, look out!"*

Khaavorn turned just in time to see the oncoming
imperial chariot before it ground against his station-
ary one, tangling their wheels. Before he could get
his shield up, the Achaysei warrior lashed out with
his sword and struck the axe out of his hand. Roaring, Khaavorn reached down and brought up a sword
of his own before the Achaysei had recovered for a
second stroke.

Unnoticed, Valdar ran behind the imperial chariot
and jumped up onto the platform. The charioteer
turned, startled. He looked even more startled when
Valdar's sword point went into his gut with a practiced twist. At the same time, Khaavorn knocked
the warrior's shield aside with a powerful blow and
brought his sword swooping around and up under
his opponent's chin to stab through the jaw, the roof
of the mouth, and the brain. Abruptly, Valdar was
alone in the imperial chariot, locked to Khaavorn's.

He brought the straining horses under control, then whooped with laughter.

"You're using one of those newfangled foreign *swords!* Don't think you'll ever live this down."

"Now I know it's really you, beard and all," Khaavorn growled. Then his face split in a grin, and he leaned over the rim of his chariot and took Valdar in a bear hug. "Is Nyrthim—?"

"Yes, he's alive too. He sent us here. But let's get away from here. There are more chariots on the flanks, and riders from the Kynaeraan plains, and their infantry is coming up."

"So is mine. Riodheg sent me ahead with his advance guard. But you're right." He looked around. The Dovnaan chariots, aided by surprise and the momentum inparted by a downhill charge, had overwhelmed their opponents. Khaavorn waved a signal, and they began to turn back.

Khaavorn got down, picked up his axe from the grass, and heaved a sigh of contentment as he hefted its weight. Then he turned back toward his chariot—a movement that brought him face to face with Andonre.

For a moment he stared, as though unsure of how he was supposed to behave. She dropped her eyes and spoke in a barely audible voice.

"I know, Khaavorn, I know. I have no right to your trust, or your forgiveness. But I'm here because I want to somehow make amends for the harm I've done. And . . ." Her voice broke. "And I've paid for it. Oh, yes, I've paid. Those I thought were my friends have Zhotiyu, and plan to kill him."

"What? Zhotiyu?" Khaavorn clamped his mouth

shut, then spoke in a very controlled voice. "You can tell me everything later. Now, let's get behind my infantry. The rest of the imperial vanguard is coming." Following his pointing hand, Valdar could see it was true. The enemy infantry was approaching at a jog trot, and in the distance the flanking chariots were closing in from east and west.

Valdar wrenched the wheels of the two chariots apart, then helped Andonre into the one whose driver he'd killed. Their touch lingered a little longer than was strictly necessary. Khaavorn gave them a sharp look, but held his tongue. Then they were off, following the rest of Khaavorn's chariots up the slope on a curving course that carried them behind a mass of foot soldiers now appearing at the crest.

Many of those, Valdar noted, were men of Riodheg's ally Taalorg, King of Ehrein. They weren't all dark and hawk-faced; the conquering Escquahar had intermarried with the natives of that island, and ruddy complexions and blunt features were common in their ranks. But if the Escquahar blood had been diluted, their tradition of archery had not. These men bore wooden self-bows, longer than the recurved composite bows of the East, and wore the traditional stone wristguards the Escquahar had brought from Ivaerisa. Stiffening their ranks were Riodheg's own men—retainers of the warrior class, the more affluent ones armed with ordinary-quality bronze axes, the less so only with spears.

The imperial infantry approached, charging uphill in their eagerness to come to grips before the Dovnaan chariot horses could recover from the battle they'd just fought, to counterattack at full tilt. As Valdar had surmised, they were unarmored men, mostly from the islands to the north and east of Schaerisa, including a number of slingers whose tiny projectiles—usually pebbles, sometimes lead—could punch a neat round hole through a human forehead. They were in loose order now, but Vaelsaru had trained them to close up quickly into the tightly packed, spear-bristling mass that even trained chariot horses were reluctant to crash into.

Riodheg had tried to inculcate the concept of disciplined fire in his war bands. The bowmen from Ehrein waited until the imperials were well within range, then loosed their long shafts in something like unison, shredding the oncoming mass. This gave the imperials even more impetus to cover the remaining ground. The slingers had time to release only a few of their deadly missiles before the two bodies of men crashed together in a roar of shouts that were soon joined by screams of pain as spears stabbed and axes rose and fell.

From the vantage afforded by their chariots, Khaavorn and Valdar overlooked the battlefield. "Their chariots are closing in," Khaavorn yelled above the din. "They want to take our footmen on the flanks. I won't lead my own chariots out into the open to meet them—they can outmaneuver us. I'll just shield the flanks."

"Right!" Valdar shouted back. "We should go and—"

"What's this 'we'?" laughed Khaavorn. "You'll stay here. And no back talk," he added as Valdar flushed and began to open his mouth to respond to what could, in their culture, be construed as an imputation of cowardice. "If Nyrthim sent you and Andonre here, it must be important that you're here—and alive. So you're too valuable to be risked." He grinned at Valdar's unconcealed frustration. "Look on the bright side: if they break through, you can die trying to protect Andonre." With a brusque command to his charioteer, he was off to lead his chariots to fend off the lighter imperial ones starting to close in like swooping birds of prey.

In the end, they had only a little skirmishing to do, for the imperial infantry began to give ground, a little at a time at first, then breaking into headlong retreat. Once the two bodies of fighters separated, the archers from Ehrein began to drive their arrows downslope again, with murderous effect.

If Khaavorn had been able to launch his chariots at the retreating men, it would have been a slaughter. But the imperial chariots, in a reversal of roles, covered the withdrawal. Presently the Kynaeraan riders approached, hovering around the left flank and plying their bows. Above and beyond the actual damage they did, their appearance set the Dovnaan to muttering uncertainly, never having seen such a thing before. So the pursuit was left to the foot soldiers, and soon flagged. As soon as it did, the imperial chariots broke off the engagement and joined the withdrawal, leaving the Kynaeraan to skirmish with any persistent pursuers.

Valdar drove his chariot to the left flank, and sought out Khaavorn. The Dovnaan chariot warriors were roaring with triumph—justifiably so, for they'd inflicted at least three casualties for every man they'd lost. The infantry had likewise recovered enough of their wind to shout obscene taunts at the imperials' backs.

As Valdar rode up to join Khaavorn, he saw that the Kynaeraan were beginning to peel off and withdraw, as the Dovnaan were clearly too occupied with exchanging boasts to present a further threat. He gazed across the field at those horsemen . . . and one in particular.

"Khaavorn, do you see that rider there—the leader?"

"Yes," said Khaavorn, following the younger man's pointing finger. He shook his head. "Outlandish! Sitting on horses! But what can you expect? Angmanu-damned foreigners . . ."

"I know that man," said Valdar. "His name is Rupaeranz. He saved my life . . . and Andonre's, and Nyrthim's. I think you'd like him if you got to know him."

"I can see that this is going to be a *very* long story." Khaavorn sighed, and decided not to let complexity spoil the good mood that battle had—as usual—left him in. "Ah, well. Riodheg will be here tonight with the rest of the army. I imagine we'll take our stand here on this ridge and wait for Vaelsaru."

"And Tarhynda," said Andonre quietly. "He and Vaedorie are with the army—and Norkhaari has joined them."

"And," Valdar added, "he's brought a whole unit of *Nartiya Ozhre*, armed for war."

"You don't say? Well, so much the better. What a glorious last stand this will be! In the meantime, Valdar, you'll have a chance to tell your tale to the High King tonight. And don't hold back! You know what I always say: never let the facts ruin a good story."

CHAPTER TWENTY-ONE

Riodheg rode his chariot into Khaavorn's torchlit camp to a tumult of cheering.

The High King already knew, from a runner sent by Khaavorn, of his advance guard's victory in the initial clash, and of the pair who had appeared so unexpectedly at the moment of that victory. So he wasn't shocked when Valdar bowed to him before Khaavorn's tent.

Valdar looked at the other chariots rolling in behind Riodheg's. The sub-kings of the high downs were there, and so were the High King's allies: Taalorg of Ehrein, and Kaailtraam of Fortrein, and . . . "Father!" he yelped.

Arkhuar of Dhulon gave an uncharacteristic grin.

His teeth gleamed against the travel-grimed darkness of his complexion and the silvered sable of his beard. With that coloring, and the slender build and elongated features he likewise inherited from the pioneering priests of the Old Empire, he was a contrast to the burly, ruddy-blond men who followed him. He was several years older than Riodheg, but stood straight in his chariot—still a form of prestige transportation in Dhulon rather than a tactical instrument, much as it had been in Lokhrein before Riodheg's reign. He stepped down from that chariot, a little more carefully than Valdar remembered, and embraced the son whom he'd thought dead.

"Father," Valdar finally said, "Wothorg is—"

"I know. Khaavorn told Riodheg, and Riodheg told me. So I know he died doing his duty as your retainer . . . and that you did your duty as his lord." For a few heartbeats, father and son were silent in the presence of their loss.

Riodheg alighted and greeted Khaavorn amid the cheers of his men. Then he turned to Valdar with a smile . . . which died as Andonre stepped from the shadows of the tent behind him. She lowered her head and said nothing.

"She came here with me willingly, nak'Udheg," Valdar said evenly. "She has renounced Norkhaari and the whole demon cult, and wishes a chance to make right what she has done. Besides, she has information you need to know. I ask you to hear her out."

"Very well. Let her join us in council." The High King's eyes gentled for a moment as they rested on his niece. Then he led the way into the tent, where stools had been set up in a circle. He sat down, followed by his allies and sub-kings and chieftains, some of them muttering darkly about the presence of a woman—especially *this* woman—at a war council.

"So, Khaavorn," Riodheg began without preamble, "what of the imperials?"

"What's left of their advance guard is still out there, encamped on the ridge to the south. They've probably sent runners to Vaelsaru, just as I did to you. We don't know how long it will take him to bring up the main imperial army."

"Then let's finish them off before he does!" exclaimed fiery young Ronedh nak'Maair, who had seen his father eviscerated by a demon in Riodheg's hall.

"No." Riodheg shook his head decisively. "It's already dusk, and our own main force is still arriving. A night attack, without preparation, would be an invitation to disaster. No, we'll wait here and prepare ourselves to receive Vaelsaru. And now, Valdar, tell us your tale."

Valdar told everything that had transpired since he and Nyrthim had parted from Khaavorn and Zhassu that night in The City. Contrary to Khaavorn's earlier admonition, and in defiance of long-established Dovnaan tradition, he supplied the story with no boastful improvements. But he left nothing out . . . with two important exceptions. From time to time, he turned to Andonre for confirmation and added details. The grumbling that greeted her first words soon subsided into a horrified silence.

"And so," Valdar concluded, "Nyrthim is still with the imperial army. He was vague about just exactly what he plans to do—you know how he is—but he clearly hopes to accomplish something involving Vaelsaru."

Riodheg barely seemed to be listening. "An armed unit of these *Nartiya Ozhre*," he mused. "Twenty of them . . ."

"I can vouch for what Valdar has told us about them, Uncle," said Khaavorn grimly. "I encountered some when I tried to steal Zhotiyu away. I'm not ashamed to say I ran." He glared around the circle. "Let any man here face them himself, and *then* call me coward!"

Valdar met the High King's dark, brooding eyes, and in that exchange of glances a great deal was said without being spoken. One of the things Valdar had withheld was the truth Nyrthim had made him swear never to reveal. Now he knew that the High King shared with him the burden of that forbidden knowledge. Riodheg knew what the Shrine of the Lake was, and what had once happened there, and why Tarhynda wanted it. And he knew that Valdar knew it.

Valdar's *other* omission had been the secret history behind the secret history, which Tarhynda had revealed to them. He wasn't about to share that with anyone, not even Riodheg, save on Nyrthim's instructions.

The moment ended, and Riodheg leaned back, stroking his beard thoughtfully. "We must make preparations. As we rode in, I noticed that this ridgeline is really a double ridge, with a dip between them." He ruminated a couple of seconds more. "I want all of you to choose some of your men—strong men, willing workers. And we need to gather tools that can be used for digging."

"*Digging?*" Kaailtraam of Fortrein scratched his shaggy head, disturbing one of its small residents, and spoke in the distinctively accented Dovnaan of his northern people. "What has digging got to do with battle?"

"I'll explain later. Plenty of time for that when the men and tools have been assembled. But for now, I must ask you all to excuse me and Valdar. It is important that I speak with him alone." Riodheg emphasized the last word, and glanced at Arkhuar as he said it.

"I think, nak'Udheg," said Valdar quietly, scandalizing the gathering anew, "that your niece should also remain."

Riodheg hesitated less than a second. "I agree." He stood up, and the others followed suit, filing out wearing perplexed looks.

"She knows too," said Valdar as soon as they were alone.

"Yes, of course she does." Neither man felt any need or inclination to say what it was they all knew. But Riodheg smiled thinly. "That was rather good, the version you gave them: that Vaedorie and Norkhaari simply want to sacrifice Zhotiyu to summon more demonic reinforcements."

"It's true, as far as it goes." Valdar's smile held as little humor as the High King's.

"And it convinced them of the sincerity of her change of heart." Riodheg turned to Andonre. "It convinces *me* as well."

"Thank you, nak'Udheg," she said in a small voice.

The High King's face grew stern. "But the fact remains that you have much to answer for. Are you truly willing to do whatever is needed to atone for your actions, and undo the foulness you have helped admit into the world?"

"Yes! I won't lie to you: I hope my expiation won't require me to betray Vaelsaru any more than I've already betrayed him. But Nyrthim assured me that it would not. I also hope that my son—who bears none of my guilt—can somehow be spared."

"Very well. If you are present at the Shrine of the Lake when they attempt to open the gateway, do you think you can prevent it? Or, at least, hinder them?"

"I don't know. I can try. But with Norkhaari herself there, and Vaedorie, who is also powerful, and Tarhynda . . ."

"You will have help." Riodheg turned back to Valdar. "No one else in the camp knows this—not even Khaavorn, who was deep in our counsels before we left Lokhrein—but Minuren is here in Arnoriysa. She departed in secret shortly before the army, and should by now have reached the Shrine of the Lake, where she will remain."

"She can't stop them," said Andonre bleakly. "Her powers are of another sort."

"But she may be able to strengthen you. Valdar, this is my command: you will take no part in the coming battle. Instead, you will depart at first light with Andonre, and—"

Valdar was so appalled that he forgot himself and interrupted the High King. "But nak'Udheg—"

"Silence! Do you think there is no more at stake here than your fame as a warrior? You are to take Andonre to the Shrine of the Lake—it's not far from here, and I'll give you the directions. You can easily reach it before nightfall tomorrow."

Valdar's face grew hot, his eyes burned, and panic

struck as he realized he was about to *cry*. "But . . . but they'll think I'm a coward!"

"No one but a fool would ever think that of you. And life is too short to spend it worrying about the opinions of fools." The sonless High King grasped Valdar by the shoulders, and his eyes held an expression the younger man found hard to interpret. "I know you have courage, Valdar. But I have plenty of men with courage. You also have something I'm afraid isn't quite so common among my followers: intelligence. Nyrthim always saw that in you, and that is what I need now. At the Shrine of the Lake, I won't be there to guide you. You must think for yourself, and take whatever action seems indicated. There is no one else I can trust with this. Will you do it?"

Valdar swallowed hard. "Whatever you command, nak'Udheg."

A messenger from the advance guard had arrived just as the main army was setting up camp, when it was too late to press on. Vaelsaru had immediately been summoned to the great tent raised beside the imperial wagon, into which he'd never been admitted.

Now he stood rigid, sweating under the glare of those strange golden eyes.

The Emperor had been in a state of extreme agitation since the previous night—the night of Andonre's kidnapping—and had commanded an immediate forced march, commencing at daybreak. Vaelsaru and Siytta had sought to make their imperial master understand that an army of this unprecedented size could not simply leap into action with the rapidity of a small war band. Tarhynda had paced and snarled,

seething with impatience, his usual studied suavity
only a memory, until they had managed to get the
great unwieldy host lurching northward in something
resembling good order.

The Emperor had recovered his self-possession,
which Vaelsaru now knew for the sham it was. Tarhynda
sat in silence, an image of cold, contained fury, while
Vaedorie raved and Malsara smirked and Vaelsaru had
to stand and take it. The general decided he'd liked
Tarhynda's earlier frenzy better.

"We have been humiliated!" the Empress shrieked.
"In their first clash with the Dovnaan yokels, your
vaunted warriors turned tail and ran like rabbits! How
do you explain your failure?"

Vaelsaru stared straight ahead and attempted to
address Tarhynda directly. "Lord, I was ordered to
send the advance guard ahead at the best speed men
and horses could stand, with no consideration but
overtaking and capturing the kidnappers. Ordinary
precautions were therefore ignored, and the advance
guard was caught off balance when—"

"Enough of your excuses!" hissed Malsara, pointing a theatrical finger at him. "Do not blame the
Emperor's instructions for your incompetence. The
recklessness of the advance guard was due to your
own eagerness to recapture your wife, which made
you forget your duty."

"Yes!" Vaedorie's eyes now held a feverish glint.
"You are a traitor! You seek to usurp the Emperor's
place!"

"Lord, I have never—"

Vaedorie slapped his cheek with all her strength.
"Quiet, traitor!" she yelled, all semblance of self-control

gone. "You will be flayed, and castrated, and then impaled while still living! I myself will—" As she ranted on, Vaelsaru held himself immobile, with an effort that made his jaw ache and his joints creak. His lack of response seemed to infuriate Vaedorie even more. She drew back her arm to slap him again.

"Enough." Tarhynda spoke the word quietly, but Vaedorie froze in mid-swing and instant silence enveloped the tent. He stood up—or, it seemed to Vaelsaru, *uncoiled*—and drew himself up to his full height. "You have failed us, Lord Vaelsaru. You have betrayed your oath. You can no longer be entrusted with our armies in this important—this *very* important—campaign. You are relieved of command. You will . . . remain in custody and be returned to The City later, for a final disposition of your case." The Emperor said this last as though it was a matter of little further moment. "In the meantime," he continued, still in the tone of an afterthought, "a new commander must be appointed." He looked around absently, like one who had misplaced something. His eyes finally settled on Malsara. "Oh, yes; Lord Chamberlain, you will now command our army."

In any other circumstances, Vaelsaru would have laughed aloud at the expression on the eunuch's face. Even Vaedorie looked taken aback. At length, Malsara found his tongue.

"Ah . . . that is . . . I cannot possibly carry out this command, lord. I'm no military man—"

"Strictly speaking, you're no sort of a *man* at all," said Tarhynda with automatic cruelty. He cut off Malsara's renewed stammering with a brusque gesture. "No matter. You will have Siytta to advise you. As regards administration of the army, you will follow his advice. In effect, you will delegate all such matters to him. The important thing is, he'll be acting under your authority—the authority of one who can be expected to execute our commands without argument." The great amber eyes held the quivering eunuch the way those of a mongoose hold a snake. "At this juncture, what we require is not military genius but obedience. *Absolute, instant, unquestioning obedience!* Do we make ourselves clear?"

"Yes, lord," mumbled Malsara, groveling.

Tarhynda's artificial smile returned. "At any rate, the army would never follow you into mutiny even if you felt so inclined." He clapped his hands, and the captain of the guard entered. "Lord Vaelsaru is under arrest. Take his sword, then escort him to his tent and post a guard around it."

The captain went pale. He was human, of course—the *Nartiya Ozhre* were still encamped apart from the rest of the army. And even though he was one of the Achaysei troops the Emperor had brought from The City, he knew what the name Vaelsaru meant. He started to open his mouth to question the order, but a glance at the Emperor's face brought his jaws together with a click. He timidly extended a hand, into which Vaelsaru placed his sword. Then, with an inaudible murmur, he gestured to Vaelsaru to precede him. Still standing as straight as a spear shaft, the general departed.

"Leave us," Tarhynda commanded Malsara. With a motion unpleasantly suggestive of a beetle, the eunuch scuttled out. As soon as he was gone, Norkhaari stepped forth from the shadows of the tent's hangings. Her expression was eloquent of skepticism.

"Do you truly think the army will follow *that*?"

"At first, they'll be too stunned to do anything else." Tarhynda's unconcern was sublime. "By the time their resentment crystallizes into resistance, it will no longer matter."

"Then you really do mean to—?"

"Yes." Tarhynda seated himself with the inhuman fluidity he no longer needed to disguise. "By the time we rendezvous with the remanent of the advance guard late tomorrow, we'll be close enough to the gateway known as the Shrine of the Lake. We can depart as soon as the battle commences, the following morning."

"So the battle itself will be a mere distraction, while we slip away?"

"Largely so. It would still be preferable for our army to win—which it will, of course."

"Under Malsara's leadership?" Even in the presence of the Minister of Rhaeie, Norkhaari danced along the edge of mischievousness. Vaedorie, she knew, hated her for her ability to so dare. But then, Vaedorie hated everyone.

Tarhynda brushed the point aside. "With a competent military craftsman like Siytta effectively in command, and given our numerical superiority, I foresee no problems. And if any do arise, the *Nartiya Ozhre* should prove decisive. They will be physically irresistible, in addition to the sheer terror they will arouse."

Vaedorie spoke avidly. "*You* would arouse even greater terror, in your true shape! Swooping down from the skies, you would—"

"I would spread just as much panic in our army as in theirs! Besides, I have no time to waste on

such pointless antics. We must leave for the Shrine
of the Lake as soon as we can do so unnoticed. It
is unfortunate that we must travel by conventional
means, but I cannot carry the two of you and the
boy in my true form. I will, however, assume that
form in due course. Now, leave me. I must con-
serve my strength, for the transformation requires
much energy."

When they reached Vaelsaru's tent, the guard
captain finally overcame his embarrassment and guilt
enough to speak.

"Uh . . . Lord Vaelsaru, I hope you realize this
duty gives me no pleasure. I wish with all my heart
that—"

"Never mind that!" Vaelsaru halted and turned
to face him, and the captain was at once under the
command of his nominal prisoner. "Just remember
the oath you've sworn to the Emperor, as I have. I
would not lead you—or your men, for whom you are
responsible—into a breach of that oath. I bear you
no resentment for doing as you are bound to do."
Without giving the captain a chance to say anything
he might regret later, Vaelsaru turned on his heel and
entered the tent.

It was a smaller tent than the one he and Andonre
had occupied. That one, he was assured, had been
wrecked in the course of the fight in which Andonre
had been abducted. He'd had trouble understanding
why that should be so, but he wasn't prepared to
pursue the point. That tent would only have reminded
him of she with whom he had shared it. He sank
down on his stool and let the numbness in which

he had been moving gradually seep out of his soul, leaving him free to feel the pain of everything that had happened to him.

"Lord Vaelsaru?"

With the blinding speed of combat-whetted reflexes, Vaelsaru was on his feet, whirling in the direction from which the voice—Dovnaan-accented, as he knew so well—had come, and reaching for the sword that wasn't there.

The man who stepped from the shadows of the tent's far corner was clearly old, with his long gray beard and lined face, but his tentative movements seemed due to exhaustion rather than to decrepitude. He wore nondescript clothes, not unlike those of many of the army's followers. Vaelsaru was sure he'd seen him somewhere; it would be difficult to forget those deeply shadowed, dark brown eyes.

"Who are you?" Vaelsaru demanded. "How did you get in here? Speak quickly, before I call for my guards!"

"Your jailers, you mean?" The man chuckled softly, as Vaelsaru stared. "My name is Nyrthim. Andonre may have mentioned me to you, as I have known her from birth. As for how I gained access to your tent . . . well, I am a member of the Order of the Nezhiy, and we have certain ways of doing things—ways which, for any number of reasons, we don't use very often." Vaelsaru's stare turned into a gape. The intruder seemed not to notice, but resumed with an air of getting down to business. "I have a great many things to say to you, Lord Vaelsaru, most of which you are not going to like to hear. So let me begin with the one thing you *will* like: your wife is alive and safe."

Vaelsaru forced control on the whirling vortex of his emotions. "How do you know this?"

"I know it because I was one of those who enabled her to escape."

"What do you mean, 'escape'?" Vaelsaru heard himself demand, from the depths of his shock.

"I think you know. I tried to do the same for your son, but in that I failed. He, too, is still alive—but he won't be for long. He is back in the clutches of the evil from which Andonre has escaped—reluctantly, for she loves you, and you serve that evil unwittingly. Or, rather, you have done so until tonight."

"What are you talking about?" Even to Vaelsaru's own ears, his voice sounded feeble. And afterwards, he would come to recognize that the realization had been gestating in his mind for so long, trapped within his inability to admit his doubts and suspicions to himself, that it had needed only Nyrthim's midwifery to bring it into horrifying birth.

"May I sit down?" Taking assent for granted, Nyrthim lowered himself onto a chest. "I'm not as young as I once was, and I've taken some rough handling of late . . . and I'm somewhat used up at the moment. And this is going to take a while."

CHAPTER TWENTY-TWO

"But why can the *Nartiya Ozhre* not vanish from sight, as they have the ability to do, and simply appear in the midst of the Dovnaan?" demanded Malsara with the eagerness of a civilian who thinks he's had a brilliant military insight. He gestured northward at the rise on which Riodheg's army awaited.

Siytta kept his mouth shut and his face expressionless. He'd had a lot of practice at that since the previous night, when he'd been awakened to hear the news he had at first thought must surely be someone's bad idea of a joke.

Tarhynda lifted a languid eyebrow and turned from his contemplation of his army's arrival behind the ridge on which the three of them stood in the afternoon sun.

"There are several reasons," he explained with ostentatious care. "For example, they would still have to cross the distance between the two ridges, and there are too many ways to detect them—their smell, for example, which invisibility does nothing to suppress. Riodheg has people who know this, and you can be sure he'll have dogs out. But more importantly, we want the Dovnaan to see them coming, and know despair. Is this quite clear?" The amber eyes narrowed, and took on the look that seemed inhuman. Malsara, unlike Siytta, knew that look was not deceptive.

"Yes, lord," the eunuch mumbled.

"Then prepare to carry out our original instructions in the morning. We leave the details to the two of you." Tarhynda swirled his cloak around him against the autumn chill and strode off down the slope. Malsara scurried after him. Siytta brought up the rear, walking slowly, his body held as stiffly controlled as his features.

To the northwest, where Riodheg's directions took them, the gently rolling landscape became less gentle, rising into the hills at the heart of peninsular Arnoriysa. Still further in the same direction, Valdar knew, lay the coast, and the westernmost cape with its standing stones, beyond which was nothing but the illimitable watery waste of the Outer Sea.

But he and Andonre weren't going that far.

"Keep the rising sun behind your right shoulder," Riodheg had told him the previous night, *"until you see a ridge ahead that looks like a reclining man."* The High King had smiled. *"The peasants here in Arnoriysa call that man 'Haerne' without having the*

slightest idea who he was or what he did. Go under his 'chin'—it's a notch in the ridge—and follow the path to the right. You'll have to leave your chariot behind."

They had traveled all day, stopping only to eat the food they'd brought. The going had gotten rougher and rougher, and Valdar's attention had been monopolized by the requirements of maneuvering the chariot over the increasingly broken country. That was one of the reasons his hand had stopped occasionally seeking hers, as it had in the earlier stages of the journey. The other reason was that she'd grown more and more withdrawn as they neared the place where her fate and that of her son would be decided.

At last the unmistakable silhouette had appeared, looming over the autumnal trees ahead. By the time they had reached the notch, trying to ride the chariot had become more trouble than it was worth. Valdar had tethered the horses with the long ropes he had brought for the purpose, giving them a wide grazing radius. He and Andonre had then proceeded on foot, passing moss-covered rocks split open over the ages by the growth of gnarled trees, scrambling along a trail that was barely discernible beneath the carpet of fallen leaves.

Now it was late afternoon, and they emerged from the trees into a valley like a shallow bowl, filled in its center with water.

The lake lay serene in its timelessness, as though belonging to another world, remote from the one they'd left. Valdar remembered Tarhynda's talk of multiple worlds, and for a flesh-crawling moment wondered if they had strayed into a world where humanity had never existed. But then he saw that there was one work of man visible. On an island in the center of the lake was a circle of standing stones, not unlike the one atop the hill of Khlaastom.

So quietly as to barely disturb the stillness of the approaching twilight, a light-green-robed figure appeared, walking along the lakeshore.

"So, Valdar, you are alive," said Minuren. "You, Andonre, I have been somehow expecting."

Valdar bowed low. Andonre fell to her knees and lowered her head.

"Holy lady," Valdar began, "she has left the demon cult willingly, even—"

Minuren raised a hand. "Let her speak for herself."

Andonre spoke without raising her head. "I have lost my husband and my son. All I have left is the possibility of helping to thwart Norkhaari and Vaedorie and . . . that which they have summoned."

"Summoned with *your* assistance."

Andonre raised her eyes, and met Minuren's. "I cannot deny it. I know I can't expect your forgiveness. But if you want to stop them from doing what they intend to do here at the Shrine of the Lake—and I think you know what that is—then I'm all you've got!"

"Why should I believe that you wish to stop them?"

"Because it's my son that they plan to use as a sacrifice, to tear open this gateway between the worlds! I know now that Norkhaari lied to me. If you want to call me a fool for being taken in by her, go ahead. You'll be telling me nothing I don't already know."

"Norkhaari is with Tarhynda and his army, not far

southeast of here," Valdar put in quietly. "Riodheg is awaiting them—we left his camp this morning. He'll try to hold them there. In the meantime, he sent us here, just in case. . . ." There seemed no need to finish the sentence.

"What about Nyrthim?" asked the High Priestess urgently.

"He lives—or at least he did night before last, when I parted from him in the imperial camp. He's still among them."

"Clearly, you two have a great deal to tell me. But it is almost dusk, and getting chilly—or so it seems at my age. So let us seek shelter." Minuren turned to the left with her usual stateliness and led the way. Lacking any viable options, they followed.

They walked around a boulder that extended almost to the water. Beyond, a whole new stretch of lakeshore was revealed, with the wooded hill slopes behind it. A makeshift raft was drawn up on the shingle. At the edge of the woods stood a crude but serviceable hut. To the side, an old but strong-looking man was turning fish over a fire. He turned and regarded them gravely from beneath shaggy brows that, like his beard, were startlingly white against his leathery, wrinkled skin.

Valdar had once been to the sanctuary of Khlaastom, and Andonre was very familiar with it. So they both recognized the boatman.

"Nechtan accompanied me here, and built the raft and the hut," Minuren explained. It was the first time either of them had heard the name of the old man, who had served at Khlaastom for as long as anyone they knew could remember. "Otherwise, I am alone. And now, you must be famished from your journey.

After we eat, you must tell me your tales. But tell me at once, Valdar: when will the battle be joined?"

"The earliest the imperials could have made contact with Riodheg was sometime this afternoon. They're probably there by now, if Tarhynda is in a hurry—"

"He is," Minuren interjected grimly.

"—but they'll be tired from their march, and it's getting dark. They'll probably attack in the morning."

"Then we have little time. I fear there'll be little sleep for any of us tonight."

It was several hours after dark when Nyrthim came to join Rupaeranz and Zhassu at the campfire beside the latter's stacked wine amphorae.

A liberal intake of that wine clearly hadn't cheered them up. Zhassu, who knew the battle was to be joined on the morrow, was in the grip of jitters. And Rupaeranz wore the same unreadable expression he'd shown the world since the change of command had been announced to a thunderstruck army.

"Zhassu," the sorcerer began with no preliminaries, least of all an explanation of what had kept him, "I have a special mission for you. Sometime before dawn, when it's still dark and the sentries are at their weariest, you will slip out of this camp and cross over to Riodheg's army."

The wine merchant gulped. If the prospect of the coming battle had made him nervous before, the notion of facing it in the ranks of the probable losers clearly terrified him.

"But," he managed, "surely you will need me here!"

"I will almost certainly not *be* here." Nyrthim

offered no further enlightenment as to his probable whereabouts. "And I cannot be with Riodheg either. He's going to need someone with some of the Order's knowledge of how to deal with demons."

"But I'm only a—"

"Yes, I know. But you're all I have. Also, I have a message for you to convey to Riodheg." Nyrthim turned to Rupaeranz, whom he studied covertly. The mercenary showed no sign of having heard the conversation. He was sitting, contained within himself, moving only to the extent of occasionally raising his eyes skyward to look at the stars. Then, as the sorcerer watched, he rose with the hair-trigger suddenness that betokened one of his impulsive decisions.

"My oath was to Lord Vaelsaru," he announced with the air of one who has found the key to a philosophical dilemma. "Not to Tarhynda, and certainly not to this dried-up gelding he's put in command of his warriors! I will lead my men back to our tribe's pasturelands."

"Will the imperials let you go?" asked Zhassu doubtfully.

"I'd like to see them catch us! Anyway, they'll be too busy at dawn to even try." The nomad's tone softened. "I was getting sick of these western lands anyway. Too damp. And all these hills and trees closing you in! I miss the big sky."

Nyrthim studied Rupaeranz narrowly. The Kynaeraan's mental universe contained no such concept as loyalty to an abstraction like the Empire. He had taken Vaelsaru as his chieftain. Now that Vaelsaru was not in command of the imperial army, Rupaeranz no longer felt himself part of that army.

"You realize," said Nyrthim carefully, "that Vaelsaru still lives. To my knowledge, nothing has released you from your oath."

The mercenary's brow furrowed with perplexity. "But he's a prisoner. I can do nothing for him."

"You never know what's going to happen," was Nyrthim's gnomic observation. He met Rupaeranz' eyes and held them. "I ask you to wait. Don't leave at dawn. Remain for the battle. I think you'll find that an opportunity may arise to help Vaelsaru after all."

Rupaeranz' eyes narrowed. "You're not telling everything you know."

"Does that surprise you?"

"In your case, not at all." The mercenary's sour expression cleared. "Oh, all right. I'll do as you ask. It ought to be quite a battle, anyway!"

"So it is. And I'm going to surprise you by telling all, for once. You'll need to know. And, Zhassu, you need to hear this too. But none of the Dovnaan must hear it, except Riodheg himself. . . ."

Dawn had not yet colored the eastern horizon, but Khaavorn was making his rounds with his brothers, inspecting the horses and testing the alertness of the sentries.

He'd been having trouble sleeping anyway, for a variety of reasons—not the least of which was perplexity as to what had become of Valdar and Andonre.

His last sight of them had been the previous night, after their private conversation with Riodheg. They'd left the High King's tent looking subdued, and he had decided to wait until morning to try and get anything out of them. But by the time he had awakened, they were nowhere to be found.

He'd finally sought out his uncle and inquired. Riodheg had been less than informative. "They are both off, about my business," he'd said in what Khaavorn had recognized as his subject-closing tone.

Well, Khaavorn told himself as he looked out into the darkness at the sea of imperial campfires on the opposite ridge, *Valdar will* have *to show up soon, if he wants to be in time for the battle. They'll attack in the morning.*

A commotion broke his train of thought. Two of the advance sentries—the ones out with the dogs— approached in the flickering light of the campfires and the torches. Between them, they half-led and half-dragged a shorter figure. Seeing Khaavorn, they flung their burden at his feet.

"We caught this one coming across the field, nak'Moreg. He asked to see you. Do you want to listen to him, before we kill him?"

"A spy!" snarled Akhraworn, stepping forward and hefting his axe.

"Wait." Khaavorn raised up the exhausted figure—he hadn't really been roughed up to excess—and held a torch to his face. "Zhassu!"

"Thank Rhaeie!" gasped the wine merchant.

"I never *did* trust that foreigner," muttered Akhraworn.

"Shut up, Akhraworn. Zhassu, what are you doing here?"

"The Nezh sent me. He still lives—"

"Yes, we know. Valdar told us."

"Ah, so he and the Lady Andonre are here!"

Khaavorn's face fell. "Well, they *were* here. But they've been gone all day. The High King sent them off somewhere."

"I see." Zhassu's expressive features lit up with understanding . . . and then immediately clamped down, as though shutting in an insight he knew must not be shared. "Well, anyway, I must see the High King. I have news. Since Valdar departed, Tarhynda has dismissed Vaelsaru and put the chamberlain of the palace in command of the army."

"That capon?" exploded Khaavorn with a guffaw, remembering Malsara from his time in The City.

"Well," smiled Khaaradh, "this sounds like good news."

"So it does," said Akhraworn sourly. Agreeing obviously took a lot out of him.

Zhassu looked from one of the Dovnaan to another. "Ah, but did Valdar tell you about the 'bodyguards' Tarhynda brought from The City?"

"He did." Khaavorn's eyes and Zhassu's met in shared memory of the night when they'd faced the *Nartiya Ozhre* in the propylon of Andonre's villa.

The wine merchant heaved himself painfully to his feet, staggering with weariness. "You must take me to the High King. I bring information from the Nezh about what the imperials plan for tomorrow. Also, I have certain knowledge that he may find useful in dealing with the *Nartiya Ozhre*."

"I *knew* it!" Khaaradh said with a grin. "I remember what you were saying to me, that day in the High King's hall before the demon appeared."

"Merely certain things the Nezh charged me to convey," said Zhassu hastily. "Nothing more."

"Well, anyway," said Khaavorn, taking the merchant by the arm and leading him off, "my uncle will certainly want to see you. So will Valdar, whenever he gets back."

Zhassu halted and regarded the big Dovnaan steadily. "I probably have no business telling you this, Lord Khaavorn. But . . . I don't think Valdar is going to be coming back."

"What? Don't be silly! Valdar would never miss such a battle as this one promises to be."

"Oh, he'll be fighting, to be sure. But his battle is elsewhere. I believe that is why your High King sent him away: to fight that battle, on which all of our futures depend." Zhassu raised a hand as Khaavorn started to open his mouth. "No, lord. There are things I may not tell you . . . things you don't really want to know."

Khaavorn gave a wolfish bark of laughter. "You're probably right. It doesn't pay to know too much. Not that I'm in any danger of that, thank Dayu!" He gave Zhassu a slap on the back that almost sent the wine merchant sprawling, and led the way toward the High King's tent.

The chill mists of the autumn dawn still shrouded the landscape as the imperial army began to rumble into its attack formation.

That formation had been worked out well in advance—a fact which did not deter Malsara from asserting his authority by issuing a steady stream of redundant commands. Siytta, standing behind and to the left of the eunuch, stonily passed those commands on to runners who might have been more usefully employed.

He barely troubled to disguise his contempt. Malsara, who had been given no choice but to endure this half-barbarous soldier, contented himself with occasional venomous glares. Siytta didn't notice. He was observing the opposite slope as the rising mist revealed it. The Dovnaan were only just getting into position. *Not that they need to exert themselves*, he reflected bitterly with a part of his mind. *We'll be lucky to get the attack started before midafternoon.*

The rest of his mind was puzzling over what he'd seen at dawn.

It had only been a glimpse, really. Two chariots clattering off toward the northwest and vanishing into the mists beyond the imperial left flank. It had been too far, and too misty, to get a close look, but he could have sworn that there was a woman in each of them, with a smaller figure in one, while the other had been driven by a very tall man. There were few men so tall. In fact . . .

No! Siytta shook his head angrily. *It's none of my affair.*

Still, he found his eyes drawn toward the hills to the northwest, beyond and to the left of the ridge occupied by their enemies.

Then the mist began to lift in earnest, admitting shafts of sunlight and revealing blue sky. In the crystal-clear distance, Siytta thought he saw a bird.

But no, it was too huge to be a bird, at such a distance. And there was something about its shape, and the way its wings moved . . . something unnatural . . .

What was it Tavazhalava said he heard, in Lokhrein?

Unnoticed by Malsara, a strong shudder ran through Siytta.

No! Madness!

But he wished Tavazhalava were with the army instead of back at Castranaenom. He felt a sudden need to talk to Tavazhalava.

CHAPTER TWENTY-THREE

In a traditional battle array, the chariots went before the foot soldiers. That was out of the question now, given the peculiar nature of Tarhynda's personal guards. In order to accommodate them and make the best use of them, Vaelsaru had devised a unique formation—which everyone, especially Malsara, now went to great pains to call Tarhynda's invention.

Thus it was that Riodheg, as he watched the advancing imperial army, was reminded of a gigantic bull's head with its horns enveloping his own army's flanks. The *Nartiya Ozhre* were in the center—the bull's "forehead"—with masses of human infantry flanking them and backing them up. To the rear came Vaelsaru's elite guard unit in reserve. On the far left and right, where there was no stench of demons to panic their horses, were the chariots—the "horns." Somewhere, Riodheg was sure, those horse-riding archers from the eastern grasslands were deployed to swoop around and complete the anticipated rout.

"Nyrthim was right," he remarked to Zhassu, who stood beside his chariot. The wine merchant nodded jerkily, inarticulate with fear.

They watched from the second ridgeline. Riodheg's chariot was one of the relatively few—Khaaradh's was another—that would be used as a reserve this day. Otherwise, the Dovnaan would fight as a footbound hedgehog. The bulk of them were drawn up before him. He gazed over their heads and across the depression at the front ridge, where a thinner line of infantry was drawn up, with most of the Companions in the center under Khaavorn's command.

It had been a battle in itself, persuading those proud chariot warriors to fight on foot. He had managed it by assuring them that they would be occupying the place of honor, facing the demons—a task for the bravest of the brave. What he hadn't emphasized was that they were the only men he had who could—he hoped—be trusted to do what he planned for them to do. When he had told them what that was, their indignation had erupted anew. He'd finally had to compromise. It was a compromise that would cost the lives of many of those magnificent men. Riodheg's way would have kept them alive, and they would never have forgiven him for it.

Now it was up to Khaavorn.

"I still say it's ungentlemanly, having some foreign spy tell you in advance what your enemy is going to do," grumbled Akhraworn.

Khaavorn ignored him and gazed at the dark oncoming masses of the imperial army. Then he looked left and right, surveying his own line. The Companions were flanked by other reliable troops, notably Arkhuar's Dhulaan, who had a tradition of fighting on foot and a reputation for steadiness. They were backed up by archers from Ehrein. The Companions weren't. Some of them would have thought it dishonorable. Furthermore, it would have been pointless. Only by wild chance could an arrow find a vulnerable point on a demon.

He turned back to face the advancing imperials. The thunder of their tread and their shouts was louder now. Loudest of all was the soul-shaking roaring from the beings loping across the shallow valley directly toward him, looming over the human imperial troops who flanked them at a skittish distance.

He looked around at his men. Their line was motionless as the *Nartiya Ozhre* came closer and closer. But it was not really steadiness. It was the paralyzing grip of fear and horror which can instantly explode into panic. Many of them had seen the demon Norkhaari had summoned into Riodheg's hall, and all of them had heard of it. But these things were far worse.

Soon the demons were close enough to make out the awful details—the four arms with the massive weapons clutched in the lower pairs of hands, the slashing barbed tails, the hideous tusked faces—that Khaavorn, alone among the Dovnaan, had seen once before. He stared at them, and that night came

crowding back into his mind, from which he'd sought
to banish it.

*I've told everyone I'm not ashamed of having run
from them. But was I telling the truth?* With the
thought came a sudden rush of cleansing, purifying
fury. *You made me run like a coward, you vermin
of Angmanu!* All at once, Khaavorn bellowed with
laughter. As his brother and the other nearby men
stared openmouthed, he ran a few steps in front of
the line, turned, hitched up the kilt of his tunic, and
displayed his naked backside to the onrushing might
of the Empire.

The paralyzing spell was shattered. A gale of inspired
madness blew through the Companions, and their
laughter momentarily drowned out the roaring of the
demons. Grinning, Khaavorn rejoined the line and
hefted his shield and axe. The demon stench was now
washing over them, but they were beyond caring.

When the impact came, Khaavorn knew what it
must be like for soft bronze being beaten into an
axehead.

Riodheg had wanted them to turn tail when the
Nartiya Ozhre came within a certain distance of their
line. But to flee without striking a single blow would
have shamed them beyond endurance. In the end, the
High King had agreed that they could receive that
demonic charge, but made them swear by Dayu that
they would run on Khaavorn's command.

Afterwards, in private, he had made Khaavorn
swear not to let the slaughter last more than a few
seconds.

Now the Companions paid for their pride as the
warrior demons crashed into them, bringing their great

crude clubs and axes down with a superhuman force that smashed shields and the arms holding them, and continued on down to crush helmets and skulls. Other inhuman hands raked with razorlike claws, drawing showers of blood.

Khaavorn, knowing better than the others what he was in for, held his shield at an angle from which a massive axehead glanced. Remebering Zhassu's words, he thrust clumsily upward with his axe, seeking the demon's throat. He must have hurt it, for the *Nartiya Ozhre* bellowed and swung its tail around. Khaavorn ducked under that swing, which continued around and pulped the head of another man.

Well, came the weirdly calm thought, *I suppose honor is satisfied.*

"Run!" he thundered over the din. "In the High King's name, RUN!" And he suited the action to the word.

The Companions—more of them than he'd expected to be alive at this point, though Dayu knew they'd lost enough, and more than enough, in that brief moment of hell—obeyed with an alacrity he hadn't dared hope for. He shot quick glances to left and right. The flanking troops were also withdrawing, to the jeers of the human enemies they'd faced.

For an instant or two, the *Nartiya Ozhre* remained immobile. They were, Khaavorn remembered, not as intelligent as men, and the Companions' abrupt flight had bewildered them. But they soon came out of it, and sprang forward with the impossible quickness of their kind. Clearly, the Dovnaan would be overtaken before they could reach the second ridgeline. Roaring with anticipation, the demons raced into the saddlelike depression between the two ridges.

Their prey were almost within their reach when the first of them plunged through the concealed lattice-work of tree limbs that could support humans but not their own elephantine mass, and plunged into the pits Riodheg had ordered dug. Their bellowing rose to an earsplitting shriek as they fell onto the sharpened stakes. Not even the incredible toughness of their hides could prevent their own falling weight from impaling them on those sharp, fire-hardened points.

Most of the demons were not so impaled. They immediately began trying to scramble out of the pits, clambering over their dying fellows. But then the ones who'd been caught on the stakes began to die . . . and, in the manner of their kind, be consumed by intense flame at the moment of their death. And, as Riodheg had hoped, the ruddy hair that covered the living ones proved to be flammable. The shrieking rose to hellish volume, and the human infantry coming up behind the demons halted in consternation.

Riodheg gave a command. The men on the flank remained in hedgehog formation to meet the charge of the chariots closing in from left and right, but the center was to advance.

Khaavorn raised his axe, and the Companions and the others in the center poured down the slope with a deep-throated roar.

The afternoon stillness of the lake was only slightly disturbed by ripples as old Nechtan poled the raft out from the shore.

Valdar and Andonre clasped hands as they gazed

ahead at the little island with its circle of standing stones. Minuren noticed, but said nothing.

It wasn't far to the island, although Valdar could tell, peering down into the water, that it was deep. Soon the raft scraped up at the foot of the shrine, whose ancient stones were partially overgrown with moss. It was, Valdar thought, as though they had drifted backwards in time, to the days when the world was young. . . .

The quiet was invaded by a sound that shouldn't have been there—a sound like the beating of vast wings. Suddenly, although there were only a few clouds in the sky, they were in shadow.

Andonre drew a horrified breath. Valdar looked up at the insane shape that had occluded the sun. His mind reeled.

The thing out of madness descended with a thunder of wings, and a backblast that almost capsized the raft. Valdar grasped both of the women by the hand and led them splashing through the shallows to confront that which stood before the stone circle.

Tarhynda's true form stood erect on its hind legs like the *Nartiya Ozhre*, but the resemblance stopped there. It was even taller, and slenderer. Instead of a second pair of arms, it had the enormous batlike wings it was now folding in from their full thirty-foot span. Instead of the unpleasantly sparse hair of the lesser demon breeds, it boasted a full coat of fur, deep vermilion in color. And the face, though equipped with the usual repulsively protruding jaws, was somehow more human. In particular, the eyes were precisely the same shade of amber into which Valdar had gazed before.

But those jaws, as they opened in a smile, proved to have the usual double row of teeth, the front row equipped with fangs. And the being possessed the usual tail, with the barbed stinger whose effect Valdar knew so well.

Valdar motioned Andonre and Minuren behind him, and drew his sword.

"You can't perform a summoning yourself. You said so. You need humans for that." As he spoke, Valdar wondered if Tarhynda could utter a human language when wearing this body.

As it turned out, the *Nartiya Chora* did indeed possess organs of speech—but different organs from those of its human semblance, for the voice that emerged from those horrid jaws was unnaturally deep and resonant and at the same time dry. It was like a voice of hot ashes.

The discursiveness was still there, though.

"Actually, I can open the gate—activate it, if you will. And I now do so." The monster stepped aside so they could look into the stone circle. Valdar looked . . . and quickly looked away, for he instinctively knew that what he had glimpsed was not for human eyes, or at any rate not for human minds. It was as though unimaginably vast distances and volumes were somehow contained, swirling, within that circle of rough upright stones.

"However," the horrid voice continued inexorably, "you are quite correct, as far as you go. Only human sorcerers can perform the sacrificial ritual that will effect the actual summoning—which, at this gateway, is open-ended, if you catch my drift. And . . . here they are!" A wingtip flicked in the direction of the lakeshore, across the water.

Norkhaari and Vaedorie were emerging from the trail through the woods, looking somewhat the worse for hard traveling. Each of them held one wrist of the struggling little boy they were dragging.

"Zhotiyu!" cried Andonre.

Once again, Tarhynda's demon face proved itself capable of smiling.

"Remember my remarks about his efficacy as a sacrifice? It is for that reason that we have cut off his supply of the drug to which he has become accustomed; he is now in a highly stressed state, and has no defenses against pain, nothing to dull it. You may also recall that the effect is further enhanced if you, Andonre, his mother, have to watch the proceedings. The emotional feedback, as it were, applies even if you have to watch simply as a consequence of being stranded here." Without warning, Tarhynda thrust his wings out again and took to the air. As he soared over them, his tail lashed out and smashed the raft. Nechtan, with an agility beyond his years, leaped free.

From above came what Valdar assumed must be the equivalent of a laugh.

"You can, of course, cover your eyes, Andonre. Or look away. But I don't think you'll be able to. Do you?"

The nightmare shape swooped over to the shore and alighted behind the two women and their captive. Vaedorie drew forth a knife.

Andonre's screams rose to a crescendo, then subsided to a sobbing wail as she sank to the mud. Minuren embraced her, and began to whisper words in her ear.

Without pausing for conscious thought, Valdar thrust

his sword back through his belt and dived into the icy water. With frantic strokes, he began swimming for shore.

Nyrthim's head jerked up.

"It is time," he said to his companion.

"You're sure?"

"Yes. I can feel it."

"Very well." Vaelsaru turned to the captain of the guard and spoke to him in low tones. They departed the tent.

Alone, Nyrthim took on a preoccupied look. He was thinking back to his conversation with Tarhynda, and reflecting on the fact—a secret from *everyone* not a member of the Order, however trustworthy—that the Nezhiy knew more about what Tarhynda had characterized as "dimensions" than the demon-emperor had given them credit for.

Not that they used that term, of course. But when the need arose, they could move *sideways* in a manner that surely was just a different application of the same thing.

Normally, they could do so only for very short distances, and at an expenditure of effort that made it hardly worth the trouble except when nothing else would serve. But when a gateway—especially the unique gateway that was the Shrine of the Lake—was opened, they could *sense* that indescribable twisting of space. Sense it and *use* it.

The sorcerer's eyes glazed over.

If anyone had been present in the tent and watching, Nyrthim would have seemed to simply vanish from sight.

~   ~   ~

The chill of the water took Valdar's breath away. He paused in his desperate strokes to come up and gasp for breath. As he did, he caught a glimpse of the group of figures on the shore.

There was a strange confusion among them. The monstrous figure of Tarhynda was visibly agitated, and the two women were staring past Valdar at the island and pointing.

Treading water, Valdar turned his head and looked back the way he'd come.

In front of the stone circle, silhouetted against hell and in some manner barring the way into it, stood a trio of figures, their hands joined. In the center was Andonre. To her left was old Nechtan, standing tall and straight in a way that made him hard to recognize. To her right was—

"Nyrthim?" gasped Valdar, nearly taking in a gulp of water.

Off to the side Minuren was on her knees, motionless but somehow, Valdar sensed, lending the others a quiet, gentle strength.

Those others were equally unmoving, their features rigid in the grip of a great concentration.

And on the shore, Vaedorie was screaming incoherently, and Norkhaari was gesticulating frantically to Tarhynda, who boomed in his terrible voice, "DO IT!"

I do not understand, thought Valdar with a portion of his mind where time had slowed to a crawl. *But I know I must help, even if I die doing it.*

He struck out for shore again, breaking the water with powerful strokes. It required only a couple of those strokes before he felt the silt under his knees. He heaved himself to his feet and ran through the shallows toward the demon and the sorceresses, who were too fixated on what was happening on the island to notice him.

Vaedorie suddenly came out of that fixation. She grasped Zhotiyu by his lower jaw, bent his head back to expose the throat, and raised her knife.

Lunging the last few feet, Valdar gripped her rising wrist and flung her aside, sprawling. With his other arm, he encircled the boy's waist and pulled him away.

Tarhynda turned, eyes burning like molten gold, and uttered a shrieking bellow of hate. Simultaneously, he brought his tail around in a swing that Valdar saw at once he could not dodge. He pulled Zhotiyu under the shield of his body.

Then Vaedorie, who had gotten to her feet, sprang forward with a howl, knife raised, eyes empty of the last vestige of sanity. She ran at Valdar—straight into the path of that swooping tail.

The barb caught her on the back, ripping off strips of cloth and flesh in a spray of blood. She screamed, and her face cleared of madness . . . only to have it replaced by horror, for she knew what that barb held. With a wail of pain and ultimate despair, she sank to her knees.

Tarhynda looked momentarily nonplussed.

In that moment, Valdar whipped out his sword and dived forward, rolling up at the Great Demon's clawed feet. Grasping his sword two-handed, he thrust upward between the grotesquely overmuscled legs, into the crotch.

The sound was too vast and too intense to call a scream or a roar or any other human word. It was like a physical blow, and it sent Valdar rolling away, still gripping his sword, which came away covered with unnatural blood. He came to rest facing the water . . . and saw that the shrine was empty of anything but autumn air.

The Great Demon spread his wings and rose awkwardly into the air.

Norkhaari staggered forward. "Take me!" she shouted. "I have served you faithfully. I adore you. Take me!"

Tarhynda gave her a look too empty of feeling to be called cold. Then, in an unmistakably offhand way, as though it were an afterthought, he struck downward with a hand whose diamond-sharp, inches-long claws slashed open the front of her torso.

Norkhaari was dead before she had time to gather a scream. Her face wore a surprised expression as she stared at the jet of blood that burst from her open heart. Then she crumpled to the ground.

The Great Demon rose in a thunder of wings and, erratically it seemed, flew off to the east.

Valdar stumbled to his feet. Vaedorie was no longer capable of the screams that had torn her throat and speckled her lips with blood. She lay thrashing on the ground, bowels evacuated, muscles spasming so violently as to dislocate her joints, eyes empty of all but the agony and torment that coursed through her.

This is a human being, Valdar reminded himself. He raised his sword and brought it down with a whine of cloven air. The Empress' head rolled free of her body in a gush of blood.

The only sounds were Zhotiyu's wracking sobs and his mother's cries to him across the water.

Valdar looked in the direction of those cries. Minuren was holding Andonre and comforting her. Nyrthim was surveying the empty interior of the Shrine with interest. And Nechtan, again the bent old boatman, was matter-of-factly gathering up pieces of the broken raft.

The imperial chariots came swirling in again and again, tearing at Riodheg's flanks. But chariots—even the new, heavier ones—were only useful as shock weapons against the kind of disorganized infantry that had, until now, typified the western lands. Riodheg had taught his men to form a solid, spear-bristling mass into which horses had better sense than to charge at full tilt. And from behind that mass, a sleet of arrows blunted the charge. So the chariot warriors swept past in repeated caracoles, hurling javelins that drew blood but did not—yet—crumple the flanks.

In the center, it was a different story.

For Khaavorn, the universe had narrowed to a process of raising his axe, drawing a shrieking breath, bringing the axe down to slice through muscle and snap bones, and repeating the process in the teeth of exhaustion.

Not all the *Nartiya Ozhre* had perished in the pits, despite the efforts of the Dovnaan to push them back down with spears into an inferno they added to with bundles of kindling. Some few had avoided that fate and continued to lay swathes of slaughter around themselves everywhere they went.

Now Riodheg finally committed his chariot reserve, leading the charge down the slope into the melee.

Khaavorn saw his youngest brother ride down a demon, his horses' hooves smashing the being into a broken ruin even as its claws and teeth savaged them, ripping out great gobbets of horseflesh. Maddened, the tormented animals capsized the chariot. The charioteer was crushed, but Khaaradh rolled free of the wreck

"Little brother!" Khaavorn called out. Khaaradh heard him and turned, grinning, to wave . . . just as another demon appeared, and sprang for him in the way that was so manifestly impossible for beings of such mass.

Khaaradh got to his feet and raised his axe—he'd lost his shield—with a cry of defiance. Echoing that cry, Khaavorn sprang to his aid.

The demon swung a club like a bronze-bound tree trunk. Khaaradh was smashed aside like an angry child's broken toy. Khaavorn's frantic efforts to reach him only brought him within the range of that swinging club. It took him on the shield, knocking him off his feet and sending his axe spinning away.

As he tried to rise and clear his head, the *Nartiya Ozhre* loomed over him with club raised, blocking the sun.

Khaavorn prepared himself for death.

Nothing happened.

Khavorn looked up. The demon was standing in a kind of bewildered listlessness.

Then Khaavorn noticed, not far away, the incongruous figure of Zhassu. The wine merchant wore the same look of furious concentration Khaavorn had seen on Nyrthim's face that night in the tenements of The City, when another demon had fallen into the same kind of disorientation.

Khaavorn drew his sword. He remembered the vulnerable spot that Khaaradh (*Khaaradh!* his soul sobbed) had used in the High King's hall. He thrust upward at the demon's neck, and still further upward, under the jaw.

With a basso shriek, the demon toppled over backwards. Continuing to hold onto his sword, Khaavorn leaped up, wrapped his legs tightly around the monstrous torso. Oblivious of the reek in which his face was buried, he rode the demon as it crashed over. Then, with all his weight behind its pommel, he pushed the sword in and up until its point scraped against the inside of the demon's skull.

"Die! Die!" Khaavorn screamed as the demon convulsed under him. Even in his madness, he remembered to roll free before the devouring flame could do more than singe him. He lay still for a moment, drained of everything.

The battle had moved on. Khaavorn saw no more demons. He looked around for Zhassu.

The wine merchant hadn't moved fast enough. He lay on his back, his rib cage crushed by one of the falling demon's flailing arms.

"I never thought I could really do that," he breathed as Khaavorn knelt over him. The words brought a pink foam to his lips.

"Lie still. I have to go. But we'll come back for you, merchant."

"Of course you will, barbarian," Zhassu whispered with a tiny smile, and closed his eyes.

Khaavorn stood up. He went over to Khaaradh, and looked just long enough to confirm what he already knew. Without allowing himself to feel anything just yet, he retrieved his axe and returned to the killing.

"Do something!" shrieked Malsara. "The Emperor will have you flayed for your incompetence!"

Siytta kept his face impassive, and his attention on the battlefield. "Everything is being done according to plan, lord. The Emperor's plan, as you have frequently reminded us."

"Enough of your insolence! The plan was the traitor Vaelsaru's. That's it! He plotted from the first to betray us. He—"

"Actually," came a new voice, "I must admit the plan was mine."

They whirled around and gaped, Siytta with joy and Malsara with horror.

Vaelsaru stood, sword in hand, with his erstwhile jailers behind him. Behind them in a half-circle, Rupaeranz and his Kynaeraan mercenaries sat their horses with nocked arrows.

"Lord," began Siytta, "you're—"

"I'm resuming command, Siytta," Vaelsaru nodded.

For an instant, Malsara stood marbled in shock. Then he blinked, drew himself up, and spoke in a voice whose steadiness surprised Siytta.

"You condemn yourself of treason out of your own mouth. I demand obedience to the Emperor, to whom you have given your oath."

Vaelsau spoke in a voice all the men behind him could hear. "Oaths are binding only between men.

And the Emperor is a demon in the guise of a man! I declare him deposed. He was summoned into this world by a foul cult of demon worshipers led by the Empress—with your knowledge and connivance."

Malsara's defiance collapsed. "No!" he bleated. "It isn't true. I never wanted to do it. But Vaedorie made me! Vaedorie and that other bitch—"

Rupaeranz' bow twanged, and an arrow protruded from Malsara's scrawny throat. The name he had been about to pronounce—the name Nyrthim had made clear he could not be allowed to utter publicly—drowned in a gurgle of blood.

Vaelsaru spared the corpse a somber look, then turned to Siytta.

"Send out an emissary to Riodheg and offer a truce. I want no more casualties. The army must be intact, to do what must now be done."

"You mean . . . ?"

"Yes, Siytta. We're returning to The City. There must be a cleansing."

"But," asked Akhraworn plaintively as they walked across the corpse-strewn field in the appropriately bloody light of the setting sun, "what *happened*?"

Khaavorn could understand his bewilderment. Almost all of Riodheg's men shared it. The desperate battle's sudden end in a truce wasn't the way things were normally done.

"I'm sure Uncle Riodheg will explain everything to us," he replied absently. Most of his attention was focused on their search. It didn't last long. They soon found that which had been their younger brother.

They went to their knees. As eldest brother, Khaavorn

grasped the axe haft in both hands, raised the head up in front of his face, and touched his forehead to it. Akhraworn followed suit.

Their retainers lifted the body onto a crude stretcher. It would be taken away and solemnly burned. The bronze urn containing his ashes would be conveyed back to Lokhrein, where Theidre would soon be giving birth to a child that would never know its father. It would be placed in a wooden barrow on the high downs. The priests would assure everyone that Mother Rhaeie had taken Khaaradh nak'Moreg by the hand and led him into the Land Beyond, where there was no pain and no sickness and no hunger and no sorrow, where warriors fought in joy and were slain only to arise again in time for the night's feasting. Then the earth would be heaped over the barrow, and there would be one more mound among the mounds of the heroes.

But Khaavorn had more searching to do, before darkness fell. Akhraworn followed him, curious. He looked around until he saw the pathetic, broken body of Zhassu.

Khaavorn knelt beside it. He touched his axehead to his forehead once again, precisely as he had done before Khaaradh's remains.

"But," spluttered Akhraworn, scandalized, "that's how you pay honor to a fallen warrior of the Dovnaan!"

Khaavorn stood up slowly, and turned even more slowly to face him. "So it is," he agreed, very mildly. "And your point would be . . . ?"

Akhraworn swallowed. "Oh . . . nothing. Nothing at all." He hastily sought for something that required his presence elsewhere.

Khaavorn remained a heartbeat or two longer, then trudged back across the field that the sunset was painting even redder than all the spilled blood had already made it.

CHAPTER TWENTY-FOUR

The scribes had departed, bearing the draft of the treaty that ended the war on a *status quo antebellum* basis. Vaelsaru gazed over the rim of his wine cup at the tent's other two occupants and spoke with elaborate casualness, in the Dovnaan tongue he had learned from Andonre.

"I'm still not entirely clear about what happened to Tarhynda. I know you've told me that your man Valdar—to whom, by the way, I owe a debt I can never repay for returning my son to me—saw him in demon form, flying eastward. But . . . *why* did he leave while the battle was still raging?"

Riodheg and Nyrthim exchanged a quick glance, which Vaelsaru pretended not to notice.

"Who's to say?" the sorcerer rhetorically asked, spreading his hands. "But that's not the important thing, is it? We can guess where he is now."

"Yes." Vaelsaru's face clouded. "He'll have returned to The City, resumed his human form, and begun consolidating his position. Nobody there knows the truth."

"Which is why your duty requires you to return there," Riodheg nodded. "But can you fight him? He'll have had time to summon more demons."

Nyrthim cleared his throat. "Remember, only humans can do that. He still has the remaining members of the demon cult in The City, but they are mere underlings. At most, they'll probably be able to summon a few *Nartiya Zhere* for him, to keep his own people terrorized. They'll lack the capability to summon any more *Nartiya Ozhre* or any of the other really formidable breeds, let alone any of Tarhynda's fellow *Nartiya Chora*. The ones who counted were Vaedorie and Andonre." Seeing Vaelsaru's wince, the sorcerer addressed him directly. "The one's dead now, and you'll have the other at your side."

"Yes. Andonre has told me everything. She's also told me she's willing to do whatever she must to win my forgiveness."

"She means it," Nyrthim told him earnestly.

"I know she does. I also know Zhotiyu needs his mother—now more than ever. No one else will ever know of her role in all this." The general finished his wine and rose to his feet. "I must go. Much needs to be done before the army can decamp."

Riodheg also rose. "Will you be emperor?" he asked bluntly.

"Never, by Dayu! I'm just a soldier. Surely there must be someone, somewhere, who has a legitimate claim—some collateral relation of old Namapa. I'll find him, with Tavazhalava's help, and put the army at his service."

"Maybe you won't be emperor in name, but . . ." Riodheg smiled, very slightly and very briefly, then turned grave. "Tarhynda is the enemy of us all. If you wish, I'll send warriors with you to—"

"No. I'm sure the offer is well meant. But the Empire must put its own house in order."

Riodheg gave a nod of understanding. "Well, if ever you need help, you know where you can turn."

"Oh, he'll have help," said Nyrthim. "I've already told him I'm going with him"

"*What?*" Riodheg stared, thunderstruck.

Vaelsaru saw at once that the High King hadn't known. "Ah . . . and now, if you'll excuse me . . ." He made his embarrassed departure.

"Nyrthim," began Riodheg the instant he was gone, "what nonsense is this? I need you."

"No, you don't. With Norkhaari gone, there should be nothing requiring my presence in Lokhrein. And if anything of the sort should arise, you'll have Nechtan."

"Old Nechtan! Who would have ever guessed?" The High King's look grew accusing.

"Well," Nyrthim protested, "I never actually *said* I was the last member of the Order left in Lokhrein."

"No, you just let everyone go on thinking so. But, Nyrthim, you're not just a Nezh. You are—or were—my chief adviser. I still need your counsel."

"Even if that were so, Vaelsaru and Andonre need

me more. There is still a Great Demon abroad in the world. Wherever *he* is, that is where I must go. It's what the Order is for. It's what *I'm* for."

Riodheg wore a stricken look that no one else had ever been allowed to see. "But, Nyrthim, I've only just gotten you back!"

"Riodheg, you're now a legend for the ages—for all time, though peoples yet unborn may give you other names and dress you in other clothes, according to their own needs. You've grown beyond me. Actually, you did that a long time ago. You just need to realize it." Nyrthim's dark eyes suddenly twinkled. "And besides, don't be so sure you've seen the last of me. I'm not *that* old, you know!"

Before the High King could muster a response, the sorcerer was gone.

"So, Rupaeranz," said Valdar, "you're leaving with Vaelsaru?"

"Yes. I'd been looking forward to seeing the wide grasslands again. But Lord Vaelsaru is back in command of the army, so my oath still holds. And besides, he says he's leading us to The City itself! What tales I'll have to tell around the campfires. Only . . ." The mercenary's enthusiasm dampened a bit, and his brow furrowed in perplexity at his chosen leader's occasionally inexplicable behavior. "Lord Vaelsaru was saying something about no looting or raping. You don't suppose he really *meant* that, do you?"

"Well, he's been under a great deal of strain lately. . . ."

"He'll come to his senses," Khaavorn put in reassuringly.

"Do you think so?" Rupaeranz brightened visibly, but then his mood changed again in its mercurial way. "I'll have to say farewell now. I only wish I could lift a last cup with Zhassu."

"I wish you could, too," said Khaavorn, almost too quietly to be heard.

"Look at it this way," said Valdar with something like his old smile. "You'll still have Nyrthim to keep an eye on you."

"Is that supposed to cheer me up?" But the shadows fled from the mercenary's face. "Good luck to you, Valdar. Too bad you had to miss the battle, but . . ." He gave an eloquent shrug, wordlessly conveying fatalism as to the inscrutable workings of fate. He turned to go, and then paused, as though mention of the battle had reminded him of something. "You know, I still don't fully understand what happened that day. Ah, well . . ." He tossed off a final wave and, with a horseman's rolling gait, walked up the slope behind which the imperial army was encamped.

"I *like* him," stated Khaavorn. Then he gave Valdar a slantwise look. "I must admit, I'm still a bit confused myself."

"Whatever do you mean, Khaavorn?" Valdar was all wide-eyed innocence. "Didn't the High King tell you—?"

"Yes, yes. He sent you up into the hills with Andonre, to keep her safely away from the battle, which was why you missed all the excitement."

"Just so. Very boring—the story of my life!"

"So I've noticed," Khaavorn observed dryly. "Still, things evidently got a little more interesting for you toward the end of the day, when you happened onto what was left of Vaedorie and Norkhaari, and caught sight of Tarhynda flying off toward the east after killing them."

"Yes. It was grim. I'm just glad Andonre and I found Zhotiyu, where they'd abandoned him."

"Indeed. You certainly earned my gratitude as well as Vaelsaru's. Only . . . what were they doing out there in the first place? And why did Tarhynda kill them and then flee?"

"How should I know, Khaavorn? Who can fathom the actions of demons, or of those who worship them? Even Nyrthim has no explanation."

"So he keeps saying to everyone, every chance he gets," Khaavorn nodded. Then, without warning, he spoke in a rush. "Valdar, I don't want you to tell me things I don't need to hear and wouldn't understand anyway. I know I'm a dullard—"

"Khaavorn—"

"No, let me finish! I don't really want to know the whole truth of what happened. Minuren once told me some knowledge is a curse, and I believe her. All I want to know is . . ." Khaavorn looked out across the field, and his strong face worked convulsively. "I just want you to tell me that all this was worth it. Zhassu . . . half the Companions . . . my brother Khaaradh, the best of the lot of us. . . . Valdar, did it all *mean* something? Did it *matter*?"

A moment passed before Valdar could speak.

"Khaavorn, there are indeed things I am not permitted to tell you. But you must believe this: what you endured, the sacrifice that was offered up here on this field—the best blood of Lokhrein spilled like water—was necessary. If Riodheg and you and the rest hadn't barred Tarhynda from conquering Arnoriysa, it wouldn't have been possible for . . ." Valdar's eyes fell, as though avoiding Khaavorn's. Khaavorn wondered why. But then Valdar raised his head and met his friend's gaze squarely. "What you did here enabled Dayu to do as we have always been told he'd do, when our need for him was great enough."

Khaavorn stared back, his face transfigured. "You mean—?"

"Yes, Khaavorn," said Valdar gently. "Dayu delivered us. Everything is all right now."

"Thank you, Valdar," mumbled Khaavorn.

Valdar smiled at him . . . and, in the distance behind him, saw the slender figure of Andonre atop the ridge.

Khaavorn followed his gaze, then looked at Valdar, who was no longer seeing him. He looked back and forth between the two of them, with the same expression of out-of-charactrer shrewdness he had worn when Valdar had lifted her into a chariot with hands that had lingered. Then he smiled, and strolled off whistling a simple old tune.

Valdar climbed the slope. Andonre now had access to her old wardrobe, and was no longer the bedraggled mother who had brought her child back from the Shrine of the Lake, but an imperial lady in outdoor dress. He halted an arm's length from her.

"How is Zhotiyu?" he asked after an awkward silence.

"As well as can be expected. Before she parted from us to return to Lokhrein with Nechtan, Minuren warned me that he'll probably have nightmares for a long time. Also, he may have a craving for the drug with which they dosed him for so long—the kind of craving that eats away everything that made a person what he was, until there's nothing left inside but the craving itself. But she thinks that, with much love and patience, he has a chance to become something like the Zhotiyu we once knew." She gave a shaky laugh. "I suppose I shouldn't complain. Any stories he tells about what happened will be discounted as just more of his nightmares and hallucinations."

Valdar looked away, soul-sick. *So it's come to this: we find advantage in the destruction of a child.*

"Yes," he made himself say. "No one must ever learn about the Shrine of the Lake, not even his father."

"I know." Andonre's voice grew even bleaker than the cloudy, blustery fall day. "I never want to lie to Vaelsaru again. But it is part of my punishment that I must continue to live this one lie with him."

"But nevertheless," Valdar ventured cautiously, "you must return with him?"

"Yes."

"And what about . . . us?"

Andonre took a step forward and touched the face he'd finally had a chance to shave. "Valdar, we sought each other when the death of the world seemed to be closing in around us. All duties, all oaths seemed voided in that onrushing doom. But now my duty requires me to go with Vaelsaru. And yet . . ." She drew in a breath that sounded almost like a sob. "If you were to whistle, I'm not sure I wouldn't follow."

Valdar caught her hand and pressed it more tightly to his cheek. Then he dropped it.

"No, Andonre. In that deserted village, there was so much death around us that we needed to affirm life itself. That need took us like a whirlwind that was beyond our control. But now, Vaelsaru needs you. Zhotiyu needs you. The Empire needs you."

"Do you need me?" she asked, very softly.

He dared not allow himself to answer her directly. "Be sure of one thing," he finally said. "If *you* ever need *me*, I will be there. In the Empire or anywhere else, I will find you."

"I'll leave half of my heart with you, Valdar," she said, reaching out to him again.

He turned away before she could touch him.

"And you, lady, take all of mine with you," he said into the wind, facing away from her. Then, not looking back to see if she had heard him, he strode off down the slope, hastening to catch up with Khaavorn.

The following is an excerpt from:

BLOOD OF THE HEROES

by
Steve White

available from Baen Books
hardcover, January 2006

CHAPTER ONE

Jason Thanou had never really cared for Earth all that much. Now, watching the blue-white-and-buff globe wax in the observation lounge's wraparound viewscreen, he saw nothing in the spectacle to make him forget his dislike.

So, he wondered, *why am I reacting this way?*

He knew he had no reason to be surprised. It was always the same, aboard a ship approaching Earth—no other planet had the same effect, not even the planet of his birth. It came at the indefinable moment when the mother planet, as sentimentalists called it, ceased to be *away* and became *down*—a world and not an astronomical object. Nor did the feeling fade with familiarity; he still felt the excited apprehension that caused the heart to race and the skin to tingle and the bowels to loosen. It never changed. Nor was it unique to him. Most outworlders admitted to the same strange exhilaration, and Jason had never found the others' denials convincing.

Still, he wondered why. Especially on this occasion, when he was here against his will and should by rights have felt nothing but cold distaste.

He decided the animus and the shivers both had the same cause: the sheer, psychologically oppressive ancientness of the place. It was a world—no, *the* world—that humans had not molded from barrenness over the past few centuries (to use the Earth-standard units of time everyone still used, which was yet another irritant). Here, the memory of billions of human lives across thousands of years permeated every acre. History had soaked into the soil like blood—an apt simile, from what Jason knew of Earth's past, which was quite a lot thanks to the job he'd once had. . . .

And to which he was now returning involuntarily. The resentment that had been simmering within him for the entire voyage boiled up anew, banishing his philosophical musings and leaving only a flat dislike of everything about this trip, especially this overripe fruit of a planet.

Jason heard a soft murmuring behind him as stewards moved among the passengers in the lounge. No blaring announcement from an intercom—this was a pricey spaceline. That, at least, was one way he'd been able to exact revenge. He had booked passage normally beyond his means, knowing he would have to be reimbursed.

"Excuse me, Commander Thanou," said one of the stewards diffidently. "We are entering our final approach pattern for Pontic Spaceport."

Jason smiled inwardly at the name of Eastern Europe's central spaceport on the steppes north of the Black Sea, so typical of the Earth fad for reviving place-names of archaic flavor. "Thank you. Has my planetside transportation been arranged as I requested?"

"It has, Commander. You have a reservation on an aircoach departing two hours after our arrival. We have made certain that you will arrive in Athens by midafternoon local time." The steward's courtesy, verging on obsequiousness, went beyond the requirements of his job.

"Excellent," Jason said absently, most of his attention on the viewscreen. The north coastline of the Mediterranean was beginning to scroll beneath the ship.

Why Athens? Jason wondered, not for the first time. *Why does Rutherford want me to report to him at his office there, and not at Service headquarters in Australia? Is it just another of his little ways of irritating me?*

Well, two can play at that game. . . .

"Thank the purser for me," he said. "And now, I think I'll return to my stateroom. I believe I have time to change clothes before we land."

"Most certainly, Commander." The Steward's attitude was reflected in the stares from Jason's fellow passengers as he left the lounge. He'd grown used to that attitude, and those stares, since the nature of his business on Earth had become general shipboard knowledge.

Time travelers had that effect on people.

"I assume you're trying to irritate me," said Kyle Rutherford coldly.

"Whatever do you mean?" asked Jason with an air of innocence whose bogusness was insultingly obvious.

Rutherford merely continued to glare from behind his desk, to the left of the door which had just slid silently shut behind Jason. Opposite the door, a virtual window provided a view of Athens from a higher level than the office in fact occupied. The location was about right, though, peering over the Philopappos Hill toward the Acropolis, serene in its ruined perfection, timeless . . . literally timeless as well as figuratively so, in the temporal stasis-bubble that enclosed it. The technology had come too late to protect it from the atmospheric pollution that had almost eaten it away in the Hydrocarbon Era. But now, with that gone, what was left stood in the unique, eerie clarity of motionless air, to be gazed at from without rather than suffering the unintended vandalism of millions of tramping feet.

Elsewhere, the office held memorabilia. To the right, the wall opposite Rutherford's desk was covered with photographs at which a visitor from a couple of generations back would have peered in deepening puzzlement. Behind his desk, a display case contained various ordinary-seeming if very old-fashioned objects . . . which, Jason decided with an inner chuckle, made it a fitting backdrop for Rutherford.

"You *know* what I mean!" Rutherford finally blurted. He nearly forgot to speak in the pedantic accent affected by Earth's intelligentsia when addressing outworlders and other vulgarians.

"Oh, this." Jason pretended to finally notice the target of Rutherford's glare. He glanced down at the uniform he was wearing—field gray, with facings of silver-edged dark green, very much in a traditional quasi-military style. "I *am* entitled to wear it, you know, being an active-duty officer of the Hesperian Colonial Rangers."

The irony was that he hadn't worn it in . . . he'd forgotten how long. The difficulty of getting the Rangers into uniforms was so proverbial that it had become a point of pride with them. They even added their own flamboyant individual touches to the starkly utilitarian and unmilitary-looking field versions. Only on very special occasions, and under extreme duress, could they be induced to put on the service dress kit in which Jason now stood, and on which he had lavished a hitherto well-concealed capacity for spit-and-polish.

"I must beg to correct you," said Rutherford in a voice as frosty as his thinning hair and neatly trimmed Vandyke beard. "You're in the Temporal Service."

"Not any more!"

"I call your attention to the agreement by which you were permitted to take extremely early retirement from the Service—specifically to Part VI, Article D, Paragraph 15, Subparagraph—"

"Yes, yes, I know! The errand boy you sent to Hesperia explained it to me in great and loving detail." Actually, Jason had known about the deliberately inconspicuous clause all along. He had just never dreamed it would actually be invoked.

Rutherford permitted himself a tight little smile of constipated triumph. "Well, then, you understand that the Temporal Regulatory Authority has the right to reactivate you under certain special circumstances. Those circumstances have now arisen, and the right has been exercised. The Hesperian planetary government has placed you on temporary detached duty with the Service."

"Not of my own free will!"

Rutherford sighed theatrically. "Let us have done with this nonsense. I recall very well that you quit the Service five years ago in some childish fit of pique, and returned to your homeworld in the . . . oh, what system is it?"

"Psi 5 Aurigae," Jason ground out between gritted teeth. Pretended inability to remember which colonial system was which was yet another grating affectation of Rutherford's type of Earthman.

"But of course. At any rate, you rejoined that system's paramilitary constabulary, from which the Service had previously recruited you for your—" (Rutherford looked like he had bitten into a bad pickle) "—undeniable talents. Evidently you had decided that nursemaiding terraformers and tracking down smugglers of forbidden nanotechnology and rescuing thrill-seekers were more rewarding than the opportunity you had previously been afforded to do something *important*."

Jason thought of his homeworld, on the outer fringes of the human diaspora, as yet raw and unfinished and needing so much, especially law and order. There—in contrast to this fossilized world—human effort could still make a difference for the future. But he chopped off an angry retort and put on the insolent smile he knew was expected of him.

"Hey, some of those thrill-seekers are young and female . . . and you'd be amazed how grateful they can be for getting rescued! Besides, if memory serves, quitting the Service wasn't purely my idea. Come to think of it, you were the one who pointed that out to me. I seem to recall words like 'disrespect' and 'flippancy'."

"True enough. I wasn't too terribly devastated to see you go, nor were certain others in the Authority whose age and learning and experience you were apt to disparage."

"Then why inflict my bad attitude on yourselves by hauling me back now?"

"I'll not insult your intelligence by claiming to be overjoyed to see you. Indeed, I would not have agreed to reactivating you had there been any alternative. Oh, and please do take a chair."

"I'd prefer to stand. And *why* is there no alternative to me?" Jason leaned over Rutherford's desk and made himself be reasonable and even ingratiating, for he thought he glimpsed a possibility of talking his way out of this. "Come on, Kyle! What can I possibly contribute that would outweigh the disadvantage of having someone on the team whose heart isn't in it? You know how I feel about—"

"Yes, I remember your vehemence about the oppressive weight of history that presses down on Earth." Rutherford took on a look of smug vindication. "Well, then, this is just the mission for you! You're going to see Earth before most of that history had happened—Earth when it was young. Slightly more than four thousand years younger than it is at present, in fact."

Without recalling having done it, Jason found that he had sat down. "Would you care to explain that statement?"

"Certainly." Rutherford leaned forward, and his

eyes glowed with an avidity that made him almost sympathetic. "We want you to lead an expedition to observe the volcanic explosion of Santorini in 1628 B.C. and its aftermath."

All at once, Jason's resentment was forgotten. "*What?* But . . . but. . . ."

"Yes, I know: it is incomparably further back than we have ever sent humans before. But there have never been any absolute, theoretical objections to a temporal displacement of this magnitude . . . or any magnitude, for that matter. The limiting factors have been political and economic. We have, with great difficulty, obtained authorization for this expedition. It helps that this project lacks the . . . sensitive aspects of some of our other proposals involving the distant past."

"Right. I remember how you had to quietly drop the idea of an expedition to Jerusalem in the spring of 30 A.D."

"Indeed." Rutherford shuddered at the recollection. "At the same time, the event in question is one of the most important in human history, and one whose effects are still very much in dispute."

Jason nodded unconsciously. One of the justifications for time travel's hideous expense was the resolution of historical controversies and mysteries. Written records tended to be incomplete, biased, self-serving or downright mendacious. Only direct observation could reveal the truth behind the veil of lies, myths, defamation and propaganda. Already, only half a century after its invention, the Fujiwara-Weintraub Temporal Displacer had forced historians to rethink much of what they had thought they'd known. And, in the process, the investigators had been able to establish a trade in items from the past that was so lucrative it helped defray the cost.

Of course, Jason reflected, *they often keep some of the choicest items for themselves.* He glanced at the display case behind Rutherford's desk. A sword caught his eye: a standard-issue early nineteenth century dragoon saber, somewhat the worse for wear and utterly undistinguished save for the fact that on a March day in 1836 a certain William Barrett Travis, colonel by dubious virtue of a commission from an arguably illegal insurrectionist government, had used it to draw a line in the dust of an old Spanish mission's courtyard in San Antonio, Texas, North America. . . .

Jason dragged his mind back to the matter at hand. "You still haven't explained why you need me, in particular. I'm not the only one with my qualifications. Almost," he added, because it seemed a shame not to live down to Rutherford's expectations, "but not quite."

"Two reasons. The first is the perennial problem of physical inconspicuousness. Of all the available persons with your qualifications—fairly rare ones, as you have indicated with your characteristic modesty—we feel you are the one with the best chance of passing unremarked in the target milieu."

"Probably true," Jason grudgingly conceded. Most of Earth, for most of its history, had not been as ethnically cosmopolitan as it had become since the Industrial Revolution. A blond, blue-eyed European in Ming Dynasty China, or an obvious African in Peter the Great's Russia, would have some explaining to do. In theory, the capability to alter physical appearances by nanotechnological resequencing of the genetic code had existed for centuries. But the crazy excesses of the Transhuman movement before its bloody suppression had placed that sort of thing beyond the pale of acceptability. The Service had to make do with what it had. For this part of the world, what it had were people like Jason, who looked as Greek as his name sounded, even though he was—like most living humans, and practically all the outworld ones—a walking bouillabaisse of national origins.

"Secondly," Rutherford continued, "the sheer, unprecedented magnitude of this temporal displacement— more than three times as far back as we have ever attempted to send humans, in fact—limits the mass which can be displaced, and therefore restricts us to a numerically small expedition."

Jason gave another nod of unconscious agreement. The tradeoff was axiomatic.

"In point of fact, we are limited to three people. The matters we wish to observe involve at least two entirely separate fields of knowledge. Therefore two members of the team must be specialists. This leaves only one position—that of mission leader—for a generalist. So that person must be a recognized expert in survival under unique and sometimes unanticipated conditions, with a proven record of resourcefulness." Rutherford paused, then resumed with an obvious effort. "Doubtless it was for these very qualities that the Hesperian Rangers found you valuable."

Jason didn't even notice Rutherford's inept best effort at flattery. His mind was too busy running through the difficulties. "But . . . this is crazy! What about language? Do we even know what they were speaking then, much less how it sounded?"

"That problem has, of course, been taken into account. I will go into more detail later, for you and the other members of the team." Rutherford's eyes took on a shrewd twinkle. "Aren't you interested in knowing who they are?"

"Not particularly," Jason pouted.

Taking the absence of outright refusal as emphatic agreement, Rutherford manipulated controls on his desk. A holographically projected three-dimensional viewscreen appeared in the middle of the air. It showed a woman's face—a high-cheekboned face of classical regularity framed by long straight hair of a very dark auburn-brown. Large green eyes gazed out from beneath straight dark brows. The nose was a graceful aquiline curve. The wide, rather full-lipped mouth wore an expression that was cool almost to the point of severity.

Jason sat up straight and stared. All at once, this job seemed more interesting.

"Deirdre Sadaka-Ramirez," said Rutherford. "A recognized expert in geology and vulcanology. And very experienced in field work on her homeworld of Mithras."

Jason's pleasurable speculations hit a bump. *Well, now I understand the severity*, he thought.

The third planet of Zeta Tucanae had been settled early, during the era of slower-than-light colonization before the invention of the negative-mass drive. The colonists had been very much on their own when they'd discovered that the planet held unsuspected autochthones. Whether or not the

nightmarish beings had been truly intelligent was
still a subject of learned debate. What was beyond
debate was the insensate ferocity with which they
had sought the extirpation of the bipedal invaders from space. (The fact that the terraforming
project was making their world uninhabitable for
them might have had something to do with it.)
The human species' survival on Mithras had hung
by a thread, and women had not been expendable.
An entire ethos had grown up around the necessity for protecting them, leading to a resurrection
of nearly forgotten social attitudes. That had been
a couple of centuries ago, and Mithras was now
part of the general cosmopolitan culture. But even
today, women from that world still had a reputation
for aggressively—sometimes abrasively—asserting an
equality that, in the larger human society, had long
ago passed beyond the need for assertion.

Well, thought Jason with an inward sigh, *I always
did like a challenge*.

Rutherford fiddled with the controls again, and a
new face appeared—a far less interesting one, from
Jason's standpoint. Male, gaunt-featured . . . and definitely middle-aged.

"Wait a minute—" Jason began.

Rutherford overrode him. "Doctor Sidney Nagel—
quite possibly Earth's premier living authority on the
history and archaeology of the Aegean Bronze Age,
despite his relative youth."

"'Relative youth'? He's—"

"I am aware that he is somewhat older than most
people we send back in time to primitive milieus. But
we have assured ourselves that he will be up to the

hardships involved. He met all our health and fitness requirements." Rutherford smiled. "He had incentive to do so, after a career spent trying to resolve mysteries by educated guesswork and inferences from a heartbreakingly few hard facts. Offered an opportunity to actually see the era. . . . Well, he would have been willing to sell his soul to the Devil for it, in an age when such things were thought possible. Nowadays, he was willing to undergo a hard regimen of physical conditioning, and pass our standard training course in low-technology survival."

Jason studied the image. There was something to be said for that kind of motivation. And yet, as he looked at the professorial face with its humorless mouth and dark-brown eyes flanking a substantial beak of a nose, he found himself thinking: *A Rutherford in training.*

"I suppose," he said aloud, "that neither of them knows anything about time travel."

"Well, I imagine they know what the average well-informed layman knows, from the popular literature on the subject."

"Which means they know nothing," said Jason dourly.

"I am counting on you to repair that lack."

"Me? But you've got all the top experts working for you."

"Experts tend to stupefy the listener with technical jargon and unnecessary detail. Certain unkind persons have even accused *me* of this sort of behavior. An introduction from someone whose knowledge is of a practical nature, acquired in the field, might be more useful."

"Some sense in that." Agreeing with Rutherford caused Jason physical pain.

"In fact," Rutherford continued, on a rising note of self-satisfaction, "you can begin their orientation at once."

"What? You mean they're here in Athens?"

"I thought it well to bring them here, in anticipation that you would wish to meet your team members without delay." Rutherford stood up. "Shall I send for them?"

For an instant, Jason's resentment came roaring back in full force. His mouth almost opened to tell Rutherford where to put this mission, to declare that he would legally contest the Service's right to order him into the past. . . .

The past when—how did Rutherford put it?—Earth was young. Jason's eyes strayed to the Acropolis. *I wonder what was there then?*

And besides, Deirdre Sadaka-Ramirez did look awfully intriguing. . . .

"Well, I don't suppose it could hurt to talk to them."

Rutherford smiled and spoke into a grille on his desktop. "Please ask them to come in."

NOW YOU'VE GOT HIM MAD!

A cry of transcendent agony from Wothorg brought the two of them to their feet. Nyrthim examined the big Dhulaan and shook his head. "The demon's venom has progressed too far. Nothing can save him. I'm sorry."

"The mercy stroke," Wothorg ground out through clenched teeth, exerting all his massive strength to hold back a scream.

"I have," Nyrthim began, "a quick-acting potion that will—"

"No." Valdar's voice was made of lead.

Nyrthim met his eyes and nodded. He belonged to the priest class, not the warrior nobility, but he understood: Wothorg was Valdar's man. He stood up and began muttering in old languages and making certain signs. The women withdrew to a corner and watched with round, dark eyes.

Valdar drew his sword and knelt over the man on whose shoulders he'd ridden before he could walk. He placed the point just below Wothorg's rib cage.

Wothorg actually managed to smile. "When you get home to Dhulon and tell them how I went, will you make up some good lies?"

"I'll do better than that. I'll tell them the truth. I'll tell them you gave the death stroke to a demon."

Wothorg smiled again. He closed his eyes, and gave a quick nod.

Valdar rammed the sword home, in and upward to the heart. Wothorg jerked and lay still, his face free of suffering. A low keening arose from the women.

Valdar stood up. His eyes were like cold bluish flame showing through two holes in a mask of bronze.

"Tell me what you want us to do, Nyrthim," was all he said.

BAEN BOOKS by STEVE WHITE

Demon's Gate
Blood of the Heroes (forthcoming)

Forge of the Titans

Eagle Against the Stars

Prince of Sunset
Emperor of Dawn

The Disinherited
Legacy
Debt of Ages

with David Weber:
Insurrection
Crusade
In Death Ground
The Shiva Option